BY SARAH ADAMS

PRACTICE
MAKES
PERFECT

PRACTICE MAKES PERFECT

A NOVEL

SARAH ADAMS

DELL BOOKS
NEW YORK

Practice Makes Perfect is a work of fiction. Names, characters, places, and incidents are the products of the author's imagination or are used fictitiously. Any resemblance to actual events, locales, or persons, living or dead, is entirely coincidental.

2023 Dell Trade Paperback Edition

Copyright © 2023 by Sarah Adams

All rights reserved.

Published in the United States by Dell, an imprint of Random House, a division of Penguin Random House LLC, New York.

DELL is a registered trademark and the D colophon is a trademark of Penguin Random House LLC.

LIBRARY OF CONGRESS CATALOGING-IN-PUBLICATION DATA
Names: Adams, Sarah, 1991– author.
Title: Practice makes perfect / Sarah Adams.
Description: Dell Trade Paperback Edition. | New York: Dell Books, 2023.
Identifiers: LCCN 2022051990 (print) | LCCN 2022051991 (ebook) |
ISBN 9780593500804 (trade paperback) | ISBN 9780593500811 (eBook)
Classification: LCC PS3601.D3947 P73 2023 (print) |
LCC PS3601.D3947 (ebook) | DDC 813/.6—dc23
LC record available at https://lccn.loc.gov/2022051990
LC ebook record available at https://lccn.loc.gov/2022051991

Printed in the United States of America on acid-free paper

randomhousebooks.com

6 8 9 7 5

Title-page art: imaginarybo © Adobe Stock Photos

Book design by Sara Bereta

This one is for the softies.
The tenderhearted sweeties.
The introverts who are afraid to shine.

To plant a garden is to believe in tomorrow.

—Audrey Hepburn

PRACTICE MAKES PERFECT

CHAPTER ONE

Annie

I am convinced dating was created by an evil villain to torture humanity. Dramatic? Not in the least. For introverts like me with social anxiety, the process of dating is equivalent to waxing your bikini line. Menstrual cramps on day two of your cycle. An emergency dental procedure you weren't expecting—and guess what: they're fresh out of novocaine.

"Again, I'm so sorry about the beer," I say to the man sitting across from me.

"It's fine," he says in a clipped way that means it's absolutely not fine.

This is not going well. Not that it has ever gone well for me in the past, but this time it really isn't. I think turning a man off in the first ten minutes of a date is my new record. Because John, the man sitting across from me with a sopping-wet, beer-stained polo and khakis from the drink I accidentally knocked across the table onto his lap, looks ready to bolt. Can't blame him.

Why did I think I could do this? It's been years since I dated, and even back then I never liked it much. I'm a person who avoids attention at all costs. Who can't think of a single thing to say when a man sitting across from her is intently staring at her.

Again, I ask myself, Why are you here, Annie?!

Oh right. It was the brownie. Well, first it was the realization that even after opening the flower shop my mom had always dreamed of, the nagging something-is-missing feeling still pesters me. So I decided it's time to put a plan in motion to settle down with my perfect someone—because that's the only box left unchecked in my life. And since I've been drooling over John (the man my sisters and I always refer to as Hot Bank Teller), I thought he might be the perfect candidate for the job.

The job in question has very strict criteria based on the bursting-with-love marriage my parents had. One, he must live in town and have roots here in Rome, Kentucky; two, he must have a stable job; three, he must be kind and also be supportive of my career; and four, he must want a family.

Those are the only things that matter to me.

So the last time I went to the bank to deposit a check, I used up my Once-a-Year Extroverted Moment and asked him if he'd like to go out sometime. He miraculously said yes, and I spent the next week recuperating from the stress and anxiety I suffered in asking.

Anyway, when I proposed meeting somewhere a little outside of Rome to have fresh scenery (and keep our nosy, single-stoplight town out of my business), he suggested Peppercorn, a nice restaurant about thirty minutes away. And when I looked it up, Yelp said this place has an excellent giant brownie. It doesn't get better than that.

The dessert is literally the only reason I'm still sitting here on this painfully awkward date.

I wish I could text my sisters right now and ask them what to do. But that requires them actually knowing I'm on a date, which would open me up to the sort of attention I've been trying to avoid.

The very minute my sisters find out about my quest to find a husband—everyone else will know too. I would really hate to have Mabel (the woman who's like a grandma to me) attempt to set me up with every eligible bachelor she knows. So I'm keeping it a secret—like most things in my life.

The only reason I'm pushing through my terrible social anxiety now is because I'm fully confident that marriage is the Thing that's missing. I wish I could call my parents to get their opinion, but because they died when I was three, that will never be an option. So instead, I'm following in their footsteps. Happily married by the age of twenty-eight. That gives me just under a year to find the person I want to spend the rest of my life with.

Too bad I have to date first.

I smile up at John, hoping that's going to lessen his annoyance at wearing my drink. But I'm Annie Walker: shy, socially anxious, introvert extraordinaire who senses this man doesn't want to spend another second in my company. And that makes my smile feel like a wobbly grimace. I imagine it resembles a snarl. My nostrils might even be flaring.

I can't do this.

John clears his throat and tries his own attempt at a casual smile. Admittedly, his is better than mine. "So . . . what's it like owning a flower shop?" He sounds bored.

I want to unzip my skin and run my bones all the way to Mexico. My heart is racing, and this swanky restaurant is too loud. I don't belong here. My sisters, Madison and Emily, however, would love it.

"Annie?" John prompts again when I don't answer right away.

Right! Conversation. You can do this, Annie. No need to clam up because the man asked you about a topic you actually like. Flowers. Easy peasy lemon squeezy.

I swallow and prepare for my answer. "Um—it's fun." John waits a moment and then tips forward slightly, clearly expecting me to say more. "Really fun," I tack on to appease his desire for a sentence with a higher word count.

I would elaborate, but now the only thing swirling around my brain is the reproductive cycle of flowers (which I find deeply fascinating), but I have a distinct feeling that John is not the type to marvel at life science. So I clamp my mouth shut again.

"So it's . . . really fun?" he asks and I nod. "Well, good." He breathes in deeply and then settles back in his chair and looks away. We bathe in uncomfortable silence. This would prompt most people to say something—anything—but not me. I freeze up even more. The weight of carrying on a conversation is too heavy for my shoulders.

I am the quiet one in my family. The one with her nose always in a book because she prefers worlds where she doesn't have to interact with other humans. It's so much easier to read about relationships than to foster them. Less dangerous too. I can't offend anyone written into a book. I can't say the wrong thing. And book characters don't make judgments about me.

When John pulls out his cell phone and starts scrolling, I realize I have to take a stab at some sort of conversation, or this night is going to be over before it starts. "So, John," I begin, and then during the next ten minutes I pretty much black out as I blabber nonstop, only regaining consciousness as I'm finishing up with, "And that's why the primary purpose of the flower is reproduction."

"Wow. Okay. That was . . . a lot of information about flowers," he says with an expression resembling something close to haunted. Clearly my stab at conversation went right through him, and he's bleeding out.

I smile timidly and glance around for our waitress. It's so busy in here she hasn't been around to take our order after getting our drinks. I could really use an interruption right about now.

Nothing.

"So—uh—do you at least have any hobbies?" he asks.

Oh geez, "at least." I'm already so far off his dating radar that he's looking for an *at least* to redeem me in some small way.

I clench the fabric of my dress under the table. I do have a hobby—but even my sisters don't know about it, so I sure as crap am not going to share it with this man who looks like spending time with me is causing him physical discomfort.

"Flowers sort of are my hobby as well as my career."

"Right," he says blandly because I've once again shut down any conversational avenues. Why am I like this? I need to talk. Ask him questions! Why can't I think of any? My brain is a whiteboard, polished clean.

But he's tapping his finger on the table now and looking away from me.

In a fit of panic, I blurt the first thing that comes to my head. "I want to get married."

Oh look, I've finally said something that gets John's attention.

He stares at me, open-mouthed and in shock, because, yep, I just mentioned marriage during a date that was already tanking.

Trying to recover, I tag on, "Oh no, not to you!" My smile fades when I see his face contort. "Well, maybe to you. Who knows? If things go well tonight anything can happen." Now I realize I've made it sound like we're absolutely going to bed together tonight, and John has to pleasure me well enough to win me over. Super.

"Sorry—no, I didn't mean you have to be good at you know what . . . for me to marry you. I'm sure there's a learning curve when it comes to that sort of thing."

Now his face drains of all color because I'm making this so

much worse. John blink, blink, blinks at me, completely at a loss for how to respond. There's no salvaging this date.

"Will you excuse me, John? I need to use the bathroom." And regroup. And possibly climb out the window and run away.

He's so relieved he will be exempt from my company for a few minutes that he eagerly nods. "Yes, take your time!"

I stand on wobbly legs and walk across the restaurant, irrationally feeling like everyone in here is staring at how awkwardly this dress fits me. It's my sister's dress, so it's a little long on me. It hugs all my curves like it's supposed to but then drowns my knees and hovers midcalves, unlike where it hits on Emily, just above her knees. She wears this dress on her many successful dates because she doesn't have an ounce of social anxiety. I stole it out of her closet and stowed it away in my purse so she wouldn't notice when I left our house and ask where I was going. I didn't have anything of my own to wear because I never go on nice dates (I haven't been on one since three years ago, when one progressed very similarly to this one).

I would have taken a dress from my other sister, but Madison is the size of a spritely fairy, and there's no way any of her dresses would get over my hips.

After what feels like a mile-long walk, I make it to the bathroom and sink back against the wall. The automatic hand dryer goes off at my shoulder, making me jump out of my skin and shriek.

"All right, Annie, pull yourself together. You can do this," I say while scooting away from the hand dryers and pulling my phone from my purse. I swipe across it to open a text conversation with my soon-to-be sister-in-law, Amelia. She's the only person who knows I'm on a date tonight.

Ever since Amelia (you might know her as Rae Rose, world famous pop star) came to town a little over a year ago and fell in love with my older brother, we've had an instant bond I can't quite explain. Like she was always meant to be in our family. And despite the fact that she's new to the family, I trust her in a way that I don't trust many other people. Which is why I text her now.

ANNIE: HELP!!!!

AMELIA: Oh no! Not going well?

ANNIE: I spilled my drink on him. And then told him I want to get married.

AMELIA: Yikes! Do you like him that much?

ANNIE: No, I hate him.

AMELIA: Hmm, confusing. Can you bail?

ANNIE: No! That's so rude!

AMELIA: Em and Maddie are coming over in a few minutes. Just tell him you had something come up and then come hang out with us!

ANNIE: I can't do that to him after spilling a drink on him and then insinuating he has to please me in bed or he won't make the marriage cut.

AMELIA: Oh my gosh. So much to unpack there.

ANNIE: I'll just eat fast. Don't start a movie without me.

AMELIA: Good luck!! Bring me home a brownie. They have the best.

I steel myself in the mirror, smooth back my long blonde hair (which at least looks really pretty thanks to Emily's curling wand, which I also stole), and then step out of the bathroom.

Unfortunately, I arrive back at the table just in time to hear John finishing up a phone call that he doesn't intend for me to hear. "Yeah, I'm telling you she's so unbelievably boring. And just sort of awkward and weird. Like zero personality." He listens to the person on the other end of the line. "I mean, yeah, I guess she's prettyish, but I don't even want to try to hook up with her tonight because she's so dull. So just call me in five minutes with an emergency. Okay, yeah. Thanks."

My cheeks flame. The lady at the table next to us heard the whole thing and gives me Pity Eyes. I hate Pity Eyes. I'd rather she'd laugh. I can handle laughter. My siblings are professional teasers, so I've been conditioned to laugh my way through life. Pity—no.

I breathe in through my nose so I don't cry—because that would really be the icing on the cake, wouldn't it?—and walk backward several steps. I count to five, and once I'm composed enough, I make a loud reappearance.

"I'm back!"

John shifts and adjusts his napkin, a new bright smile on his face (most likely so he can be convincingly sad he has to leave after his emergency call). "Great. Do you know what you want to order?"

"Probably just a brownie," I say more to myself than to John before the corner of my eye catches a couple entering the restaurant. I look up and do a double take.

It's . . . the pirate.

CHAPTER TWO

Annie

O r no. Not a real pirate but Will Griffin—former bodyguard of pop star Rae Rose—also known as my brother's fiancée, Amelia. Noah and Amelia met a little over a year ago when her car broke down in his front yard. They've been pretty inseparable ever since. So after Amelia's last tour, when she decided to officially move to our little town of Rome, Kentucky, to live with my brother, Will came with her for a few weeks until she settled in and the press cooled off. Without there being much of a threat to her safety, Will was transferred to provide security for another high-profile celebrity.

Before that, he was Amelia's bodyguard for five years on and off as she needed him. During that time, he became kind of famous for being one of the hottest bodyguards in the world. And a dangerous one. If you google Hot Dangerous Bodyguard, Will's picture is the first one that shows up, along with a slew of videos of him pinning against walls scary people attempting to get to Amelia, or showing him tackling a guy to the ground who pulled a knife when he was guarding a politician. There are lots of terrifyingly brave images and videos of him doing his job thoroughly and successfully. And then there's the BuzzFeed article, which is my personal favorite. They devoted an entire piece to the many looks of Will Griffin. It's basically a rotation of images and GIFs where he's either stern or swoony. Will has perfected the balance between I-will-knock-you-flat-if-you-try-to-cross-me, but my-hands-can-be-oh-so-tender-on-your-body.

There's also the *People* magazine article showing photographs of him with several different women on various dates around the world. And there are many. I don't love that article as much.

Amelia—the one woman in the world who seems immune to his charms—claims he looks like a street fighter, but she's wrong. Street fighters have chunks missing from their ears and chipped teeth and meaty fists. Will Griffin is . . . beautiful.

He has these strong inky black brows that slash over mischievous blue-gray eyes. A muscular lithe body, and a playful mouth that looks absolutely wicked when he smiles. And there's his left arm, covered in beautiful, ornate, black-line floral tattoos that wind all the way down his toned arm to end at a butterfly spread over the top of his hand and knuckles. I don't have to look now to confirm the butterfly is there. I studied it enough times to have memorized its shape when Will wasn't looking at me over those weeks he was around town.

Will has the kind of face that dares you to cross him because he would adore the chase—craves the adventure of it. No, he's not a street fighter, he's a roguish, wild fiend. A pirate. At least, he is in my fantasies. Also, in said fantasies, he has an earring and wears tight buckskin breeches with an open-collar, white linen shirt that reveals the chest portion of his tattoos that I'm assuming exist.

Did I mention my hobby is reading historical romances? Specifically in the piratical genre.

As Will and his gorgeous date step into the restaurant, it seems like the whole place suddenly hums to life. His soft grin sends a swirl of electricity through the air. When he places his hand on his date's lower back, I feel a phantom of that same touch against my skin. Time slows as Will and the woman glide through the restaurant to their table—so secure and confident that they seemingly don't even notice everyone staring. Maybe he's used to it.

Right on cue, John's phone starts buzzing. I smile to myself as he puts on an Oscar-worthy performance. He casts his eyes down at the phone, and etches a tiny frown between his eyebrows. A funny little *hmm* escapes him. "I wonder why my roommate is calling me. Do you mind if I answer?"

"No, not all," I say weakly, distracted by the sight of Will removing his skin-licking suit jacket and draping it over the back of his chair before rolling up the cuffs of his shirt. Holy Guacamole, those forearms are glorious.

John answers his phone, voice dripping in alarm as he says, "Hello?"

Immediately his face morphs into something frowny, and I replicate it because I want an Oscar too.

"Seriously? What happened?" He holds up a be-right-back finger to me and then stands up from the table, walking away to anxiously chat with his roommate or whoever is on the other end of that line.

I finally flag down the waitress who seemed intent on avoiding us all night and ask for the check as well as a giant brownie to go.

Then I busy myself with folding my napkin into a perfect little square.

"Annie?" comes a familiar male voice from above me.

My heart hiccups, and I lift my head to look right into the mystical eyes of Will Griffin. I've never heard him say my name before—it was magical. I didn't even plan to say hi to him because I wasn't sure he would remember me.

As Amelia's bodyguard, he was every inch the focused agent. Sure, he'd smile kindly and always winked at the old ladies, making Mabel absolutely swoon; but he never really engaged in chitchat. He always hung on the outskirts in his reflective aviator sunglasses and looked ready to take a bullet for Amelia at any moment. I get chills just thinking of it.

"Will Griffin. It's you. Hi."

He smiles. "Annie Walker. Hi back."

"What are you doing here?" I look around hoping to see Adele, but no. Just the gorgeous brunette he came with looking over her menu. I turn my eyes back to Will and that's when my gaze sweeps over him. His tailored suit pants hug nicely muscled thighs, and a formfitting black button-down shirt covers his top half. It's snug to his shoulders, unbuttoned at the collar and rolled up to his fore-arms. An artful sleeve of magnolia flowers and foliage wind out from under his shirt and descend to his wrist.

Holy Potato, I bet Will has all the other men in this restaurant clutching their ladies for dear life, just hoping Will doesn't decide to run away with one of them.

"I'm on a date actually," he says, signaling to the lovely lady at his table.

"You're on a date thirty minutes away from Rome? Is that a coincidence?"

He grins, and two creases—not quite dimples—bracket his smile like even his body understands how outstanding a smile it is and wants to emphasize it. "Not really. Gretchen and I were both passing through this area so we met up for the night, and then I'll be headed to Rome tomorrow. Did Amelia not tell you? I've been assigned to her again for a while."

"Oh. I didn't know." Why didn't she tell me? Then again, why would she tell me? No one knows I've had a thing for Will since I first met him.

"Her team is anticipating a rise in media around the town with the wedding approaching. They wanted me near just in case."

"Good. I'm glad you're coming back." And then I realize how that sounded and add, "I mean, for Amelia's sake."

He grins softly and my stomach swoops.

I swallow thickly. "And nice you'll get to be so close to your girlfriend for a while," I say, trying to distract him from accidentally admitting I'm glad he'll be around town again. Around me again.

He looks over his shoulder briefly and back. "Gretchen isn't my girlfriend—just a date."

But he said he's staying the night with her . . .

Oh! Right! They're just hooking up. Cool, cool, cool. *Totally* cool and normal and the thought of Will taking off all his clothes doesn't at all make my skin burn hot and weird and tingly.

"So are you here alone?" he asks, eyes sweeping over me and then the table and empty chair.

In the next moment, John steps back to the table. Before he opens his mouth, I speak for him, "Well, I was on a date. But I think John is about to leave because he has an emergency." I look up into John's wide eyes. He thinks I'm a psychic now. "Is your house on fire? Grandma's in the hospital? Or does your roommate have a flat tire?" I ask cheerfully.

He hesitates a second. "Uh—the flat tire one."

So much for that Oscar. Under Will's suddenly dark stare, John's acting skills are deflating along with his courage.

"Hate when that happens," I say kindly as the waitress brings our check and my to-go brownie. She sets it down with a double take at Will. She's momentarily shocked by his handsomeness. Get in line, ma'am.

"Well, John, good luck helping your friend. Drive safe!" I reach into my purse for my wallet to pay for my drink and dessert before I leave—more than eager to get out of here and put this date behind me.

John shifts on his feet, and taps his keys on the side of his leg. "Yeah. Thanks for understanding."

"No problem." I wave him off while still digging in my purse.

I look up when I hear a throat clear and see Will's shoulder pressing lightly against John's chest, keeping him from walking away like he was apparently attempting. Will's head hitches toward the table in some unspoken Man Language, and then John whips his hand into his back pocket, pulls out his wallet, and tosses a fifty on the table. "Uh—I'll catch the bill since I'm the one having to bail."

"But I spilled—"

"It's fine. Have a good night, Annie." And then John is gone so fast there's a smoking streak left on the carpet.

I sling my purse over my shoulder and stand. Will hasn't moved yet, and I've never realized how tall the man is until right now. I come up to his shoulder. But that isn't necessarily hard to do when you're only five foot three inches.

"You okay?" Will asks with pinched brows.

I smile. "Yeah. Why wouldn't I be?"

"Because that jackass seemingly just made up an excuse to bail?"

"Oh. Yeah. He definitely did."

Will eyes me closely for signs of distress. "And that doesn't bother you?"

I think about it and then answer honestly. "A little, but not much. We were both having a terrible time. I wouldn't want him to stick around if he was miserable." I shrug. "Hopefully he'll recover his night now."

Will laughs a short, disbelieving laugh. "You're serious?"

"Should I not be?"

He smiles and again it shoots down into the pit of my stomach. Geez, what would it be like to date a man like him? All charisma and confidence. I would definitely embarrass myself.

"I think maybe you're too nice?" He says it like a question.

"My sisters would agree with you, but one peek inside my head during traffic . . ." I whistle lightly and let the implied villainy dangle.

"So what about you? Are you going to have a bad night now?"

"Can anyone really have a bad night if they have a giant brownie to eat on the drive home?" I raise my plastic container as evidence.

Oh no. Now he's giving me Pity Eyes. "Yes. That absolutely makes it worse. Do you want to join me and Gretchen for dinner?"

That makes me laugh audibly. "No—thank you, but not in a million years. That would be so embarrassing," I say, inching my way toward the exit of the restaurant. Will hangs at my side, matching me stride for stride, and I can't quite figure out why he's still talking to me. Oh right, pity. "Don't worry about me. Seriously. I'll have a spectacular night. There's a book I've really been wanting to finish."

It's a half-truth. I will most definitely cry on my way home from the sting of John's words, but then I do have a steamy romance to finish where a pirate has just stolen a lady, and she's about to turn his world upside down with witty remarks and a bewitching personality.

"A book," he repeats incredulously.

"Uh-huh."

"A book is going to be fun?"

I chuckle as we continue to walk. "Are you one of those non-readers? The movie is never better, I assure you."

"I wouldn't say I'm a nonreader. Reading just hasn't been on my radar before."

"But now it is?" I ask hopefully, glancing at him.

"Maybe." He smirks.

I make it to the door and think this is the moment where Will and I will part ways, but to my surprise, he leans forward, opens the door for me and then follows me out, tossing a glance back at his date and looking for the signal that it's okay for him to walk me out. She gives him a little wave to go ahead. Nice gal.

The air is hot and muggy like all summer nights in the South, and my heels *clip-clop* on the concrete sidewalk. I can't help but laugh. It's not at all the usual soundtrack of my life. My normal shoe of choice is a pair of white Converses. Attire: one of my five different-color overalls with a T-shirt underneath. If you look up the word *comfy* in the dictionary you will find a picture of me.

"So which book will it be?" asks Will when we make it to my truck and I pull out my keys.

I laugh lightly. "What?"

"What book are you going to read tonight?"

I glance briefly back at the restaurant, wondering why in h-e-double hockey sticks he's out here with me trying to join my secret book club instead of back in there with his date. It almost feels like he's stalling—trying to lengthen our conversation. But no, I'm sure he's just being kind. There's no way a man like him would be interested in a woman who was just dumped mid date because she's unbelievably boring, prettyish, and not even hookup material. I'm sure Will is just paying the nice girl a little attention before going on his way.

I squint an eye and smile. "Well, I'd tell you—but then I'd have to kill you. And I'm really not a fan of murder, so I think I'll just keep it to myself."

Will coughs a laugh. He has no idea what to make of me. And that makes two of us because I suddenly realize that I'm standing here having an effortless conversation with Will Griffin and I have no idea how I'm managing it. All I know is that somehow, it's easy.

"Well, for what it's worth, I hope you really do have fun reading your book."

Will opens my truck door and I feel momentarily upset—only because this five minutes with him has already been better than any date I've ever been on, and yet I'll never get to have it again. And now on every date I go on I'll hope they get the door for me—which they won't, because half the women in the world hate it when a man gets their door and the other half love it, resulting in the man panicking and cannonballing into his side without ever asking what the woman actually prefers. I've never particularly cared either way, but now, after having Will do it for me, it's decidedly in the like column.

Even worse, I'll hope my next date has bluish-gray eyes like Will's—but not just any blue-gray but grayish blue with a thick dangerous rim of black around them. I'm not even sure what that means, I just know I feel it down to my toes that that rim is dangerous.

It's possible I'm reading too many romances.

I smile. "And I hope you have fun with Gretchen in all your amorous adventures." Oh gosh. I grimace when Will's eyes widen.

If it's not abundantly clear already, I'm a virgin. Just feels important to note in this moment.

"I probably shouldn't have said that. Sorry. Residual first date awkwardness. I'm going to go before I tell you about the reproduction of flowers."

Will doesn't cringe or look away. He smiles fully and it slips right into the fleshy part of my heart, inflating it like an emergency flotation device. "Well, I guess I'll be seeing you around town, Annie."

"I guess you will."

Then I hop up into my truck. But I hop a little too high and slam my head on the doorframe.

CHAPTER THREE

Will

"How's your job going these days, Annie?" My date blinks back at me with wide eyes, and I immediately realize my mistake. "Gretchen! Shit. Sorry. That was—"

"The second time you've done that since you walked her outside," Gretchen says quietly, but with an edge. She was completely fine with me spending a few minutes with Annie outside, but after the first name slip, things quickly went south. Understandably.

What a douchebag move to call a date by the name of a different woman. What the hell is wrong with me? I can't get Annie Walker out of my head for some reason. I keep spacing out and picturing her soft blue eyes and then realizing I'm just staring at the salt and pepper shaker on the table.

It's an unresolved attraction, that's all.

During my stint working in Rome, Kentucky, it was always difficult to not pay attention to the youngest Walker sister. The sweet one, everyone says. The quiet one. The cute one. I've heard folks in that town refer to Annie as every possible synonym of those words—but never once did they give her the adjective that always sprung into my head when I saw her: *gorgeous*.

We'd never really talked before because first, I don't socialize while on the job, and second, I've known since the moment I laid eyes on Annie that I needed to stay the hell away from her. Something about her attracts me in an I-could-get-feelings-for-her kind of way. And I don't do feelings.

But tonight, I talked to her, and it was a colossal mistake. I can't stop thinking about her.

Even just that short talk with Annie outside of the restaurant was the most I've enjoyed a conversation with anyone in a long time. Which is a problem because I'm currently on a date with a woman I can't seem to focus on. I just keep thinking about how Annie's entire face lit up and reflected her thoughts. Her wide eyes. Her pink mouth. Her nervousness. I wanted to talk to her all night. Hell, I would have settled for sitting and watching her read her book. I bet she makes all kinds of faces while reading.

And now I realize I've done it again. Gretchen said something, and I don't know what it was. Shit, I don't deserve to be on a date with her tonight. "Uh—" I smile at her, trying to search my brain to see if any part of it heard her. "Damn, I'm sorry Gretchen. I'm distracted tonight and missed what you said." I hate that I'm not giving her my full attention. Annie did something to me—she scrambled my brain.

Gretchen pats her lips with her napkin. "It's okay, I just said that I got a promotion at my job."

"That's great. You deserve it."

"Yeah," she agrees and then frowns. "To be honest, Will, I feel like I'm having dinner with a brick wall. Is it because of her? Annie?"

I lie, mostly because I want it to be true. "No. Well, sort of. Annie is a family member of the person I'll be providing security for again starting tomorrow."

"Rae Rose," Gretchen says flatly. "You've been her security on and off for five years, Will, it's not a secret. You can just say her name."

Yeah, but I'll never do that. I take my job protecting Amelia seriously—and that means never dropping her name. The number of dates I go on where they recognize me from that damn BuzzFeed article is absurd. They always want to know the gossip about Amelia. What's she like? Is she sweet? Have I ever hooked up with her?

It's wild to me the intrusive questions people will ask about a celebrity because they think their life is open for public consumption. And by the way, the answer to that last question is a resounding no. I have never, nor will I ever, sleep with Amelia. Like I said, I take my job seriously and sleeping with the person you're protecting is unprofessional. Not to mention I like to think I have good morals, so sleeping with someone who's engaged is not appealing. And third, after working for Amelia for so long now, she feels like the little sister I never had.

I don't want to offend people, though, so I sidestep Gretchen's statement just like I do everyone else's. "Anyway my head jumped into work before it was supposed to after seeing Annie. I hate to do it, but I think I'm going to have to cut our date short tonight and head out after dinner."

Gretchen frowns. "Wait. You're not going to come back to my hotel?"

I get why she's upset. Gretchen and I don't see each other regularly. She works for a pharmaceutical company and travels a lot for it. We hook up occasionally when we're in the same area, and usually go on a date before. There is a difference. But I'm not into it tonight. Annie is, for whatever reason, stuck in my head, and I don't think it would be right to go to Gretchen's place when I'm preoccupied with someone else.

"Yeah—I think I just need to get some sleep tonight."

She scoffs with a smile, pulling her napkin from her lap to set it on the table. "Wow. She must have really made an impression."

"I'm sorry, Gretchen," I say again, and I really mean it. I didn't intend for this to happen, and it's never happened before.

Some of Gretchen's icy demeanor cracks and she smiles genuinely. "It's fine. Really. I don't know why I'm acting so jealous all of a sudden. You and I have never had that kind of relationship, and I don't want it either. I guess, I just . . ." She pauses, looks down at her plate and then back up at me. "The look you've had on your face while thinking about her—" She shrugs lightly. "For a minute I thought it would be nice to have someone look like that while thinking about me. Maybe I'm realizing it's time to readjust my intentions."

Wait, I've had a look on my face? That's not good.

Gretchen sighs and continues, "Do you ever think of committing to someone? I don't mean me . . . just someone in the future?"

"Never," I say quickly. "Long-term relationships are not for me and never will be."

I take a drink of my water, suddenly feeling like my throat is too dry to speak. Mainly because Gretchen's question is ringing loudly in my ears. Annie did make an impression—and I'm not happy about it. I like women, I like dating, and I like to think I'm a good guy who appreciates and respects women. I make sure everyone knows my intentions up front, and I only sleep with women who have the same goals in life as I do—singlehood.

But lately I have noticed when I sit still, there's a feeling I can't quite pinpoint—or more accurately, maybe don't want to pinpoint. It's why I like staying busy with work and adventures. It keeps my head from wandering.

Tonight, however, after talking to Annie and then watching her drive off, I found myself rubbing my chest to ease that damn feeling. I hate it. I want to pay for dinner and take Gretchen back to her place and spend the night tangling up with her until the feeling goes away and I never have it again.

Instead, I pay for dinner and walk her to her car. We have an unmemorable conversation on the way and I sigh with relief when I get into my SUV and drive away from her—straight for the town that I hoped I wouldn't have to go back to. Straight for the woman who now feels like the most dangerous person in the world to me.

Ten minutes into my drive, my phone rings and I answer it over my car's Bluetooth.

"Hey, man," I say to Ethan after answering. He's two years younger than me, and we look nothing alike. Where I have dark hair and blue eyes that I've been told look grayer in certain lights than true blue, he has dark brown eyes and dirty blond hair. Other than how we look, though, we're very much alike.

We don't see nearly enough of each other because my job keeps me busy (read: I like staying busy) and he lives on the other side of the country in New York, with his own busy career. He's a divorce lawyer, which is both fitting and satisfying given the way we grew up.

"What are you up to?" he says like it's totally normal for him to be calling to shoot the breeze rather than getting straight to the point. We're not phone talkers, which means if we call, it usually goes like this:

Hey, man.

Hey.

You okay?

Yep. You?

Yep.

Okay, see ya later.

And then we text each other memes on occasion to let the other know we're still alive.

"I'm currently driving back to Rome, Kentucky. Which, by the way, gets really shitty service, and my call could drop at any second." Yet another reason I'm dreading going back there. When I say this town has no service, I mean it's like a black hole. If you want to make a call, you have to walk around with your phone extended above your head just hoping the cell phone gods will bestow a single bar. My agency told me it's gotten a little better since I was there last with the help of several shops that installed wifi in their establishments, which I guess is better than nothing.

"I thought you weren't going until tomorrow?" asks Ethan.

I adjust my grip on the steering wheel. "Decided to go tonight instead."

I intentionally leave out the part about dinner, and seeing Annie, and then bailing on my night with Gretchen. Mainly because it isn't a big deal, and I don't want him to make it into one. I'm just tired and distracted, that's it. Annie happened to throw me off balance a little, and all I need is a solid night's sleep before my job starts tomorrow to get my head in the right place.

"Cool," Ethan says and then goes quiet. The pause grows and grows until it feels tangible. Something big is coming, I can feel it. And if he's stalling this much, it's because he knows I'm not going to like it.

"So . . . uh—listen." He stops. "I need to tell you something."

"Okay."

"Um . . . shit, I'm just going to say it. I asked Hannah to marry me last night." Another pause. "She said yes."

My throat closes. A cold sweat breaks out on the back of my neck, and my hands grip the wheel so hard my knuckles turn white.

"Come on, Will. Say something," Ethan urges when I stay silent too long.

But I don't want to say anything. I want to scoff. I want to curse at him and hang up.

I squeeze the steering wheel tighter. "I don't know what you expect me to say to this. Congrats? So happy for you? I can't do that, and you know it."

Ethan sighs heavily. I hate disappointing him like this, but he knows where I stand on marriage, and until a few months ago, he stood right here beside me in avoiding it.

"I don't expect you to congratulate me, but maybe to . . . I don't know, just try to hear me out."

I grind my teeth and stare out at the dark road. "Dammit, Ethan. I don't want to hear you out! You practically just met her. Like what, three months ago? How in the hell is that long enough to know that you can spend your life with her? You're a divorce lawyer for shit's sake, you know better than this."

"Yes, I am, so you know that I'm going in with my eyes wide open. But I love her, man. I gotta take a chance because . . . I'm helpless to do anything else."

Helpless to do anything else. I want to punch him in the face.

"Well, now I really know it's a mistake. Tell me it's for practical reasons—that she needed to go on your insurance or you wanted a tax break. Anything other than you're doing it out of a misguided romantic notion—then I could come around to it. But helplessness? Ridiculous."

"Why does it have to be misguided?" he asks sharply.

"You know why!" My voice is hard as granite. I can't believe I'm even having to explain this to him. "You and I grew up under the same damn roof, Ethan. Our parents were serial cheaters. They were toxic and they blamed all their shit on us. Or maybe I shielded you too much for you to remember? Maybe I should have taken the headphones off your ears and unlocked our bedroom door when they were screaming at each other in the kitchen and we were upstairs scared out of our minds?"

"I remember just fine," he says, but I wonder if he really does.

We both go silent as memories swim through our heads. Mine

most likely different from his because unlike him, I took most of the brunt of our dysfunctional upbringing, always trying to create at least an illusion of normalcy for Ethan. Our parents both worked at low-paying jobs that required them to be gone most of the day—sometimes nights too. I took care of my brother more than they ever did. I cooked most of his meals. I did our laundry. I made sure that he had help with his homework. And then when they'd come home exhausted and angry, they would tell me I was the one who messed up by not cleaning up the dishes after I made dinner. My perceived laziness would kick-start my parents' fighting. My dad would drink. My mom would leave and go to whichever dude she was sleeping with at the time—and in the end, they'd always come back together and tell me and Ethan that they were going to make it work for us.

There was very little happiness in our home when we were growing up, and there sure as hell wasn't love. Maybe marriage works for people who grew up in ideal homes with parents who support and care for each other; but for people like me and Ethan, we wouldn't even begin to know where to start to have a good relationship. I've tried it a few times. I never make it past the three-week mark before either I'm ending things or she is because we can't stop fighting, or that initial spark has faded. It's why I don't even bother trying anymore. I don't know how to love—not even sure I'm capable of it. In fact, I don't know that I believe in it.

And until three months ago when he met Hannah at a concert, Ethan felt the same way.

"I'm sorry, but I won't support you in this. You're making a huge mistake, and I can't sit by quietly while you do," I tell him plainly—hating that I have to upset him but incapable of not being honest with him at the same time. I love him too much to watch him potentially ruin his life like this. "Why not hit the brakes a little and take it slow? Keep dating for a while and see if your infatuation holds up—because most likely, that's all this is, and soon the fight-ing will kick in or she's going to cheat, or—"

"Stop. I'm choosing not to be hurt right now because I know where you're coming from, but I won't listen to you talk negatively about Hannah. As someone who understands better than anyone else, I hoped you'd be willing to listen to me and trust me when I say that I was wrong about relationships and marriage. We had a terrible upbringing, but not all relationships have to be like that. My relationship with Hannah is really good, Will. We communi-cate, we both give and take, and it's so nice to know that at the end of the day I have someone to love me through every—"

I end the call.

Later I'll text him and tell him I lost service, but for now I can't stand to hear him say any more about it. I hate that he's running full steam ahead toward something that could really hurt him, all because of feelings that are still brand-new. And I really hate that he doesn't seem to be as scared of it as I am. How is he able to move past it so quickly when it's something I'm affected by daily?

It doesn't matter. Because the fact is, when I started keeping people at arm's length was when I started really finding happiness—and I've never met anyone who's made me want to challenge that decision.

No one.

Not Gretchen, not the woman I met in Italy last year, not Jada from Texas, not Allie from Indiana, and not even . . .

My thoughts snag on the one name I can't bring myself to lump in with the others for some concerning reason:

Annie Walker.

CHAPTER FOUR

Annie

After leaving the restaurant, I go straight to Amelia and Noah's house for an Audrey Hepburn movie night with the girls. Before going in, however, I change out of Emily's dress and back into my usual overalls and T-shirt in my truck, and then shove the dress into my purse. It's fine—it's dark. No one saw anything.

My sisters and I have adopted Amelia's practice that if anything goes wrong, hurts, or makes you feel cloudy, you turn on an Audrey film and inject her smile into your heart until it heals. Or you know, just generally have a girls' night and gossip and eat popcorn.

That's what's happening tonight, while we're all four curled up in various parts of Noah's living room (or I guess I should think of it as Amelia's living room now) watching *Funny Face*. When Amelia first came to town a little over a year ago, we had never seen an Audrey movie. Amelia, however, is capital *O* obsessed with her. And after watching her movies, my sisters and I are too.

"Nope," Amelia says abruptly over the sound of the movie as she points to the hallway off the living room. "I saw you. Go back into your room."

My brother Noah emerges from the hallway wearing a sulky face. "Come on. Just let me watch this one with you guys. You can't keep me from my own damn living room."

Amelia has been very firm in protecting our early tradition of girls' night, and her engagement to Noah hasn't changed it. The funny thing is, I don't think he actually wants to watch the movie. He just loves to push Amelia's buttons, and she loves to have them pushed. Match made in heaven.

"Excuse me—it's my living room, too, now. And this is girls' night. No boys allowed."

Noah rolls his eyes. "Fine. I'm going to James's house." James is Noah's best friend and like our second brother. He owns Huxley Farm next door (*next door* meaning several acres over).

"I'll send a courier pigeon when we're done," says Amelia.

Noah slaps a ball cap on. "Just call."

"We'll flash the lights twenty times when it's safe to come back and get frisky, Lover Boy," says Maddie with a devious smile. Noah hates the nickname we gave him when he was first falling for Amelia. We'll never let it go.

Noah frowns. "Call me when it's over so I can come to bed. Some of us are not teachers on summer break and have actual jobs in the morning."

Emily cups her hands around her mouth to get a good projection going. "I'll turn on the hose and shoot a stream of water at James's window when we're on our way out, so you know the coast is clear to come home and make sweet, sweet love to Amelia!"

Noah tries his very best not to smile, but we can all see it there, lurking. He looks at me next. "Nothing from you?"

I shrug. "Tell James I said hi."

My sisters and Amelia all boo, and Noah just grins at me. "I like you the best."

He turns and leaves, but no sooner has the front door shut

behind him than it opens again. Noah storms back inside. He walks around the back of the couch where Amelia is sitting, puts his hands on her jaw, and tilts her face up so he can kiss her goodbye.

When I first saw Noah and Amelia together as a couple, I was shocked. Well, we all were. The affection between those two was so easy and freely given. I've never seen Noah like that with anyone else. It's inspiring watching the way they have managed their long-distance relationship all while dating within the limitations of Amelia's fame.

"Ew," says Madison with a disgusted laugh. "You're going to kiss her Spider-Man style? It wasn't a good look for Tobey, and it's not a good look for you either."

Emily throws a pillow at Maddie, and she deflects it with a karate chop.

"I love you," Noah says in a whisper to Amelia after the kiss, but I'm sitting close enough to hear it.

I smile down at my lap because I adore Amelia and Noah's relationship. I think it must be similar to what my parents had. Sturdy, deep, and dependable. And they sure look at each other with hearts in their eyes just like I've seen in all the photos of my parents. It's the kind of love that just works and makes everyone around them envious. It's what I want. The superglue-sticky, not-going-anywhere, till-death-do-us-part relationship. Someone to step up beside me and lend me his hand where we'll walk happily together through life.

Noah eventually leaves, and Amelia's cheeks are completely pink as we watch my personal favorite out of all of Audrey Hepburn's films, *Funny Face*. I deeply relate to Jo—the character Audrey plays. Jo works in a bookstore (which would be my dream job if I didn't already have a dream job owning my own flower shop), and she is considered quiet and introspective, maybe even a little plain.

But in the movie, Dick Avery (who is played by Fred Astaire), a famous fashion magazine photographer, spots Jo and sees something in her that isn't plain or quiet at all. Together, he and Maggie Prescott, the editor of *Quality* magazine, sweep Jo off to Paris, where they pull her out of her shell, turning her into a model and teaching her how to dress and pose and carry herself like a woman of Quality. Of course, in the end, Jo and Dick fall madly in love and live happily ever after—ending like every good story should.

"See," I say with a big sigh as I point to the TV after the final scene of Audrey and Fred dancing to the song "'S Wonderful." "That's what I need."

Maddie and Emily are in the kitchen and out of earshot.

"An old man to fall in love with you?" asks Amelia with a chuckle.

I gasp. "Don't you dare slander the great Fred Astaire and the hero of my favorite movie."

Amelia grimaces and leans forward to grab another handful of popcorn from the coffee table. "Normally, I wouldn't say a word against an Audrey movie. But even I have to admit the pairing is odd here. Audrey was in her twenties and Fred was definitely in his fifties."

"Oh. Deflating," I say staring at the screen again.

"So anyway, why do you want a major age-gap love affair, Annabanana?"

I pull my legs up onto the couch and wrap my arms around them. "I don't want an age-gap love affair. I just want a love affair in general. So I'm saying I wish I could have someone like Dick Avery or Maggie Prescott swoop in and teach me how to be the Quality woman everyone wants to date. Or at least I want my dates to not say I'm boring and then have their friends call and make up excuses to leave."

"What?!" says Amelia a little too loudly.

"Shh!" I hiss, looking over my shoulder to where my sisters are busy cooking something in the kitchen. Actually, Madison is cooking, and Emily is hovering around her and badgering her with itinerary questions for their upcoming trip to Mexico for a vacation with a few of their other teacher friends. They've been saving for a year to afford it.

"Is that what happened tonight?" Amelia asks me in a whisper this time.

"Yes." I rub my hands up and down my shins. "But don't blame him—"

"I do."

"I was a terrible date. I barely talked and then when I did, I sprung marriage on the poor guy. And then even after all of that, Will made him pay for the drinks even though I dumped John's in his lap. It was a disaster."

Amelia sits forward abruptly. "Wait, wait, wait. Go back. Did you say Will?"

I nod. "Yeah, Will. You know? Will Griffin."

"Will Griffin, as in my bodyguard Will Griffin? He was on your date?"

"No." I pause. "I mean, yes. Your bodyguard was at the restaurant where I was having the worst date of my life, but he appeared to be on a very successful date of his own."

"But he hung out with you?"

I raise a shoulder. "Well, sort of. He came over and said hi, but that was right in the thick of John getting the heck out of Dodge, so then Will walked me out to the truck and we talked."

"You talked. To Will?"

"Why do you keep repeating my statements and forming them as a question?"

"I'm just trying to picture it." She circles her hands in the air like she's trying to conjure up an instant replay. "He's always so businessy with me. I practically have to pry friendship from him, and here he is just strolling right up to you and chatting."

I frown and take another bite of popcorn. "It was only for like five minutes tops. Not a big deal," I say, completely disregarding the slightly too alert look in Amelia's eyes. Maybe she thinks I have a thing for Will and is worried I'm going to try to date him? *Ha!* A hilarious thought. "Anyway, he went back into the restaurant pretty quickly and said he's staying the night with the woman he was on a date with and that he'll be in Rome tomorrow." I nudge her knee. "I didn't know you had hired him to come back, by the way. Are you having safety issues?"

"Not really. A few paparazzi have been getting too close lately, but I haven't felt worried. They're just hungry for wedding details. Keysha is the one who thought it was time to call in a mobile guard until things settle down again after the wedding."

Keysha is Amelia's manager. She hired her a year ago after finding out her old manager had been doing some shady business behind her back. I think Keysha has been really good for Amelia—as is Claire, the personal assistant Amelia hired to help her life run a little smoother.

"But you're wrong," says Amelia abruptly. "Will isn't coming tomorrow. He's here now."

Wait, what? I try not to look too excited at that prospect and mentally intimidate my cheeks into not blushing at just the mention of his name. "But he told me he was staying with Gretchen tonight."

Amelia looks like she's studying me for answers before a big test—expecting to find them written all over my skin in red ink. "Interesting. All I know is about thirty minutes ago, Harold, the night shift guard, texted me and said that Will had arrived at the surveillance trailer and got his emergency satellite phone"—which they keep on hand because service is spotty around here—"and then went on to Mabel's Inn for the night and would be ready to start at eight A.M. tomorrow. So he must have decided to cut his date short."

Amelia is in the process of having an actual guard shack built on their premises, but it won't be ready for at least another month or two. Until then, her security team always stays down the road at Mabel's Inn.

Also, I will choose to not read anything into the fact that Will didn't stay the night at Gretchen's place.

I. Will. Not!

Do you hear that, you romantic schmuck of a heart? There's absolutely no way Will coming to Rome a night early has anything to do with me and our meetup earlier tonight. For all I know, they hooked up super fast and he left. End of story.

"What are y'all talking about?" Maddie asks, popping her head over the back of the couch.

Without looking the slightest bit suspicious, Amelia says, "My bodyguard—Will Griffin. I was just telling Annie that he's going to be back in town and sticking with me until after the wedding."

Maddie's eyes light up and, for some reason, it makes my fingers twitchy.

Emily rounds the corner and sits back down in the armchair. "Wait, who?"

"The hottest bodyguard in the country," says Maddie, also coming to take a seat in the living room.

"Oooh, Will Griffin?"

Again, I don't love that she immediately knew who Maddie was talking about. But I'm not sure why I care. It's not like I have hopes where he's involved. And, honestly, my outgoing, gorgeous sisters have way more of a chance with him than I do. Oh, and you know, the most important part: I want a stable relationship. Will in no way equals stable.

Propping her face mischievously on her fists, Maddie aims a look at Amelia. "Okay—be honest with us, did you and Will ever hook up?"

"Gross, no!" Amelia says with a genuinely disgusted look. "First of all, Will is like my brother at this point, and the thought of that literally makes me gag. Second of all, I've just never been attracted to him."

"Never?" asks Emily with a studying expression. "You're telling me that even when he started working for you, you never once found that beautiful muscular man attractive?"

Amelia shrugs. "I don't know what to tell you. He just never did it for me. I think he's a great guy, but he's not my type. Noah on the other hand . . ."

We all three groan.

"We're going to kick you out of our group if you continue to act lovesick over our brother," says Maddie.

"I am lovesick over your brother. Hence the upcoming wedding!" She pretends to flick Maddie in the skull.

"But that's no excuse to act like it on girls' night. I mean, dammit, Amelia, at least do the polite thing and pretend you're sick of him for our sakes," says Maddie before wincing.

Emily is already handing me a pen as I flip open my spiral pocket notebook and add a tally next to her name.

"How many more do I have until I have to pay up?" Maddie asks.

"Three." I close the No Swear Notebook and wish I could throw it off a cliff. What started off as an attempt at humor on my end has turned into a full-fledged part of my character that my siblings won't let me escape. Everyone gets a tally mark when they say a curse word and then has to pay twenty bucks when they hit their twenty swears in a month. It hasn't made anyone swear less, to be honest. Instead, it's made us regular contributors to various nonprofit organizations around the town because that's where I donate our spoils each month after everyone pays up. Just call us a bunch of philanthropists.

"Back to Will, do you think he likes slightly bossy women with blonde hair?" Emily asks, obviously kidding but still kicking up an urge inside me to jump to my feet and yell *No! You can't have him!*

I stay quiet.

Maddie apparently has the same thought as me. "No way! If anyone gets to date Will, it's me. Obviously, he's the bad boy type and needs someone like me to complement him." She bats her eyelashes playfully. I love her dearly, but I'm dreaming of plucking out each one of those lashes in this moment.

Amelia—bless her—then looks at me. "You know, I think he'd do better with someone like Annie."

Madison barks a laugh at this. Emily chuckles too. "Annabanana and Will Griffin? No. Absolutely not," says Maddie, chuckling the whole time.

I smile softly and try very hard not to show that my stomach is twisting up in a tight knot.

"I think I have to agree with Maddie on this one," says Emily. "Annie is so soft and sweet and virginal. Can you imagine her with someone like Will? He'd eat her alive."

I think Emily meant for that to sound upsetting, but for some reason, it's not sounding all that unappealing to me. Something I would never admit to my sisters, because, yes, they unfortunately know I'm a virgin and remind me every day of my life.

"Hmm," says Amelia, with narrowed eyes and a soft smile in my direction. "What do you think, Annie? Would you and Will be good together?"

Immediately my cheeks go hot. If I say yes, my sisters will laugh and continue to point out all the obvious reasons we're not right for each other. I already know all the reasons (I'm a homebody—he's adventurous. He has dated countless women—I can't even get a guy to finish a date with me), so I decide to skip the embarrassment. "All I want is a nice guy who is going to be there for me every day."

"See," says Madison with a playful scoff. "Definitely not Will—BuzzFeed's sexiest bodyguard and serial dater. And because Annie will wait until she gets married to have sex, and Emily is too bossy for Will, I think I should be the one to bring Will home for a night."

Emily hits her with a pillow. "How about none of us bring Will home, and we all remain friends?"

"Deal," I agree a little too quickly.

"*Fine*. Damn party poopers," says Madison before going to get the brownies she was baking from the oven. In the presence of chocolate, all men are forgotten.

The next hour is spent talking about the wedding and going over final details we've been meaning to plan with Amelia. I'll be providing the flowers, and I couldn't be more excited. Well, I could be more excited if I also had a date to take to the wedding, but I guess that's beside the point.

Later, after we're all heading out for the night, Amelia stops me at the door once Emily and Maddie are walking to their trucks. "Okay, so I've been thinking about your dating predicament and what you said after the movie."

"Do you think I should visit a senior citizen center to find an old man to marry?"

Amelia frowns. "I'm disturbed by how quickly you said that. Makes me think you've been contemplating that idea all along."

"Continue with your thoughts."

Amelia smiles. "I'm still putting all the pieces together in my head right now, but if I had a way to help you get better at dating, would you want to do it?"

"Sure," I say easily, because honestly, I trust Amelia with my life. I'd do anything she asked of me. In some ways, I feel closer to her than I do my sisters. I don't know how it happened, but when Amelia came into my life, our bond felt like one that had been forming since childhood. "All I want is to marry someone as perfect for me as Noah is for you and my dad was for my mom. If you can help me make that happen, I'll do anything you say."

Amelia gives me a wide (slightly devious?) smile. "Perfect. I'll let you know when I figure it out."

CHAPTER FIVE

Will

After a sleepless night, it's finally a normal hour to get up for the day. Five A.M. (Okay, so it's normal for me at least.) It carries over from my military days. I served in the Air Force for six years on active duty as a Security Forces specialist, and two years in the reserves while training and starting my career as an executive protection agent, aka an EPA. To be honest, I entered the military for all the wrong reasons. It had never been my dream, but when I needed a path to take quickly, it was there. I don't regret my time in the military, but it just never quite felt right for me. There wasn't a lot of happiness in it for me. And now here I am, year five as an EPA and still not sure this is what I'm supposed to be doing.

I open my eyes and have to reorient where I am. Right. Rome, Kentucky, sleeping in the room that will be mine for the next month. I roll my head to the right and am assaulted with a piece of embroidery art hanging on the wall: Bless This Mess. It's really too bad the guard shack isn't finished yet, and I have to sleep at the inn.

Since I was here last, Amelia and Noah have made a lot of alterations to their property. Not only did they install a top-of-the-line security system around the house and the perimeter of their property, but they are building a security house on the premises. For now, there is a small surveillance trailer at the front of the property where Harold monitors at night and then trades off in the morning with another guy, Sam, to monitor during the day.

I've worked for several celebrities during my career as an executive protection agent (or bodyguard, as the masses call us), and every celebrity approaches their security differently. Some think having a security team is a waste of money, and they don't put nearly enough into their own protection. I hate seeing that. Usually it takes something really awful happening to wake them up and show them that more money needs to be thrown into their security budget.

But then there are people like Amelia, who have always taken their safety seriously (except for the time she bolted in the middle of the night and didn't tell any of us where she was going). Fortunately, this town is safe for the most part, and no one, not even the press, knew where she was for a while. She was never in serious danger. Plus I'm confident Noah would have beat the shit out of anyone who came near her. But now word has gotten out as paparazzi have spotted her here in town, which, unfortunately, has put Rome on the map. So Amelia puts an enormous amount of her income into security, which is why I'm here. I'll follow Amelia around through the month and make sure she stays safe and unbothered.

On tour, my job is exciting nearly all the time. I sweep locations before she goes in, and then I accompany her everywhere, constantly scrutinizing the people around us, and sometimes intentionally blocking the paparazzi's view if she doesn't want to be photographed that day. And during concerts, I hover backstage, ready to help restrain any overzealous fans who get past stage security and onto the platform.

I generally only work eight hours at a time unless we have a concert at night, but I get more breaks than you'd think. Usually when Amelia is just hanging at home or in her hotel room, the surveillance guys take over. That's when I get downtime to explore whatever city we're in and meet all kinds of people. Thanks to my job, I've gone skydiving in Paris, snorkeling in the Bahamas, and ATV riding in Cape Town. I always try to do at least one exciting thing that each city is known for.

But now I'm in Rome, Kentucky, staring at a white ceiling in a frilly bed-and-breakfast where absolutely nothing exciting takes place. There's only one bar in town and nothing else. Forget adventure. Looks like I'll have to take up embroidery.

It's only a month, and it's for Amelia, I remind myself.

I throw on a pair of athletic shorts and running shoes and spend the next hour jogging through this backwoods country town. My bad mood slowly melts away as I watch the sun come up and highlight the wheat and corn fields. Everything is gold for a few minutes, and although I've always been more of a city guy, even I can admit that summertime in the country is beautiful. The grass is so green it almost doesn't feel real. Eventually I loop my way through the town just as shop owners are opening their doors.

And that's when I notice it: eyes peering at me from all directions. Through shop windows. Peeking out entrances. Around corners. Even though I'm drenched with sweat and dead tired, I pick up my speed because I swear everyone in this town is moving out of their shops like a freaky horror movie to stare at me as I run by. What the hell?

When I finally make it back to the inn and am bent over, hands on my thighs trying to catch my breath, a pair of black flats enters my line of sight. They stop right next to the big drop of sweat that just fell from my forehead to the pavement. It's so hot out I swear it sizzles.

I look up and find none other than Amelia Rose in her dark jeans, black-and-white-striped tee, and a travel coffee mug in hand—a big bag with a logo for the local diner hangs off her arm. Her eyebrows lift, and I'm still too out of breath to say anything more than, "Hey. I'm back in town."

"I see that," she says, amusement coloring her tone. "I was just picking up some breakfast from the diner and thought I'd come by and make sure you got settled in. But here you are." She sips her coffee, looking like she could laugh.

"Here I am." I can barely breathe still.

"So you jogged through town like that?"

"Like what?" I say, finally standing to my full height and using my wadded up T-shirt to soak up the sweat from my face and neck.

"Bare chested and a walking billboard for your tattoo artist?"

I look down at my abdomen as if I'm just realizing I'm not wearing a shirt. "Yeah," I say, looking up at her and still breathing heavily. "Is that bad? Is there a dress code around here for running?"

Again she smirks. "Not officially. But I better get back home so I can field all the calls about to flood my landline."

"Wait, why?" I ask her retreating back.

"Because the gossip train is going to be chugging along at warp speed this morning. Gotta catch it before it gets too far!" She raises her mug. "Come up to the house after you get changed. We've got lots of breakfast to share!"

Executive protection agents are not supposed to enjoy sit-down breakfasts with the people they are protecting. And yet Amelia has always been determined to add me to her circle of friends if it's the last thing she does.

Half an hour later and freshly showered, I knock on Amelia and Noah's front door. She opens it with her landline phone stuck to her ear. "Uh-huh. Absolutely. That's an excellent point, Harriet, I'll be sure to pass that along." She smiles and waves me inside.

I have to step over the curly phone cord that is running from the kitchen around the small island, disappearing around the corner wall, and then down the hallway and up to the phone she's holding. It's also looped once around her waist.

Amelia points toward the living room, gesturing for me to go in and have a seat. She spends the last bit of her conversation on the phone unraveling herself from the cord. I hear a door open and shut behind me, and when I see Noah appear from the hallway, I stand.

"Will," he says coming into the room and extending his hand. I clasp it, and we give each other a firm shake. "It's good to have you back."

I genuinely like Noah. Amelia dated a few guys before him whose teeth I wanted to knock down their throats. But this guy is legit. He's loyal and puts Amelia first. I trust him and he seems to trust me.

"It's good to be working for Amelia again."

He grins. "I'm not sure the town shares your joy."

"What do you mean by that?" My eyes track his gaze over my shoulder to where Amelia is still on the phone, nodding absent-mindedly to whoever is blabbering her ear off.

"That's her fourth call since you got back from your run."

We both turn our attention to Amelia as she finishes her call, slowly moving the phone from her ear, closer and closer to the receiver at every word. "Yep . . . Uh-uh . . . Absolutely . . . Okay . . . I will . . . Bye now!" She hangs up and sags dramatically against the wall, sliding all the way to the floor. And then she points, leveling her finger at me. "You!"

"Me?" I say with lifted brows, pointing at myself.

"Yes, you! You just had to run this morning with your shirt off, causing an uproar in the entire town."

"Are you kidding?" This has to be some sort of joke.

Noah shakes his head. "Nope. Town's in a tizzy. You really did it this time."

Amelia stands and walks into the living room. "I just got off the phone with Harriet, who did not at all appreciate the way you paraded your nakedness around town—inviting the unmarried young ladies to stumble into lust."

My jaw falls open. I'm speechless.

Noah shakes his head at me. "So unthoughtful. Are you trying to seduce them? Your first day on the job?"

"Who? The young ladies?" I raise my hands. "No. I swear. I just got hot and took off my shirt like I normally do, and . . ." I pause when I hear both of their barely contained laughter. "And you're messing with me."

Noah nods this time, smirking. "We're messing with you." He walks by and claps me on the shoulder. "Welcome back to Rome. Where no one has anything to do but complain about one another."

He passes Amelia and stops to kiss her on the mouth—not a long kiss and not a short kiss either. Just . . . heartfelt. I rub my chest. "I gotta get to work. I'll see ya after a while. And Will," he turns back to me. "Please do your best to keep your damn clothes on today."

"I'll try."

Once he's out the door, Amelia pours me a cup of coffee and I sit at their little kitchen table. We catch up for a few minutes, and she tells me what's been going on in more detail with the press and a few superfans who get a little too close for comfort. We set up a game plan for the month and decide that we'll go on a day-to-day scheduling basis. A morning meetup to see what her plans are for the day, and then I'll be around to escort her into town and anywhere else she needs to go, but I don't need to hang around while she's home or in her studio. She's apparently working on a new album and will spend a lot of time here, and I'll be left to my own fun while she does. Goody.

She's hopeful that after the wedding, everything will calm down. Either way, I plan on asking to be transferred to a different client after the month is up. Not because I don't like working for Amelia—I always have—but I won't stay put in this town for a minute longer than necessary. Boredom does not suit me.

"So that sounds good to you?" she asks.

I nod. "Sounds great. I'm here for anything you need. Seriously, yard work? Gutters cleaned? I'm your guy. You know I get stir-crazy when I have nothing to do."

Amelia laughs. "I do know. Which is why I'm happy to hear you say you'd be willing to help out with other things in your downtime."

I sit forward, eager to know what she has in mind. "Yes, anything. Name it."

If I'm not mistaken, her smile turns a little mischievous. Anyone else would see that smile and think she was implying something sexual. But knowing Amelia as I do, it's definitely not that. It's something different. Something tricky. Something I'm not going to want to do.

"Great. For starters, do you mind taking a letter into town for me?"

"Sure," I say, dragging out the word to let her know I'm onto her. "Like to the post office?"

"Nope." She grins wider. "To the flower shop, actually."

And because there's only one flower shop in town, that means I'll be seeing Annie Walker today. Shit.

If I wasn't on edge before, on my way out the door with a discreet little white envelope in hand, Amelia calls out, "Hey, Will!"

"Yeah?"

"Don't say no, okay?"

"To what?"

"To what's in that envelope." The look on her face is all plea and genuine something. "Please don't say no."

CHAPTER SIX

Will

This time for my trip into town, I'm fully dressed. It doesn't seem to stop everyone from popping their heads out of storefronts to stare. I wave at a lady who emerges from the quilt shop. She blushes and waves back. A little farther down, a man rushes out of the hardware store (I think I remember his name is Phil) and asks if I need any tools. Tape measures are on sale today, he informs me eagerly and with eyes that can only be described as slightly feral.

"I'm good for today, thank you." I try to step around him, but he steps too. I think maybe he wants some insurance that I'll only shop in his store for anything handyman related while I'm here, so with a wide smile, I tag on, "But I know where to go if I need anything."

"Sure you do!" he beams back, slightly over the top in a disconcerting way. He then yells over his shoulder to a guy about his same age writing in chalk on their propped-up street sign. "Todd! I said tape measures are on sale today. Not screwdrivers."

Todd sighs and silently wipes away his intricately detailed handiwork, starting over. Man—poor Todd.

"Right, well, I'm actually headed toward the flower shop, so . . ." Kindly get out of my way.

His eyes narrow. "Ah, going to see our Annie, are you?"

"Sort of—but not specifically." I move to the right of the sidewalk, and he moves with me. Again.

"Sure, sure. I get it. The kids are all against commitment these days. It's supposedly cool to keep your options open." He does air quotes when he says cool.

I shift on my feet and eye him, feeling like I'm missing something here. I chuckle in an easy-natured way, though. "Listen, Phil, right? I'm just running an errand for my boss." Everyone knows I work for Amelia, but I'm careful anyway. "An errand which I really need to be getting to. So if you don't mind, I'll need a raincheck on our chat." Kind but firm. The ever-present tightrope I walk.

I try to edge around him but abruptly stop when I feel Phil's hand splay out across my chest. I slowly look down at his fingers and every ounce of congeniality I feel dissolves. Now I'm fighting the urge to wrap my hand around his wrist and twist it behind his back. I hate that that's my first instinct when I'm touched without warning. Part of me wonders if maybe I've been doing this job too long. But what else would I do?

I force myself to breathe and relax—because this is Phil, a man who has lived in this town his whole life and has likely watched Annie grow up. So instead of shoving him backward with a warning to not touch me again, I look him in the eyes and listen.

"Our Annie is a sweetie, you know?" He's saying it in a cheery tone, but there's an edge to it that I don't miss. Unspoken words of warning: our Annie is a sweetie, so don't mess with her, or I'll cut off your balls with the chain saw we have on sale today for 50 percent off. Phil and his blue-and-white-striped collared shirt, khaki shorts, tube socks over his ankles, and dad tennis shoes is threatening me. Me—a highly trained executive protection agent who specializes in hand-to-hand combat, evasive maneuvering, and weapons training. And guess what? It's working. Phil has the fatherly stare down that makes my blood curdle.

"I know," I say honestly, because only one look in Annie's soft blue eyes is enough to inform a person that she has kindness and empathy spilling out of her soul.

Phil nods. "I don't want to hear of anyone—and I do mean anyone—hurting our girl. Understand?"

I respect Phil and his tube-sock-wearing self more, even if I am a little irritated at his insinuation that I would purposely hurt her. Or any woman. "I understand, sir."

He pats my chest and removes his hand. "And wear a shirt when you jog from now on. You about made Gemma pass out into her clearance fabric bin this morning. Woulda never found her after that."

One month. I can do this for one month. Thirty days. I've endured worse.

CHAPTER SEVEN

Annie

Heaven will undeniably be made up of flowers.

There's nothing in the world that boosts my mood like standing in my flower shop and taking in a deep breath of flowers. The morning sunshine spills through the large, shop-front windows and kisses the rainbow of blooms bursting from every corner of my little shop.

I wish my mom could see it. She adored flowers—and was even the one who started the flower crop on our local farm where I buy my wholesale flowers. She's the reason my shop is named Charlotte's Flowers. And as strange as it sounds, I tried to match the space to my mom's smile. Bright, open, welcoming, hopeful. I barely got the chance to know her, and yet I ache for her often. To know what she'd think of the wooden buckets filled with long-stemmed flowers lining the perimeter of the shop. Would she like the light wide-plank flooring? I think she would love the giant old farm table in the back center of the room I found for a steal at a flea market.

What would Mom say about the void I can't seem to get rid of?

Somehow I feel like I've betrayed her by opening her dream flower shop and realizing it's not enough for me. It's got to be that my heart is ready for love and marriage and a family, and when I get all of those things, I'll be content. I mean, one look at a picture of my parents would tell you that they had everything they needed in each other. They exuded joy and peace. I want that.

Currently I should be finishing the bouquet James called in earlier that he'll be picking up soon; instead, I'm busy with Very Important Work. (Sneaking in a chapter of the latest pirate romance I can't put down.)

> Coraline's breasts were heaving above the tight bodice of her gown in a manner that drove Allistair mad with desire. Unable to keep himself away any longer, he snaked his arm around Coraline's waist and pulled her tightly to him. "Coraline," he whispered, his mouth only a breath above her own. "Please. I beg you. Allow me to—"

The bell above my shop door chimes, and I barely manage to not audibly groan from how annoyed I am at being interrupted right as Allistair was begging Coraline to let him . . . what? Kiss her? Make love to her? I need to know!

I look up, gasp, and throw my book over my shoulder, somewhere into the abyss of my storage room.

There is a man standing in my shop with a roguish smile and a sleeve of tattoos.

"Hi," says Will Griffin looking far too amused. "Am I interrupting something?"

"No." I answer too quickly.

He smiles curiously. "But you did just throw a book behind you, right?"

"No." Again, too quick. I swallow and tell my skin to stop

boiling. "But if I did—hypothetically speaking—it would be because I don't want you to know what book I'm reading. So please don't ask any more questions."

His smile widens as he advances into the shop to stand right in front of my worktable. "I see. The illusive if-I-tell-you-I'll-have-to-kill-you book. But you should know, it's torture in and of itself not knowing what book it is."

Gosh. Speaking of torture. It's nearly unbearable to look right into Will's eyes. It's like staring at the sun. Too powerful for mere mortals.

I purposely change the subject. "What can I help you with, Will? Are you here for flowers or are you on bodyguard duty?"

"Executive protection agent."

I frown and he sees my confusion.

"We prefer to be called executive protection agents. But currently I think I fall more under the title of errand boy." He extends a small envelope across the table to me, and my brain momentarily blanks when my gaze connects with the black ink of his butterfly tattoo so close to me. Something about it feels illegal. Like it's so sexy that this man's hand should be on a list of Most Dangerous Males hidden in a top secret filing cabinet of the FBI.

"I have no idea what's in it," he admits when I finally take the letter from him—careful to make sure our hands don't brush in the process because I have no desire to spontaneously combust right here in my flower shop. "Amelia just asked me to bring it to you and for you to open it while I'm here."

"Seems kind of odd," I say, and Will just shrugs his shoulders—white T-shirt straining against his muscles as he does.

His eyes wander from me to the buckets of flowers against the wall before he tucks his hands easily into the front pockets of his jeans, turning away to explore the shop. I realize this is the first time he's ever been in here. When he was in town last, he always hovered outside whichever establishment Amelia was in, only entering if there was a large crowd. But this is Rome, and there is never more than one or two people in an establishment at a time.

Even though I'm curious why Amelia would send me a letter via her bodyguard, it takes me a minute to peel my eyes away from Will and the way he's taking in every detail of my shop. He touches petals and stems. He looks up, exposing the long column of his throat to look at the thick crown molding around the top perimeter of the shop. Taps his foot against the wide plank floors. I could watch him do this all day.

Instead of being creepy, however, I force myself to crack open the seal of the envelope and read Amelia's handwriting. After quickly scanning her words, I promptly fold the letter and consider putting it in my mouth and swallowing so it's never seen again.

"What's it say?" Will asks, having turned around and, apparently, watched me read it.

"Nothing." My voice is suspiciously prim. I walk to the shop door and fling it open. "Well, I'm sure you've got lots of things to do today. Don't let me keep you. Thanks for bringing this by!"

"I don't think so." He takes hold of its handle and slowly closes the door. He turns his eyes to me. "What was in that letter?"

I give him a nonchalant smile. "Oh, you know, nothing important. Girl stuff."

He steps closer, and I take one instinctive step away. Not because I feel threatened, but because I feel . . . the opposite of threatened.

"I know that letter had something to do with me."

I talk out of the side of my mouth like a ventriloquist. "Someone's a bit of a narcissist."

"Annie. Show me the letter." Will's tone is calculatingly easy and his smile is dripping with seduction. He's baiting me.

I don't know what comes over me, but before I can stop myself, the words, "You can't make me," fly out of my mouth.

His smile melts into something roguish and challenging. "Wanna bet?" He steps closer, and an excitement I've never known twirls through my veins.

There is absolutely no way I'm letting Will Griffin get ahold of this letter. What was Amelia thinking? It's embarrassing! It's a terrible idea! Which makes the letter *Terribly Embarrassing*.

Will steps closer—slowly—and with every step he takes, my skin sizzles happily. Which is confusing because this is not the time to think of happy sizzles.

I pinch the letter fiercely between my fingers using every muscle my poor little under-toned fingers will provide, and then tuck it behind my back. "This letter isn't for you, sir."

"But it's about me, right?"

"No." I hold my chin higher.

He grins. "You're lying."

"And how would you know that?"

"Because I've watched you. I know your tell."

The floor swoops under my feet. "You've . . . watched me?"

He doesn't look embarrassed or like he's just admitted something creepy. He states it like a fact. "It's my job to watch and listen to everyone Amelia interacts with. And that includes you. Which is how I know that when you're not telling the whole truth, you always lift your chin slightly. Like you have to muster up the courage to tell a lie. It's cute."

Ugh, I wish he wouldn't say "cute." It's disorienting. Compliments from him make me dizzy. Ah, but that's his motive, isn't it?! He's like the snake in *The Jungle Book*, growing closer with swirly hypnotizing eyes.

"We both know I'm going to get that letter, Annie, so how about you hand it over and save us both some time." His voice is so charming and playful that I could melt. And with him this close, I can smell him. A mix of body wash and deodorant—but not cologne. A subtle masculine and clean scent that's so good it hurts.

"You'll have to try to steal it from me if you want it. Because there's no way I'm giving you this letter."

He chuckles soft and low—like I'm adorable for even considering going against him. "I'm not trying to steal anything. I am succeeding in stealing it. Your first mistake was ever letting me get this close."

"Oh? Then how is the letter still in my hand?"

"It's not. You dropped it a minute ago."

I gasp and break eye contact to verify that the paper is in fact still pinched between my fingers, and when I do, Will uses my momentary disorientation to lurch forward fast as lightning and slip the paper from my grasp.

"And that's how you lie without a tell, Annie Walker," he says with a gleeful smile. "Now let's see what Amelia wrote about me in here, shall we?"

He barely gets his last word out before I launch myself at him, intent on ripping that paper from his hand, and then tearing it into a million little unreadable slivers. But I forget that I'm five foot three, and he's at least six feet or more and easily holds the letter above his head to begin reading as I jump like a child trying to pluck an apple from a tree.

He clears his throat dramatically. "Dear Annie! Remember when I said I had a solution to your dating problems?"

"Give me that letter!"

"Well, I've brought him right to your door. I'm convinced Will is exactly who you need too—"

"*William!*" I yell loudly, my own voice scraping against my nerves as I continue to hop and tug and circle him for that letter. "You can't read this! It's embarrassing."

This time he lowers the letter in front of my face like bait. It dangles lightly between his finger and thumb. I purse my lips together knowing full well he's going to pull it away the second I go for it, but I still do it anyway. And yep, he immediately yanks it to the right—out of my reach. We're chest to chest now. My face is tilted up and his is tilted down. I could kiss him right now if I wanted to.

Where in the world did that thought come from?

"What makes you think my name is William?" he says quietly, like we're lying together in bed rather than duking it out in a flower shop.

"Fine. Please give me the letter, Wilson," I whisper in return.

He grins. "Definitely not after realizing I'm the solution to your dating problems. I'm so intrigued I could never give it back now."

I growl and lunge for the paper. He rainbows it up over his head and to the other side.

"Wilbert, please give it to me right now or I'll be forced to . . . say rude things to you."

"So polite to warn me," he says in an impressed tone of voice. Like he's seconds away from laughing. "I think I'd like to hear the rude things."

This time I grab his bicep and haul it down. Given that he's twice my size and I haven't exercised anything more than my wit in years, I know he's letting me do it. But I use his pity to my advantage and twist his arm over my shoulder, whirling so my back is to him and I can grab the paper from his hand dangling in front of me. I experience momentary triumph where I'm sure I'm the world's newest Strong Woman until Will wraps his other arm around me and holds me in a backward hug. His hands cover mine, so now we're both holding the paper. I feel his breath against my ear. "What's your rude comment, Annie?"

A shiver ripples through me. I've never felt so alive.

"It's going to be awful," I taunt—struggling to breathe normally with the feel of his strong yet gentle arms encircling me and the butterflies whirling around in my stomach. "Super mean."

"I'm braced. Let me have it."

I swallow and turn my chin so I'm looking at his eyes—so close I could use a ruler and measure that black rim around his blue-gray irises with precision. "You're acting . . . like a . . . stingy . . . butt munch!"

He gasps. "Butt munch? You've cut right through my heart. I don't even know what that is but I'm devastated."

I'm laughing so hard now that I can barely stay upright. My knees are buckling, and Will is using his arms to hold me up as he laughs too.

"Fine," I say stumbling out of his hold to wave him off. "I give up. You're clearly not going away so just read it and get it over with."

He catches his breath, watching me with only the suggestion of a grin as he unfolds the paper. "You know, I thought you were supposed to be shy."

I shrug. "I am with most people." *But, oddly, not you,* is what I leave unspoken.

Will reads the letter, and I watch him closely as his eyes scan the words. Because I read it first, I know that Amelia (a woman who has lost her marbles) suggests I ask Will to be my dating coach. She thinks we should go on practice dates, and he can help me navigate my First Date Anxiety. She helpfully points out that Will has not had any shortage of dates over the few years she's known him, and he's considered a pro at it. She adds that despite the tattoos and menacing persona, he's a fantastic guy and would absolutely say yes. To this, I mentally laugh because I don't find Will menacing at all. Enticing, yes. Would look incredible on the cover of a historical romance? Absolutely. Afraid of him? Nope. Not a bit.

Amelia ends the letter by telling me to be brave and then asks me what Audrey would do. A cheap trick, Amelia Rose.

It's not bravery I'm lacking—the issue is the loud alarm ringing in my ear, warning me that this is a bad idea. I can't ask Will to practice date me because, well, just look at him! I clearly have a major crush, and judging by how my body reacts when he's around, this suggestion has disaster written all over it. I'll get feelings all tangled up and then be confused about what my goal really is. I'm a self-aware gal, and I know my flaws. Falling quickly for hunky mysterious men who look like pirates and don't do relationships is definitely one of them.

But I also can't fall for Will because he's not the kind of man I want to marry. I need dependable, sweet, and cozy. Someone to match my vibes. Someone to be a great dad to our future children and help with math homework and play catch in the yard. In comparison, Will is dangerous, and sexy, and exciting. The only thing he'll catch is my heart before he tosses it onto the ground and stomps it into a million tiny little pieces before sailing off into the sunset.

He's taking forever to read this letter. I dissect his expressions hoping for a clue to what's going on in his head. He gives me barely anything because he has a very good poker face, which I assume was learned from years of body guarding. His jaw flexes and mine does too. His eyebrow twitches and I twitch mine. And then abruptly his eyes cut to me, and he grins because he was watching me from the corner of his eye the whole time.

Well.

He turns away from me to finish the letter, and I roll my eyes.

The bell above my shop door chimes, and my attention is forced away from scrutinizing Will's every move to see my favorite and most challenging customer stroll in. "Buckle up, Buttercup! I've got an order for you that's either going to make you cry tears of joy or distress. We'll see."

Ms. Mabel, my grandma's best friend of more than fifty years and also the woman who helped raise me and my siblings, steps through the door—floral print dress clinging to her voluptuous form and swaying lightly at the hem. She's breathing heavily, like she power walked here, and has her leather purse clutched to her ample breast.

"Good morning, Mabel! What sort of order—"

I'm cut off when suddenly the shop door flies open like a saloon door. I half expect Mabel to whirl around and draw a six-shooter from a garter under her skirt.

"I need fifteen flower arrangements in colors of pink and white by tomorrow night!"

"Damn you, Harriet! I got here first," Mabel huffs.

"Don't curse at me. It's not my fault you dawdled." These two have been bickering since I was born. Not sure what started it, but I'm confident it will continue until they're both in their graves. Maybe even past the grave. Mabel will haunt Harriet's burial site, drawing inappropriate pictures on her gravestone, and Harriet will retaliate by bringing in a heavenly choir to sing at the top of their lungs around Mabel's resting place.

Mabel puts her hands on her hips and scowls. "I'm in charge of flowers for the ladies' tea. And I want purple flowers."

Harriet, with her chest heaving under her very appropriate gray A-line dress that perfectly matches her gray tightly coiled hair, fully enters the shop. "Standing up from the table in the middle of our planning session and running for the flower shop the second Deloris mentioned needing arrangements doesn't make you in charge of flowers."

"Now, ladies," I say in a soft tone. "There's no need to argue.

Mabel, put down that rose. Respectfully, if you smack Harriet with it, you're going to have to buy it." Mabel harrumphs and resheaths the rose into its rightful bucket. "How about I put your names in a hat to decide who's in charge? Or better yet, we can do half the arrangements pink and white and half purple and white."

"Or," Mabel says as she inches toward the door, her leather support loafers squelching lightly with each step. She puts her hand on the door handle and continues, "We can put it to a vote at the planning committee. I'll go tell them! Nice to see you back in town, William!" She flings open the door and makes a mad dash through it, heel-toeing it past the shop window and down the sidewalk.

"That dirty cheat! She's going to promise Deloris the use of her dining room for bunco night if she votes for her before I get there." And out she races in a dash of bland grayness.

With a smile on my face, I turn back to the store, nearly jumping out of my skin when I see Will staring at me.

He levels me with a look so potent I think I'll fall flat on my back.

"My answer is no. I can't be your dating coach."

CHAPTER EIGHT

Will

Annie's hands go to her hips. "Well, for the record, I thought it was a bad idea at first, but why do you think it's a bad idea?"

I can think of a million and two reasons. But the first and most important is that I'm miserably attracted to Annie and need to stay as far away from her as possible over the next month. I haven't been able to get her off my mind since last night. I even dreamed about her.

Damn that dream.

I absolutely can't get involved with her. Not only because she's Amelia's soon-to-be sister-in-law, but because Annie represents everything I avoid. Commitment. Relationship. Longevity. My brain sees her and superimposes a big *Nope!* sign above her head. Absolutely not.

"Because," I say, wishing that was enough of an answer. "Have you never seen the movies like this? The woman always has to do a bunch of shit she doesn't like to do, like go to places that make her uncomfortable, change her style, and step outside of her normal world. And then, by the end of the movie, the guy falls in love with her and everything gets complicated. No, it sounds like a terrible idea. Not to mention I'm opposed to the whole love thing. I don't want a relationship with anyone ever—and why are you smiling at me like that?"

Her blue eyes are sparkling with dangerous ideas. "Oh my gosh. Amelia is right. You are perfect for the job."

I stare incredulously at her. "Were you even listening just now?"

"Yes, and I heard a man who's very qualified to be a dating coach."

I shake my head. "No, I'm not. I'm not doing it."

"But what if I promise I won't fall in love with you?" she says as if that's a flattering option. "You're not the kind of guy I'm looking for anyway."

"Wow. I feel great now. Thank you."

"Come on, Will! It's perfect."

"Annie . . ." Instinctively I take a step back, but she follows. I've never felt hunted more than I do at this moment. I wish I couldn't say I don't like it.

"Wildon, please be my tutor."

I shake my head, trying not to laugh while skirting around her. A minute ago I was the one holding all the power, and somehow she flipped the script and has me crossing to the complete opposite side of the shop to escape her. "Why do you need a tutor so badly?"

"Because I'd really like to get married before I'm eighty, and my last date was a disaster."

"It couldn't have been a disaster."

"A disaster," she repeats firmly, with eyes wide open. "Remember how he left at the beginning of the date? Before that I overheard him on the phone tell his friend that I was unbelievably boring. Too dull to hook up with."

Rage swiftly and furiously sweeps over me. "What a dick. Tell me his name. I'm going to—"

"He didn't mean for me to overhear it," Annie says, sticking up for a man who doesn't deserve it. "And the fact is, he wasn't wrong. I thought back on the date, and . . . I really was boring. I couldn't think of anything to talk about. I need help learning how to be fun on dates."

But as I look at Annie's flushed face and sparkling eyes, her words still don't sit right. She shouldn't have to change herself.

I lean closer. "If any jackass thinks you're boring, that's his problem, not yours."

She looks away. "You only say that because you've never been called boring, or dull, or wholesome. One look at you and everyone knows you're the antithesis of those words. But me—I need some help or I'm never going to find someone. I need a coach."

The longer I stare at Annie, the more I itch to destroy the man who made her doubt herself. "No. Absolutely not. You deserve more than the kind of guy you went out with, and I'd die on this hill. You'll find someone who sees you for who you really are."

Annie completely disregards my thoughtful monologue.

"Ugh. Please, Will!" she asks in an over-the-top beg that makes me have to smother a grin.

"No."

She props her hand on her hip. "Are you worried you're going to fall in love with me?"

"Nope, I'm not."

"Well, then, we don't have any issues!"

"You're not listening to me. I have issues because I don't want any part of this plan. It's a bad idea to change yourself." And even more, I don't want to see any part of Annie change. Not a single thing. I've never met anyone like her before—and it would be a damn shame for her to morph into some popular social construct of what a woman should be like on dates. I hate it. If some jackass doesn't take the time to peel back her layers of nervousness to find out who she really is, he doesn't deserve to have her when she's at her most comfortable.

Annie follows me across the room—holding her letter in front of her like she's gathering signatures for a petition. "I wouldn't be changing myself. I'd just be getting more comfortable being myself on dates. Plus maybe a little changing here and there as needed."

"I would rather wax off my eyebrows completely."

"Rude."

Without thinking, I place my hands on Annie's shoulders. The shock of her soft warm skin against my rough palms momentarily sets me off-kilter. A hum of desire pulses through me so strong and sudden that I have to pull my hands back. Further evidence that I cannot be some sort of dating tutor for her. Fantasies are built on that kind of shit.

"I'm not doing it," I say firmly. Final. End of story.

Annie's shoulders sink, and I feel bad for letting her down. But still—I won't be a part of the reason she's not Annie anymore.

"Fine," she says, stiffening into a more stubborn pose. "Then I'll just have to hire someone else to do it." She turns and starts walking back toward where I assume her storeroom is located.

"Like who?" I follow her.

She rounds the worktable, and I go around the opposite side until we meet in the middle. She cuts her eyes to directly look into mine. "Someone." She blinks twice. "Someone good at being sexy who can help me be sexy too." Two more blinks. "Maybe a male escort."

I whistle quietly. "A male escort? No way is Annie Walker going bad. Are you going to pay extra for the sex too?"

Her eyes flare ever so slightly, but then her chin lifts. "Absolutely I'm going to pay extra for the . . . sex." She drops her voice to a whisper on the last word, making me laugh.

"I gotta see this. Promise me you'll bring him around once you've hired him?"

"Oh, I doubt I will," Annie says as she heads into the storeroom. I follow again and then stop abruptly in the doorway when, faster than I expected, she surfaces holding a small bouquet of pre-arranged flowers. We're standing together, bookended by either side of the doorway. "We'll be too busy for me to bring him by with him teaching me all kinds of things."

I narrow my eyes and tip forward to lean my hand on the doorframe over her shoulder. "Just to clarify and make sure I understand the whole picture. You're saying you'll be too busy with your male escort?"

"Yes, with my . . ." She briefly glances at my forearm beside her head and then weakly finishes her sentence, "male escort."

"Because he'll be teaching you all sorts of things. Sexual things I'm assuming, but correct me if I'm wrong."

Her nostrils flare and she sucks in a fortifying breath. It's too much fun to mess with her. There's no way Annie is any kind of serious. She's just trying to ignite some sort of protective instinct in me, hoping that I'll agree to be her coach.

"Probably. I mean, yes. Definitely lots and lots of . . ." she swallows, "sexy times on the horizon."

"Wow, that's going to be great. You'll have a blast," I say, enjoying this taunting way too much before noticing Annie's eyes drop to my lips. And just like that, she steals the entire show again. All of my thunder is gone and I can't think straight with her eyes fixed on my mouth like that.

I try to hold still because I know she's thinking about kissing me right now, and I can't let her. I want to—oh God, I want to—but I can't. Every single one of my skin cells ache for me to step forward and press our bodies together. But I can't do that because I'm scared what will become of me if I do.

But neither of us steps away, and somehow the knuckles of my free hand brush against hers. Her fingers respond and lightly move against mine. Our fingers never intertwine; we just let our skin brush a controlled fire against the other. How is this the most erotic thing that's ever happened to me? And now, to hell with it, I have to kiss her. No, I have to do more than kiss her—I need to press her against this doorframe and feel our bodies collide.

She lifts her face and I lower my head and—

Outside the shop, a car door slams and makes both of us jolt, heads whirling guiltily toward the shop window.

"Oh, it's James," she says breathily. "He's coming by for this bouquet." The one she's clutching to her chest with the hand that wasn't just torturing mine. "He called and ordered it this morning."

I nod absently—my lazy movement matching her lazy tone because we're both stuck in a sensuous, unrelieved haze. My arm is still resting behind Annie as I turn my eyes to watch James round the large white truck with the logo for Huxley Farm on the side. From everything Amelia has told me, he owns the farm now after it became too much for his parents. Apparently, he's Noah's best friend and has pretty much grown up with the Walker siblings. I assume he's like a brother to them.

Or maybe he isn't . . .

"Oh wow," Annie says, also watching James but sounding less hazy by the second. "He's wearing a suit!"

Yeah, he is. And even I can admit the man looks good. It's a nice suit that's accentuating his farmer's body. He's tall, muscular, tan. And even more important, when I look down at Annie, she's looking at him like she's never seen him before. My pulse jumps angrily. Possessively.

She steps away from me to go to the counter as James opens the door to the shop.

"James, hi!" she says in a cheery tone, while setting the bouquet on the counter and pulling out a piece of brown paper to wrap around it. The weird part is, she never even looks at what her hands are doing. She's staring at James the entire time. Not necessarily like she wants him—but like she's contemplating him.

Shit. I'm afraid I know what's happening now.

"Morning, Annie! Thanks for having this ready for me." This man has Town Golden Boy written all over him. The dazzling smile. The open face. The twinkle in his eye of a person who's never been jaded by the world. Irrationally, I hate him.

"You look amazing," Annie says with way too much emphasis, if you ask me. "Where are you going?" Her fingers work to delicately wrap twine around the brown paper—and all I can think about is how those fingers felt moving softly against mine. What they'd feel like dancing across my chest. Clutching at my back.

"With Mom to a wedding for one of my cousins."

"Your dad okay?" she asks, sweetness and concern coating her tone.

What's it like to have someone like Annie worry about you? I doubt James even appreciates what he has.

He chuckles lightly. "If you count stubbornly refusing to go to the wedding because it has a black-tie dress code and Mom won't let him wear his John Deere hat, then, yes—he's fine. I, however, am going to be miserable all afternoon after being guilt-tripped into going."

"And yet you're still taking her a bouquet of flowers. What a guy," she says with a soft chuckle. "But you'll have a great time. I've seen you on the dance floor, and I know you'll have all the ladies lined up by the end of the night."

James laughs again, and their camaraderie is making me feel a little ill.

"We'll see," James says before winking at Annie in a blatantly Matthew McConaughey kind of way. And now I want to run him over with his own truck.

Am I jealous? No, I'm never jealous. You can't have a series of no-strings-attached hookups with women for your entire adult life and be the jealous type. It's impossible. And yet, as I see Annie eyeing James in an assessing way and coming to some sort of conclusion, I realize I am absolutely jealous.

"Hey, James?" she begins thoughtfully. "I have sort of a random question to ask you. And feel free to say no, but would you—"

"I'll do it," I say quickly, cutting Annie off.

She whips her head in my direction and stares up at me. "You will? But you just said—"

"I know. I changed my mind. I want to do it." She blinks and smiles up at me, and my heart fills with something that feels like lava. "But I have one condition."

"Name it."

I grin. "I get to walk out of here today with your book."

"My book?" she asks, hoping she heard me wrong.

"The book." I smile as I watch two pink splotches hit the apples of her cheeks.

For a beat, there's nothing but silence. Painful, thick silence. And then slowly Annie's sweet smile tilts ever so slightly into a devious grin, and I realize I just got epically played. "You've got a deal, bodyguard."

"Executive protection agent."

James clears his throat. "Why do I feel like I just missed out on an important opportunity?"

Because you did. Now, get lost, she's mine.

CHAPTER NINE

Annie

I dramatically throw open the door to Amelia's studio and then lunge to catch the handle before it slams against the wall. The point was to make a shocking entrance—not a hole in the wall.

Amelia whirls around on the piano bench, wide-eyed.

I hold up the letter. "This was unacceptable, you little . . ." She leans closer to see if this will actually be the moment I say something cutting. "Meddler! Beautiful meddler actually, because you're honestly glowing today—but that doesn't change the fact that I'm mad at you!"

Amelia smiles. "You are looking beautiful today too."

"Don't try to butter me up. You're in trouble. You Funny-Faced me!"

"Yeah, I did!" Her smile grows. "What was his answer?"

I move to sit on the little couch against the wall and run my hand back and forth over the soft green velvet of the armrest. "You don't get to know. Meddlers don't get rewards."

"You agreed last night to let me come up with a plan, remember? You said you wanted someone to swoop in and teach you how to get good at dating, like Fred taught Audrey to be the Quality woman. So I found your Fred."

"But you weren't supposed to present the plan to me in front of Fred!" I shake my head. "I mean, Will—where he would bodily wrestle me for the friggin' thing."

Amelia takes in a happy gulp of air. "He said yes, didn't he?"

I fold my arms, eyeing the space around me and choosing to let her dangle a little in uncertainty. It's the best form of torture I can think of at the moment. "The studio turned out nicely. Are you liking it?"

Her studio really is adorable. It's one room with an attached bathroom. Amelia said she didn't want anything too fancy, just a quiet space with natural light to work on her music when she's home. There's a piano, a few guitars, and a desk with equipment for recording in the corner. But my favorite part of the space is this little cozy lounging area composed of a green velvet couch and a few floor poufs scattered around for extra seating. Above the couch there's a giant poster of our queen—Audrey Hepburn—standing in a cream-colored dress in front of a wall of pink flowers.

"Yeah, yeah, the studio is great. Tell me what Will said."

I squint at various parts of the room. "You need more plants in here. I think a fiddle-leaf fig in the corner over there would be nice."

"Annie . . ."

"And a succulent on your piano."

Amelia stands up from the piano bench and launches herself onto the couch with me. She tackles me in a hug. "Don't be mad at me, Annie! I can't take your polite chitchat. It's worse than a cold shoulder."

I resist her hug, tucking my arms tightly against my sides. Must resist the affection. She hugs even harder. Squeezing the daylights out of me. When I can't stand it any longer, I blurt, "Fine! I give. Will said yes," and then I return her hug, because not many people understand this about me, but I love affection.

Amelia squeaks, squeezes one more time, and then jumps up to do a quick happy dance—or maybe victory dance?—and then shoots finger guns at me. "I knew it! I knew he would."

"Whoa! Careful, there." I reach forward and pretend to carefully remove her finger guns, turning on the safety and then putting them away under the couch. "You're dangerous when you're gloating."

Laughing and slightly out of breath, she sits back down beside me. "So when do you guys start?"

I shrug. "Not sure yet. He said he'd be in touch."

"What a Dick Avery."

I sputter a laugh at her play on words. "Okay, but for real, Will Griffin is not Dick Avery."

"Why not? Will is kind. He's outgoing. He's an expert in his field—all attributes that our tap-dancing pal Mr. Avery shared."

I chuckle. "You mean he's an expert at playing the field. There is a difference."

The mere thought of Will Griffin and Fred Astaire (aka Dick Avery) lined up in comparison is hilarious to me. Will only has to walk into a room and make direct eye contact with a woman for her panties to go up in flames. Fred Astaire looked as if he would really enjoy a nice cup of herbal tea before turning into bed early. To be honest, I'm more suited for someone like Fred Astaire.

Will feels . . . dangerous.

Amelia shrugs. "You're not trying to marry Will, so the playing-the-field bit is irrelevant in any other aspect than that it serves your purpose—which is to get comfortable at dating. He's perfect for this job." When I don't answer immediately, she nudges my leg lightly. "He is perfect for this job, Annie."

"Uh-huh. You keep saying that—and I was inclined to agree—but the more time I have to think about it, I'm not so sure."

Amelia pulls her feet up on the cushions. "Okay, well let's talk it out. Tell me your worries."

Even though Amelia has only been in my life for a little over a year now, I somehow feel closer to her than I do my sisters. I adore Emily and Madison, and have that special sister connection with them, but with Amelia, it's not just a sisterly connection but that of a close friend too. She views me differently than my sisters do. She values my opinion and seems to understand me in a way that Emily and Madison never have. With them, everything always gets boiled down to one clear-cut outlook: Annie is our sweet baby sister, a little plain and unexciting. It doesn't matter that I'll be thirty in a few years; they treat me like I'm ten years old. Which is why I keep a lot about my life to myself. Sometimes I don't want to hear the let's-poke-fun-at-sweet-Annie banter they always reply with when I tell them the truth.

Amelia doesn't do that to me.

However, in this situation, I still don't want to tell her the truth. Because the truth is, today when Will's hand touched mine, my entire body felt electrified. When he had his arms around me, I breathed deeply. I breathed deeply, people! And honestly, having him play-fight with me over the letter was the most fun I've had with a person in . . . maybe my whole life. Which is not good because Will is absolutely not the man for me, and I'm not sure I can trust myself not to grow feelings for him over the next couple of weeks when I'm already so clearly attracted to him.

I can't tell Amelia any of that because then she'd be over on the sidelines watching me a little too closely. Even worse, she might tell Will, and then he'd pat me on the head like everyone else does and tell me my attraction to him is cute. No, this secret is better kept to myself, where I can work alone on squashing any desire toward him.

"I'm worried it's going to be weird," I say, keeping my chin nice and level as I deliver that lie because I know for a fact it's not going to be weird. No part of talking to Will over the last two days has felt weird. In fact, it's felt good.

"Weird how?"

I sigh. "Weird like . . . embarrassing. A man who is super good at dating is going to see how terrible I am at it and internally laugh at me. Possibly externally laugh too. There might be pointing and chortling."

Amelia shakes her head. "You're looking at it all wrong. A man who is super good at dating is offering to systematically walk you through the steps so you can go off and date someone else non-awkwardly and fall deeply in love so you never have to date again. And really, you have nothing to lose. You're not trying to date Will, and he's not even into relationships, so there are zero prospects or expectations on the table. It's a no-pressure, stringless way to learn how to date."

I take in a deep breath. "You're right."

"I know I am," she says with a sassy smile. "But now the question is, are you going to tell your siblings?"

"No." The answer comes out quickly even though I haven't previously given it any thought. It's a knee-jerk reaction but feels like the right decision when I say it out loud. I want to do this privately.

I adore my sisters, but in addition to the way they often treat me like a child, they tend to be overly opinionated when it comes to my life—and this is one situation I'd like to navigate on my own without their input, suggestions, or teasing. I can see it now: Emily would create a long list of all the reasons this plan isn't going to work, and Maddie would make crude jokes about the Bad Boy tutoring the Good Girl, and I just . . . ugh. I'm tired of it. I'm so tired of that narrative looping around me day in and day out. I'm tired of everyone so neatly placing me in a box and tying a silk ribbon around it and then telling me to sit and stay.

If I want to spend my days learning to date with the dangerously sexy bodyguard, I will.

So no, I'm not going to tell them. I'm not going to tell anyone because this isn't open for discussion.

CHAPTER TEN

Will

"What's so bad about the town?" asks Liv Nolsen, my boss, from the other end of the phone line. She is trying to persuade me to extend my stay in Rome, Kentucky, as one of Amelia's permanent agents rather than transferring to Washington, D.C., and guarding a high-profile politician after the month is out, as I'm requesting. I've been here one weekend, and I'm already bored to death.

Usually I'm placed with other celebrities when I'm not working for Amelia—partly because they request me after having seen me on either BuzzFeed and social media, or met me while I worked for one of their famous friends. Amelia is the only celebrity who hasn't made me want to rip my hair out, though.

And truthfully, my favorite assignments have been providing security for politicians. Why? Because shit gets real for them. It's rarely dull guarding someone whom half the country hates. And when I'm busy, I don't have time to stop and think about anything else. I don't have time to worry whether I'm lonely or whether I made the right career choice. I just work and stay on the move, and my mind remains blissfully clear.

So about ten minutes ago when my boss said she was contemplating keeping me in Rome at the request of Amelia's team, I felt sick. Not because of Amelia—I'll gladly provide security for her on each and every one of her tours. But in this sleepy town longterm: no.

"Uh—let me put it this way, I'm talking to you from a landline in the coffee shop because the cell service is so spotty. And the room I'm staying in is filled with frilly embroidered phrases on the walls and a *Chicken Soup for the Soul* book beside the bed."

There is wifi, but you have to have the damn password for it. And no one in any of these establishments will let me have it. Apparently, you have to be one of them to gain access, and they don't trust me ever since I jogged with my shirt off.

"Damn. I love Mayberry towns," says Liv. She may be a stoic agent, but she's also a romantic. She always claims she's going to meet the perfect woman on a mission someday and fall in love James Bond style. I've pointed out that James Bond never has the same lover in the next movie, but she always just waves me off.

"Then why don't you come and take over if you love small towns so much?"

"Because Ms. Rose specifically asked for you when her manager said she wanted an agent to stay on for a while even after the wedding because they will be announcing the upcoming album. And because she happens to be our highest-paying client, I will literally do anything to keep her happy, including selling my kidney or forcing my best agent to live in her town for a while. Rae Rose wants someone she can trust to keep her safe and be discreet with her personal life, and thanks to your years together, you achieve that for her, so suck it up, Griffin."

Great. This is what being reliable and hardworking has gotten me. It's high school all over again, where I practically killed myself to get the highest, most impressive grades in the class just so my parents would notice. Whether it was out of a need to make them proud, make them see me, or make them stop fighting so damn much and get along for five seconds, I still don't know. Probably a heavy combination of the three. Either way, it didn't help. It worked against me. My parents didn't notice my good grades, they noticed the random low ones instead and would chew me out relentlessly for slacking off even though they knew I wasn't.

I run my hand down the back of my hair, rubbing at the tension building in my neck. "Does this mean I have no choice? You're really not going to let me transfer to D.C. even after the wedding?" If that happens, I don't know what I'll do. Quit most likely. I'd sooner change agencies than be forced to kick my feet in a rocking chair for the rest of my damn career.

She breathes out a long breath. "I'll think about it. For now, make the best of it and pick up a hobby in your downtime. It'll be good for you. You've been working like a dog for, well, since you joined the agency ten years ago."

"I don't want a hobby."

She scoffs. "Get a girlfriend then."

"That's definitely not going to hap—" As if on cue, I look out the front café windows and spot Annie across the street. She's walking up the sidewalk from the communal parking lot, and I'm able to see her perfectly through these giant picture windows. Today she's wearing jean shorts and a pink tank top—long blonde hair down and straight.

She smiles and greets everyone she passes before pausing outside of the hardware store to talk with Phil for a minute. He tells her something that makes her tilt her head back as she laughs. That ache in my chest cinches tight. She looks happy and warm and . . . so damn sweet. It's exactly the distraction I need from my boredom. I might not be able to have Annie in the way my body wants, but I can at least have fun with her in the way she requested.

At some point I realize I've completely tuned Liv out. "Griffin. Hello? Are you there?"

I clear my throat. "Sorry. I . . . lost service for a second."

"I thought you were on a landline?"

"Right. Actually, I was distracted by some suspicious activity."

She shuffles papers. "You're the suspicious activity."

"Liv—sorry, I need to run."

"Check your email. I'm sending over some new info on stalkers and fans to watch."

"Will do," I say, putting the phone on the receiver just as the barista calls out my order and sets Amelia's iced latte on the counter. This is what I've been reduced to: an errand boy. And no, Amelia didn't make me come into town just for her coffee—I begged her for something to do while she's working in the studio today. So here I am.

"Would you mind putting it in the fridge for a minute?" I ask the barista. "I'll be right back."

CHAPTER ELEVEN

Annie

I pull a box of Fruit Crunch off the shelf and jump out of my skin when I hear a male voice behind me. "Hello."

I squeal in appropriate inside-voice terror until a butterflied hand extends over my shoulder and grabs a box of shredded wheat. My eyes track the box all the way into the empty shopping basket hanging beside Will's leg.

"What are you doing here?" I sound accusatory only because I wasn't expecting him, and I need a full five minutes to prepare for his company before I see him. You know, mentally gird my loins and all that.

He cocks his head. "Well, this activity is most widely understood as grocery shopping," he says, lifting the basket as evidence.

I frown down into his basket instead of acknowledging his sarcastic remark because he has selected the single worst type of cereal, and I can't allow him to continue living his life in such a depressing way. I remove his choice, put it back on the shelf, and place a box of Fruit Crunch in his basket.

"What I mean, Wilbur, is what are you doing here shopping in the middle of the day?"

He pulls the shredded wheat from the shelf again and puts it in my basket this time, looking down at me with playful indulgence. "You need fiber, Annie Walker."

"You came all the way to town today because you had a strong suspicion my fiber intake was low?"

"All the way to town, yes." He grins lazily and I realize there's nothing quite like the sound of this man's voice when he's teasing.

And mother of pearl, he looks great today. His deep green T-shirt stretches across his shoulders in a way that gives me the urge to lightly sink my teeth right there on the rounded curve of his muscle. What kind of unhinged thought is that? Another reason to place Will in the not-for-me category. He disturbs the status quo of my sanity.

And although the black cargo joggers he's wearing do him all kinds of favors, it's those tattoos that are steering me down the path of no return. I trace the lines of the flowers and vines until they disappear under the sleeve of his shirt, and that's when I feel irrationally angry because I have no idea where they end. Do they extend over his shoulder? Down his back? Over his chest?

I'll never know, and it's that thought that has me turning away from him feeling frustrated.

He catches up to me quickly. "Are you on your lunch break?"

"Yep. Mondays are my day to visit my grandma, so Jeanine works the shop for me for the second half of the day while I cut out a little early to do my grocery shopping, grab my grandma a box of her favorite vanilla wafers, and then head over to the assisted-living center to check on her."

Why did I tell him all of that? He only asked if I was on my lunch break, and here I go sharing my entire schedule. Clearly my social skills are worse than I thought. Any second now he'll smile pleasantly and then turn away. He'll put a sticky note on my front door saying: Can't help with lessons anymore. You bore me.

Will walks beside me. "How's she doing?"

"Um—okay. She has Alzheimer's, you know? So she has good days and bad. But overall she's always declining. It'll be like that from now on." I stop in front of the oral hygiene section and stare blankly at the boxes as an unexpected wave of grief envelops me. I don't often let myself think about the true state of her health—that one day the woman who raised me will be gone. It's gut-wrenching.

"That sounds really tough," he says gently, his body nearer to mine than a moment ago, like he wants to comfort me but doesn't know how. I look up at him, and his warm gaze does nothing to help the sudden building emotion behind my eyes.

I blink and reach for a box of toothpaste and dump it into my basket. "It's all right. I just enjoy the moments I have with her now," I say, strong-arming those bad feelings out of the way. Feeling them doesn't help anything. It doesn't make her disease go away. It doesn't bring back my parents. It's easiest to not pay attention to them.

Will seems to want to say more but grabs the same brand of toothpaste as I did and puts it into his basket instead. He then selects a box of denture cleaner and drops it into mine before walking away.

I quickly replace it on the shelf and catch up to him. "Your turn. Why are you shopping in the middle of the day?"

He cuts a quick glance at me over his shoulder and slows his pace so I can catch up. "Amelia is in the studio, so I had some free time. Thought it would be the perfect moment to bless Harriet with my presence."

We both round the aisle, and at that very moment we intercept Harriet's cold glare aimed at Will. He smiles at her. "Looking beautiful today, Harriet!" he says, making her scowl harden.

"See. She loves me," he says through his pearly white teeth.

I laugh and steer us down the next aisle, knowing that Harriet not only doesn't love Will but openly dislikes him. Could that be part of my draw to him? I've seen the movies. Good girl gravitates toward bad boy because she can't be bad herself?

That's the easiest explanation, so I'll go with it and ignore the quieter voice in my head that says I feel a connection to Will.

We pass a feminine hygiene section, and I grab a pack of overnight pads, bank-shotting them into his basket before walking the other way and trying not to laugh at the flat look on his face. With a devious smile, I round the corner, and when Will meets me halfway down the next aisle, the pads are nowhere in sight.

I face the snack section and try to decide between spicy or cheesy chips.

He stands shoulder to shoulder with me, and we look like we're lined up for a general's inspection. I cut my eyes to him and try not to grin when I see he's doing the same. And then he tilts toward me. "By the way, I finished the book."

Shock whips through me, and I drop the bag of Lay's I was holding.

Will casually and softly sets a box of Imodium in my basket and strolls away.

Embarrassment, horror, and curiosity all war inside me. Ever since I handed the book over to him in the flower shop and watched his eyebrows shoot up at the sight of a scantily clad woman draped over a well-muscled half-naked man, I've been dying a slow death of dread. And now I know—Will Griffin read my steamy romance novel. Suddenly an image of Will lying shirtless in bed reading some of those incredibly sexy scenes has my skin boiling. I don't think I want to know whether he liked it or not.

Wait, yes I do.

No, I absolutely don't.

I catch Will on the next aisle. "What did you think of it?"

Okay, apparently I do.

My heart races as I wait to hear his answer. I try not to get my hopes up because I know that most likely he hated it. In fact, I'm prepared for ridicule and teasing for the rest of his time in Rome.

I'm not prepared for his slow melting smile. Like he's re-enacting for me the look he had on his face while he read. "Honestly, I couldn't put it down. I stayed in all day yesterday just reading."

I pull in a deep happy breath through my nose. I would bounce on the balls of my feet if I didn't think it would make me look childish. "Are you serious?"

We're not the only shoppers in here today, and a woman I've definitely seen before whose name I can't remember starts down our aisle. Will steps closer to me to avoid her, and his chest presses against the side of my body. Fire sweeps me. I can barely think straight when I feel his breath against my temple. "It was sexy as hell."

I keep my eyes fixed straight ahead on the loaves of honey wheat bread because if I look at Will right now, my skin will melt clean off my body. How dare he talk to me like that! Like . . . like I've always secretly dreamed of someone talking to me.

The woman passes and Will steps back again, taking a loaf of bread with him. "But it was also a lot of fun. There was more adventure than I expected. And there were a lot of profound moments too. Felt like free therapy."

"Right?!" I say, turning to look at him and feeling absurdly pleased that he read the book and not only liked it but connected to it. "What was your favorite scene?" I reach into my basket and move the diarrhea medication to his instead.

"The fight sequence on the boat was pretty awesome."

I grin and narrow my eyes. "What was your favorite scene, Will?"

He steps a little closer, a taunting look in his eyes. "The scene in the pub?"

"William," I chide gently, knowing full well his favorite scene was the one with the ladder. I absolutely should not be trying to get him to mention it—but I can't help it. Something about Will brings out a different side of me.

The air between us grows arms, reaching out to grab the fronts of our shirts and tug us closer until we're so close that our baskets fit together side by side. Grocery basket Tetris. I catch a glimmer in Will's eyes and the corner of his mouth tugs.

"You wouldn't be trying to lure me into inappropriate conversation, would you, Angel Annie?"

In an instant, any playfulness I feel dies away with that awful nickname. It's one thing when everyone else calls me that or taunts me with it—but from Will I can't stand it.

"Don't call me that, please," I say, allowing myself a rare moment of honesty. "I don't like it."

I'm not looking at Will, but I can still feel his gaze. And then I can feel his fingers lightly clasp my elbow as if he were afraid I was about to drift off, and he needed to keep me there beside him. "Annie. I'm sorry." His voice is low and genuine. "I didn't mean it in a negative way."

I force a smile and look up at him. "I know. No one ever does when they call me by those names. And I've heard them all: Saint Annie, Angel Annie, Goody-goody Annie. It's never meant in a bad way, but that doesn't mean I don't feel a negative connotation when they say it." I shrug slightly like it's no big deal, even though . . . I guess it *is* kind of a big deal to me. "It feels like they're saying I don't have as much substance as everyone else. That because I'm sweet, I don't have as much to offer. I constantly feel underestimated, and I'm so tired of it."

Will's thumb glides tenderly against my skin. His voice drops until it's intimately quiet. "I won't do it again."

I breathe out. How was that so easy? I've always had trouble telling people the truth of what I'm feeling when I know it's going to be uncomfortable for them to hear—so I usually just keep it bottled up. But I want Will to know what's actually happening beneath the surface. Maybe it's just because I know there's no real threat to a relationship that doesn't exist in any permanent way with him?

"Thank you." My eyes shift to Will's mouth, and that's when I realize we're standing inappropriately close for two friends in a grocery store. I smile and pull away to continue my shopping.

Will trails behind me. "I can relate, though."

This makes me laugh. "You can relate to being seen as too sweet?"

"Well, no. But to being underestimated."

"How so?" I say, looking back at him and enjoying our joint shopping excursion way too much.

Will shrugs. "Usually people see the tattoos and the videos of me forcefully removing an aggressive fan from a situation, or that damn BuzzFeed article, and they think they know me. They assume I'm nothing but a fu—" he catches himself and grins before amending, "a player who probably didn't finish high school."

I can see that—not that I've ever thought that about him, but other people might. It's evident by the way Harriet is now lurking around the store and popping her suspicious eyes through every peephole like she expects to find Will slipping merchandise into his pocket at any second. Or better yet, like he's going to throw me over his shoulder and steal me—the sweet town golden girl—

away into the night where he'd lay me down in a bed of wildflowers and make love to me until—

Oh wait, huh? That's not what we were talking about.

I adjust my shopping basket onto my forearm and shift a box of crackers on the shelf, closing off Harriet's view. "So what is the truth about the illusive Will Griffin then?"

"Really nothing special." He walks to a new corner of the store and this time I trail behind him. "Grew up in a cave in Alaska. Was raised by a pack of wolves. You know? The standard."

I groan. "Oh come on."

He spins around at the end of the aisle with a smoldering grin. "Winters were cold, but I learned to get by after killing bears with my teeth and wearing their fur on my back."

I shove him while laughing. "Terrible. Does PETA know about you?"

His face grows too serious to be genuine. "It's really rude to laugh at someone's childhood, Annie. Have a little compassion."

My face hurts from smiling so much. "All right, Wolf Boy. If you're not going to tell me the truth, I have to check out now." But as I pass by Will, his hand shoots out and lightly catches mine. A hot zing shoots through my fingers all the way to the pit of my stomach. When I look at him, I'm afraid he can see in my eyes just how affected I am by his touch.

"I did finish high school, for the record. With a 4.0 GPA, and then I joined the Air Force afterward and served as a Security Forces specialist because I couldn't stand the thought of going to college and continuing on with my miserable existence as an achievement-seeking perfectionist."

"I see," I whisper, trying to absorb all of that rapid-fire information coming at me. But my knees keep nearly buckling at the mental image of this man in uniform. How commanding he must have looked. How . . . is mouthwateringly delicious fair to say?

Will continues before I can say anything I'll regret.

"And my favorite moment in the book was absolutely the ladder scene." He pauses briefly. "I'm willing to bet all of my money it was yours too." My heart thumps painfully at the nearly wicked look in his eyes as he accurately reads my thoughts.

"How would you know that?" No one else in the world would ever suspect my favorite scene was the steamiest one in the book, but Will does because for some reason, he doesn't see me quite like everyone else does. In fact, no one else would even guess I like these kinds of books. It's a secret not even my sisters know because I've kept my box of romance novels neatly tucked under my bed, out of sight for years.

And yes, I realize that I'm supposed to be loud and proud about my romance-reading ways, but when you've grown up with siblings like mine and those siblings have given you the nickname of Angel Annie and would absolutely roast you every single day for the rest of your life if they knew you loved steamy books with *Big Duke Energy,* you'd hide the book under your pillow too. This is a secret (along with the box of romance books under my bed) I will take to my death. If anyone ever robs my grave, they'll be shocked to find me blanketed with shirtless pirates fiercely embracing a lady in a gown that is not even remotely accurate for the era of the book.

But now Will knows my deep dark secret. My body heats up at the thought.

His eyes hold mine. "Because contrary to what everyone seems to say about you, I can see a mischievous spark behind your soft blue eyes, Annie Walker."

Will's eyes drop to my lips, and I'm speechless for three heartbeats. Desire fills the air like smoke—thick and heavy—making it difficult to breathe.

"But . . . you won't tell anyone, right?" I ask quietly, making

Will's gaze rise up to my eyes again. "Not even about our lessons? I don't want my siblings to know."

"Why can't they know?"

I glance down. "They'll . . . they just can't." I shake my head. "If they find out, they'll be full of opinions and suggestions that I don't necessarily want." I can hear Emily now—initiating twenty questions until she knows every detail of what I'm planning and suggesting a better way to go about it until I end up caving and doing things her way so that I don't hurt her feelings. And Maddie will demand to take over as my tutor, and somehow I'll fall right into the shadows as I always do when my siblings are around.

I look up into Will's eyes and nearly flinch at how unwavering his gaze is. He's waiting for me to say more. "I just want to do something for myself for a while—is that bad? It feels wrong."

"I don't think it's wrong, but then I'm an innately selfish person, so maybe I'm not the best person to be asking."

"You don't seem selfish to me."

His fingers tighten ever so slightly around mine and his expression looks almost desperate. "Annie, I need you to know that I don't do relationships. Ever. And I never will. If we do these lessons you want, they will be as friends and nothing else."

His words shouldn't sting. I already know this about him, and I also know that I'm looking for a man completely opposite from him. And yet I feel them like shards of glass. He can't know that, though.

I lean in even closer. "And I only do relationships. So we're in perfect agreement."

His eyes search mine. "So . . . friends only?"

"Friends only."

"Great. Then we can start lessons tonight if you're available."

It takes all my self-control to not audibly gulp. And because I don't trust my voice, I simply nod.

I don't miss the moment his thumb glides over the skin of my hand before he releases it. "I'll sneak you into my room. Around six thirty?" I barely register that he tosses a little box into my basket because I'm too busy internally panicking over his last statement.

"But how?" I ask while fast-walking down the aisle to catch up to him. "How will you sneak me in? This town has eyes everywhere."

"Just wait outside the inn for my cue." Will doesn't glance back at me. He sets his basket down and leaves the market.

I look down and realize his basket is now empty.

Did he only come in here to talk to me?

At the checkout counter, I set my basket down and begin pulling out items for Harriet to scan. And too late I realize I'm holding, courtesy of Will Griffin, a box of condoms—ribbed for her pleasure.

With burning cheeks, I look up directly into the scowling face of Harriet. This is why my sisters buy all of their intimate items on Amazon.

"You watch yourself with that boy, Annie. He's no good for you and definitely not the kind of man you need in your life."

I turn to the window just in time to see Will laughing and walking away from the market—so proud of himself and his prank.

I think Harriet's right. Will Griffin is absolutely not the kind of man I need.

Too bad he's very quickly becoming the man I want.

CHAPTER TWELVE

Annie

I t's go time.

Looking from my left to my right, I exit the alley that runs behind my flower shop and into the parking lot. Immediately I see Phil and Todd—the mouths of the South—so I duck behind my truck to avoid them. It's hot as blazes today, thick humid heat rising up from the pavement and boiling everything exposed. When I lean against my truck's bumper, it singes the back of my arm like a hot iron.

Welcome to the South, friends, where you get third-degree burns from leaning against your vehicle. Worth it to avoid being spotted, though. I'd for sure be the talk of the town. Did you hear that sweetie pie Annie Walker spent the evening in Will Griffin's room all alone? *The Scandal!*

The thing that bothers me is that if it were Emily or Madison, no one would think twice. But because it's me, I'd have fifteen visitors the next day warning me to guard my heart.

Phil bickers at Todd about something (it's always something), and I wait until they are safely in their truck and driving away to surface from my hiding spot. They're the last shop owners to leave for the day, so I know the coast is clear. I waited to come back into town until after closing time so I could give everyone a chance to get into their vehicles and go home. Because, not to be dramatic, but tonight is the night when everything changes for me. Will is going to teach me to be a master dater, and I'll snag a husband in no time.

Will dropped off a note at my door earlier (which made me laugh considering I have a cell phone he could have texted) that said tonight we're going to write out a formal plan for the lessons. That gave me chills because there's nothing I like more than a good bullet point list. The letter also came with a hand-drawn map and time stamps of when each part of the mission should be completed. I half expected the note to self-destruct after I finished reading it.

One thing is for certain, the man is thorough. Which begs an intriguing idea of what it would be like to kiss him or even . . .

Nooooope. Not going there.

Back to the plan. I'm supposed to be outside of Mabel's Inn at 6:30 P.M., when Will is going to distract her so I can get inside without her seeing me. Apparently, he'll give me a cue and I'll know it when I hear it.

Listen, this is high-stakes stuff. Even Jason Bourne would be sweating if he were faced with the potential of Mabel's discovery of one of his missions. If she finds out, I might as well go live on Instagram with it because everyone from here to the edge of Kentucky will know about our secret lessons before my foot has time to cross his threshold.

My watch says I have four minutes until I need to be outside the inn. Once the parking lot is empty, I rush across the street. I can't decide if I should walk normally or hurry while crouching, and I'm afraid the result will look like Annie is about to poop her pants. I'm really hoping Will isn't watching out his window right now.

A few more blocks and I'm at my destination: Mabel's Inn.

It's a gorgeous old Victorian house with a white picket fence around the small lawn. It has the look of a home that was built before the town, and has been a second home to me since childhood. Every Sunday after church, my grandma Silvie would bring us all over here to Mabel's for lunch. Mabel didn't go to church, so she was able to spend the whole morning cooking up a huge feast—and I remember thinking how incredibly rebellious she was. Not going to church?! Gasp! I asked her about it once and she just told me, "If I wanted to see a bunch of people wearing fancy clothes and acting fake, I'd go to a steeplechase." That was that, and I call dibs on being Mabel when I grow up.

The irony is that while Mabel won't set foot in church, she plays poker with the church ladies at Hank's Bar every Monday. Unfortunately, she won't leave here for that event until eight o'clock, so I have to sneak by her.

Instead of following the sidewalk, I hop the side picket fence and plaster my back to the side of the house like Will instructed. No sooner than I'm in place does the front door of the inn open. And then I hear Will's voice.

"It's over here, Mabel! Follow me," he says loudly.

"Well, shit, son. No need to yell. My hearing aids are already turned all the way up," says Mabel in her scratchy sweet voice that always makes me smile.

"Sorry about that."

"Apology accepted. Now show me this worrisome piece of siding."

"Yeah, it's just over here—" Will's voice cuts off as he rounds the side of the house where I'm standing.

In unrelated news, I'm not so great at reading maps.

Our gazes meet and Will's eyes go wide. I frantically start waving him away, and he whirls on his heels just before Mabel turns the corner. "Whoops! Wrong side. Totally forgot it's . . . on the other side." Their shadows are projecting onto the grass, and I see Will place his hands on Mabel's shoulders and guide her the opposite way.

She whistles lightly. "Now, William. At least take me to dinner first."

The only person in town who is a bigger flirt than Will is Mabel.

"Believe me, Mabel, if I thought I had a chance . . ." Will says, making Mabel chuckle and me roll my eyes. Their voices grow more distant, and when I believe the coast is clear, I peek my head around the corner.

Nope.

Not clear.

Of course Noah is walking up the front sidewalk of the inn, holding a pie box. "Mabel? You here?" he hollers.

"Yep! Right here," she says, coming around to the front of the house and leaving Will on the side.

"Brought your pie."

"Oh good, just set it on the porch, and come look. William was showing me a bad piece of siding on the house."

"Really? Didn't you just have the siding replaced last month?"

Mabel lowers her voice. "Lord, yes. But between me and you, I think the boy is lonely. Inventing excuses to spend time with me and all that. Better come humor him with me."

"What's going on?" And that would be the voice of Emily as she walks up to the inn, coming to join the circus. What the Frankenstein are my siblings all doing around town this late? Don't they have lives?!

"Will is showing us a bad piece of siding on the inn," says Noah.

Emily scoffs. "No way. I thought Mabel just had it all replaced last month. And Darell is the one who did it. He never does a bad job."

Looks like I should have brought a tent, at this rate. Sweat is gathering on my neck. My shorts are sticking to my legs. Just how I wanted to show up for this night with Will—as swamp woman.

"Mabel thinks Will is just lonely and is trying to get attention."

Emily laughs. "I highly doubt that. From what Amelia has said, he has lots of female company whenever he wants it."

Her statement makes my skin itch uncomfortably.

"What's going on over here?" Oh geez. Do we really need to throw Harriet into this mix? "Is this another impromptu town meeting without me?" She still hasn't forgiven Mabel after the last one.

"Does this look like a town meeting, Harriet? Do you ever use your brain?" asks Mabel ruthlessly.

"At least I have one to use! And if it's not a meeting—why are y'all standing around here?"

"William is going to show me a piece of bad siding."

"Didn't you just have the siding replaced last month?"

"Yes," everyone says in unison, including me under my breath.

Finally, I hear Will's voice. "Mabel, are you—oh, people. Look at that." I smile to myself, imagining the look of annoyance on his face. I would bet my entire life savings that he rakes his butterfly hand through his hair.

"Yes, William, the gang's all here. Now, show us this rotten siding."

"Good. Right. Glad we all get to see it." He pauses and clears his throat. "Follow me, everyone."

I wait three breaths, peek around the corner again, and then hightail it up to room number four. Will's room.

CHAPTER THIRTEEN

Annie

The moment I'm finally inside Will's room, panic sets in.

Did I just willingly enter the room of the great seducer (which no one calls him but absolutely should) Will Griffin? I'm not prepared enough for this. What if he proposes we take our lessons to the bed? Oh gosh—what if he was serious about those condoms, and he intends for us to sleep together?! Am I going to be able to resist the temptation of all that is Will? Do I want to resist? If I didn't, it would require admitting I'm still a virgin, and I think that's something I'd rather he never know.

But then I look around at his room and relax with a little laugh. There's one of Mabel's standard quilts on the bed (courtesy of Gemma's quilt shop, Comfort Quilts), and there are several decorative trinkets on the dresser and bedside tables. A random owl. An antique clock. A pillow embroidered with the words *Pretty as a Peach* sitting in the middle of the neatly made bed where the top edge of the sheet is folded down primly. The only evidence that Will stays here is the cell phone charger plugged into the wall and the folded clothes on the dresser. Other than those, nothing suggests a modern-day version of a rake is staying here.

Clearly, I have nothing to worry about.

The door suddenly opens and Will rushes in, closing it behind him.

He leans back against it like he just outran a bear. In his butterfly hand is a piece of white siding. "Damn, Annie, what are you turning me into? I'm now at a new level of awful after having to deliberately rip off a piece of Mabel's siding before they all came to look! Of course I told her I'd fix it for her—but I feel like I'm going to have bad dreams after seeing how proud she looked at me for offering to fix it after I was the one who ripped it off." He's still wearing the same black cargo pants and green tee from this morning, but now he has a roguish, excited smile in place. It fades when he takes in my expression. "Why are you smiling like that?"

"Oh, it's nothing," I say, waving him off and still not able to hold back my chuckles.

He cocks his head skeptically and tosses the piece of siding onto the bed. "Okay, it's clearly not nothing. What's with the laughter?"

I shake my head and give in to it, laughing until little mist droplets form in my eyes. "It's silly. But I was a little nervous to hang out with you in your room tonight because of your reputation. But then when I realized you're living in one of the Golden Girls' rooms, I didn't feel so worried anymore."

"Whoa, whoa, whoa," he says, looking highly offended now. "Why don't you feel worried anymore?"

"Because!" I say, laughing again as I think of Will trying to seduce me on top of that blue-and-white-checkered quilt. "Look at this room! The only thing you could hold in here is a Bible study."

"Psh," he says looking away and then back again with a grin I've come to know as a precursor. "You think this decor matters one bit? If I wanted to seduce you, the frills on a pillow aren't going to stop me."

"Nope—sorry, I call bull crap," I say, sitting on the end of the very wholesome and unsexy bed. "Here I was thinking that Will Griffin would live somewhere with satin sheets and a record player in the corner where he could offer to show me his favorite slow jams that would set the mood. A real den of iniquity—"

"Well, I don't love that name."

"But really, it's just getting me in the mood to go to the farmers market! Does this thing even . . ." I bounce on the mattress a few times. "Oh my gosh! It doesn't even squeak, Will! What kind of a ladies' man are you?!" I lose it, falling back on the mattress with a devastating laugh.

He watches me with a smile. "Are you enjoying yourself?"

"Quite. Because, you, sir, are a disgrace to bad boys everywhere by living in a room like this! I'm tempted to take pictures of you standing there with the Bless This Mess embroidery behind you and then sell them to BuzzFeed."

Will steps toward me with a lazy smile. "All right. Get your ass up."

I feel drugged and loose-limbed from joy as I sit up and take his outstretched hand. "Where are we going? To make some jam in the kitchen?"

But then my breath catches in my lungs when we get to the door and Will whirls me around so that my back is flat against it. "Because you've insulted my very carefully practiced reputation, your lessons start now. I'm going to demonstrate a few things— skipping lesson one, which I'd planned as light first date flirting— and we'll jump all the way to lesson seven: postdate seduction for when you're ready to take someone to bed."

Oh Lordy.

"But first, I believe in absolute consent at all times. So I need to know if it's okay for me to touch your hands—and only your hands?"

I swallow and nod, feeling my pulse throb against my neck.

"Words, Annie. I need to hear you say yes."

I clear my throat. "Yes."

"Great." He steps closer—so close that his chest is almost brushing mine, and his bluish-gray eyes are searing through me. That suddenly feels like way too much distance. Will's gaze holds mine—mesmerizing me as he intertwines our fingers. Slowly. Intentionally. Never has my skin felt so alive.

His hands are big and calloused and warm. Slowly he raises both of my hands above my head and presses them back against the door. Not too hard, not too soft. Just the right amount of pressure. Speaking of pressure, my body is now dying for him to close the gap between us. To press me to him and . . . I don't know, just do something!

My lips part and Will's eyes lower—watching the moment as it happens. The smallest of curves touches the corners of his mouth before he drops his lips to the side of my face. His breath brushes against the shell of my ear and tickles every nerve ending in my body—fertilizing them and somehow growing more. New sensations I've never known surface in the pit of my stomach and . . . lower. He smells so good. Feels so good.

"First things first . . ." Sweet molasses, his quiet, rumbly bedroom voice is hot. "It's never about the room. The room doesn't play a part in sex." His voice is deep and amused and confident. This is exactly how I imagined he'd be in this situation. No—better.

As promised, he touches nothing but my hands. I am slowly perishing.

He continues—his breath hot and heavy against the side of my face. "In a bind, a closet, a bathroom, even a car will do just fine." His mouth lowers even farther to breathe against my neck now. Never touching me, just breathing. "Decor doesn't matter." He moves up my throat as he speaks, and on to the other side. I angle my head like I want to make sure he reaches every spot and crevice. "Because if I've effectively captured her attention through the date, from the moment we're alone, her pulse will be racing, and her mind will be absorbed with touch and breath and so much desire that the color of my damn bedspread won't even cross her mind once."

His mouth is at my ear again, and his hands continue to hold mine pinned above my head with a delicious gentle pressure that makes me squirm. One I didn't know I liked. Didn't know I needed. Now I'm afraid I'll feel deprived of it for the rest of my life.

Will moves from my ear, fanning his breath across my jaw to hover just in front of my lips now. "Annie, open your eyes and look at me," he commands, and until that point, I didn't even realize my eyes were shut.

When my eyelids spring open, I feel drunk. His gray gaze is dark now and heavy on mine. I feel desperate for him to tip forward and kiss me. His thumb tracks back and forth over the inside of my wrist. I barely remember what I was here for today or what my name is, for that matter. All I know is my pulse is drumming loudly in my ear, and it seems to be saying the same thing over and over again. Kiss me. Kiss me. Kiss me.

With his mouth only a centimeter apart from mine, he smiles. "Believe me?"

I nod silently.

"Great," he whispers and then releases my hands. My arms fall limply at my sides because I am a sack of Jell-O at this point. Will, however, is completely unaffected and goes back to the couch. "Come sit down so we can talk about the lesson plan."

For a moment I can't do anything but stand here and lean against the door. My insides are blazing. My stomach is all twisted and bunched, and I feel absurdly let down that he's over there and I'm over here.

"H-how did you do that?" I say, finally finding my voice as my feet carry me in a daze back to the couch. My brain isn't working right yet, so instead of sitting, I stand here like a robot waiting for its next command.

Will grins and hooks a finger in the baggy back pocket of my shorts and tugs me down to the couch. I sit, wide-eyed.

"Confidence," he says, picking up his laptop and opening it.

I lean over and shut it again.

He chuckles.

"But how?! What if you don't feel confident?" I'm not sure I've ever felt confident a day in my life.

"You fake it, Annie."

"No way." I shake my head in disbelief. "You don't fake that kind of confidence. All of that . . ." I circle my finger toward the door where the ghost of Annie who had never been seductively entranced by Will Griffin still lives, ". . . was natural for you."

He grins. "Not true. I was nervous."

I take in his pirate eyes with the dangerous black rim around his irises, the tattoos wrapping down his arm with the masculine veins that universally turn everyone on, and last but not least, the rebellious wave of hair that flops down above his brow every time he rakes his hand through it. "I don't believe you for a second."

Will's eyes narrow on my face, jaws clenching as he debates something. And then Will raises his hand level between us. That's when I see it. His hand, that beautiful, strong, inked hand, is trembling. Will Griffin is shaking from touching me.

"If I waited until I felt confident to live my life and do the things I want to do, I'd never live." He stares into my eyes. "This lesson is one as old as time: Fake it till you make it. If you want something, pretend you're the kind of person who's not scared of it."

I let out a *huh* sound as I sink back against the couch. "You do that?"

"All the time," he says, still looking at me. "You should have seen me the first time I went skydiving. I actually thought I was going to shit my pants on the plane." We both laugh. "But I told myself I was Tom Cruise at that moment and somehow it worked. Ended up being one of the most fun things I've ever done."

I'm mesmerized by him. I pull my legs up onto the cushion, fully facing him. "You seem like a thrill seeker."

He smiles. "I absolutely am. It's addicting."

"Were you that way as a kid too?"

Will looks away. "You mean when I dropped out of elementary school and joined the circus to work as a lion tamer? Definitely . . ."

Okay, that's the second time he's deflected a question regarding his childhood. Apparently, that means any conversation surrounding his adolescence is off the table. Interesting.

"What other adventurous things have you done?"

He takes in a deep breath, his chest expanding under his soft T-shirt. Oddly, my brain nose-dives to how nice it would feel to sink onto him and rest right there—in the crook of his shoulder. To have his arms encircle me and just hold me.

"Let's see . . . during Amelia's last world tour, I went ATV riding on the Atlantis Trail in South Africa. I'm scuba certified and have gone diving in a lot of places—but I think Mexico was my favorite. And hiking in Red Rock was awesome."

"That's a lot of *ing* words," I say, suddenly realizing how little I've done in comparison to him. Once again, Will unhelpfully reads my face. He knocks his knuckles against my knee.

"There's still time for you to do anything you want to do."

I shrug. "I don't think adventure is the life for me. Anyone who knows me will attest that I'm more built for a steady, safe routine. My dream is to get married to a nice man and have babies whom I can eventually pass down my flower shop to. Soccer games on the weekend and harvest parties in the fall. And all of it taking place right here in Rome. That's my future."

He holds my gaze and smiles softly. "Hmm."

"What?"

He tips his head to the side. "It's just that I'm not totally sure what you said is true."

"It is," I say, feeling a frown between my brows.

"Okay."

"Really!" My voice is an octave higher than usual. "That's what I want."

He tips a brow, looks down, and opens his laptop. "If you say so. Now, for these lessons. Do you want to—"

I slam the laptop shut. "You really don't believe me?"

The challenge in his smiling gaze cuts directly to mine. "No. I really don't."

"Why not?"

Will's eyes feel like a caress on my face. "Because you told me not to call you Angel Annie. Because you wrestled me in your shop and then masterfully maneuvered me into being your dating coach. Because you read books about women who are pulled from their average lives and thrust into huge adventures where they thrive and find passion. Because even though you say you were relieved when you realized I lived in this old lady's room, I could see the disappointment in your eyes." His gaze drops to my lips, holds for two seconds, and comes back up again. "It seems to me, Annie, that you are just waiting for someone to give you permission to be yourself out loud."

My heart trips over his words. I stay quiet. I wasn't disappointed at the sight of his room—I was relieved. Right? Sure, I've had a crush on Will this whole time, but it's not like I'm harboring any secret ambitions to be anything more than friends with him.

No, none of what he said was true. It can't be true—because if so, then this void I'm feeling is not going to go away with the future I described to him. It's going to get worse. And with Grandma's health failing and so much change already happening all at once to Noah with his wedding, my family won't be able to handle Annie having an early life crisis on top of it.

So I'm going to put his words out of my head and not dwell on them. All I need are these dating lessons so I can snag myself a husband and get married and live happily ever after just like my mom and dad. That's it.

I look down when I feel Will's hand gently splay across my knee. "I didn't mean to upset you."

"You didn't," I say quickly, swallowing my feelings and looking up at him with the best smile I can muster. He nods slowly and turns his eyes to his laptop, opening it once again. This time I let him.

Without looking at me, he adds, "Tell you what, Annie. We'll get you your committed relationship and your white picket fence, and if for some reason it doesn't feel right and you want that adventure after all—" He looks at me. "Call me and I'll come hold your hand on the flight."

His words wrap around my heart and squeeze. And it's in this moment that I realize BuzzFeed wasn't able to capture the most wonderful expression I've seen from Will yet—tenderness.

CHAPTER FOURTEEN

Will

"As much as I appreciate it, you didn't have to repair the siding, you know? Would've had Darell come back and fix it," says Mabel. She's hovering behind me in her pink pullover gown, steaming cup of coffee in hand.

"Believe me, I did." There was no way I was going to make her pay to have something replaced that I intentionally broke. I didn't even intend for Mabel to know I was the one who fixed it (or plans to fix it). But about five minutes ago she heard me as I attempted to fit the siding back onto the house and came marching out in her gown to ask what the hell I was doing out here at the crack of dawn. It's around eight in the morning. Hardly dawn. But sometimes I forget that the rest of the world doesn't share my same early morning rhythm of waking up at five and going for a jog.

Today it was raining when I woke up so I tried to stay in bed later. But then my thoughts took over and dove down every avenue I try to avoid. Like Ethan getting married to someone he barely knows, and wondering how I'm going to respond to the text he sent me before bed last night: Please don't freeze me out. I need you during all of this.

I honestly don't know what to say, though. I'm not ready to welcome his new fiancée with open arms, and I'm starting to realize it might not have anything to do with Ethan or Hannah. Last night as I listened to Annie talk about the kind of future she wanted, I felt that relentless tug in my chest again. Not because I want the harvest-parties and soccer-games life she mentioned, but because I want the ability to dream of a life with someone like Annie where my immediate thought isn't: *But how is it going to fail?* Ethan seems to have unlocked some new part of himself that can just move past what we went through, and I think I'm wildly jealous of him for it. Maybe even a little bitter. Because the only difference in our upbringing is that he had someone older to take care of him—to make sure he was loved and hugged regularly.

I had no one.

Even now I have no one, but the difference is I've stopped waiting for someone to fill that role, and I'm better for it.

After I pushed thoughts of Ethan out, new ones—equally unwelcome ones—took their place. Ones that starred Annie Walker. The feel of her hands under mine. The way she smelled during my demonstration. Ugh. That damn demonstration. Before she showed up, I had promised myself to behave. Keep things buttoned up and businesslike. But of course Annie had to be Annie and throw me a curveball and make me act irrationally.

Now I'm stuck with the memory of her soft skin and parted lips and dilated pupils. She wanted me to kiss her. Badly. And I wanted to kiss her just as much. Probably more. And the worst part is, I'm not just physically attracted to her. I can't get enough of hearing her talk, and I want to read every book she has stashed away, and I want more than anything to take her on an adventure she'll never forget.

At least we finally got a real plan in place for these lessons. It was not an easy task, though, because I told Annie we should get her signed up for online dating—to which Annie spent a good portion of the time explaining how she in no way wanted to be sent pickle pictures. I told her to call them dick pics like the rest of the world, but she only grimaced and refused, saying that she didn't even have any selfies to upload for a dating profile. That made me irrationally upset. Why doesn't she have photos of herself? Because no one takes photos of her or because she's not comfortable enough to be in them? I made a silent promise after that to take photos of Annie while I'm in town. And we vetoed the online dating completely. Instead, I'm going to take her out in a few days so I can officially see what sort of a "bad date" I'm dealing with, and we'll continue from there.

Anyway, back to this morning. I was sick of fighting my thoughts, so I got up and jogged in the rain, and then when the weather cleared, I got a jump start on fixing shit on Mabel's Inn.

Now she raises her mug to her lips and watches me as I hold up the siding, wondering how in hell I attach it. I found a hammer and some nails in the inn's storage closet, but they're sitting uselessly at my feet. I think I'm missing something crucial here—because as I look at the other pieces of siding, I don't see a single nail.

"You don't know what you're doing, huh?" Mabel asks.

"Not a bit."

She snorts. "It's a good thing you're pretty."

I give her a side glare and drop the siding to the ground next to the hammer and nails that I don't think I'll be using. "I might need the number of your siding guy," I admit, even though I'd rather eat my shoe than force someone else to clean up the mess I made.

"Like I said, you're not responsible for this. I'll call Darrel. You go about your day." She makes a shooing motion with her hand.

I shift on my feet uncomfortably. "I'd like to help, though. If you'll just give me his contact number, I'll get him to fix it and I'll pay for—"

"You ripped that siding off to create a distraction to sneak Annie into your room, didn't you?" The wrinkles in her forehead multiply as she skewers me with a look and waits for my response.

My mouth falls open. I flounder for an answer. "How did you know?"

It's not worth it to lie. This woman has abilities that are clearly not to be underestimated.

She gives me a slow grin—masterfully perfected from years of wielding it. "I know everything in this town."

"Terrifying."

"Isn't it?" She sips her coffee.

"I guess you'll want to know why she was sneaking into my room?"

"Would you tell me if I asked?"

"No," I say honestly. "Annie asked me not to. So I have to keep my promise to her."

And for some reason, having Annie's trust feels like holding the world. I never want to break it.

"Good man. I knew I liked you." She raises her mug. "Woulda lost a lot of respect for you if you'd caved right away." Her eyes shift to the missing siding, and laughter springs to her eyes. She shakes her head with a smile. "Fool. You could've just told me Harriet was on her way to the bar early to take my place at poker night."

"Damn," I say genuinely, also turning my attention to the eyesore on the side of her inn.

"Next time." She drinks from her mug and then turns away. "I won't tell anyone," she says loudly in her scratchy voice. "And the siding guy's my nephew. Let me call him because it'll be a hoot to tell him his handiwork didn't hold up and then threaten to call his daddy." She pauses and looks back at me with lifted brows. "Now get to work before Amelia fires you and you have to leave town and Annie behind." The corner of her mouth twitches, and I think her brain is drawing all sorts of conclusions it shouldn't. Ones with wedding bells and babies and deep, deep roots.

"Nothing's going to happen between me and Annie," I say, just to make sure everyone is on the same page.

She laughs. "You're aware it's only eight in the morning, right? That means it's too early for your shit talking. Now I'm going to go finish my coffee while watching *The Price Is Right*, so get out of here."

I laugh even though I'm a little terrified of Mabel. Terrified and in awe. "See you later, Mabel."

With her back to me and fluffy pink gown swinging as she walks, she raises her mug in the air. I'm not fully convinced there's actually coffee in there.

"You look ridiculous," Amelia tells me as we wind our way around the greenhouses at Huxley Farm.

"No, you look ridiculous," I say, looking Amelia up and down. She's wearing homemade cutoff shorts, brown work boots, a gray tank top, and a big oversize floppy hat—so opposite to her usual classic tailored look. "Like a hillbilly."

Normally I would never dare speak to a client so freely. But this is Amelia, and we've worked together for so long now we're practically related. And Amelia is the furthest thing from a stuck-up celebrity as you can get. The first day on the job with her, she threw everything I was taught out the window. The woman refused to walk in front of me, falling in step with me, asking an endless string of questions like, So where were you born? How many siblings do you have? What's your favorite hobby?

After a year of that, Amelia became my friend whether I wanted one or not. Never anything more than that. Yes, I would absolutely take a bullet for the woman, but I would never in a million years sleep with her. And I'm a thousand percent sure she feels the same way.

She strangles a guttural laugh in her throat. "Better a hillbilly than what you're wearing. You look like a city slicker straight out of a Hallmark movie who needs to learn a lesson in the country. Who wears white sneakers to a farm, Will?"

I look down and cringe at the dirt smudges already forming. "It was an oversight for sure. But it's better than dressing like Elly May Clampett from *The Beverly Hillbillies*. I don't even know who you are anymore."

I give her shit about it, but the truth is, I like this new side of Amelia. She seems lighter and more fun. Country life suits her the way adventure suits me. I just didn't realize until she was here with Noah how much she needed this place—these people.

She touches the brim of her straw hat. "It's basically farm dress code. Don't worry, you'll learn."

"Don't think so. I'll be out of here before there's enough time for any of this to rub off on me once you persuade my boss to let me go." The grass crunches under our feet as we walk to a wide clearing behind each of the greenhouses where Amelia and Noah are planning to hold their ceremony and reception.

Amelia squints up at me. "You really don't want to stick around after the wedding?"

This morning, on our drive to the farm, I talked to her about the conversation I had with my boss. That's one of the perks of having a nontraditional relationship with the client. I can be honest. Amelia wasn't too thrilled, though. The only thing that seemed to ease her mind was when I told her to call me when she's ready to tour again.

"I can't," I say, looking down at her with a genuinely sad smile. "You're hands down my favorite person to work for—and a good friend—but you know me. I need a fast-paced life. I've only been here a few days, and I'm already pulling my hair out." Sort of. Okay, in truth it hasn't been all that bad, but I don't want to admit that to Amelia, or she'll be like a kid in a candy shop.

"Is a fast-paced life really what you need?" she asks, surprising me with the seriousness of her tone. She has spiritual guide eyes right now, and she's freaking me out.

I turn toward her and frown. "What does that mean?"

"Never mind."

I don't trust that "never mind" one bit. "Will you tell my boss you're okay with being assigned a new EPA?"

She looks at me with a meaningfully sharp expression and a taut smirk. "I'll consider it."

Meaning no.

She raises her hand to the top of her hat as she turns her gaze to the open field. "So what do you think? Great place for a wedding, right?"

I look out over the sprawling green grass dusted with little white wildflowers and dandelions that fade into a lush tree line under dark blue skies. "It's beautiful."

Even a cynic like me can appreciate how perfect this spot is for a wedding.

"I think so too." Amelia bounces lightly on her feet and then starts out in front of me, excitedly describing what's in her imagination. "We'll have a row of adorable wooden folding chairs here. And one here. This is where the center aisle will be." She points to her left. "Over there we're having a temporary dance floor installed, and there will be all these dreamy lights and velvet fabrics draping over it like a canopy. And then over there is where we'll have the food."

I watch silently as Amelia bounces around the empty field—

joy bursting from her like sunlight as she describes her wedding. What's it like to feel that unbridled excitement toward sharing your life with someone else? To be full of hope and anticipation rather than dread and cynicism. I envy her.

"All right, are you getting bored over there?" she yells across the expanse of grass.

I shut my eyes and pretend to snore, making her laugh.

"Fine, let me just take this picture and we can go," she says, fishing out her phone.

The whole reason we are here right now is so she can take a picture of the area for her wedding planner, who has been working remotely, and then I'll escort her into town, where she's going to spend the afternoon with Noah in The Pie Shop. And then I'll be on my own for the rest of the day. Where that thought used to cause dread, now I feel a stir of anticipation. I wonder what Annie's doing?

Once Amelia is finished with her photos, we make the trek back through the farm toward her truck. We fill the silence easily as usual.

"It's a nice farm," I say, pretending I know anything about farms. "Good grass."

Luckily, Amelia shares my brand of sarcastic humor. "Right? That's clearly the best tractor too."

"Yeah. The . . . green is good."

"I've driven it," she says proudly. "It's pretty slow."

I hum noncommittally as we again approach the greenhouses full of produce and one of flowers. In my limited knowledge of farms, this one feels massive. It has outdoor crops in addition to the greenhouses. Some dairy cows too.

Amelia and I continue to make farm-ignorant comments back and forth until I see a figure several yards away in one of the rows of huge pink flowers. My eyes are snagged immediately, and I do a double take. Annie. Her blonde hair is braided to the side, her face shielded by a big straw sun hat. She's wearing work gloves and holding a pair of gardening scissors. Today she has a tight white short-sleeved shirt underneath her cutoff jean overalls. I swear the sunlight hits this woman differently than other people. It seeps into her skin, makes her glow.

I imagine running my hands over that sun-warmed skin, and desire punches me in the stomach. Or rather, somewhere farther south than the stomach. I stare—and everything gets worse as Annie bends over to clip a few long stems from the row of flowers. My gaze sweeps over the soft curve of her ass, down her tan legs to her brown work boots. She looks mouthwateringly sweet.

"How come you're not commenting that she looks like Elly May Clampett?" asks Amelia, bumping her shoulder into my arm.

"Who?" My voice comes out as dry as the desert. Amelia barks out a laugh, and I shake myself from the daze to look at her. "I was just trying to figure out what the name of those flowers is."

She smirks. "Uh-huh. Sure. Why don't you ask the woman you're gawking at?"

I wiggle my fingers in front of her smug face. "Can you do less of this please?"

She bats her eyelashes. "Less of what?"

"The matchmaking. I can feel it. This town has seeped into your brain and turned you into a disgusting hopeless romantic."

"And I can turn you into one, too, if you'd just quit fighting it so hard. You're not going to want to be a player forever, you know? And if you happen to meet a cute blonde flower shop owner and want to give dating a go . . . well, then—"

"I knew you had ulterior motives by asking me to be Annie's dating coach. You're going to be very disappointed when this doesn't work out the way you want. I'm not going to fall in love with Annie or whatever it is you think is going to happen."

"Yeah . . . the love part. That's exactly what I think will happen."

"Like hell. I don't think I'm built for love."

She narrows her eyes, still not convinced. "Then why did you say yes to helping Annie?"

Why, indeed. Because she has a hold on me that I can't figure out. Because her eyes do this sparkly thing when she's excited and the light hits them just right. Because the curve of her bottom lip is perfect. Because I feel desperate to know what wild thing she's going to say next anytime she's around.

"Because there's absolutely nothing to do in this town, and I need something to keep me busy when you don't need m—"

I cut off, my eyes drifting to follow the new scene playing out in front of me. James appears out of nowhere and walks down the row of flowers toward Annie. He's carrying a bucket full of cut roses and the muscles in his arms bulge obnoxiously. He smiles at Annie and she looks overjoyed to see him. He sets down the bucket, and she launches herself into his arms for a nice big bear hug. The squeeze he gives her in return feels like a bit much.

Amelia hovers in my vision again, following my gaze. "Someone feeling a little jealous?"

"Not in the least."

"Your jaw just flexed."

"It does that naturally because it's so square."

"You mean it does that naturally when you're jealous." She drags out the word annoyingly.

I sigh and close my eyes, tilting my face up toward the sun, wishing it would burn me up. It would be better than having to endure Amelia on a mission. Last time this happened it was over tacos. I made the terrible mistake of telling her I didn't like them—which happens to be her favorite food—and she proceeded to stop at every acclaimed taco place during a U.S. tour and made me try one from each restaurant until I found one I liked.

Unfortunately, I do like tacos now, but it's annoying.

Amelia laughs, and I'm afraid that if we stand here much longer, they're going to hear her evil cackle and notice us.

I open my eyes and put my hands on Amelia's shoulders, steering her in the direction of the car—opposite to the way of Annie and James. "All right. Time to go."

"Because you're raging with jealousy and about to throw your fist in James's face?"

"Because you're clearly having a heatstroke and growing delirious. I'm not into Annie." I'm not, I'm not, I'm not. Or if I am, it's purely lust. Lust that I will not act on because that feels like an awkward situation waiting to happen. You can't have a one-night stand with someone in a town of this size. Not to mention the situation that Amelia just inserted me into as Annie's dating coach. All signs point toward *don't*!

Amelia is relentless, though. "You know what? Now that I think of it, Annie and James do make a cute couple. I should ask him to help her with her practice dates instead."

I leave her in my dust, eating up the ground to get to the truck faster. "It's a good thing you found Noah," I call over my shoulder.

"Don't you want to get one more look at her before you leave?" Amelia taunts cheerfully.

"Nope. I'm good."

"Oh my gosh, Will, they just kissed! So much tongue I can see it from here."

I roll my eyes and keep walking. But when I get to Amelia's truck (she refuses to ride in the company-provided SUV), I glance briefly over my shoulder.

Annie is by herself again among the flowers, and for some reason, that makes me breathe a sigh of relief.

CHAPTER FIFTEEN

Annie

Jeanine sets down the plate of French toast I ordered right next to the plate of pancakes. I have to scoot the omelet with a side of bacon a little to the left to make room. The bowl of fruit balances off the opposite edge of the table, but I reach my foot under and use the toe of my shoe to scooch it back on.

"Hun, this is a lot even for you," says Jeanine, pushing her gorgeous red ponytail back over her shoulder. Jeanine is one of those women I'd like to shadow for a day and take notes on how she does . . . *everything*. She has that natural sway to her hips when she walks that screams confidence. A smile that is innately flirtatious. And she once went with me and my sisters to a bar in the city where the woman came away with ten phone numbers! Ridiculous. Inspiring.

"They're not all for me. I'm meeting someone."

If there was a record playing, it would have screeched to a stop. Jeanine's sharp blue eyes whip to me. Phil and Todd, sitting two booths down, angle their faces in my direction. Greg, behind the breakfast bar, nearly spills the coffee he was pouring.

Jeanine smiles then. "One of your sisters?"

"Nope." I shift the plates around, needing something to do with my hands. "Someone else." My knee bounces under the table and I'm sweating. Because today, I am meeting Will for a practice date.

He swung by the shop earlier this morning and asked if I'd like to meet him for a low-key practice date. And despite the fact that we're meeting at the local diner, I'm still buzzing with nervous energy like I'm meeting him at a three-star Michelin restaurant, and it's going to be filmed for live TV. I couldn't focus on my work at all. I spilled my coffee from how much my hand was shaking on the way into work. I've had a constant buzzing sensation in my stomach that makes me feel as if I'm about to take flight.

"Someone else, you say?" Jeanine prompts, clearly wanting me to dish all the gossip so she doesn't have to dig it up on her own.

In that moment, the Someone Else in question walks through the door. His presence fills the place like a sudden gust of summer wind. Will steps into the diner, removes his sunglasses in slow motion (okay fine, it's regular speed but a girl can imagine), his biceps flexing under his black short-sleeved shirt as he does. He turns his head, scouring the diner until his blue-gray eyes find me. A smile tugs the corner of his mouth as he hangs his glasses on the collar of his shirt.

I have melted into a puddle in the booth. I am no longer human—just a blob of desire.

And now he's walking toward me, and Jeanine's face is a study in shock and awe. Everyone—and I do mean *everyone*—watches Will Griffin and his inked body walk to my table. Clearly, they thought it was okay when he was silently guarding Amelia, but meeting me for a solo lunch is too much to stomach. Angel Annie and bodyguard Will? It's a big concept. Even I'm struggling a little at how we ended up here.

It's all fake, that's how!

"Hi," he says as his laughing, roguish eyes land on me.

"Hi yourself." Oh geez, it comes out a little more flirtatious than I intended, but the shadow of our afternoon in his bedroom is still shielding me from reality. I smile up at him as he stops beside the booth, not able to take his seat because of how Jeanine is blocking it—staring in thick silence. She's trying to process why Will Griffin is meeting me for lunch.

"Hey, sorry, do you mind if I . . ." He gestures toward the bench she's blocking.

Jeanine shakes herself from his hypnotic eyes and practically leaps away. "Sorry! Yes. Have a seat, honey!" She calls everyone honey. It's her thing. It's why she goes home with ten phone numbers from the bar.

"Can I get you anything?" she asks Will, still in a daze.

He laughs, eyeing the table. "Normally I would say yes, but it looks like the whole menu is already here." He looks up at me inquisitively, one brow lifted. So impressive, that ability.

I fidget with the napkin beside my plate. "I was nervous while I waited. So I went ahead and ordered a few things for us . . ."

"Just a few," he repeats with a smile in my direction and then looks back up to Jeanine. "I think I've got everything I need here. Thank you."

"All right, darling, well . . . just holler if you need anything." She gives me a speaking glance and then slowly pulls herself away to return to the area behind the counter.

Will leans forward slightly. "What was that look for?"

I shrug my shoulders even though I know exactly what that look was about. And then I push my full plate away because suddenly I can't even entertain the idea of eating. "All right. Let's do this. What's first?"

Will's gaze moves from my plate to my face, a cautious smile in place. "What do you mean?"

I gesture between us. "Dating. What do I do first? You've sat down, I ordered you everything you could possibly need. What do I do now? Especially with my hands because I'm getting the urge to wave them around for no reason."

And wow, that's *so* freeing to say to someone. Normally, on dates I have to keep those thoughts in my head, but in this scenario, I can spill my guts and nothing bad happens. Amelia is a genius.

"You don't need to do anything with your hands."

"It feels like I do. How's this?" I perch them on the table, and he watches, tracking my movements as I adjust them again. "No? How about like this then?" I spread my arm over the back of the booth. I scrunch my nose. "This feels manly. Do I look manly? Does this look like I'm asserting dominance, because I can tell you right now I'm a beta all the way."

Will reaches across the table and pushes my plate back in front of me. "How about you just eat this?"

"I can't eat. I'm too nervous."

"What's there to be nervous about?"

"You," I say honestly before I remember to filter. Something about Will does this to me, though—I can't help but say exactly what I'm thinking. "Or . . . you as in men. A date. You get it."

He picks up his water glass, presses his lips to the rim, and takes a quick drink. "I have a secret you might like to know. It's related to your pirate books."

I have never needed to know anything more in my entire life. "Tell me," I say leaning over the table and splaying my hands on the surface like I'm willing to push the entire thing away if need be.

He grins and nods toward my plate. "Take a bite and I will."

I eye him sideways, seeing right through his tactics. "I'm not one of those girls you have to worry about eating, you know? I like food normally. Enjoy it often. Could probably clean most of these plates myself if this weren't a practice date making me feel like barfing." I wince. "I said barfing at the table. On a date. See, this is why I opt for silence, usually. When you get me going, there's no filter."

He shakes his head—seemingly unfazed by my barf comment. "It's just me. You can't mess up because there's nothing to mess up. I'm your practice person, remember?" He holds my gaze. "You're safe with me."

His gentle tone has all of the tension in my body melting away like butter on toast. I take in a deep breath and release it. "Okay."

"Okay." A smile. "Now eat."

As if on cue, my stomach growls. With a revived appetite, I switch my plate of eggs for the burger and fries. After biting into the burger, I wipe my mouth with my napkin and raise my eyebrows at Will. "A bite for a secret. Let's hear it, Wolf Boy."

He points lazily to his ear. "I used to wear an earring."

My mouth falls open, but then I remember there's food in there and clamp it shut. Sudden vivid images of Will in a pirate outfit, pistols hanging off a leather belt around his waist, shirt gaping open over his inked chest, and now . . . a silver hoop in his ear. Or no, it would be something gaudier. An emerald. A ruby he stole from a lady in a ballroom. The same ballroom he spots me in, and then decides he needs me. Can't live another second without me. To the screams of the entire room, he snakes his arm around my waist and hoists me off the ground, stealing me away into the night. He takes me to his ship (which is somehow docked nearby), where he pushes me back against the railing and then his mouth crashes over mine. I wrap my arms around his neck and—

"What the hell is going on in your head right now?" he asks, pulling me from my fantasy.

My face flames. "Nothing. Let's change the subject." I squirm in my seat, suddenly feeling both hot and awkward. Will can never know what was going on in my head.

He hums, grinning like he somehow already knows. I wad my napkin and throw it at him. "You don't know."

"I think I do." He circles a finger around his face. "You wear all your thoughts on your face. So openly. You were taking my clothes off in your head."

I gasp like an outraged matronly woman. "Absolutely not."

His eyes sparkle. "How naked did you get me? All the way or just to my underwear?"

I bury my face in my hands. "Moving on! What's next?"

He has pity on me, leaning forward and resting his elbows on the table. "All right. Tell me what you're most insecure about when it comes to first dates. What's your weakest point?"

"Is everything too broad?"

"A bit, yeah."

I take in a deep breath and think back to my date with John. "Conversation, I think. I'm so used to my family and the way there is never a quiet moment with them that I don't know how to handle lulls. So I usually try to fill it as quickly as possible."

"And that gets you into trouble?"

"I gave a Ted Talk on the reproductive cycles of flowers on my last date."

Will gives a valiant effort to not burst with laughter. But I see it there, hovering below the surface. His nostrils flare. His cheek twitches. "Is it too much to ask to hear this monologue? Please tell me flowers are into kinky stuff?"

"Stop!" I say, laughing and stretching my foot under the table to push his knee. Chuckling, he captures my ankle instead of letting me kick him. His thumb glides softly across the tender skin of my ankle and at the same moment, our laughter fades. The air cracks between us, and he lets go while I clear my throat and sit up straight.

Silence blankets the table.

Will pops a fry in his mouth and then licks the salt off his lips. Before I realize it, I'm watching oh so closely. For research! Obviously. Noting how the pros do it.

This time he does the manly look I tried but couldn't master: arm hooked over the back of the bench seat. So casual and composed. Like maybe his shoulders are tight from a long workout and he just needs to stretch them. My eyes track down that long arm as it spans out over the top, putting his floral tattoos on display for me.

Will clears his throat. "It's okay to let the conversation go quiet for a bit, by the way. The ability to be silent shows confidence." As if to illustrate a point, he shifts, picks up his water glass, and takes a long drink. His Adam's apple bobs against the long column of his throat, and now I'm convinced I need to jump into a pool full of ice because I am way too hot and bothered for a casual lunch at the diner. What is happening to me?

I lean my forearms on the table, sitting forward. "How are you so good at this?"

"Practice. Everyone thinks a good date is something that comes naturally, but it's not. It's taken time for me to learn the best tactics. Like the other day in my room when we . . ." He trails off and looks down briefly. "Anyway, yeah. I know my strengths now, and I'm confident in them."

Interesting. He's avoiding remembering that moment too. Did he feel as affected by it as I was?

A thrilling concept.

"Hey, can I ask you a random question?"

"Sure."

"Is there something between you and James?"

A startled punctuated laugh jumps from my throat. "Me and James?" I'm sure my eyes are bugging from my head. "No way. That would be like me falling in love with Noah. Gross."

"Really?" he asks, looking a little skeptical.

"Really. I can't think of anything less appealing. No offense to James." I smile as Will nods. "Why do you ask?"

He shrugs. "No reason. Just thought it would be good to get the whole picture. If we were trying to specifically help you snag James, then we could tailor our lessons."

Makes sense. But no—James may not be my brother by blood, but he's my brother all the same.

I pull my legs up in the booth, crossing one over the other. "Okay, speaking of lessons. After I've learned to bask in silence confidently, then what? What about when I need to talk? I don't think my sexy flowers are as interesting to other people as they are to you."

He laughs and grabs a napkin. "Do you have a pen?"

After digging through my purse, I find one and hand it to him. Will then writes a series of sentences on the napkin and hands it to me. "These are the questions I have memorized that I ask on every single date. Questions about family are always awkward and have too many potential pitfalls, and no one really wants to talk about their job. So I like to ask fun icebreakers instead. Works every time."

I read the napkin out loud. "What was your favorite TV show to watch as a kid? What's something you've always wanted to do but have been too scared to do it? Would you rather skydive or read a book?" I lower the napkin. "You have these memorized?"

He nods.

"And they really work?"

He doesn't answer. Instead, he tilts his head and watches me like there's a question that's been nagging at him for years. "Annie, what's something you've always wanted to do but have been too scared to?"

Immediately the answer comes to mind. One that I can't voice. One that he can't know.

Instead, I nibble on a fry and make a thinking noise. And then my eyes rest on his forearm and a more appropriate answer surfaces. "I've actually always wanted to get a tattoo."

He sits forward, looking excited and a little pleased. "Really? Why haven't you?" He asks like it would be as simple as just getting a haircut.

"I don't know. A combination of being afraid it will hurt and not sure what I'd get." And because I just can't. I'm Annie—it would be shocking. It would be so out of character for me. It would be . . . fun.

Suddenly Will's words from the other day ram into my memory: "It seems to me, Annie, that you are just waiting for someone to give you permission to be yourself out loud." I'm afraid to admit how right he was. How much I haven't been able to get our conversation out of my head no matter how hard I've tried. How the more I think of it, the more fear I have that the future I described to him won't be enough. That marriage isn't going to give me my happily ever after. And if that's true, what in the world is causing this hollow feeling?

"It doesn't hurt that bad," he says before taking a big bite of pancakes. "I'm sure you can handle it."

My eyes trace his arm all the way down to the butterfly. "How did you decide on your flowers?"

He answers too quickly for me to believe him. "I don't know— I've just always liked them."

"If I lift my chin when I lie, looking a little too nonchalant is your tell. What's the truth, Will Griffin?" I ask, mirroring his leaned forward position so we're eye to eye.

He stares at me, his expression never changing. And then he shocks me with an honest answer. "In my yard growing up . . . we had a magnolia tree out back. I used to hide out there a lot. When I needed to get away. It was sort of a haven for me."

Oh.

Something in Will's eyes and thoughtful tone tells me that he visited that tree often. And it wasn't just a haven but a safe haven. A place he needed too often. As I picture a younger version of this man hiding up in a magnolia tree all by himself, my heart bleeds. I want to climb up there with him and hold his hand. I want to know every reason that drove him up those branches—and I want to make all that pain go away.

He sits back abruptly and smiles. "Of course that was before I found my wolf family. After that I was too busy roaming the land and hunting to climb trees."

The more I get to know Will, the more I realize his charming playfulness is not always real. Sometimes I think it's a mask. It's a smile drawn on a sticky note and pasted on his face. If I were to pull it off, I would find a frown beneath.

"Come on—don't give me that look, please." He glances over his shoulder toward the fellow diner goers watching us with hawk-like intensity. He flashes someone a beaming smile. Waves at another.

"Am I giving you a look?"

"A heavy one," he says before turning his eyes back to me. "Let's move on and figure out what tattoo you should get."

I don't want to make him feel uneasy, so I push down my growing, desperate need to know this man in front of me. It's for the best anyway. Empathy is the first step toward feelings. And Will Griffin is not someone I can have feelings for.

"Hmm. Well at the risk of you thinking I'm trying to be your copycat, it would be fun to get some flowers. Maybe a little bouquet on my wrist." But then a new idea hits me, and excitement surges right to my belly. "Or even here." I pull my shoulder forward and tap the back center of it. Will's eyes track my finger and a smile like lava melts across his mouth. For a minute he's lost to whatever mental image he's conjuring up. And then his blue-gray irises connect with mine—the black centers dilated. "You should definitely get that. It would be very sexy."

My stomach clenches and I blink at him. "You think I would be . . . sexy with a tattoo?"

He laughs one short laugh, and for a second I'm scared he's laughing at me. Maybe he never said sexy. Maybe my brain added that word all on its own out of hope. If that's true, I'm going to need to join the witness relocation program.

"No, Annie. Don't get it twisted. I already think you're sexy without a tattoo. So I know for sure you would be with one."

My lips part on a sharp happy inhale. Did he really mean that? I've never once in my entire life been referred to as sexy. Always nice or the girl with a good heart. Never sexy. Never anything that made me feel quite so womanly as the word he just used to describe me. But then with a flash of disappointment, I remember how this whole conversation started.

Again, this was a demonstration. Practice. He's showing me how well the lines work and how he effortlessly flirts because of them. Was the story about the tree real? Or is it just all a part of the mechanics.

Ugh. My heart is racing and my skin feels clammy. Like I'm going to cry. Oh God, am I going to cry?

I give a stilted laugh while dropping my gaze and blinking a hundred times at my plate as I shift it around to wipe a nonexistent drop of water from the table. "Nice. Good line."

"Wait, what?" he says sounding confused.

I clear my throat and flash him an imitation of his own fake

smile a minute ago. "I see what you did there. With the demonstration about the line and then the subsequent flirting. It worked
flawlessly," I say, overly cheery. "I'll definitely have to remember it.
Well done."

"Annie . . ."

"You know what? I need to get back to the flower shop. I just
remembered someone is coming by to pick up a big order. Huge
order." I shoot up from the bench. "Tell Jeanine to put my half on
my tab."

"Wait—Annie!"

"Sorry! I really just have to go. Thanks for the lesson!"

I'm in such a rush to leave the diner that on my way to the door,
I run straight into Phil's chest. "Hi, darlin', how are you this morning?" he says with a big smile.

Sweet Phil. He helped me learn to ride my bike, and gave me my
first summer job, restocking shelves in his store. Phil wears dad
sneakers and khaki shorts every day of his life—even in the winter—
and I think if I were to go open his closet, I'd find fifteen identical
pairs lined up on hangers, pressed neatly and ready for action. I
truly adore Phil, and I don't want him to know I'm upset. Mainly
because there's no reason for it. Will was only doing exactly what I
wanted him to do—teach me how to successfully flirt and converse
on a date.

But for some reason, hearing the words I've so desperately
craved coming out of his mouth and knowing they weren't true,
that they were just to prove a point—well, it hurts.

"I'm great!" I say to Phil, most likely doing a poor job of con-
cealing my emotions based on the way his brows are crunching
together and he's looking over my shoulder to where Will is talking
to Jeanine at the booth. I want to wave my arms around to distract
him. I go for the next best thing. "How's your sale on bolts and
screws going today?"

It's a new sale every day, and it's the highlight of my mornings to make a guess about what the sale of the day will be. My sisters and I even have a dry-erase board on our fridge where we post our guesses. Loser (the person who gets the fewest correct guesses in a seven-day period) gets grocery shopping duty that week. Unfortunately, I'm the loser this week.

"Selling like hotcakes! Who knew bolts and screws would be so popular? I haven't had a sale this successful since rakes last September. Stop by the store later, Annie girl, and I'll give you a packet of bolts. Never know when you're going to need one."

"You're the best, Phil."

He frowns again. "Annie, has that boy said something to upset you?"

Shoot. The last thing I need is for the whole town to suspect that Will is hurting me. They'll run him right out of here if they think I'm heading for heartbreak.

Am I?

I hazard one last glance over my shoulder and find Will standing up from the table while throwing cash on the check. Because I'm a coward, I turn and practically run out the door.

CHAPTER SIXTEEN

Will

I t's nighttime before I can get away to find Annie.

I still don't fully know what happened this afternoon. Everything seemed to be going well, and then I called her sexy and everything fell apart. She said something about it being a nice line and working perfectly. But I'm not sure what about that would have hurt her so badly.

All I know is that the look she had before she shot up from the table gutted me. She was smiling with tears in her eyes. One glance at those blue eyes filled with emotion, and I wanted to beg her to stay so I could fix whatever happened. I haven't been able to shake the image from my head all day. And now I'm finally off work, and I've been trying to hunt Annie down. I checked her house first, but her truck wasn't there. And then I drove by Hank's, and she wasn't there either.

Even though her shop is closed, I decided to come by anyway, and sure enough, there she is. The town is dark, but her shop is lit up like a glass box. I see her in there standing in front of the wooden worktable, shoving stems of greenery into a vase like it personally offended her. Her long blonde hair is piled on her head in a messy jumbled heap, and she's wearing a light pink oversize sweatshirt that's draping off one of her shoulders. I've never seen her undone like that, and it's making my pulse race. My fingers ache to sink into the back of her messy hair and wreck it even more. Seeing her bathed in light and surrounded by flowers from out here in the dark makes me feel like a man who slipped out of hell and is glimpsing heaven.

Annie takes a step back from her worktable and presses one sweatshirt covered fist to her mouth, appraising the bouquet she's been working on, and then apparently deciding she hates it and ripping all the stems out again.

I try the door, expecting it to be locked, but it's not. The bell chimes above my head as I step into the warm shop.

"We're closed," Annie says without even checking to make sure a serial killer isn't about to murder her.

"That's too bad because I really need to buy a bouquet for a woman," I say, and Annie's body stiffens. "It's an emergency."

Slowly she turns to look at me. Her face is a study in embarrassment, but I don't know why. I've never wanted to crawl into someone's head and read all of their thoughts like I do with Annie. My need to understand her, to know every desire, every hope and fear and longing, scares me.

"What kind of bouquet do you need?" she asks, tugging the sleeves of her sweatshirt—which I can now see has a slightly faded Charlotte's Flowers logo on the front—over her fists and bunching them up at her chest.

I squint one eye. "An apology bouquet."

Her face softens and her hands fall to her sides. "Will . . . you have nothing to apologize for."

"I do, though—I said something that really hurt someone, and I don't know why." I take two steps closer. "But I want to fix it. I want to make her feel better. So if you could make her a bouquet that you would like to receive, I'd be so grateful." She watches me closely as I edge even closer to her. "Or . . . if you're too busy, maybe I could make her one myself?"

A warm smile curves her full lips and more than ever I want to press mine to hers. I want to lick the sweetness right from her skin. "You don't need to do that, Will."

I lift a brow. "Very presumptuous of you, ma'am. You don't even know the lady."

She laughs and shakes her head before shifting on her feet. "Fine. I think if the lady in question was hurt—it probably wasn't your fault."

I step closer and my senses fill with Annie. She smells like sunlight and sugar cookies. "It was. I called her sexy and it offended her. I think I crossed a line."

Annie presses the heels of her hands to her eyes. "No. Oh gosh—I'm so embarrassed. Let's just forget it, please?"

I'm close enough now that I'm able to tug her hands down. "I can't do that. What happened, Annie? Are you upset that I think you're sexy? Are you afraid it's going to change things?"

She squeaks and her eyes clamp shut. "No! I'm upset that you keep feeding me that line over and over."

I frown. "It's not a line."

"Yes, it is. We were in the middle of practicing, and you lured me right into your perfect trap of seduction with your question and then made up the story about the tree and then hooked me with the line about being sexy, and it was just too much. And then I felt silly because I was the one who asked for all of this, but then I got so caught up in it I forgot it was a demonstration again, and—"

I press my hand to her mouth. "None of that was a lie. None. I swear to you—I wasn't even setting a trap of seduction or whatever you said. The story about the tree was true and something I've never told another soul. And the part where I think you're wildly sexy is true too." And then I notice tears welling in her eyes again, and now I'm completely lost. I shift my hand from her mouth to clasp the side of her jaw and rub my thumb under her eye—wiping away a tear. "Annie, why does that make you cry?"

She closes her eyes and shakes her head desperately like she's hoping it will shake her emotions away. "Because . . . because no one has ever said that about me before." Those blue eyes open again, and a burst of potent feelings hits me in the chest. "They say it about my sisters—but never me. I'm always praised for being so nice and kind and tender. I'm the girl next door with the sweet face. I'm never viewed as a woman, Will. Instead, I'm just the one men butter up so that I'll introduce them to Emily and Madison. Even John said . . ." she trails off.

"What did John say?" I ask feeling every muscle in my body go rigid.

"When I overheard him on the phone telling his friend how boring I was, he also said I was only prettyish." She smiles sadly.

"I'll murder him."

"Will!" Annie reprimands me with a surprised laugh.

"I'm serious, Annie. That guy doesn't deserve to go on living after making you feel so shitty. Especially after he wore the ugliest baby-blue polo I've ever seen on a date." She laughs, and I shift my hand around to the back of her neck—not willing to let her go yet. "And he's just plain wrong. First, he was wrong about you being boring. You don't even need dating lessons, Annie, you were so perfect on our date. Even when you think you're doing something wrong, you're so damn adorable I wanted to pull you into my lap and do things with you in the middle of that diner that would have put me in jail for public indecency. Second, he was so wrong about you being only prettyish. God, Annie, you're drop-dead gorgeous. So beautiful it's hard to look at you and continue persuading myself that kissing you would be a mistake because of our agreement. And third, your ass."

She gasps. "What about it?"

"Your ass is a work of art. Two absolutely perfect slopes of soft curvy sensuality that absolutely kill me, Annie. Your ass kills me. And I need you to know that if we weren't doing this just-friends thing—I would have already . . ." I let the sentence dangle as my eyes rake over her, implying everything I've dreamed of doing with Annie but not saying it out loud because I think I've already said too much as it is. And the thing that scares me the most is how desperate I am for her to know all of this and believe it. I'm so good at playing games. At strategically moving pieces around so I can be seductive without ever really having to be real. Without truly risking any feelings. But just now I was more honest and ineloquent than I've ever been in my life.

I'm not playing games with Annie—I'm spilling my heart out.

When our gazes lock again, her tears are gone. Instead, her cheeks are rosy and she's pressing her smile into her knuckles.

I gently angle her face up to look at me. "Do you believe me?"

She nods silently. And then her eyes drop to my lips. "But you were wrong about something."

"What's that?"

"It wouldn't be a mistake to kiss me."

My heart rams into my ribs. "It wouldn't?"

"No. In fact, I think we should kiss because I could use the practice."

"Annie, practicing dating is one thing but—"

"I want to change our original terms too." She shifts on her feet, and her eyes continue to flit back and forth between my eyes and my mouth. "This whole thing started off with me wanting to get good at dating, but . . . the more time I spend with you, the more I feel something coming to life inside me. Something I can't quite pinpoint but I don't want to lose either. You make me feel different, and I like it. I feel free with you—adventurous and curious."

She pauses and I don't dare say anything. I need to hear where this is going without inserting any ideas of my own.

"So I was wondering if you'd be the someone to help me practice taking risks with, doing new things, and . . . maybe finding who I am now?"

"Be your all-encompassing practice someone?" I ask, letting my thumb drag against her bottom lip.

"If it's not too much to ask," she says in a quiet whisper.

"And tonight . . . you want to practice kissing?"

Her chest fills with a heavy breath and she nods. "I haven't done it in a few years. I need to shake out the cobwebs. See if I'm any good at it."

This news is astounding to me.

Even as I'm wrapping my arm around her and splaying my hand against her lower back to pull her up close to me, I ask, "No one has kissed you in years, Annie? How is that possible?" I've wanted to kiss her every second since I met her.

I feel her tremble against me. "Maybe there's something wrong with me. No one ever tries. Even my college boyfriend broke up with me after three weeks without ever really touching me. I think my reputation makes people think I don't like this stuff."

"There's nothing wrong with you." I push back the hair that's falling around her face and do what I've been dying to do for days—sink my fingers into the mass of blonde hair behind her head. I bend down and whisper against the corner of her mouth, "Nothing."

"I might be bad at this," she warns with her eyes wide open, watching me as I tease the corners of her mouth.

"I'm prepared." And then just as I'm about to finally close the gap, an idea hits me and I pull away. She looks disappointed, like she thinks I'm changing my mind. No damn way. "In light of what happened at the restaurant, I think we should have a clear cue for when we're in practice mode. So there's no confusion."

She looks relieved. "Good idea. Like . . . time in and time out?"

I hum. "Perfect."

The tension between us is crackling, and I can tell she wants me to rush this and kiss her already, but the truth is, I love drawing it out. I love taking my time and torturing us both. And if Annie hasn't been kissed in years, I want to make this one really count.

I sink my face down to her throat and lay one soft kiss at the base. Her breath catches and I move to kiss under her jaw, opening my mouth to feel her warm skin against my tongue. She shivers, and I smile, moving up to kiss the corner of her jaw and then her mouth. The moment her warm, plush lips press into mine, my world tilts. Any finesse or control I feel dissolves, and suddenly I am at her mercy.

Her body sways toward mine, and even though I'm not taking it further than a press of our lips, it feels outrageously good. I slide my hand a little deeper into the back of her hair and force myself to keep this light despite a frantic need building below the surface.

I only intended for it to be quick. A luxurious kiss on the mouth to make her body heat. But damn. Her lips respond to mine as she rises up to wrap her hands around my neck and my blood thrums under my skin. My fingers curl into her hair and the back of her sweatshirt until I'm unconsciously pulling her flush against me. She's so damn soft, and as I slant the kiss, I can't help but taste her mouth just once, letting my tongue glide lightly across her bottom lip.

Annie sighs a moan and parts her lips and that's when I drop my hands under her thighs and hoist her up. She wraps her legs around my waist and our kiss quickly turns from chaste to devouring. I'm carrying her to the storage room, head swirling like I've had four shots of tequila and savoring every sigh, every flick of her tongue, every intentional press of her mouth. And as I adjust to walk through the doorframe, my shoulder knocks against it and shocks me back to reality. *What the hell am I doing? I can't take Annie in there. This was only supposed to be a kiss.* I want so much more than a kiss from her, though, and that's why I break the kiss and slowly lower her to the ground. She doesn't protest, seeming to agree with my thoughts.

"Time out," I say, when I release her and pace away a few steps, rubbing the back of my neck, trying to settle my body and clear my head.

Get a grip, Will. It was just a kiss. Just practice.

"Was that okay?" Annie asks, self-consciously, and the very question is as absurd to me as the fact that she feels any reason to doubt her skill.

With my hand still hooked around my neck, I look over at her knowing she can plainly see on my face how absolutely wrecked I am by that kiss. I give her one scoffing laugh. "Yeah. It was great."

Annie turns away a fraction and smiles to herself, and then does something so open, so honest it tears my cynical, terrified heart in half. She rests the tips of her fingers against her smiling mouth.

Before she has time to notice, I pull out my phone and snap a picture of her standing there in the warm overhead lights of her shop.

"Out of curiosity," I ask later as she's locking up and I'm walking her to her truck. "What is your favorite flower?"

She drops her gaze to her white Converses and smiles. "Magnolias."

CHAPTER SEVENTEEN

Annie

I park my truck right next to my siblings' trucks in the town's communal parking lot. It's a rainbow of burnt orange (Noah's rusty old truck), powder-blue and white (mine), red and black (Emily's), and olive-green (Madison's). It's an unwritten rule in this town that if you share our zip code, you must drive a truck. Doesn't matter if it's new or an old dinosaur, you've just gotta have one.

As I walk toward The Pie Shop, where I'm meeting my siblings for our weekly Saturday night hearts tournament, everything feels so familiar and comforting. The hot summer night licking at my skin, the darkened town square empty of busybodies, and avoiding the same large sidewalk crack that's been there for a decade.

It's all the same, but somehow I'm the part that feels a little different. I feel a ghost of Will's kisses on my mouth, and there's a promise, a hum, a prickle of something new in the air around me. It's making the world seem sharper. Sort of like the first day of your senior year of high school. You can sense the change around the corner, but it's not in your grasp quite yet. Somehow it makes me appreciate the wave of comfort I feel while stepping under the blue-and-white-striped awning of The Pie Shop. How is it possible to crave change and relish familiarity at the same time?

My brother, however, despises change. Everything about The Pie Shop, which he inherited from my grandma, is exactly the same as it always has been since my great-grandparents started it in the sixties. When you step inside, a little bell, softer in sound than the one at my flower shop, jingles above the door. There's a high top table in front of the single large front window, where Phil and Todd sit every Monday morning at eight thirty to share a slice of fudge pie before they open their hardware store. An antique pie case divides the front half of the shop from the back, and there's a wooden countertop connecting the case to the wall. My favorite part is still the small section of the counter that lifts up so you can walk through to the back. Until the age of sixteen, I never lifted the counter—I always limboed under it while my grandma warned me that one day my back was going to break doing it. I'd give anything to hear her say that now (and to have the ability to limbo like a sixteen-year-old).

There are only two things I can think of that Noah has changed about the shop since he took it over. One, the register, because even the starchiest of modernizing resisters doesn't want to perform math on a piece of paper. Two, he added a large decal of a pie on the shop window. And by "he added" it, I mean that he let me place it on the window after I'd had too many beers and online-shopped my drunken heart out. But listen, I gave the Etsy shop their first sale, and I'll never regret it.

Anyway, Noah doesn't like change. So the day he told me he was having wifi installed in his house and at The Pie Shop so he could keep in touch with Amelia while she was on tour, I knew he was in love. And now when you look at his quaint country house, you see a big intimidating gate at the front of the driveway and a sign announcing the sensors all around the seven acres of his property line. And then there is the guard shack they're building, which is worth mentioning because it's bigger than the peanut shell me and my sisters live in together. All of this is direct evidence that my brother has absolutely devoted his life to Amelia Rose. Those two are in it to win it, and it makes my squishy, romantic heart wild with the double *J*s. Joy and jealousy.

I open the door to The Pie Shop and am immediately met with my brother's voice. "No," he barks, and at first I think he's talking to me before I see his green gaze narrowed on Madison. "Absolutely not."

"Oh, come on!" she says, nudging his knee with her foot under the little folding card table we set up on Saturday nights. "Don't be such a party pooper."

"What's going on?" I ask, joining them at the table.

Emily grins. "Maddie is trying to get Noah to have the whole wedding party do a choreographed dance down the aisle."

"Not gonna happen," he says sternly, crossing his arms.

"I already told Amelia, and she said she wanted to do it."

Noah grunts. "Over my dead body. No way in hell am I going to prance down the aisle to some poppy-gumdrop song. Besides, I know you're lying. Amelia would never suggest it because she'd know it would give me ulcers just thinking about it."

"Ha! Pay up!" Emily shouts, extending her hands to Maddie. Em grins at Noah. "Maddie bet me twenty bucks she could persuade you to say yes to a dance mob." She cuts her gaze to Maddie. "And by the way, fabricating Amelia's support was definitely cheating."

I should have known. Those two are always betting over something.

Noah folds his arms. "I'm getting married—not giving up my dignity."

"What's Amelia doing tonight?" I ask, taking the seat next to Noah and hoping he doesn't read the underlying context of my question: Is she out somewhere that requires her to take Will?

"She's in the studio working on her album."

Despite our best attempts to convince Amelia that she's welcome to join our sibling hearts night, she has refused to come. She wants us to have our time together—just the four of us. The woman is too thoughtful for her own good.

"Great. And how are things going with wedding prep?" I ask, raising my beer to my lips.

"Fine. The wedding planner seems to have everything covered. Amelia and I have been staying out of it as much as possible."

I nod slowly. "Great! Good. That's good. And . . . everything else? No security issues?"

Noah shakes his head and begins dealing our hands. "Nope. Everything's good."

"That's good. . . ." I pause, telling myself not to say it but losing my own internal battle. "So her bodyguard . . . what's his name again? I can never remember. He's good too? Settling in okay?" It's been a few days since our kiss in the flower shop, and as odd as it is to admit, I miss him. He's been busy with Amelia and then I've been busy in the evenings working on arrangements for the wedding and trying to get the design just right. He left a note taped to my shop door that I found this morning, though. It said, "Let's practice something fun tonight."

No time or place to meet. Just those few words. I've been left tingling with anticipation all day.

Unfortunately, everyone notices my pointed question and eyes me speculatively. They look like a sibling gang—all setting down their beers and about to crack their knuckles before they shake me for information.

"Okay, what the hell, Annie?" asks Noah.

I sigh with relief because Noah just unknowingly saved the day.

"Oooh!" Maddie proclaims loudly, pointing a finger at Noah. "That's number twenty for him! Pay up, bucko."

"No. That was only nineteen. I have one more until I have to pay." (Noah says this every month after he's the first one to burn through his allotted twenty swear words.)

"Let's take it to the notebook. Annie?" Emily prompts, sitting forward and resting her forearms on the table like she's about to be witness to an incredible show.

Even though this notebook has begun to wear on me, I reach in my purse and pull it out, grateful for the change of subject. I thumb through the pages and land on this month's tally chart. Everyone holds their breath while I add them up. Making sure not to tip them off, I keep my face solemn and clear my throat before snapping the notebook shut and setting it on the table. They're dying of anticipation, each tilted forward and eager to hear Noah's sentence. It kind of makes me want to drag it out. Really make them ache for it.

But when I finally open my mouth to reveal the answer, a shadow of someone walking across the street catches my eye. A man. Tall, lean build, tattoos down one arm.

My heart hiccups.

He pauses across the street, makes eye contact with me through the shop window, and then hitches his head. It's time!

"I'm suddenly not feeling well," I say, jumping up from my chair and clutching my stomach.

"Oh no," Emily says, eyes searching me head to toe for any unseen ailment. "Do you think you're sick?"

"I'm afraid so. I feel like I'm going to barf." I gather my purse and walk toward the door.

Emily stands too. "Here, I'll come home with you."

"No!" I say, whirling around. "No, you should stay here. I'm fine. It's probably just my period about to start or something. I'll call you if I need you."

I can practically see her Antenna of Suspicion rising from the top of her head. At all times Emily is scanning for potential danger that could befall us siblings. And if that's the case, I imagine her warning system is beeping off the charts with Will Griffin close by. I force my smile not to be too big.

"I promise I'll be okay, Em," I say, and Madison comes to my aid by telling Emily to sit down so they can start their game before midnight.

And then I leave The Pie Shop.

It's completely dark outside except for the light of the moon and a few (but not enough) streetlamps. I mention it because it's a big thing. At the last town meeting, it was put to a vote to install more streetlights or add a speed bump on either side of the town square and, of course, a speed bump won even though no one in the town wanted it. It's no surprise that Harriet was in charge of counting the votes, and the implication of her tampering is *heavy*.

I've never contributed to the rumors that circled around Harriet's manipulation because I don't like to see anyone slandered behind their backs. But now, as I'm searching for Will in the dark and can't see him without the help of an extra streetlamp, I'm ready to spray-paint *It Was Harriet!* in bold red letters across the windows of the market.

"Will?" I whisper into the stale night air while looking all around. *"Williamson!"* I don't see him anywhere. Surely I didn't just imagine him. Oh gosh, if I only imagined him out of my desperation to see him, I will have reached a whole other level of infatuation. Because yeah, I can at least now admit that it's more than a crush on Will.

I like him.

A lot.

I keep trying to tell myself that I don't, but the more times I say I don't, the brighter his eyes look in my memory. The more I picture his face while reading my steamy books, the more I dream of him holding me at night. Actually, after our kiss the other night, I dream of a lot more than him simply holding me.

"Will! Where are—"

A hand shoots out from a narrow alley and tugs me in. I know it's Will before I even see him because my skin has memorized the feel of his. The subtle calluses at the top of his palms and the way his hand swallows mine. And then there's his smell. It's so distinctly him, like he did his laundry in the ocean. Someone could blindfold me and spin me around and set me loose in a room full of people, and I'd still be able to find him.

I land in the alley, chest to chest with him. I can see his smile even in the dark.

"Hello, Annie Walker," he says and uses his hand to brush my hair back from my face. A hot thrill spins like a tornado in my stomach. It's so good to be near him again. I want to wrap my arms around his middle. I want to press my face into his neck. I want to clamp my legs around him and not let go.

Instead, I stand here and look up at him. "Hello, Will Griffin."

"Have you had a good day?" he asks, and the attentive question shocks me.

"I have. I think I finally figured out what was missing with Amelia's bridal bouquets."

He lifts a brow as his fingers brush along my jaw. "And?"

"It needed a pop of pink."

"Pink is always the answer," he says with a grittiness to his voice that makes me want to lick it from his lips. What in the world is happening to me? Who is this woman who's so full of desire and excitement? The astounding thing is, I think Will would let me if I asked him. He'd lower his mouth for me to get a better angle because it wouldn't mean anything to him. This may all be new and exciting for me, but for him, kissing a woman in an alley would probably be normal for a Saturday night. And I'd do well to remember that.

"What are we doing tonight?"

He grins mischievously and his blue-gray eyes shine. "Something you've always wanted to do but have been too scared to."

My stomach tenses. "You don't mean . . ."

"You're finally getting your tattoo tonight."

"What?!" I say, instinctively taking a step away from him. "No. I can't do that."

"You can." He reaches out and takes my hand, lacing our fingers together, and my body immediately softens. "I already made you an appointment with an artist right outside of town who seemed really good. And I'll be with you the whole time. Trust yourself. You said you wanted flowers—let's get your damn flowers, Annie." He lifts my hand in his and pulls my wrist to his mouth, where he leaves a tender kiss on the vulnerable skin below my palm. His easy affection stuns me as much as it delights me. "You can do this. If you want to . . ."

I do want to. I really do.

Normally, I would need time to think about it. Weigh the pros and cons and get my siblings' input first and then eventually get talked out of it, completely. But I'm now committed to this experiment of trying to find myself by following my impulses. Plus I'm still actively looking for a husband and practicing my dating skills just in case that's the thing I really need too. The answer has to live down one of those paths, so why not try them both, right?

I breathe in and smile. "Let's go."

I try to walk away, but he tugs me back with a chuckle. "We don't have to go now. I didn't mean to take you from your time with your siblings. Go finish what you were doing and we can go after."

"They'll be okay without me for one hearts tournament. I want to be spontaneous with you tonight."

CHAPTER EIGHTEEN

Will

I expect Annie to hesitate outside the tattoo parlor. It doesn't look like the friendliest place, but the options were slim within a fifty-mile radius of Rome. Luckily, the highest rated parlor according to Google was this one, only twenty minutes away.

Annie let me drive her truck—and I enjoyed it more than I thought I would. I get now why people are addicted to these gas guzzlers. There's something about the feel of an old leather Ford steering wheel with ridges all around that's way more satisfying than a new smooth one. Even better if it comes with a beautiful blonde woman hanging her arm out the window and letting her hair fly all around her face as you drive.

It's not safe, and I don't condone it, but I took a picture when she wasn't looking.

When we pulled up to the parlor, I put the truck in park and looked over at Annie, expecting to see some trepidation in her expression. I couldn't have been more wrong. She jumped out before my eyes even had time to land on her.

"Come on," she says, excitedly waving me forward. "Why are you moving so slow?"

I close the truck door and meet her on the sidewalk. "Are you sure you want to do this?" I ask, looking in the lit-up parlor and feeling a pang of remorse for instigating this. Not even sure why. It's just that the thought of Annie in all her softness going into that place and being inked forever has me suddenly feeling like an overprotective mother. What the hell? I've never been one to over-think any choices in my life. I joined the military when I went to the grocery store for milk and the recruiting tent was parked out front, for God's sake.

And yet . . . something about being with Annie makes me want to be cautious for once. I have the distinct feeling of holding something precious and not wanting to let it drop. I feel protective. Possessive even.

Annie laughs and eyes me speculatively. "Yes! I'm *so* sure. Let's go."

In an ironic turn of events, Annie grabs my hand and tugs me along behind her. We go into the parlor, and it smells old. Nothing like the updated, trendy, and clean places where I've gotten my tattoos. This is a backwoods country parlor through and through, and who knows what sort of disease she could get from just sitting in one of their chairs? Are their needles sterilized? How long has this artist been in business?

I can't let Annie do this.

"Hey—on second thought, why don't we wait and go somewhere in the city?"

She only has a second to frown at me before a burly man with a biker beard comes around the corner. "You a walk-in?"

"Yes, sir!" She chirps happily, and I instantly clench my hand tighter around hers. She's about to mark her body forever. Because of me. By a man I absolutely don't want anywhere near said body. Look at the size of the paws on him.

I've never felt the weight of being a bad influence before. Normally, I thrive on it, actually. But not when I'm looking at Annie's perfect blank canvas of soft skin and imagining her stuck with a tattoo she might hate for the rest of her life. All because I made it happen.

"Follow me," the man says, and there's zero tenderness in his voice. He doesn't care that the woman in front of him is sunshine in the flesh. He looks like he's going to make it hurt twice as much simply because she smiled at him. Why isn't Annie scared? I'm scared, and I've sat through more than twenty hours of tattooing. I can't let her be in pain tonight.

Annie starts after him and I tug her back. She whirls around and nearly bumps into my chest, her soft smell flooding my senses and illustrating her perfect contrast to this disgusting place. "What's wrong?"

"This is a mistake."

"What?" she asks with a laugh. "No, it's not. It was the best idea. I'm so glad you thought of it."

I wince. "Exactly. I thought of it. A tattoo should be your idea. Not something I push you to do."

"But you're not pushing me." She looks down at where my hand is tightly holding hers. "Currently you're actually holding me back."

"Let's just go," I say, slicing my gaze over her shoulder to the burly man pulling out a cigarette and lighting it. "You don't want a tattoo from him. Come on, I'll drive you into Nashville on a different day and take you to my tattoo guy. We can make a weekend of it." I sound desperate and I don't know why.

Annie's face tilts up to mine. Determination and a warning

flash through her eyes in a way I have yet to see from her. It makes the hairs stand up on my arms and my heart race. And my knees go a little weak.

She pokes me in the chest. "Don't you dare, Will."

I frown. "What are you talking about?"

"I see what's happening right now. You're treating me like everyone else. Like I'm too sensitive and sweet for this. And I'm warning you . . . don't. I can handle it from everyone else—but not you. Never you."

And just like that, my apprehension melts. She's right. And hearing that my opinion means more to her than anyone else's . . . damn, give me the tattoo gun and I'll do it myself. I'll single-handedly make sure all her dreams come true this very night. She wants to travel? Let's go. She wants to hike Mount Everest? I'll get the gear.

I push Annie's hair behind her ear. "Go get your tattoo, Annie."

"Thank you," she says, looking so proud of herself she's practically glowing. "And actually, I think I want you to stay out here."

Apprehension returns.

"No. I'm coming back there with you."

She raises one saucy brow that sends heat spiraling through my veins. "Let me rephrase. I'm going back there by myself—and I'm going to surprise you with what I get. End of story, Will Griffin."

I clench my fist at my side but not because I'm angry. Because I have to physically restrain myself from taking that hand, cupping her jaw, and taking her mouth in a frenzied kiss. I've never felt an urge so strong. An attraction so intense.

Every day Annie reveals a new layer to herself—and dammit if I don't like each one more.

I have no choice but to stand back and smile as I watch Annie's perfect ass stroll away from me.

Thirty minutes later I hear footsteps. I look up in just enough time to see Annie blaze past me—power walking out the front door. "Let's go," she says quickly. "I paid in the back."

What in the world?

I follow her out, quickening my strides to catch her. "Annie! Hold up. What happened?"

She doesn't answer. She thrusts open her truck door and jumps inside, slamming the door behind her.

I practically run to the driver's side and hop inside. Worst-case scenarios are flying through my head. And then when I twist to fully look at her, and I take in her crumpled expression, fury and rage overtake me.

"What did that asshole do to you? Did he hurt you? Was he inappropriate? I'm going to kill him!" I say, putting my hand on the door latch and preparing to open it. Annie tugs the back of my shirt before I can.

"Stop. Grady didn't do anything wrong. He was so nice, and I'm going to provide flowers for his six-year-old daughter's princess birthday party next month."

I relax only in the slightest measure because now Annie has a tear streaking down her cheek, and I'm inadvertently the cause of it. I pushed her to do this tonight. I'm the asshole.

"Then why did you storm out of there?"

For the first time, her misty blue eyes slip to me and she smiles sadly. "I needed to get to the truck so I could cry."

"Because you hate the tattoo?"

Her smile widens, big tears pooling in her eyes. "No. Because I love it so much—and I'm so proud of myself for getting it. Thank you for making this happen, Will."

I expel a breath as the tension in my shoulders releases. So this wasn't a bad thing for Annie after all? In fact, it was good. I want to dive further into that logic but decide it's not safe. I might come to conclusions in the end that I shouldn't.

I put my hand against Annie's jaw and chuckle, wiping the tear from her cheek. "I would have committed murder for you just now."

"I do appreciate it," she says with a laugh too.

We're both laughing and she's crying and I've never experienced this kind of emotion with anyone else. It's so fragile and vulnerable. I feel guilty that I'm the one who gets to experience it with her. And yet I'm greedy for it at the same time.

"Can I see it now?" I ask, dropping my gaze to her wrist. But there's nothing there.

She nods and adjusts a little away for me in her seat, gathering all of her long hair and tugging it over one shoulder. And then my breath catches as she tugs the neck of her shirt down, revealing her beautiful bare shoulder.

Well . . . her bare shoulder inked with the cutest small tattoo I've ever seen.

"I got a book," she says, sounding like she just won a million dollars. "I was going to get the flowers we talked about, but then I realized flowers were always my mom's dream—not especially mine even though following it has worked out nicely for me." She pauses and I admire the fine lines of a book, lying open with its pages fluttering like the wind caught them. "I wanted something special to me. Just me."

I smile at the sight of Annie poised with her shoulder presented to me—the profile silhouetted by the streetlamp outside the truck. And her soft mouth curled up in a gentle smile. I'll never forget this moment. And before I can stop myself, I tip forward and kiss the skin just beside her tattoo. Annie sucks in a breath, and I memorize the feel of her skin against my lips, as smooth and blazing as a shot of expensive whiskey. I want to kiss every square inch of her. I want to lick the base of her shoulder. I want to kiss my way up the side of her throat all the way until I find her mouth, and there I'll linger, caressing so thoroughly that our lips sting afterward.

If I had it my way, I'd pull this warm, sweet, tenderhearted woman over onto my lap and show her just how in awe of her I am. I would worship her body.

Instead, I pull away and gently pull her shirt back up over her shoulder. "It's perfect, Annie."

CHAPTER NINETEEN

Will

I'm at the farmers market today and I'm not happy about it for two reasons. First, there are so many people. These sorts of places—open-air venues with endless numbers of entrances and exits—are my nightmare. Tickets aren't required, so I have no way of checking everyone in attendance to make sure none of Amelia's stalkers will be here. But I have their faces memorized and survey everywhere we go for any signs of them. She's wearing a hat and sunglasses, as is Noah, but obsessive fans will still know it's her. In fact, there's a man with a backpack eight feet to her right. He's noticed her three times now. Even if no one is here to do her harm, these sorts of crowded locations can turn into a fan mob in a second if we're not careful.

I don't like the guy with the backpack.

The second reason I don't want to be here is because Annie is working a booth for her flower shop. It's the whole reason Amelia wanted to come out and support her, and that woman is the distraction I don't need today. And I mean that in the current literal sense, and the metaphorical long-term sense.

I'm using all of my willpower to focus on my job right now, and it's torture. Just like every second when Annie is anywhere near me lately. I've only seen her once since she got her tattoo. Amelia and I were in town, and while she was visiting with Noah at The Pie Shop, I dipped into the flower shop next door to see Annie. Her eyes lit up when she realized it was me, and now I'm afraid I'll replay that image on a loop for the rest of my life.

I'm trying to put her in the same category as all the other women who have moved like water through my life. But it's not working. She's quickly becoming special to me—like something rare and precious you want to put in a safe place so you never lose it.

That's why I can't look at her today. My eyes need to stay focused and alert to my surroundings.

And then Annie cackles from her booth, and like a damn siren call in the night, I turn right to her. My gaze lingers, and I don't understand how just the sight of someone can feel so good. God, she's beautiful. No overalls today—which is oddly disappointing— but instead she's wearing a pair of distressed jeans and a white T-shirt with her shop logo on it. Her hair is pulled up in a ponytail, and a few little strands have fallen out and cling to her neck because of how humid it is out here.

She looks so damn good.

And sounds good.

And for the first time in a long time, I wish I weren't stuck here doing my job. I want to be over there with her. I want to know how her day has gone and if she's having fun. How her tattoo is healing and if she remembered to put lotion on it today. I want to touch my lips to her glimmering neck and taste the sweat from her skin. But I can't—not only because that's not the kind of relationship we have but because I'm on duty right now.

But before I look away and mentally commit to not looking at her again the rest of the afternoon, I take out my phone and snap a picture of her laughing behind her booth. I'm collecting all these photos and will send them to her when I leave town because the woman deserves to have pretty pictures of herself. I'll delete them from my phone once I send them to her. I will. I really will. There would be no reason for me to keep them after I leave because I'll move on and get back to life as normal. I won't let myself miss Annie. I won't.

I pocket my phone and turn to watch Amelia, and . . .

Shit.

I lost sight of her. She was standing with Noah over by the produce booth and now she's gone, and Noah is over with Annie. Where's backpack guy? He's gone too. Adrenaline kicks through me as my eyes scan the crowd from behind my sunglasses. I keep my face neutral and try to project a relaxed demeanor even though inside I'm running in circles and thinking up worst-case scenarios. But the last thing I need is for anyone watching us to know I've lost track of her.

I'm suddenly thumped on the back. I spin around and find Amelia. I'm torn between sighing with relief and chewing her out for slipping out of sight.

"Why are you standing so far away from us today?" she asks with her hands on her hips.

I steady my breathing and glance around again. Always watching the perimeters. I messed up just now losing my head for a second, and I won't let that happen again. "Could you please stay where I can see you at all times?"

Amelia's eyebrows fly up when she detects my curt tone. "Sure. But you know? It would be a lot easier to keep track of me if you'd just come hang out with us."

I refrain from grinding my teeth together. "I can't effectively do my job that way."

"Why are you talking to me like a robot?"

"Because," I say looking around the area again. "I'm on the job. You shouldn't even be talking to me now. You're going to draw attention." I have two modes. Playful and serious. And despite the fact that I love to socialize, love to flirt, and would absolutely enjoy every second of hanging out at Annie's booth with everyone, I'm working and therefore fully committed to serious.

"We're in Rome, Kentucky, Will. There is practically zero threat."

"*Practically* being the key word there. Your management wouldn't have hired me if they thought the threat was zero."

Amelia sighs. "Just come hang out for a minute with us. I feel weird having you stand so far away when we're all over there."

"Why the hell would you feel weird? It's how we've always operated in places like this."

"Yeah, but . . . things are different now."

Ah—now I see.

I look sharply down at Amelia and then away. "I'm worried about you, Amelia. You seem to be under the illusion that I'm suddenly a different person since coming to Rome. But I am still very much me—an EPA doing his job until he gets released and sent to a new one. So please go back over there and hang out with your fiancé and don't slink off again."

"You're crabby today."

Yeah, I'm crabby today. I'm crabby because I just messed up on the job for the first time in . . . ever. And although nothing came of it—I'm well aware of everything that could have happened. The worst part is, I'm trying as hard as I can to take this anger and project it onto Annie in a way that will make me repulsed by the idea of her and want to pull away. But I can't. Instead, I'm just grumpier because I have to focus even harder now and not go over there and spin her around and kiss her watermelon-pink mouth.

A large part of me worries it'll be like this from now on. Will I leave Rome and my attention will be torn between where I am and wondering what the hell Annie's doing? This wasn't supposed to happen. I'm not supposed to feel things. I never have before.

Unhelpfully, my brother's words fly through my head: "I'm helpless to do anything else." Is this what he was talking about? This intense magnetism my body has for hers? Surely it's just desire, and if we were to finally have sex it would go away. Right?

But what if it's not? And what if I chewed my brother out for the very thing I'm starting to feel about Annie?

"Plus this is probably the only time you'll get to see Annie for a few days," Amelia adds like she's removing an ace from her sleeve and tossing it on the table. She has a smug expression when I look down at her.

"Why?"

"We're going to L.A. tomorrow for three days because I've been booked for a few television interviews. I was going to tell you on the way back, but I figured I should tell you now because—"

We're interrupted by none other than the approach of backpack guy. I immediately step around Amelia, intercepting his approach. "Can I help you?"

He has nervous eyes, darting back and forth between Amelia behind me and my reflective glasses. I set my jaw and square my shoulders, reading his body language, and mentally mapping eight different ways I can take him down if necessary. "S-sorry to bother you, but I was wondering if I could get a picture—"

"She's not available for photos today," I say, cutting him off with finality.

He smiles shyly. "No . . . sorry. I didn't mean with her. I meant with you. I saw the BuzzFeed article, and I'm a huge fan of . . . well, your face." He blushes.

Behind me I hear Amelia stifle a laugh.

Well, this is unexpected.

"Thank you, I'm flattered, but I have to decline. Have a nice day."

"I understand." He turns to walk away and then whirls around briefly. "Can I just take a candid one from a distance?"

Amelia peeks around me. "Yes, but please only photograph him from the left because that's his good side. Gotta have the tattoos in the picture."

I turn a slow glare down at Amelia. She laughs. Dude takes this moment to snap a picture and then scurries off.

"If I weren't tasked to protect you right now . . ."

Amelia gives me a smile that's the equivalent of the little yellow smiley emoji baring all its teeth. "Now that the major threat is neutralized, it looks like you can say hi to Annie."

I inhale in a long slow breath through my nose and turn my body toward the crowd again. "You gotta knock it off with the matchmaking, Amelia. You're just going to be disappointed. And besides," I say, scanning from the west to south entrances, "three days is nothing. Definitely not enough to make me compromise your safety by needing to talk to her before we go."

But it is enough to have me sneaking out of Mabel's Inn after dark that night and driving to Annie's house—leaving my truck on a side road and then cutting across lawns to get to her window.

CHAPTER TWENTY

Annie

A light tap sounds against my window. At first I think it's a bug trying to get in, but then it happens again and again, growing a little louder each time. I go to the window and peek through the curtains, and then smother a scream with my hand. There's a man outside my window. But then I register the blue-gray eyes and the dark brows and the tattooed hand as he raises a finger to his lips. It's William Griffin.

Why is he outside my window at ten o'clock at night? Even worse, I'm all snug in my banana-print pajamas. He can't see me like this. It doesn't seem like I have a choice, though.

Quietly I unlatch the window and raise it. The sound of crickets, the feel of the humid summer night, and the dangerous smile aimed at me all combine to make sure this becomes the strongest core memory of my life.

"Hi," Will says in little more than a whisper. "Can I come in?" He asks this like he's standing at my front door—perfectly normal. Allow me to take your hat and coat, sir.

"Um, yeah, of course, come on in." I step back and watch in awe as he easily drops a leg over the windowsill, folds his tall frame, and ducks his head under the window. He maneuvers the rest of his body through until he's here, standing in my room with me.

"I remember that being easier when I was sixteen."

My eyes widen. "You snuck through windows when you were sixteen?"

"You didn't?" And then his eyes drop to my PJs and his grin widens, confirming the answer to that question for him. "You have bananas all over your pajamas."

I clear my throat lightly and regret all of my life choices. "Uh, yeah. Well, I wasn't expecting company, so I got ready for bed as usual."

A small smile touches his mouth, and then my breath catches when he reaches out and pinches the hem of my sleeve between the fingers of his butterfly hand. "Your usual being banana-printed sleepwear?" He doesn't say it in a mean way. More as a curiosity than anything.

"My full name is Annabell. So my siblings call me Anna-banana. I have an entire drawer full of banana-themed PJs." And underwear. "It's basically the only kind of sleepwear I own. Is that pathetic? Should I burn them all?"

I've always loved my banana PJs. I generally like who I am as a whole, but standing here in front of Dark and Mysterious Mr. Tattoo has me feeling the need to defend myself. To question whether this is a strange way to live as an adult woman or not.

Will is looking down at me as if stuck in a daze as he rubs his thumb back and forth delicately over the fabric of my sleeve. Every so often his thumb brushes my wrist, and I feel like the physical manifestation of static electricity.

"Anna-banana," says Will quietly. He couldn't help trying out my nickname at least once. His eyes pop up to me, and I see something compellingly honest in them. "Promise me, no matter what you decide to change about yourself, this will not be one of them."

I let out a sigh of relief and then laugh before I realize his solemn expression. He's dead serious. Not laughing in the least. He wants me to promise I'll never stop wearing these bananas. Will a contract be drawn up next?

"Okay, I'll keep them." Oddly, something in me relaxes and settles in a way I normally can't around other people. And then I ask, "What are you doing here? And . . . how did you know this was my room?"

Will releases the hem of my shirt and steps back. "I didn't," he says with a crooked grin. "Every other room in the house was dark, though, so I thought I'd try my luck with this one first. It was a gamble."

"What would you have done if this was Emily or Maddie's room?"

He shrugs. "Pretended to be drunk and lost."

I laugh. "You really gave this some thought."

"Always be prepared—that's my motto."

"And by yours you mean the Boy Scout motto."

"Is that where I've heard it?" He makes a skeptical thinking noise before turning away to make himself at home in my room. He's not shy about it, strolling around like he owns the place. Maybe this is the bodyguard side of him that's used to sweeping locations and inspecting every inch before letting Amelia enter. Oddly, there's something sort of fun about watching him as he lazily peruses everything inside these four walls.

"Your room is pretty," he says softly. My knees go weak because the word *pretty* coming out of his mouth feels like the most enticing juxtaposition. It's achingly tender and innocent—which forcefully combats his worldly and dangerous appearance.

Chills dance down my arms, and I blame it on the night. The darkness and the quiet are what's responsible for the intimacy right now. For the charge in the air and the way I can't seem to get a full breath. For the heat swirling low in my stomach that absolutely has no business being here. It's not Will making any of this happen, it's just science. Or biology. Or . . . physics. Basically any other subject besides Will!

I'm mesmerized watching him smell the bouquet of flowers on my side table, run his fingers over the plush blanket on the end of my bed, pick up the trinkets on my dresser to examine them closely before setting them back down gently. He's so tactile. I imagine he touches and feels his way through life, whereas I usually keep my hands right where they are now—safely tucked behind me, alone in the corner of the room.

But then Will picks up the framed photo on my dresser—the last picture ever taken of my entire family before my parents died—and my feet move in his direction. He stares down at it and I know what he's seeing: three happy kids lined up in front of two beaming parents; and me, only three years old, on my mom's hip and smiling up at her instead of the camera.

"That's the last photo that was taken."

Will looks down at me over his shoulder and his gaze holds mine. "I'm sorry, Annie."

I shrug. "It was a long time ago."

"But I'm sure it still hurts."

I breathe in—trying to push away the sudden rush of emotions his words rip from me. I don't want to cry in front of him. Actually, I don't cry in front of anyone. So I blink, and blink some more until the threat is gone. "Sometimes."

He sets the frame down and looks at me. I'm scared he's going to ask if I'm okay, which I really hope he doesn't because I will absolutely cry. I'm usually the one who provides comfort in my family—which is, honestly, fine because it's a role I chose when I was very young and my siblings were all falling apart and I didn't quite understand why. They knew my parents better than I did—so it became my self-appointed job to lessen their pain. I could hug them. I could make them feel better. I could make sure that I never did anything to add to their worry. And then that, in turn, made me feel better. But a side effect of being the one who listens and comforts is that people rarely offer to listen or comfort me. I've been living this way for so long now that I'm not sure I'd be any good at expressing myself even if I were asked to.

Just when I think Will is going to make me talk through my feelings, he lightly grasps my bicep, pulling me into his chest. And that's it. No prodding questions. He wraps his big arms around me and holds me here in my room until my body melts against his. It feels so good to be held by him. To breathe him in and feel his heart beating against my chest. Too good.

And then he presses his lips to my forehead and my entire heart wrenches.

"What are you doing here, Will?" I ask when I can't take the sweetness of this anymore. It's too confusing.

He releases me. "I'm going out of town for a few days with Amelia for work." I'm surprised at how disappointed I feel by this news. Which is ridiculous. Absolutely absurd.

He continues, "And I realized I don't have your phone number."

"Oh."

"And I thought I should have it . . ."

"You did?"

He nods, still watching me. "In case . . . you have any tutor-related questions."

"Right." I give a firm nod. Makes sense. Perfect sense. "Where's your phone? I'll put my number in it."

He fishes it from the back pocket of his jeans and hands it to me. Something about holding Will's phone just feels so . . . personal. More personal than anything he's ever let me see before. His lock screen is a photo of a mountaintop view, and his background is a photo of an ocean. They're obviously pictures he's taken on his adventures—and suddenly I'm overcome with desire to know everything about these trips. To see him standing there in those places and witness the smile on his face when he reached his final destination. Maybe even go with him on one.

Instead, I create a new contact and type my number in and quickly hand his phone back. He frowns lightly at the contact name and deletes Annie Walker and replaces it with Annabell. We're not even going to acknowledge the obscene surge of butter-flies that rushes through my stomach when he does.

In an attempt to make myself feel normal and not buzzing with physical awareness, I walk back toward the window and open it again. "Okay, well now that you have my number, feel free to . . ." my words trail off when I turn around and find Will toeing off his shoes and sitting on my bed ". . . stay."

Will leans up against my headboard, shoes kicked off, long legs stretched out, and one ankle crossed over the other. Will is in my bed.

In. My. Bed!

"Is that all right? If I stay?" he says with the confidence of a man who already knows the answer.

I would love to surprise him and kick him out. *No, you may not stay! Out you go!*

Yeah, not happening. I want him here more than I've wanted anything before.

"Of course. But . . . why?"

He came here for my phone number, and he got it. Task accomplished. He should be on his way.

Will smiles at me—bemused. "To hang out with you."

"I repeat, why?"

"Because you're fun to hang out with."

I have to press my lips together and divert my gaze, so I pull out the chair from my desk and sit so that he doesn't see the way my soul beams from that response.

"Are you going to stay all the way over there?" he asks.

I look up into his playful sparking eyes. "It's not way over here. You make it sound like I need a map."

"Annie." His tone is gently inquisitive. "Is something wrong?"

I blink and shake my head. *Nope. I'm great. Everything is great,* I should say. My head isn't spinning at all. My heart isn't hammering and my palms aren't sweating. This is totally normal. Will and I are just hanging out. With no purpose. No specific practice. Just . . . two friends in a tiny room together for fun.

"It's making you nervous that I'm on your bed, isn't it?"

I grimace because I really need for him to stop doing that—reading my mind so easily. "It's not that—" I cut myself off before I attempt to lie and realize he'll know. He'll see right through me immediately, as he always does. "All right. Yes, I guess it's freaking me out a little." I gesture between us. "I'm not good at all of this, remember?"

"All of this?"

"Yeah . . . the socializing. Friendship. Secret late-night meetings." I pause and then add quietly. "Men in my bed."

"Right. Well, lucky for you, there's only one man in your bed tonight. The others won't be here until tomorrow." We both grin. "Seriously. It's just me. No need to be nervous. But if you want me to leave, I will. I never want to make you uncomfortable."

I think about this for a minute, exploring how I would feel if he left now. I picture myself watching him go and then lying awake the whole night wondering what would have happened if I'd let him stay. I feel the disappointment so acutely it's like it already happened. "Don't go."

The weight of those words hangs in the air between us and they don't settle. They stir up questions and implications like a storm.

This time, I have the pleasure of watching Will squirm. Or the closest he's likely ever going to get to squirming. He swallows, lightly clears his throat, and then turns his eyes away—searching. Most unfortunately, they land on the book that I left open on my bed. He picks it up and to my horror, starts reading it right there in front of me. Unacceptable. Because I happen to know what was written about on the page I was reading when he arrived: the couple's first kiss. And that may sound sweet, but that's only if you've never read a historical romance before.

I knew this kiss was coming, and I wanted to be comfy and cozy in bed before I read it, so I set the book down and got up to get changed and brush my teeth. And now Will is reading it . . . before me. What if it's really steamy? What if there is dirty talk? *Oh my gosh, what if there is other stuff?*

I need to think of a discreet way to distract him. Something really casual and easy so that he sets the book down but isn't suspicious.

"Stop reading!" I blurt.

Super. Really discreet.

Will's eyes flick to me, and then a grin that I've come to know all too well spreads on his face. His fingers clutch the cover a little harder. "Why, Annabell? Something wrong with me reading this book?" His eyebrows lift.

"Wilton, put the book down."

His expression says it: not a chance.

And then—the jerk—cuts his eyes to the page and begins

reading. Aloud. "A growl sounded from the back of Captain Cutler's throat as he stared down at Lady Eloise's full, erotic mouth . . ."

Without thinking, I leap onto the bed. *"Oh my gosh, stop reading!"* I try to yell in a whisper at Will, who then hops off the other side of the bed.

Laughing at his own words, he continues. "If he didn't take her then and there, he was sure he was going to die," Will reads while racing around the front of my bed to evade me. He raises the book above his head. "So dramatic, this captain. I mean I know the feeling, but I've never thought I'd die from an erection before."

"Oh my gosh! Don't say *erection*!"

"Boner then?" he supplies—knowing full well that word is not better—while doing a spin move to get around me and lower the book to continue reading. "Her breasts heaved above the bodice of her gown, and Captain Cutler knew she wanted him too." He pauses again, long enough for me to ram into him like a linebacker and lay him out flat on his back on the mattress. He laughs harder, eyes sparkling dangerously, and extends the book above his head as far as he can as I crawl over him to grab it. "I see lots of consent red flags in our dear captain. A man should never assume a woman wants him."

"He's a pirate! He's used to pillaging and murdering! I'm not sure that consent is on his radar!"

"And that makes it okay?" he asks, still laughing at my attempts to get the book.

"No—definitely not. In real life I'd be horrified. But this is a book. And books are . . . different." That last word comes out like a grunt as I manage to latch onto the book and valiantly rip it from his hand. I hold it over my head—breathing like I just finished a triathlon. I smile victoriously. "You lose!"

And then we both realize I'm straddling him.

CHAPTER TWENTY-ONE

Annie

My smile slowly fades as the playfulness in the air dissipates and reality grabs hold of me. Will is currently horizontal on his back, and my legs are on either side of him. On my bed. His face sobers as our eyes connect. Heat and something fierce that I'm terrified to admit is want zips through me. Will's hands are still above his head, and my eyes drop to where the cap of his sleeve has bunched up over his shoulder, proving that his tattoos do continue up past his bicep. But how far? To what end? I need to know.

Will's eyes blaze, knowing exactly what I'm wanting. "Go ahead."

I briefly look to his eyes—making sure he really gave me permission. He nods once. And then with shaking hands, I brush the hem of his shirt before grasping it as lightly as humanly possible to push it up. Slowly his skin is revealed like a curtain rising to display a million-dollar art installation. A taut, smooth, defined abdomen, followed by a chiseled chest and—gasp!—a peek of inked foliage across his left pec. He flexes his stomach muscles lightly, and I'm not sure if it's in an attempt to impress me or because my hands are cold. Either way, it's quite the sight.

Will abruptly sits up, and my breath catches as I fear he's going to push me off or say he's offended at how bold and handsy I'm being.

But he doesn't.

He lifts his arms in the air for me to continue peeling the shirt completely from his body. A thrill surges through me.

When it's off, Will and I are face-to-face, and his bare torso and shoulders and chest are all here too. Skin. Warm male skin right here for me to touch. I lift my hand to press into his chest and hesitate. My hands shake and my nerves tell me this is wrong. I shouldn't be able to do this or to enjoy it. I'm Annie Walker! Annie Walker is sweet. Annie Walker doesn't even desire these sorts of encounters. Annie Walker is—

Will's hand covers mine as he presses it to his skin. I give in and shut my eyes from how incredible this feels. But now all I want is more. Slowly my hands memorize the feel of his raised tattooed skin and marvel that it has a texture—a memory. I glide my fingers delicately up and over his shoulder, stopping to feel his prominent collarbone along the way and then the curve of his neck all the way up into the back of his rebellious hair. Will's face turns and his jaw presses into my palm. Something is happening between us, and I'm incapable of stopping it.

His hands are on my hips now—fixed there, unmoving. "Annie . . ." Will says quietly. "I need to ask—you're a virgin, aren't you?"

The truth falls between us.

I swallow and wish more than anything I could lie. Or maybe I don't. "Yes. How'd you know?"

"Well," he says with a crooked smile. "For one, your reputation.

And two . . . the way you kissed me the other night." He pauses and I'm terrified he's going to say he knew from how bad it was. How inexperienced. But then the corners of his mouth curve and his grip tightens. "You were so responsive, like you were experiencing passion for the first time. It was incredible."

My face heats and I drop my gaze. But Will touches my face, angling it back toward him. "Is there a reason you've been waiting?"

The quiet presses in around us, but I don't feel uncomfortable. I feel completely safe with Will just like I always do. I normally shy away from this topic at all costs because, honestly, it's embarrassing; but now that it's out in the open with him, I feel nothing but relief.

"I've been waiting because I've been too scared." I say those words out loud for the first time in my life, never really knowing until this moment the reason why. "Actually, I'm not even sure *scared* is the right word. I've just never known anyone who made me feel safe enough to share that part of myself with them."

I've always been made to feel like my virginity was silly—not that my siblings have ever said that in so many words, but they've said it in the little jabs about how angelic I am. How I'm the only one of us who will likely make it through the pearly gates. Like somehow my need to wait was just me trying to prove I was sweeter and holier than everyone else because I don't succumb to desires and needs like everyone else.

Will doesn't do that. He nods, seeming to understand that it's always been more about protecting myself and my emotions than proving anything to others.

Will's eyes drop to my mouth. "Time in?" he says quietly, and my stomach swoops. The steady sounds of our breathing are the only soundtrack for the moment.

"Time in."

"If you want to kiss me again, Annie, I want you to. Take as much as you want, and I'll keep my hands right here"—he grips my hips again—"unless you tell me to move them."

I fill my lungs with air—feeling and knowing this is a pivotal moment in my life. The question I'm afraid to answer is why do I feel safe enough to even consider taking this further with Will when I know he won't be here forever? When I know that with him it can only ever be passion and nothing else. I shouldn't want this with him because there is no option for happily ever after and babies and white picket fences.

And yet . . .

My eyes travel up his chest and shoulders and neck, and then decide to take a leap. "You can move them."

Four little words. Deadly words. Desire pulls the strings on my fingers and raises them to the sides of his abdomen with the lightest pressure, but I still feel his ribs expand under my hand. He holds absolutely still. I'm trembling and nervous as I slide my palms up farther, following the trail my eyes and fingers paved a moment ago. I've never felt anything quite like his warm skin before.

"I always keep my hands to myself because no one expects me to want any of this," I say more as a realization than a statement. "But with you . . ." I frown contemplatively, letting my statement dangle.

"Kiss me, Annie. Please."

His voice, raw with longing and restraint, excites parts of me I didn't know existed.

Before I lose the nerve, I tip forward and press my lips to his. We've kissed before, but this is different. It's intimate and loaded. The moment we connect, I am lost to the darkness behind my eyelids and the desire pooling in my body. His lips are warm and soft. He doesn't assert himself, he only responds to my soft kisses.

Exploring little presses. It's not that I'm a complete amateur when it comes to kissing—it's that I am an amateur at kissing Will. And if this is the last shot I ever get, I want to make it count and not rush a single second.

I pull away to look at him, he looks back, and then I lean in again, eyes open—kiss. I pull away once more, note the fiery look behind his blue-gray irises, tilt, and kiss again. He smiles lightly after the third one, catching on to my pattern. He raises a brow before being the one to lean in this time. He kisses me and lingers, slanting and coaxing. Here. It's even better this way.

My eyes close again and I sink, sink, sink.

He pulls away, and our lips peel slowly, like they don't want to let go. And this time, when I go in for the kiss, I linger too. I initiate a new rhythm—something deeper and more exploring.

I slide my arms all the way up around his neck so my chest presses to his. I want—need—to get closer. My consciousness is slowly swirling away from me as I lose myself to this kiss, and I hold on to him for dear life.

And then for the first time, Will's hands slide up from my hips under my shirt to splay across my bare back. They tug me up even closer, his rough thumbs gliding over my soft skin. I have never felt more alive as Will holds me and kisses me—breathing deeply from time to time like he loves the way I smell.

I'm terrified. Thrilled. Embarrassingly needy.

Will's mouth leaves mine to kiss my jaw and then my neck. My head lulls back and his hands roam down over my thighs and around to my backside, where he cups my butt and pulls me up to him. I gasp and he catches it in his mouth. A thread snaps and we're lost.

Will holds me tight and flips us so he's hovering over me and my back is against the mattress. My pulse is in my ears, heat is flooding every corner of my body as Will's kisses extend to any part of exposed skin he can find, like my neck. The V of skin peeking out from my pajama top. And then the small section of skin on my abdomen where my top has ridden up. Just when I think I might pass out from the pure ecstasy of this, Will asks, "Why are you smiling?"

I shake my head and tug him up so that we're face-to-face again. "I just embarrassed myself with my own thought."

The black centers of his eyes grow. "Say it."

I bite my lip and tell myself there's no turning back now. "I was just wondering if you'd maybe . . . kiss me . . . passionately," I ask, barely getting the words out and feeling so embarrassed by them that I could combust. "Less controlled. I can feel you holding back . . . and I don't want you to."

He stares down at me—his unruly lock of hair falling over his brow and his dark tattoos competing with the perfect, dangerous rim around his irises. And then like a riptide swallowing me whole, his mouth slants over mine and demands as much as it gives. I make a sound and he makes a sound, and I think I might die from how wonderful this is—from how much more I need. I don't care about anything besides taking everything that Will wants to give me. And that's when I realize that never again will I be able to set-tle with simply nice and soft and stable. I mean, yes, I want those things still. But I also want this. Dangerous, untethered, and demanding. How did I ever think I didn't need this?

I grasp at his shoulder blades and then pull away with surprise. "Your tattoos do extend over your back!" I peek up and over and am delighted to see that these beautiful flowers completely wrap his shoulder.

Will's eyes are unfocused when he looks at me, resting on his forearm and pushing my hair back from my face with his other hand. "You've been wondering?"

"Every night since I met you," I say, solemnly. "Sometimes I can't sleep because I lie here imagining where they end."

He stares at me, barely breathing. "I wasn't expecting that."

And then his head lowers and swiftly takes my mouth for a kiss so intimate, so demanding, so fevered that my toes curl and my legs lock around his. His tongue parts my lips and glides over mine until I'm consumed by him, and everything I knew about myself vanishes and begins redrawing new lines. I want more. Everything.

While we kiss, Will's hands fumble with the buttons of my shirt, starting at the bottom and working their way up. There's only one left when I grab his hand. "Wait. Time out."

He pauses immediately and pulls back.

"I'm not ready yet," I say in a nervous rush. "I'm sorry . . . I thought I would be, but then as things started progressing—"

Will immediately cups my face, cutting me off. "Don't apologize. No explanation needed."

"I feel bad."

"Don't." He adjusts to his side, resting on his forearm and then using his free hand to pull my hand to his mouth. He kisses my inner wrist with a tenderness that surges to my soul. "You don't owe me—or anyone else—anything, Annie. Just kissing you is a gift. One that . . ." His brows pinch together and he pauses, idly playing with my fingers. When he looks at me again, I see something so raw in his eyes I never expected to see: fear.

I never do learn what he was going to say. I expect Will to leave, but he sighs and pulls me over to rest my head on his chest, holding me so tight it feels like he's afraid I'm going to fly away.

CHAPTER TWENTY-TWO

Will

Sunlight hits the back of my eyelids, and I drag in a quick inhale. I've been sleeping like a rock. Like the dead. Like . . . I'm not alone.

Shit, shit, shit.

I open my eyes to the sight of bananas and blonde hair. Annie is tucked up close to me, leg draped over mine, head in the crook of my bare shoulder and hand splayed out on my chest. She's breathing deeply—sound asleep. We must have fallen asleep together after . . . Damn, I don't even know what to call last night. It definitely wasn't just a kiss. It was devastating.

This is not good.

And by not good, I mean the Entire Situation is not good. I'm overwhelmed. There's a lot happening inside me that I don't know what to do with. I'm feeling things for Annie that I didn't know I was capable of feeling. Normally, by now, I'm bored in a relationship. This isn't even a relationship with Annie, and I'm clawing out of my skin with a need to be more for her. To always be around when she needs me. To be the kind of man I never saw modeled growing up.

And yet—can I trust it? Can I trust myself with her? Would she even want a man like me with so much baggage and heartbreak to share a life inside her white picket fence? I feel like the biggest hypocrite alive to be desiring more with Annie when I just told my brother to pump the breaks with the woman he loves. But I didn't realize . . .

Maybe there is hope for us.

Or maybe I should take a step back and think about it without this lushly curved woman pressed up beside me.

It was a bad idea to ever come back to Rome. To let Annie touch me. Kiss me. Turn me inside out. It was so much easier when I thought I wouldn't like a relationship and that I didn't want to run the risk of ending up in a position similar to my parents'. Because what other option is there for someone who endured eighteen years of a hate-filled marriage between his parents? When infidelity and emotional abuse were all I saw? There was no tenderness. No patience. There were insults and harsh reprimands and me wondering if that night was going to be the one when all their yelling was going to end with my dad hitting my mom or her leaving us for good to sleep with some other guy.

But neither of those things happened. Ethan and I were always just waiting on the precipice of something terrible—wondering when it would break. It never did—and I guess I'm thankful for that. Instead, their marriage fizzled out in an anti-climactic way that led me to believe that maybe what they had was just normal. They divorced after Ethan and I left home and then acted as if all the hell they put us through never happened. Like I never became a man who avoids real relationships at all costs because all I've ever known are painful ones. A man who in no way trusts himself with a woman as good and hopeful and lovely as Annie.

Until I met her and held her in my arms, I never knew I could be capable of so much tenderness. And I'm not talking about sex. I'm talking about tender conversations. Tender words. Tender understanding. Even the way she breathes against my neck while she sleeps is tender—and I want it. All of it. I'm just not sure it's sustainable or that I want to find out if it's not. Ever since I realized I could climb that magnolia tree in my backyard, I've been very good at protecting myself and avoiding anything that could cause me more pain.

The woman I'm holding has the potential to cause me more pain than anyone else ever has. And I sure as hell can do the same to her. I have no idea where to go from here.

For now, I need to get moving. The sun is still soft and warm, just beginning to rise, which means it's around my usual early morning wake-up time. If I hurry, I can still get out of here without anyone noticing. Maybe even before Annie notices.

But when I look down, trying to assess the best way to extricate myself, instead of moving away, I watch my fingers curl tighter around her side. I notice everything about Annie that I shouldn't. Like how her eyelashes curl on the ends and are blonde at the base. How she has lots of small freckles across the bridge of her nose. And I notice the way she curves into me perfectly. I honestly didn't take Annie for a snuggler. *"I always keep my hands to myself. . . . But with you . . ."* Those words echo loudly in my head.

She's draped fully over me, weighing me down in the most incredibly affectionate way. I keep my fingers light against her side even though I want to curl them into the adorable banana-printed fabric of her PJs and then proceed to peel them off one by one. I want to roll her over and wake her up with kisses down her neck and over her stomach. I want to kiss her and not stop.

Time to get up, Will. Get out! And get far away until I can think clearly again. And I absolutely cannot be the one to take her virginity. Not only because it would complicate things with Amelia and my job with her, but I'll for sure be out of here by the end of the month (as soon as I get Amelia to agree) and then I'll be off to Washington, D.C. It's going to be high-stress, high-stakes, and fast-paced work. My favorite. No time for roots or relationships.

Carefully, I slide out from under Annie and simultaneously pull the pillow into the place where my shoulder was holding her head up. She doesn't move or stir. As much as she'd hate to hear it, she looks like a sleeping angel with her soft pink lips relaxed into a pout and her eyelashes curling against her cheekbone. Her hair is half in, half out of the bun she was wearing last night, and somehow it makes the whole sight look even more attractive.

I stand up from the bed, slowly working my shoulders in a few circles to ease some of the tightness. The sun is higher now, and it spurs me to get out the window and back to my SUV down the street before anyone notices it. When I make it to the window, I lift the pane as quietly as possible, happy it doesn't squeak or scrape. I drop my leg over the side just like the way I entered and pause only long enough to look at Annie one more time.

My breath catches when I realize she's facing me now, eyes open, smiling softly. She doesn't say anything, and neither do I. Her blue eyes sparkle in the morning sun, and the most domestic images rush through my head: of her pouring a bowl of cereal, me topping it off with milk, and then her sitting in my lap while we eat together at the table—because I'm a clingy son of a bitch like that. That is all wrong. That's not the sort of fantasy I should be having about her. It should be all sexual. All primal and fleeting. Instead, I'm rubbing my chest and telling myself to get the hell out of here before I accidentally ask her to have coffee with me on the porch while the sun comes up.

I give Annie one last smile and then duck out through her window and close it behind me.

I can't go back to my room yet until I'm certain Mabel is gone. She'll be hovering around the front desk this morning waiting to catch Terry lazily throwing the newspaper on the lawn instead of onto the front stoop. So I make a detour to the diner for some coffee before I go back, biding my time until Mabel leaves for her nine o'clock exercise walk around the town.

When I get near the diner, I park in the communal lot and then start my trek through the town toward it. My eyes are peeled, and I'm ready for someone to pop out and spring a sale on me I have no interest in, but, thankfully, it's quiet. There are no noses pressed to windows, no eyes peeking from corners, no one really in sight.

The diner is empty except for Noah, who's sitting at the bar. He comes in here almost every morning for coffee before going over to The Pie Shop and making even more coffee. I take the barstool two down from him just as Jeanine bursts through the door, rushes back behind the bar, then throws her apron over her head with a megawatt smile. "Morning, darlin's!"

We both nod at Jeanine, and mirroring Noah's mannerisms feels weird.

"Having a good morning?" asks Jeanine.

We both grunt a response.

Jeanine retrieves her notepad and pen and tucks them into her pocket. "Riiight. Okay, so the usual for Noah: coffee, black as tar. And what about you, Will?" She raises her brows at me and flips her long auburn hair over her shoulder, waiting for my answer.

I glance at Noah and back at Jeanine, wishing I didn't have to put my order in with him listening. "Uh, coffee too."

"Black?"

"Yep." I lean forward slightly. "Plus cream and sugar."

I catch Noah's grin.

"Shut up," I tell him and he raises his hands.

"I didn't say a thing."

"Your smirk did. It's sexist of you to think I can't be manly and also enjoy cream and sugar."

Noah cuts his eyes to me, still holding a look of complete disinterest. "I can't work in a pie shop, wear an apron every damn day of my life, and also be sexist."

"I'm starting to think it's all a front. You and your black-as-tar coffee are sexist as shit."

Jeanine chuckles and turns toward the coffeepot to pour our drinks. "Aren't you two just bursts of sunshine this morning?" Jeanine slides Noah's black coffee to him first and then mine to me. "Noah's always grumpy, so that's nothing new," she says, leaning over the counter to be face-to-face with me. "But you've always got a smile for me. Where's my smile, Will?"

She's not coming on to me—I don't think. It's just Jeanine. She's naturally flirtatious, and naturally flirtatious people are usually drawn to me. Probably because I'm one of them. I learned it from an early age: flirtatious people are widely loved, and I've been in the business of getting love from anyone and everyone I can since the day I went to school and told Teressa Howard she looked pretty in her Lisa Frank shirt, and she hugged me. It had been weeks since I'd had a hug, and I still remember it feeling so damn good.

I sip my coffee, and grin around the rim—not quite feeling it today. "Sorry, Jeanine. Long night."

Her eyes twinkle, and she lifts a brow before standing up straight and giving a soft whistle. "And who's the lucky lady you ditched for a solo breakfast? Anyone I know?" I don't miss the calculated easy grin. She's fishing to see if it's Annie because we had lunch together here at the diner.

"I didn't—" I catch myself, remembering that the brother of the lady in question is sitting only a barstool away from me—and he also happens to be my boss's fiancé. I need to watch myself. "It wasn't that kind of a long night."

Jeanine laughs harder this time. "I see. Now the grumpy mood makes more sense." Annoying that she's implying I'm in a bad mood from not having sex with Annie. I could care less about that, and I'm glad Annie was honest and said she wanted to stop. I'm grumpy because my night with her was better than anything I've ever experienced before, and I don't know what to do about it. "All right, well, I'll leave you two alone to your man time. Holler if you need me, honeys." Jeanine disappears into the kitchen.

Noah and I sit in silence for several minutes, and I'm thankful for it. It gives me time to consider what I'm going to do about Annie and the magnetic hold she seems to have over me. Part of me insists I need to bow out of offering to help her. After last night—and then falling asleep next to her—it's clear that I need to clamp down on my boundaries if I'm going to stay on the path I've made for myself.

"So . . ." Noah's voice pulls me from my thoughts. "You spent the night with Annie, huh?"

I choke on my coffee. A full-on coughing, eye-watering, gasping-for-air choke.

Noah—the asshole—laughs. "Calm down. I didn't mean it to come out like a threat." He's maybe the only person in the world who could make me feel threatened. I've stared down some pretty terrifying people, but Noah has this quiet confidence about him that tells me he could make my life hell if he wanted to.

I take another drink of coffee to try to ease my coughing and press the back of my hand to my mouth. After my life has stopped flashing before my eyes, I look at Noah. "How else am I supposed to take that question?"

He doesn't say anything, just smirks into his coffee. Not a

threat, my ass. He knew what he was doing when he said it, and I won't dare lie to him or try to convince him I didn't spend the night with Annie. But I at least can be honestly innocent in front of him. A first for me.

"I didn't sleep with her, just so you know." I pause. "Well . . . we did fall asleep together, but I didn't—"

Noah holds up his hand, cutting me off. "I don't need to know details. It's none of my business."

I eye him skeptically. "It isn't?"

From what I've seen, it seems like everything in this town is everyone's business.

Noah smiles from under his beard—and I would damn well trade all of my tattoos for the ability to grow a beard like that man's. It isn't fair. I'm the former military man turned bodyguard—I should have the manly beard. The only facial hair I can grow excellently are eyelashes. They're long and thick, and women always note them. A damn shame. Note my muscles, note my square jaw, note my ass for goodness' sake—but please, for the love of God, do not comment on the length and volume of my lashes.

"Annie is a grown woman. I don't need to keep tabs on her or monitor who she does or doesn't date." Noah turns his casual gaze to me and tips a shoulder. He takes a drink of his coffee, and then sets the mug down and stares into it. I've seen him and Amelia together and it's hard not to root for them. To be wildly jealous of them. They're good for each other.

Would I be good for Annie?

Instinctively, I know she would be good for me. But I worry that I would drag her down. I wouldn't know how to communicate well, or I'd feel an itch to leave when things got tough—because I'm self-aware enough to know that I avoid all confrontation and discomfort like they're diseases. It's why I haven't called my brother back. It's why I haven't been home to visit either of my parents in years. It's why I chose a career that allows me to be a happy-go-lucky nomad, where I can float from woman to woman and place to place, and never get attached enough to have to deal with real life.

Jeanine glides through the swinging kitchen door and sets my eggs in front of me with a smile and a wink. Only after she crosses the diner to take another table's order do I ask Noah, "How did you know? That I spent the night with Annie, I mean."

"Saw your truck."

"You live on the opposite side of town."

"Didn't say *I* saw your truck." He looks at me and grins—reminding me that this town's meddling goes deeper than I can even imagine. "James saw it on his way out for deliveries this morning. Considering the gossip around the town that y'all have started dating and then seeing your truck down the road from my sisters' house . . . it doesn't take a rocket scientist to put two and two together."

I'm not sure whether this is good or bad. Annie confirmed she's a virgin last night—and I'm not sure how many other people in her life know that or if it even matters to her at the end of the day. But I'm not the kind of guy you hear has been sleeping in a woman's room and assume nothing happened. Then again, she did want to change her reputation around this town.

"Do you think James told anyone else?"

Noah stifles a laugh and gives me a face that says, you poor dipshit. "Don't let the farmer look fool you. James is every bit the gossip that Mabel is." He pauses and tips his head sideways and then back like he's remembering something. "Plus there's the fact that Tony—our sheriff—saw you climbing out of Annie's bedroom window this morning."

"Shit."

"Yep."

Speaking of James, a minute later he walks into the diner,

whistling. James has the most open smile I've ever seen on anyone. There's no ulterior motive to it—it's like he's just genuinely happy all the time. Strange.

"Morning, Jeanine!" he calls from the door. I notice he's carrying a clipboard in his hand, but he goes to the far end of the bar and drops it off by the register before coming to take the stool next to Noah. He slaps Noah on the back. "Good morning, sunshine. Dream about me last night?"

"Uh-huh," Noah says and then takes another sip of his coffee. "Dreamed I ran you over with my truck."

"Well, this is a treat, James," says Jeanine, coming over to take his order. "I never see you here in the mornings."

"I had some business in town to tend to."

Noah looks at him with a frown. "What business? You don't deliver to my shop until tomorrow."

"You'll see," he says with an unnerving grin. Maybe I'm thinking too much about it, but paired with the town's unnaturally quiet disposition this morning, I feel a prickle of unease. "I'll take the morning sampler, Jeanine, thank you." James leans around Noah to look at me. "You two been having a stimulating conversation?"

"If you count Noah subtly threatening me, then, yeah, it's been great."

James laughs. Noah shakes his head, gazes forward. "It wasn't a threat."

"I bet it was," says James. "If it was concerning Annie and your slumber party last night, it absolutely was a threat. And just wait until the sisters get wind of it."

"Nothing happened!" I say, suddenly feeling like I need a lawyer present.

"Quit shaking." Noah tips his mug up high, gulping down the last bit of coffee and then turning toward me on his stool. "I like you, Will. I always have. I know I'm supposed to be the protective older brother who warns the guy with the reputation to stay the hell away from his baby sister, but that's just not how I work. I swear I'm not trying to threaten you—because like James said, my sisters will do that just fine without my interference. But more than that, I trust my sisters to know what they need better than I do. And the fact is, whatever is going on with you and Annie, I support it."

"You do?"

"Yeah." Noah stands and faces me. "To be honest, I'm more worried about you than about Annie."

"Why's that?" I say, even though I agree wholeheartedly with him.

"Because I can guarantee you've never met anyone like her," Noah says ominously and then turns to leave, pauses, and then goes to the side of the bar to look at whatever James dropped off. I hear his grunt of a laugh before he flashes me a look, shakes his head, and leaves without exchanging any other words.

"For what it's worth," James says around a bite of eggs, "I do plan on threatening you." He aims his smile at me, and suddenly it doesn't look quite so sunny anymore. It has the same glint a sword has. "Hurt her, and I'll kill you and bury your body as fertilizer for my plants."

I nod once, slowly. "Noted."

I toss a ten-dollar bill onto the counter and finally go over to see what's on that clipboard. I curse under my breath. "Did you make this?"

He laughs, not even looking at me as he continues to dig into his eggs. "Nope. That would be Harriet's doing."

"When did they all have time to do this?"

"About thirty minutes ago at their impromptu town business owners' meeting. There's one in each establishment."

"Of course there is." And this would explain why it was a ghost town out there today. They had all gathered to make a petition to keep me and Annie apart. Across the top in bold letters it reads:

We, the town's people, demand that Annie Walker and Will Griffin hereby forfeit their new relationship on the grounds of Annie Walker being a sweet darling and Will Griffin being . . . not a sweet darling.

Below that, there's a pretty nice little slander campaign that lists all the reasons I'm not to be trusted (see the grainy copy and pasted BuzzFeed article) followed by all of Annie's superlatives. I'm impressed that she led the children's literacy fundraising campaign at the library. But not surprised. And getting Harriet's market to switch from plastic to bring-your-own reusable bags is cool too. At the bottom there's a plug for Davie's Print Shop.

Nice.

"Is this even legal?" I ask James.

"Doubt it. But never underestimate the power of the town of Rome to meddle just enough to get shit done. Plus Harriet bought fifteen boxes of Girl Scout cookies from the sheriff's daughter, so I imagine he's willing to look the other way on this petition." He eyes me closely. "So if you want to marry Annie, you better put your best foot forward and show us you're worth it."

I groan. "I don't want to marry Annie! This is one big misunderstanding." A ridiculous one that's quickly getting out of hand.

He looks back down at his eggs with a smile. "Sure you don't."

CHAPTER TWENTY-THREE

Annie

I get home after work to the smell of fancy baked chicken. The moment I open the door, the beautiful aroma smacks me right in the face and I make a beeline to the kitchen. I love summer because it means Maddie and Emily are out of school. That's wonderful for two reasons: one, I get to see more of them, and two, Maddie has more time to cook.

I groan as I walk into the kitchen and find Maddie in front of a pot of simmering something. "What is that amazing smell?"

Maddie turns to me, oversize messy bun bouncing as she does. "It's a new recipe I'm working on: Spicy Honey Butter Chicken. Here, try the glaze and tell me if it's good."

She raises the wooden spoon to my lips, and the moment the glaze hits my tongue I decide no other food will ever live up to it. "This is it for me," I say solemnly. "My peak food experience ends with this recipe."

Maddie laughs and hip checks me. "You're too nice, though. You would never tell me if it was bad anyway."

"Not true. I would just get really quiet and compliment the initiative you put into it. Either way, I really do love it."

I take a seat at the bar and graze on the appetizer Maddie whipped up. Spinach-artichoke dip. It's glorious. Heavenly. I am undeserving.

"How was your day?" she asks, coming over to dunk a chip in the dip too. Her eyes squint up slightly after she takes a bite—trying to figure out what it's lacking. It's lacking nothing. She's just a perfectionist when it comes to her food.

Her question sparks a series of memories. Will climbing into my room. The devastating press of his mouth against mine. And then waking up in his arms.

All day my mind has been playing that kissing session over and over again but adding new fantastical details with every pass. Like instead of being in my room, Will enters the shop after fighting off several henchmen. A drop of blood drips down his cheek from a small cut across his face left by a sword. Naturally, I rush to his side and pull him into the shop, where I tend to his wound. He stares down into my eyes, I stare up into his, and then our kiss explodes like a cannon. Not sweet or timid but hot and frantic.

I clear my throat. "It was good. How about you?"

"Good too. Just spent the day online shopping for our trip next week. Hey—in unrelated news, how long is it morally acceptable to wear an outfit with the tags still attached before returning it because you're too broke to actually afford it? Wait! Don't answer that. You'll tell me to return it immediately, but I don't want to."

Maddie and Emily are finally going on their Mexico trip with their teacher friends. I keep telling myself that's the only reason they didn't invite me—it's a teachers-only trip. But somehow, instinctively, I know it's because they're assuming I wouldn't want to go. They think I'm superglued to this town like Noah. And probably assume I'd be a buzzkill too.

It's fine, though. I couldn't go even if I wanted to, what with how much flower prep I'm doing for Amelia's wedding and how busy the shop has been lately. Not to mention these lessons with Will.

My stomach swoops as it has every time I think of him. It's like I'm on a constant roller coaster. I need my body to hurry up and get used to his presence because I can't take much more of these butterflies.

Mid chip to mouth, our front door opens and Emily storms in. "*You!*" she yells, pointing at me. "You and Will Griffin have a thing going on and he slept in your room last night and you didn't tell us!"

"What?!" Maddie squeals, hopping down from the bar into an immediate battle stance. "We've been in here talking for five whole minutes! I asked how your day was, and you said, 'It was good.' *Good!* When the first thing out of your mouth should have been, 'Oh, hey, sis, I got laid by the hottest bodyguard to ever grace *People* magazine, and I'm no longer a virgin!'"

"First of all, I'd never say 'laid.'"

Emily throws her purse on the kitchen counter. It makes a loud *thud,* and I know it's because she has the thing so loaded down with everything she could ever possibly need (including a first aid kit and emergency water bottle). "That man was under our roof last night in your bed deflowering you, and you never thought we should know? I'm disowning you! I can't believe I had to hear it from Holden Jones that Will was sneaking out of your window at sunrise!"

I raise my brows. "Holden? Wow. Made it all the way over to the library?"

"Yes. And he heard it from Cathy Bryant—"

"Lee now. She got married last month, remember?"

"Who heard it from Harriet when she was spouting off about your decaying hussy's soul in the market, who heard it from Terry, who saw the whole thing with his own eyes when he was making his morning newspaper rounds and caught sight of Will climbing out of your window!" Emily is fuming. She hates being the last to hear about anything concerning us siblings. I half expect to find a tracker planted on my person one day.

I would open my mouth to reveal the truth, but I know it's no use. My sisters need to get their words out first, or they'll combust. "Harriet said what about Annie?" says Maddie, her soft ivory skin turning a nice shade of reddish purple.

"Don't worry, I already went by the market to give her a piece of my mind. But Mabel beat me to it. She was laying into Harriet when I walked in, so I just grabbed the dishwasher pods we needed, signed the petition, paid, and came home."

My ears perk up. "I'm sorry—what petition?"

"You haven't seen it? The town put together a petition to vote on your and Will's relationship," says Emily. "It's actually way more extensive than the one they did for Paul and that woman he was dating for a while. This one has an entire facts list attached for why y'all aren't well suited for a relationship." Emily finally notices the dip and slides onto the stool beside me to dig in. I scoot the bowl a little closer to her.

"Wait, wait, wait. It's a relationship now?" Maddie dives her hand through her hair. "My head is spinning. Are you telling me that you and Will are dating? You were too shy to talk to Hot Bank Teller, so you bypassed him and went straight for Sexy Bodyguard? I need all the details."

My sisters stare at me expectantly. I know that this is the moment I should tell them the truth. I should burst out laughing and explain that Will is just my practice person. But for some reason, the words won't come out. Because right now, my sisters are looking at me like I'm the opposite of boring. Like I'm maybe . . . fascinating. Like I'm not their sweet baby sister, and maybe there's more to me than they realized.

And I'm not ready for that look to fade when I tell them I wasn't too shy to talk to Hot Bank Teller, that he, in fact, thought I was too boring to date, so Will is just being kind and helping me.

And that's why I lie.

"Yeah. It's not a big deal," I say, looking down to scoop another chip in an attempt at looking casual. "He came into the flower shop the other day, and we hit it off, and . . . now we're . . . dating." Oh gosh. What are you doing Annie? Will is never going to go for this. "It's just casual, though. Could end any day really."

"Casual?" Emily repeats with a quizzical frown.

"Uh-huh."

"Annie," Madison says, like she's gently trying to tell me the people I'm seeing in the room aren't really there. "You don't do casual. You're Monica in the episode of *Friends* where she reveals her wedding scrapbook. You and casual do not belong in the same sentence."

"Well, we do now." I tip a shoulder like it's no big deal. But even I know that what I'm saying is a very big deal. It's also untrue. I feel a tug of disappointment as I deny being true to myself, but I squash that feeling under my Converse sneakers because what has being true to myself gotten me besides blown off in the middle of a date?

My sisters look at each other—obviously freaked out by this deviation in character and uncertain how to continue.

"Huh," Maddie says.

"So you and Will can . . . what? See other people?" asks Emily, testing me.

"Yep."

"And you're okay with that?"

I shrug. "Of course. The more the merrier!"

Nope. And I'm also a little worried at how the thought of Will (the man who is not my real boyfriend) dating anyone else sends a boiling surge of jealousy through my body.

Apparently, that was a bridge too far because Maddie and Emily share a look. One of the looks that always makes me feel so mad to be excluded from. The one that I can never understand the meaning of, but they seem to comprehend perfectly. How is it possible to share DNA with someone and still feel so "other" from them—and yet still love them with my whole heart? It's too messy.

They turn to me and cross their arms—a habit we've all adopted from Noah for when we mean business. "All right. Fess up. What's going on? Did you and Will actually sleep together last night?"

My shoulders slump. "Fine. He slept here, but nothing happened. In fact, I don't think anything will ever happen between us."

Madison melts dramatically to the floor, pretending to weep as she says, "Annie. You're killing me. You're literally murdering me slowly. Please start from the beginning!"

Ugh. Here we go. The truth.

"Okay, okay, okay. Amelia set the whole thing up. Will is my dating coach for a few weeks to help me practice because . . ." Because I went on a date and it was a disaster and I'm boring. Nope. Still can't bring myself to tell them that part. They'll laugh. Or they'll make a joke about Angel Annie being too saintly for a bank teller. Or even worse, they won't be surprised at all. "Because I'm ready to start dating seriously, but I'm nervous. He's just helping me get over the nerves." I don't mention how dating lessons have melted into something else entirely, though. And I don't tell them about the tattoo or how Will has offered to help with any other kind of practice I want because all of that feels too personal. As misguided as it might be, it feels like something special between me and Will, and I don't want to include anyone else in it.

Emily frowns lightly—her ever-present mom mode trying to carefully dissect every possible obstacle I will have to overcome and then determine whether I'm emotionally strong enough to handle a situation like this.

Maddie leans her hip against the counter. "Please at least tell me it's like a sexy dating-coach thing? Like y'all are going to practice having sex too?"

"No, it's not a sexy dating-coach thing." But when I'm confronted with memories of me and Will making out in my bed last night I realize that statement isn't totally true. But it stops with kissing. No sex will be happening between me and Will because as I'm realizing in the light of day, that would only complicate whatever mission I'm on to find a husband or myself or . . . ugh, I don't know. It just wouldn't be good, okay?! I have to stop thinking about it.

"So what do you practice?"

I shrug. "Just like regular stuff. Datey stuff, you know? Good topics to bring up on dates. How to flirt. Those sorts of things."

Madison's nose wrinkles. "Oh. I guess that makes more sense."

"What do you mean?" I ask, having a bad feeling that I already know the answer.

She laughs lightly because she thinks I'm in on this joke. "It's you; and it's Will Griffin! You guys are polar opposites. He's all sexy-fun-adventure, and you're our quiet sweet-little-introvert. I'm just saying it's probably for the best that you guys aren't really dating because you'd rather be inside on a Friday night reading a book, and he'd probably be drunk in a club."

She and Emily laugh, and I try to muster one, too, but all that comes out is a weak attempt at a smile.

"Which isn't a bad thing at all. It's just who you are. Our tender-hearted sweetie pie," Emily adds, laying her head on my shoulder and squeezing affectionally around my waist. "But listen, I fully support your endeavor to get comfortable at dating so you can find someone right for you. Maybe this fall we'll have a new student enroll with a single dad with a heart of gold and lots of love to give."

"Oooh," Madison says, lighting up. "That's perfect for Annie! Brownie points if he's a doctor."

"A pediatric doctor!" Emily adds.

"A pediatric doctor who's waiting until marriage to have sex again and also has a nonprofit helping stray puppies on the weekend!"

I can't decide who makes me feel more upset right now. My sisters for once again telling me who I am and what I want—or me for smiling and nodding while they do. I love my sisters so much—which is why it hurts to not feel seen by them at all. I just want to be their friend and not their baby sister all the time. I want to be valued and taken seriously. But how do I do that without opening an entire can of slimy, messy worms? Or potentially hurting them when I tell them they've been inadvertently hurting me for years? I don't want to seem whiny or fragile.

And please explain to me why I can't for the life of me picture myself standing next to the man they just described, but I can perfectly picture a man with a pair of mischievous blue-gray eyes, a tilted smile, and tattoos hovering over me in my bed as he kisses my mouth again and again for the rest of my life.

Crap.

CHAPTER TWENTY-FOUR

Monday

WILL: The town still holding up while I've been away?

ANNIE: Who is this?

WILL: It's Will. We literally exchanged phone numbers just last night.

ANNIE: Sorry. I think you have the wrong number.

WILL: Seriously?

ANNIE: No. I was just messing with you.

WILL: Ha ha, funny girl.

ANNIE: Everything is holding up. But the scenery is oddly a lot less hot.

WILL: Annie Walker. Are you . . . flirting with me?

ANNIE: Maybe. Or maybe this is a forty-year-old man's number and I'm catfishing you.

WILL: If you are a dude, are you at least sexy?

ANNIE: How do you feel about loafers with little tassels on the front?

WILL: *Bites fist*

Tuesday

WILL: Have you seen the petition yet?

ANNIE: OMG, you've seen it already?! I've been all worked up worrying about how to tell you. I was afraid you'd be upset.

WILL: Why would I be upset?

ANNIE: Because the town thinks we're a couple and is voting against it.

WILL: Again. Why would I be upset? I'm clearly getting the better end of the stick in this scenario. You're the one dating a debauched bodyguard.

ANNIE: Debauched!! What a good word.

WILL: Learned it from your pirate romance book. I like it.

ANNIE: It suits you. But don't worry, I'll set the whole town straight with the truth one by one.

WILL: Or . . .

ANNIE: Or???

WILL: We could not say anything. And just let them believe what they want to believe. You said you wanted everyone to stop seeing you as Sweet Angel Annie . . . this might be just the thing to do it.

ANNIE: You'd do that for me?

WILL: I'm quickly learning I'd do anything for you.

Wednesday

ANNIE: Hi.

WILL: Hi. Whacha doing?

ANNIE: *Picture of boutonniere options*

ANNIE: Which one do you like better for the groomsmen?

WILL: The one on the left.

WILL: While I've got you . . .

WILL: *Picture of palm tree and blue sky overhead*

WILL: At the risk of sounding a little too poetic and sappy, the color of California's sky is the same blue as your eyes.

ANNIE: Oof. That *was* sappy.

WILL: Dammit. I thought so.

ANNIE: I'll let it slide this one time.

WILL: Changing subject now. Have you ever been to L.A.?

ANNIE: Nope. I haven't traveled much.

WILL: That's a damn shame. You need to come to California, Annie. So many cool flower shops. You'd love it here.

ANNIE: I want to, but I'm scared of flying. And going to new places. And meeting new people.

WILL: My offer stands to hold your hand.

ANNIE: I do like your hands.

ANNIE: Oh wow. Pretend I didn't say that. I'm super embarrassed now. GAH! Why is there no unsend button.

WILL: I like your hands, too, Anna-banana.

Thursday

ANNIE: I had the funniest dream about you last night.

WILL: Funny? Hmm. I'd prefer sexy.

ANNIE: Well, you don't get to choose. And this one was funny because you and I were in high school together, and I kept failing the same test over and over so you wrote the answers out for me on a piece of paper and gave them to me.

WILL: Sounds like something I'd do. Did we get caught?

ANNIE: Yes. And then we had to spend detention in Harriet's Bible study.

WILL: Yikes.

ANNIE: Did you ever cheat in high school?

WILL: No.

WILL: It was sort of hard to cheat in a wolf pack. Our tests
consisted of preying on other animals and the best way to
lick your coat clean.

ANNIE: Are you never going to tell me anything about your
childhood or teen years?

WILL: I was shorter back then . . .

ANNIE: You're impossible.

WILL: Thank you :)

CHAPTER TWENTY-FIVE

Annie

I twirl a long-stemmed rose between my fingers as I lean against the worktable at the flower shop, but my mind isn't here. It's stuck in an alternate world where a sexy, funny, outgoing man is my boyfriend. And then there's the texts. I know I shouldn't read too much into them, but those texts have felt meaningful this week. Last night he texted me before bed, just: Good night.

That was it.

It's so confusing. He says he isn't relationship material, and then he goes and texts me "Good night."

I jab the rose into the bouquet I'm assembling and tell myself to get a grip. It doesn't matter whether he wants a relationship or not. I'm not into him like that. There's absolutely no feelings stirring up in me. Anything I feel so far is just attraction. I mean who wouldn't be attracted to Will Griffin? It's got to be a law of nature or something. Nothing to worry about—but I definitely need to keep my head on straight and remind myself that all the kissing and cuddling and texting is just a part of the process of my transformation.

He's Fred and I'm Audrey. But in our movie, the credits will roll after my transformation is complete and I've found the wholeness I've been looking for. Romance subplot, removed. Admittedly, it would be easier to picture this analogy if Will weren't so freaking hot. I need to draw some wrinkles on his face and strap him in tap shoes and high-wasted trousers. That'll cure my attraction.

My attention goes to the shop door when the bell rings and a nice-looking man steps inside.

"Hi! Let me know if I can help you with anything," I say while continuing to mess with the bouquet. I try not to crowd shoppers because no one likes a hovering sales associate.

"Thanks," says the man and immediately I take note of his voice. It's a nice voice. And because it caught my attention, I try to discreetly assess him as he wanders around the shop.

> Nice light brown hair cropped close to his head but with
>   enough play on the top to style it
> A well-groomed beard
> Button-down casual dress shirt
> Nice jeans
> Clearly works out
> No wedding ring

He looks up and catches me looking, so I'm forced to say something. "Um, those premade bouquets are half-price."

"Great," he says with an easy smile. "Thanks."

The arrangement I'm working on is missing something. It looks nice and all, but I think it's lacking a standout element. Something that grabs me and doesn't let me look away. Something exciting. It's missing a dangerous black rim around its irises . . . and wait, I'm not thinking about flowers anymore, am I?

I barely refrain from groaning into my hands. Of course I would be thinking about Will while a handsome (possibly single) man is roaming around my flower shop.

"Hey, could I get your advice on something?" the man asks, approaching me at the worktable.

"Of course! I'd be happy to help."

He frowns, looking around the shop. "What sort of bouquet is appropriate to buy for a woman who just had a baby?"

Oh.

He's a dad.

Well, that's that.

"Actually, for a sister-in-law who just had a baby," he amends like maybe he saw my face and wanted to clarify.

Things are looking up again.

I walk around the worktable and go to the far corner, where I have a few freshly assembled, colorful flowers. "I think any of these would be perfect. They're beautiful but not over-the-top."

"Great." He leans in and selects one—treating me to a sniff of his cologne. And it is cologne. He definitely owns a fancy bottle of something cinnamonlike and spritzes it once—maybe twice—before he leaves the house.

I think I like it. Or I could like it.

It doesn't smell anything like . . .

No! Not finishing that absurd thought. Now is my chance to use a little bit of the newfound confidence I've been practicing.

"So are you from around here or just in for a visit?" I say, wondering if this has been an appropriate amount of eye contact.

"I've actually just moved to town. Or the town over, to be exact. My family lives around here, and I felt ready to settle down. So I moved my clinic here and bought a house."

This is starting to feel like a lot of eye contact. Too much. Oh gosh, I need to look away. And please tell me why I never have this issue with Will? With him I never want to look away.

I take his bouquet to the counter to ring it up. "Oh, are you a doctor?"

"Veterinarian," he says, and that earns another *ding, ding, ding* sound in my brain because I love animals. Even better—a man who loves animals too. And he's apparently a family man who is looking to put down roots! My sisters would definitely be giving me a thumbs-up right now and telling me to go for it.

"That's great news!" I say a little over the top.

"Oh yeah? Do you have any animals?"

"Well . . . no, but it's great news for everyone else who does." He laughs and hands me his credit card. "Brandon Larsdale," I say, shamelessly reading the name on his credit card out loud.

"No fair. I don't get to scan your credit card to learn your name."

I smile up at him, feeling my cheeks turn pink in a way that I really wish they wouldn't. I think he's flirting with me now too—and the familiar discomfort of talking to a new guy is settling over me. Must push through. "I'm Annie Walker."

"Nice to meet you, Annie." He pauses only briefly as he picks up his bouquet from the counter. "Listen, I realize this is really forward of me, but . . . you don't happen to be single, are you?"

My heart trips. Is he about to ask me out? Is this really happening? Do I want it to happen?

Also, what constitutes "single"? If you ask anyone in the town, they would say I'm dating a dangerous-looking bodyguard. *But that's not real, Annie.*

"I am single," I say and then realize my chin is lifted. I promptly level it.

Brandon smiles. "Well, then, would you be interested in going out sometime? I know we just met, and this could come across as super creepy, so no pressure. Also, I'm on Instagram if you want to look me up to make sure I'm legit."

I should say yes. *Say yes, Annie!* He's ticking all the boxes so far, and if I want to get married, I have to go on a date again. But I don't want to end up on a date with someone who's only looking to hook up at the end of the night, because no matter how amazing making out with Will has been lately, I'm realizing I'll never be the first date hookup kind of person. And maybe that's okay?

Honestly, this could be perfect. I wanted to pursue both paths (one, being dating, and the other, giving in to self-indulgence) in hopes of figuring out which one brings me the peace I've been looking for—and it looks like one of those paths is currently illuminated with a blinking sign above it reading WALK THIS WAY.

I decide to throw out the truth to see if this man will be a waste of my time or not.

"I need to be up front with you, Brandon. I'm not looking for anything casual."

His smile grows. "Me neither, actually." Brandon reaches into his back pocket to fish out his wallet. "Here," he says, and then takes out a very official-looking business card with his veterinary clinic's logo and information on it. "Do you have a pen?"

I hand him one, and he quickly jots down a number on the back. "This is my cell. Text me if you think you'd like to go out. Or if you just want to talk and get to know each other."

"Okay, I will. Thank you," I say taking his card and giving him one more smile before he turns, telling me to have a nice day and he hopes we see each other again.

The second he's out the door, I drop the card on the counter like it's a poisonous leaf.

"Well," I say, rubbing the back of my neck as I stare down at the little rectangular card. "This is unexpected."

CHAPTER TWENTY-SIX

Annie

Hank's is lit on Friday nights. The whole town comes out to line dance and drink and socialize. If you're not at Hank's on a Friday night, you're a certified loser. It's why even I manage to turn up. (And I enjoy being here, so there's that.)

I've done this enough times to know how to manage it, though. Hank's is one of my comfort spots. Me and my sisters show up a little earlier than most—somewhere around seven, drink a few beers and catch up on our weeks even though we see each other literally every day and know nearly all of each other's business at all times. But . . . I guess I have things they don't know about right now. Why does that send such a thrill through me?

It suddenly makes me wonder if they have things I don't know about their lives too.

I glance around the table, assessing my sisters with fresh eyes. Sherlock eyes. What are they hiding? On the outside Emily looks normal. Her blonde hair is parted down the middle, tucked neatly behind her ears, curls she created with her wand this morning are brushed out into soft luscious waves. But her strong features, high cheekbones, and knowing eyes remind you that she could kick your butt in a second. Emily is our fierce protector. Although my grandma raised us, at the end of the day, she still felt like a grandma more than a mother figure. But Emily always feels more like a mom than a sister to me. I've never known anyone to keep it all together like she does. And in case anyone needs any more convincing that she's a fierce queen, Emily has taught second grade for nine years with twenty or more children in class each time. Superhero status.

So what is she hiding? I've often wondered why she hasn't married. It's not for a lack of men trying, but as far as I know, she's only ever loved one person. Her high school sweetheart. None of us really know what happened there. It was all very hush-hush. One day he was the love of her life, and the next, he was packing up his truck and leaving Rome for good. I remember Emily spending an entire twenty-four hours crying in her room, and then she wiped her tears and never mentioned him again. Didn't let us mention him either.

And then there's Madison. Just look at her. A sprite if I've ever seen one. A spunky little brunette with a bouncy shoulder-length haircut, wild brown eyes that are always seeking trouble, and a small adorable nose that is all too boopable. Maddie looks like a sugar cookie, yet she's wild to her core.

But she's hiding something, I'm convinced. She looks at me and smiles, I smile back. *I'm onto you, lady.* So what is it? Hates her job? No, wait, that's not a secret. Madison has always been quick to follow in Emily's footsteps, even when the rest of us can see it's clearly wrong for her. Madison also teaches second grade at the same school as Emily, but she complains about her job 90 percent of the time—usually while anger-cooking us something fantastic in the kitchen.

So . . . Madison, what's your secret?

"Annie, are you okay?" Emily asks. "Your smile is super creepy."

I wipe my face blank. "I was thinking about a . . . movie I just watched."

"Was it a movie about a serial killer? Because those are the vibes you're putting out."

I scoff. "It was clearly not a serial killer's smile. You guys just don't know your smiles."

Amelia suddenly pops over my shoulder and pulls out a chair at the table, slightly out of breath. "Hiya! I'm back from L.A.! Who has a serial killer's smile?"

"Anna-banana."

Amelia grins and settles into the chair. "It's always the quiet ones you have to watch out for."

With Amelia's presence comes a spike in my blood pressure, because if Amelia is back in town, that means Will is back too. I'm more confused about that man than ever. He and I have been texting nonstop since he left town a week ago. And the weird part is— I miss him. A lot.

I'm not supposed to miss him. He's my no-strings-attached practice person. It's not supposed to be difficult to keep my face forward rather than craning my neck to see if he's anywhere in this bar.

And then Noah steps up, tosses his keys on the table, bends down to kiss the side of Amelia's neck in a lingering not-safe-for-work way, and then tells her he's going to grab them drinks from the bar. Her eyes give him the most I'm-desperately-in-love-with-you look as he walks away, and all of us sisters notice, sharing a knowing smirk. I'll bet all my money that they leave this bar early tonight.

Amelia notices us giggling like schoolgirls at her expense, and her face turns beet-red. "Stop! All of you. Stop it right now!"

We're all laughing obnoxiously now as Madison makes over-the-top making-out gestures. Amelia throws her hands over her eyes. "Y'all are so mean. You're not supposed to point out stuff like that."

"Hard to miss it when Noah is chomping on your neck like that," I say, taking a sip of my beer.

Amelia peeks over her hands to flash me a playfully offended face. "You too? My sweet Annie is going to stab me in the back like that?"

I reach over and fix Amelia's sweater, which is a little askew. "Sorry. Your bodyguard is being a bad influence on me."

Maddie grins and raises her beer in a toast. "And speak of the devil." She nods over my shoulder.

My stomach leaps into my throat and tap-dances. I don't need to turn to realize he's here. I can feel him. The temperature changes, the air grows thick. (Which shouldn't be happening because he doesn't mean anything to me.) *Remember, Annie, No Strings Attached!*

"Oooh, he can sit with us now that he's off the clock, and he's dating Annie, right?" Maddie says with way too big a gleam in her eye while air quoting the word *dating*. Maddie's hand shoots up in the air, waving frantically. "Will! Your woman is over here!"

"Hush, Maddie! You're making the whole bar look."

She flashes a self-satisfied expression that lets me know that was her aim in the first place.

I can't take it anymore. I peek over my shoulder—just one quick, tiny little glance to the side. But my eyes instantly connect with his, and I shoot my gaze forward again, pulse rushing in my ears. That tiny glance was enough to take in every inch of Will, and it's making everything worse.

Tonight he's wearing black jeans, white sneakers, and a denim button-down shirt rolled up over his forearms. His hair is sort of purposefully messy, and he's wearing a black watch on his tattooed wrist. He looks too good to be real. And now that I know what his skin looks like and feels like under that shirt—the way the lines of his tattoos are subtly raised to add the most delicious texture—my face heats.

"Annie's been saving your seat!" Madison says unhelpfully, making me sound desperate even though I had no idea he'd be here tonight. I widen my eyes to signal her to cool it, but she just grins her mischievous smile back at me.

Amelia points over my shoulder at Will. "Okay! Rules first. You can hang out with us, but you have to interact like a friend and not a bodyguard. No subtly protecting me!"

And then Will's butterfly knuckles enter my vision, and my skin curls up with tension. I keep my eyes on the table—hand wrapped around my drink. "Deal. If a fight breaks out, I'll use you as my shield."

Will takes the seat beside me, and his shoulders are too broad for this small space. He's almost touching me. Out of the corner of my eye I see him look at me. I cut my gaze to him for a fraction of a second, and his mouth suggests a smile—a hidden one. Secrets.

"Annabell," he whispers making the hairs rise on the back of my neck.

"Wilfred."

We grin quietly at each other until Maddie's voice breaks through our moment. "Hey, did you see the latest articles floating around about you from this week?"

"No. I try to stay off social media as much as possible," Amelia says, and then her expression turns weary. "But what are they saying now?"

Maddie chuckles. "Not you, pop star. Him." She nods toward Will. "There's a fresh batch of photos of him guarding you at all of your events from the past few days, and they are calling him . . ." her smile grows, "A stern brunch daddy."

"A what?" Will asks, sounding horrified. "Wait—do I want to know? It sounds disturbing."

"What's disturbing?" Noah asks, finally making his way back to the table, and this time, he has James in tow.

Amelia looks up at Noah as he sets down a beer in front of her. "Will is a stern brunch daddy."

Noah looks like he just stepped in cow manure. "I can't even begin to know what that is."

James, however, takes a chair from the table beside us and whips it around to straddle it, forearms resting on the back. He steals one of Maddie's fries, earning her glare. "A *stern brunch daddy* is a term romance readers use to describe a character type. It's when a dude who looks scary is actually all soft and sweet to the person he loves."

Noah looks at him in dismay. Actually, we all do.

Madison plucks the fry out of James's fingers. "Stop acting like you're a super progressive man who knows about romance. You only know that because I showed you the article ten minutes ago at the bar."

James shrugs. "But I get points for actually listening." He pauses and looks up at my scowling brother. "Actually . . . now that I think of it, Noah, you're kind of a stern brunch—"

"If you say the word *daddy* one more time, you're going to be scraping your teeth off the floor."

James pretends to shiver with delight. "I love it when you go all alpha."

I wish I could say I'm enjoying this conversation, but the truth is, I'm hardly listening. The majority of my consciousness is laser focused on the place Will's knee is resting against mine. A soft, yet almost intentional, pressure that I try not to overthink. But the thing about quiet people is, we're only quiet because our brains are so busy overthinking everything.

Does he know his leg is touching mine? Does he want his leg to be touching mine? *Tactile, Annie. He's just tactile, remember?* The man needs to be touching something at all times. He's probably touching Emily's leg on the other side. I glance under the table to sneak a peek, but nope. Their legs could fit an entire watermelon between them. And then my gaze shifts to his hand resting on his thigh. I have the strongest urge to reach over and run my finger over the wings of the intricate butterfly. To take that hand and put it back on my hip and tell him to squeeze because it's the memory of that touch that will likely haunt me until I'm in my grave.

And then his hand flexes, and I realize I've been caught staring. I suck in a breath and shoot my gaze up and forward. But in the corner of my eye, I can see Will looking at me. He turns forward abruptly when Amelia addresses him. "I bet you're wishing you'd never sat down right about now."

Will laughs and it's warm and inviting. "Nah—I kinda like the absurdness. It makes me miss my brother."

"You have a brother?" she asks. "How did I not know that?"

"I don't get to see him a lot. You know . . . working and all that."

The look on Amelia's face says she feels personally responsible for his lack of time with his brother, but I know better. I heard the hesitation in his voice and the blasé way he delivered that sentence—there's more there that Will doesn't want unearthed. I have the deepest urge to take a shovel and get to digging.

Will interprets her expression too. "Amelia, don't worry. You're not overworking me."

Her face skews up. "I feel like I am. You need a break! Take one now. Starting today, no more working until after the—"

"Like hell I will. I like working. It's what makes me happy. Now, enough about me. Please." This man really hates talking about himself. He has deflected any sort of personal revelations from the day we met. And yet I've still managed to understand him more than he'd like me to. I know that he kicks all the covers off when he sleeps because his body heats up to the temperature of the sun. I know that he adds extra salt to his fries—and that he hates soda. I know that he's an early bird and wakes up with the sun. And I also know that something in his past hurt him because he used to hide in a magnolia tree but absolutely won't discuss it. I think he has scars he keeps safely hidden behind his charm.

Suddenly I realize my family is all staring at me like I have a horn sprouting from between my eyes. "What?" I ask, alarm running through my voice.

"He just said a cuss word. Why doesn't he get a tally in the sacred notebook?" Emily asks.

"Oh. Well, because . . ." I turn my eyes to Will and contemplate it. The answer springs to my mind immediately, but I know I can't say it out loud. Because I like it when he does. So instead, I smile. Not even meaning to, really. And Will smiles, too, like he can read my thoughts. Like he's remembering our secret stolen moments together in the flower shop, in my truck, in my room—and that just maybe he knows me in different ways than my siblings do. "He gets one freebie."

That seems to appease everyone enough for their attention to turn away from me.

"Speaking of freebies!" Amelia starts. "Guess what I brought y'all back from L.A."

I tune out as Will leans in close to my ear. "Is it okay that I'm here? I figured it would be because everyone in the town thinks we're dating now. But maybe I assumed wrong, and you want to keep our hangouts on the down-low?"

Hmm, is it okay that he's here? That his warm breath is caressing the shell of my ear and making my head spin? That just the nearness of him has the blood in my veins pumping with fire? No. It's not okay. And I think it's only fair that he move far, far away because whether he means to or not, he's slowly wrecking my plans.

"I'm glad you're here," I say with a quiet grin. "And my family knows we're not really together now. They guessed it the other day, so there's no pressure to act like it at the table."

"Hmm," he says making a deep noise in his throat. "That's too bad."

And something happens to me that I've never experienced before. The world around me falls away, and for once, I'm not worried what anyone is thinking of me. All I know is Will's eyes are fixed on mine, and his mouth is curving softly and his hand is dropping to my leg where it splays out like it's been in that same spot a hundred times before. And before I know it, I'm tipping forward. He meets me in the middle and our lips brush.

It's not enough, though, and instinctively my hand raises to clutch the back of his neck, my body curving toward his as his hand contracts against my thigh. Our mouths move and press and it feels so right. So hot—his touch burns me from the inside out. I feel the subtle glide of his tongue across my mine and that's when reality grabs me by the scruff of my neck. Oh my gosh, we're making out at the table in front of my family. *Me!* Annie Walker is making out in a public setting. I rip my mouth away from Will's and pat my lips with the back of my hand.

Everyone—and I do mean everyone in this bar—is wide-eyed, staring. They look like cartoons with jaws unhinged.

Emily speaks first as a laugh courses through her voice. "Well, I think Hot Bank Teller is wishing he'd asked you out right about now."

"What?"

My eyes fly over Will's shoulder, and sure enough, John is here, watching—looking just as shocked as everyone else. Of course my sisters don't know that I actually went on that date with John and that it was a disaster, so they move on from Emily's statement pretty quick. But because I did go out with him and he damaged my self-esteem by leaving mid date, a whole new layer gets added to that public make-out session with Will.

I didn't do that to get John's attention or prove anything to him—but knowing that he's having to eat his words, that maybe I'm not as boring or awkward as he suspected, has a surge of joy rocketing through me. But would I have kissed him in public? Would I have felt safe enough with him to ever let him touch me the way I let Will? I don't think so.

Will notices my triumphant expression and turns his face to see where my gaze is landing. And I can feel the moment all the dots connect for him. His body stiffens slightly, and when he looks back to me—his face is a little too void of emotion. "That was the guy, right?"

I don't need for him to expound. "Yes."

He nods a few times. "Nice. I think you successfully made him jealous," he says in a low voice so the rest of the table can't hear.

"No, Will, that's—"

"It's exactly what I would have done. Great job. All this practicing is paying off." He gives me a smile that feels so fake I want to wipe it off his face. I hate that smile. That's not his smile. That's a shielded self-preservation smile. And it only serves to remind me that Will doesn't want me to know him. He promised me from the beginning that this would never be anything more than practice, and he's reestablishing those boundaries now.

I hate practice.

CHAPTER TWENTY-SEVEN

Will

It's been a few days since the kiss in the bar that completely shook me. No, I'm not being dramatic, and no I'm not exaggerating. I don't think I've ever thought about a kiss for longer than twenty minutes after the fact. But Annie's kiss . . . that one soft, vulnerable kiss, has been playing through my head for three days now. It was perfect in a way that I can't describe. I know that public attention is hard for her, so to have her initiate that kiss because she wanted it was too much.

But then she looked over my shoulder, and a jealousy I've never known gripped me. It was for show. And of course it was. She didn't do anything wrong. In fact, like I told her, it's exactly what I would have done if someone I would want to make jealous was nearby. I just wish I could say it didn't sting to realize it meant so much to me, and was only part of a maneuver on her end.

I thought . . . never mind. Doesn't matter.

Postkiss, I went to the bar for a beer. But if I'm being honest with myself, I went to meet the jerk sitting at the bar who had the audacity to leave Annie in the middle of a date.

And I know he's a jerk because when I walked up and ordered a beer, he asked me if Annie and I were exclusive. For a long minute, all I could do was stare at him. Stare at him and imagine punching the shit out of him because he only wanted Annie after he saw her make out with me in public. He's not the kind of man who's going to savor her or treat her well or peel back her layers to gain her trust. He's looking for a quick good time with her, and that's too much to stomach.

But if that's what Annie wants, it's not my business to get in her way no matter what I think about him. So I was honest. "Nah—it's not serious. I'll most likely be leaving at the end of month." And for some reason, saying that last part had every muscle in my body tensing.

His eyebrows had gone up in a look of anticipation that made me hate him more. "Really?" He smiled as he took a drink of his beer. "Cool. I guess I misjudged her."

And then I hated myself in that moment, too, because I felt like a disrespectful asshole for talking about Annie without her present. For throwing her to a shark all because I'm terrified to admit that holding her in my arms is the closest I've come to feeling truly happy in a very long time. I didn't even know I was lacking happiness. But now that I've realized it, I can pinpoint it with scary accuracy.

I don't know what this means for me now or where to go from here. Nowhere, maybe?

And that's why I've been hiding and avoiding her the last few days. I invented a bogus fan threat and told Annie I needed to stay parked outside of Amelia's studio while she worked, and that we couldn't go into town. Even Amelia didn't question it because this kind of thing happens from time to time. Our agency keeps a close watch on her known stalkers, and we get alerts when they are in a certain radius to her. Do I feel bad about adding potential unnecessary worry to Amelia's life by suggesting said stalker is nearby, no. Because I'm not the good guy—even though spending time with Annie makes me feel remarkably close to one.

Today we're headed into town, though. I couldn't keep up the pretenses of a potential threat much longer. Currently I'm escorting Amelia down the sidewalk toward The Pie Shop. The paparazzi sightings have been pretty minimal lately, and even now I can only spot one carrying a long lens on the opposite side of the square, but I spoke with my agency last night, and they predict a steep rise over the next two weeks leading up to the wedding.

I'm in full work mode when we're out in public, keeping an eye around us at all times for any potential threat. Zero percent of my brain is focused on Annie or what she's doing or what her days have been full of or why she hasn't even texted me at all. And that's when my foot hits a divot in the sidewalk and I trip, nearly busting my ass on the pavement before I catch myself.

"Holy crap, Will!" says Amelia, stretching out a hand to help me up. I don't accept her hand and instead pop up on my own with extra exuberance, brushing my slightly raw palms against my jeans. "Are you okay? I've never seen you trip before."

"I'm fine, let's keep going."

Amelia's mouth is open and she looks near laughing. "You're blushing. I've never seen you blush either! I didn't know you could be embarrassed." Now she is laughing and I hate her for it. Are we sure she isn't actually my annoying little sister after all?

"Come on, we don't need to stand here. There are paparazzi over there." Who most definitely caught my spectacular fall on camera and will publish it ASAP. Cool. Just the sort of image I want buzzed around the internet. Clumsy Blushing Bodyguard.

This is Annie's fault. Another reason I need to get my head out of the clouds. Relationships interfere. They're bad for people. They're—

"Where the hell is Annie?" I ask Amelia when we pass her flower shop and see a Closed sign on the door.

"She's sick."

"What? Since when?" My voice sounds a little too eager.

Amelia points to the little sticky note on the door. It's in Annie's handwriting. Only in a town this small would someone leave a note like this: "Out sick! Be back when I don't feel like I have plungers up my nose anymore."

I look sharply to Amelia. "How long has she been sick?"

"I think since the day after Hank's."

Shit. I had no idea. Now I feel terrible. This whole time she's been sick, and I haven't checked in on her at all. Wait. No. It's not my job to check up on her. I'm her dating coach, not her boyfriend or her nurse. If it were anyone else in the world, I'd never think twice about someone having a cold. In fact, I'd stay even farther away so I wouldn't catch anything. I'm just going to put her out of my mind and see her when I see her.

We walk in silence a few steps.

"Do you think she has a fever?"

Amelia chuckles to herself. "She did . . . but I don't know if she still does."

I tap my thumb on the side of my thigh and try to stay silent again. "I just don't understand why no one told me she was sick."

She pauses and turns to me with laughing eyes. "And I didn't realize I was supposed to give you updates on Annie's day-to-day health."

"Well, now you know. I always want to be kept in the loop about . . . everyone's health."

"Okay. Now I know," she says, with deep satisfaction. We walk a few more steps before Amelia breaks it. "Davey's son broke his arm last week."

"Who?" I frown down at her.

"You know. Little Charlie?"

"No."

"And Mabel said she had a tickle in her throat the other day. I wonder if she's catching what Annie has."

I breathe deeply to counteract my annoyance. I see what she's doing.

"Oh—and I heard Gemma is going to have to have surgery for some of her bunions later this month!"

"Amelia."

"What!" She laughs. "I thought you wanted to be kept in the loop about everyone's health. I'm just looping you in per your request!"

I groan. "I say this with all due respect as someone who works for you—please, shut up."

As soon as I say this, Noah steps out of The Pie Shop. "She doesn't know how to. I think it's physically impossible for her, actually." He grins at her and she steps into his arms, angling her face up to kiss him. Right out here in broad daylight where the paparazzi get their fill. These two don't care, though—they're in a lovesick bubble. So sick that Noah came outside to greet Amelia like an overeager golden retriever. That'll never be me.

Amelia looks at me over her shoulder once they're finished with their PDA. "Thanks for walking me in, Will. I'll be here all afternoon with Noah and then ride home with him. So you're off the clock for the rest of the day to go . . . wherever you like—and see . . . whoever you'd like to see."

Noah frowns lightly. "You're talking about Annie, right?"

She lightly pinches him in the side. "I was trying to be subtle."

"I love you, but there was nothing subtle about that. Leave him alone and come bug me instead," says Noah, pulling Amelia away as she tries to stare me into spilling my guts on her way into The Pie Shop.

Only when she's out of eyeshot do I turn around and take off jogging down to the market.

I set a box of tissues on the checkout counter, followed by a box of cold medicine, a few various types of hot tea, and some random produce; and then let my eyes trail over to the town petition, trying to stop me and Annie from dating. So far, it's looking grim. Three votes in favor (Mabel, Emily, and Madison) and over a hundred votes against. Why does that make my stomach sink?

I shake it off and look up into the most terrifying eyes I've ever seen: Harriet's. This woman is severe and calculating at all times. And she really hates me.

"Hmm . . . cold medicine," she says in an odd way.

I nod and fish my wallet out of my back pocket as she begins scanning everything besides the cold medicine.

Suddenly a scratchy voice sounds from the right of my shoulder. "A lot of cold and flu products there, William. Feeling under the weather?" Mabel. She's everywhere.

"Uh—no, ma'am."

"Then why do you need all this cold medicine, hmm?" says Harriet, lifting her brows to her hairline. "Are you planning to make drugs with them?"

I frown at the single box of Tylenol Cold + Flu Severe. "I think you're thinking of the medicine that contains pseudoephedrine."

Her eyes narrow on me, down to my tattoos and back up to my face. "You would know, wouldn't you?"

This makes me laugh. Yes, my sleeve of intricate flowers and foliage paired with the butterfly really falls into the usual profiling for meth addicts. I wonder what this town, or the general public for that matter, would think if they found out I was the valedictorian of my graduating class. That I had scores so high and excelled at so many extracurricular activities (hello, science club) that I got into MIT. That I didn't even go on my first date until I graduated from high school and decided I was tired of living my life to perfection only for it to still not help anything.

I look back at my younger self and cringe remembering how I thought bringing home straight A's would help my parents fight less. That doing lots of extra chores around the house and taking care of my younger brother would remove some stress from them so maybe they'd actually enjoy being around each other. Yell less and smile more. Nope. Instead, I had zero fun in high school for nothing. The second I graduated, I hit a wall. I couldn't bring myself to go somewhere and continue to work for something I didn't care about. That's when I joined the military.

"Harriet, what are you thinking? You're being suspicious about the wrong thing," says Mabel, pushing her way up beside me to put her hands on her hips. "The man isn't trying to make drugs, you ding-dong. He's trying to make love."

"I'm sorry—what?" I ask, but Mabel isn't paying attention to me anymore.

"Don't call me a ding-dong, you old kook. And that's even worse if he's trying to make love to a box of medicine."

I shake my head. "No—I can assure you both, I'm not—"

"Gross, Harriet. Not to the box. To Annie! The woman he's dating. He's clearly buying all this shit to take care of her because he loves her."

"No. Again, I don't—"

"That true?" Harriet looks up at me—trying to decide if I'm going to do unspeakable things to this box of cold medicine or not. I can't decide whether she thinks that's better or worse than doing it with Annie instead. "Are you taking all of this to our Annie?"

I sigh, really wishing I didn't have to bring the whole damn town into this poorly thought-out decision to take care of my fake girlfriend. "Yes. It's all for Annie."

She hums as her lips purse tightly together. "I don't really take you for a nurturer."

"You and me both. But here we are," I tell her in a rare moment of vulnerability.

"Just a minute, William," says Mabel, disappearing into an aisle before returning with an armful of ingredients and setting them on the counter with a firm nod. "I'm going to teach you how to make her favorite soup. It'll cheer her right up and get you a few extra brownie points."

Do I want brownie points?

Dammit, I do.

I thank Mabel with a smile and then turn back to Harriet. My smile falls. I nearly jump from the stern look in her eyes. Like she's slowly extracting my soul and weighing it. Silently, Harriet comes to some sort of conclusion about me, and then grabs the box of cold medicine and begins scanning.

Bizarrely, I find myself feeling relieved by that. Maybe even a little proud.

There's clearly something in the water of this damn town.

CHAPTER TWENTY-EIGHT

Annie

O kay, Annie. You can do it. You can get your booty off the floor and get to your doctor's appointment.

This is what I get for needing water. I thought by now I had trained my body to not need it anymore—to live on a strict coffee-only diet—but no. The little weasel decided to defy me and demand rehydration.

After drinking my obligatory sip of water, I thought I just needed a little rest, so I sat down on the floor in the kitchen, and then that turned into lying on the floor of the kitchen, and now here I am . . . thirty minutes later, still lying here, head pounding, ears feeling like someone took a baseball bat to them, and nose so stuffy it's possible I'll never breathe through my nostrils again.

My sisters left for their Mexico trip yesterday, and now I'm wondering if this is where I'll die and how my sisters will find me when they come home glowing and suntanned from the beach. They'll hover over my body and laugh that I died wearing banana-print underwear and matching tank top. But it's not my fault that I can't sleep in PJ bottoms, and it was too hard to bend over and pull them on before walking into the kitchen because my body has no energy left from expending it all trying to breathe.

But I have to get up. Must get up. I have a date tomorrow with Brandon—the guy from the flower shop. I vetted him on Instagram, and then we texted a few times and set up a date for Saturday, which is tomorrow. So far, I don't feel exuberant sparks when we talk, but I'm sure that'll come later. *No need to worry, Annie.* Earlier, I managed to call Dr. Mackey and get an appointment for this afternoon, so maybe she could prescribe something to get me better before the date—but how in the chicken potpie am I going to get there?

At this moment, there's a knock on my door. I don't answer it because I'm only 50 percent conscious. I think it might actually be a burglar because I heard the doorknob jiggle, followed by its opening. Good. I'll ask him for a ride to the doctor.

"Annie?" A voice hovers over me, and I cringe because I know that voice, and I also know that I'm pantsless. I hear a *thunk* as he drops to his knees. "Shit, Annie. Talk to me—are you okay?"

"Will? Are you kidding me?" I crack my eyes open to find the world's most attractive man kneeling down beside me, looking relieved that I'm not dead. That's sweet.

I know I should feel upset to see him without my pants (especially because I know he's been avoiding me since that misinterpreted kiss at Hank's the other night), but instead, I feel a deep sense of peace. "I wasn't trying to make him jealous, you know," I say, because I've been dying to tell him the truth for days. But I didn't want to do it over the phone.

"Shh—it's fine, Annie."

He pushes my hair back and I catch his wrist. "It's not fine. It's important to me that you know it wasn't a game."

Will takes in a soft deep breath and then nods. "Okay."

I smile—feeling a hundred pounds lighter now that that's off my chest and close my eyes again. "Okay, now leave. You're not supposed to see me like this."

"Like what? Pantsless? Wearing underwear printed with little yellow banana characters on them?" he asks with a crooked grin. "Cute. They match your PJs."

I groan and toss my arm over my eyes. "Leave me to die."

"That's one option. But then who would service everyone's flower needs in town?"

"The keys are in my purse. The shop is yours now. Please don't give anyone ugly carnation bouquets."

A low rumbly laugh sounds from his chest, and all I want is to press my face to it and feel the vibrations against my cheek. "I don't love flowers as much as you."

"Says the man who has them tattooed on his skin for eternity."

"Good to know you still have your sense of humor." I feel his hand rest over my forehead and he hisses. "Geez, you're burning up. Have you taken anything lately?"

"No. I can't move. My body doesn't work anymore."

Will's hand brushes affectionately over my hairline, pushing my sweaty hair away from my face. "Why didn't you call me to come take care of you? Or Noah?"

I grimace. "And risk getting any of you sick? No way. I'll be fine. I have a doctor's appointment in an hour."

"Good. But how do you plan on getting there?"

"I'll hitch a ride on the back of a turtle."

"Very practical," he says with the backs of his fingers lingering against my neck. "Let's get you off the floor, sunshine."

Sunshine. Am I hallucinating or did Will just call me by the sweetest name my ears have ever heard?

Will's strong arms scoop under my bare thighs and back, lifting me off the floor and carrying me to my room, where I'm deposited gently on the bed. I'm immensely grateful for the gently part because my head feels like it's going to explode. I would be able to appreciate all of this tenderness so much more if I wasn't near death. Unfortunately.

I hear Will shuffle around through my closet for a minute and then return to my feet. "Annie, I'm going to slide these pants on you so I can take you to the doctor, okay? Can you give me a sign of life that it's all right for me to help like this?"

I grunt an affirmative, and then Will gently tugs my feet and legs into my PJ bottoms. He slides them all the way up my body until they're sitting below my hips. I use the last of my strength to lift my butt so he can slide them the rest of the way. The strange thing is, I'm the most modest person you'll ever meet, but I don't feel the least embarrassed that he's seeing me half naked. I trust him in a way I shouldn't. In a way that I know is just going to hurt me later when he reminds me he's not the relationship type. That he hates marriage. That he's absolutely not returning the feelings I've caught.

The sun is down and I'm feeling more like myself and a little less like a walking corpse. Will took me to the doctor, where I was diagnosed with a sinus and double ear infection. After bringing me back home and tucking me into bed, he went to the pharmacy and picked up my antibiotics. I took them and then slept for the entire day, thinking I'd wake up to a lonely house again, but instead, I leave my room to find Will in my kitchen . . . cooking.

"What are you doing?" I croak out—immediately reprimanded by my seriously dry sore throat.

He frowns lightly and comes around the kitchen island to put his hand on my forehead again. "Seems like your fever broke. That's good. Medicine must be working."

I lightly push his hand away because all I want to do is lean into it. "Will, what are you still doing here?"

"Making dinner." He turns back to the pot he was stirring. It smells good enough to rival one of Maddie's soups. "You should go sit down. I'll bring you a bowl in a few minutes."

I want to cry. My usually well-guarded feelings are sitting on the top of my skin, exposed and raw. "No. I mean what are you still doing here? As in . . . you shouldn't still be here."

"Why not?"

"Because . . . because!"

"You don't say?"

I slump and wrap my arms around myself for extra comfort and stability, because, yes, the medicine is working, but I still feel like a bus ran over me. I can't tell Will that he shouldn't be here because we've kissed three times and they were all so good that I really think I'm going to need a fourth. Or even worse, that I want him to stay and talk and snuggle and laugh with me all night.

After Hank's, I told myself I was going to take a step back from Will because if we continued on that trajectory we were on, it would spell disaster and heartache for me. So no texting. No potential run-ins. No practice anythings until I could wipe the feel of his lips from my brain and his smile from my heart because I'm starting to severely doubt my ability to keep Will in the casual category, where he wants to belong. And now here he is, making everything more complicated with soup.

"You'll catch my cold. You need to go."

He narrows his eyes while looking around the countertops. "Do you have any pepper around here?" His butterfly flutters all around the kitchen.

"You should be at work."

"I looked in the spice cabinet, but it's not there."

"I found antennae growing out of my head."

"And the salt for that matter. They're both gone."

I sigh and open the cabinet above the stove and pull out the salt and pepper shakers. "Maddie says they're a married couple and deserve the privacy of their own house. And you're not listening to me."

Will smirks, gently taking the spices from my hands. "I have a very strong immune system. Amelia gave me the day off. And you'll look very cute with antennae."

"Willington . . ."

"Annie." His happy-go-lucky demeanor melts into something serious. Unguarded. He puts his hands on the sides of my arms and then slides them down to my fingers. "Please. Just let me be here. I don't know why, but I can't be anywhere else. I tried but my feet keep bringing me back here to your door." He pauses, looks to the soup and then to me. "This . . . isn't something I would normally do, but I just need to take care of you. Please let me."

Well. With a response like that, how can I say no? What's another little fracture to my heart? I'll go back to building boundaries tomorrow by going on my date with my potential perfect soulmate, and everything will be fine. "The bowls are in the cupboard to the right. And you better put that paring knife back in the same place you found it, or Maddie will have your neck when she gets home."

He releases a breath, lets go of my hands, and smiles. "Got it. Completely rearrange the kitchen drawers before Maddie gets back. Now go sit down before you decide to camp out on the floor again."

I do as I'm told, taking a big fuzzy blanket from an oversize basket beside the couch and wrapping it around my shoulders. I sit down, laying my legs out across the cushions, resting my face against the back so I can peer at Will over the top. His shoulders work as he ladles out the soup, and I wonder if I can blame it on my sickness if I ask him to remove his shirt while cooking.

I lose the nerve, and Will brings a steaming bowl over to me on the couch. He sets it on the coffee table and then takes the seat at my feet, lifting them up and pulling them into his lap. I blink, stunned at his easygoing physical touch. Tactile. He's just tactile.

"Will?"

"Hmm?"

"Are you this affectionate with everyone?" I ask, nodding to where his hands are now resting over my shins.

"Pretty much," he says, hesitating before bringing his blue-gray eyes up to meet mine.

I'm instantly both disappointed and jealous. There's no reason I should have hoped he was only like this with me—and yet here I am. A little sad. I blame the cold and the fact that I'm only like this with him.

Will frowns. "That's not what you wanted to hear?"

I nuzzle the side of my face against the overstuffed pillow we keep on the couch. "I don't know what I want to hear. I'm sick. It's messing with my head. And you're nurturing me, which is catnip for softies like me."

The right side of his mouth rises in a grin. "You're not normally affectionate, are you?"

"I wouldn't say I'm not affectionate. I've just never really had anyone to be affectionate with. I think I must accidentally put out an invisible force field that tells people I don't want to be touched. And it feels too awkward to all of a sudden start after all this time."

Will looks down at my bare feet and then gently begins rubbing over my arches and up my calf. It feels so good I want to cry. All of the muscles in my body have been cramping from dehydration today. And Will's hot hands are exactly the thing they need to relax. Unfortunately, it's also working in the opposite way—winding my body up into a tight coil.

"You can be affectionate with me. I won't read into it," he says casually, like he didn't just hand me keys to a golden palace. Because the truth is, I love physical touch. Crave it more than I want to admit. But my shyness and social anxiety often keep me from reaching out for it first. I wait for other people to initiate, and sometimes that leaves me waiting forever.

I force my tone to sound calm and not at all excited by this all-access pass to Snuggle Town. "Right. Because you're my practice person. I can practice initiating snuggles."

"Exactly." He looks up at me.

"Like Fred and Audrey before the ending."

He frowns. "Now you lost me."

I wave him off. "Don't worry about it."

We sit in tense silence for several minutes before Will breaks it by leaning over and gently moving the bowl of soup from the table to my lap. "It's cooled off by now. You need to eat a few bites if you can. The doctor said hot broth is good for your throat."

I'm not at all surprised to find out Will is caring and attentive. But I think he is . . .

The first sip is salt and butter and carrots. Chicken soup—my favorite. Will came to my house, put pajamas on me, took me to the doctor, and made me chicken soup. *Don't you dare read too much into that, heart.*

My heart snootily pushes a pair of glasses up the bridge of its nose. *He may be affectionate by nature, but he doesn't normally do this with other women,* it reminds me unhelpfully. I kick my heart in the shins.

"It's really good, thank you."

"It's Mabel's recipe. She cornered me in the market and forced ingredients into my hands after she learned I was headed over here. She also followed me out to the car and wrote the entire recipe on the back of the grocery receipt, which was good because I've never made soup before and it definitely would have ended up tasting more like cat pee than anything."

I laugh and then wince when my ears, head, and throat all scream. I set down the soup and then rub my temples to ease some of the never-ending pressure. It's quite possible that a pathetic whine also escapes my mouth.

"Come here," Will says, not waiting for my response before he sets my feet on the ground and starts adjusting me around. He puts a pillow in his lap and then eases my head down on it. And then he gently runs his fingers over my scalp and my neck in soft massaging strokes. His hands are warm and secure as he moves them over me—but it's more the fact that he seems to care so much that is making my heart squirm.

"Were your parents affectionate too? Is that where you got it from?"

His fingers pause in my hair, and I think maybe I scared him off. There's going to be a Will-shaped hole in my front door any minute now.

"Only as affectionate as wolves can be, you know?" he says, trying for levity and coming up short.

I look up at him. "No more jokes. Please tell me."

He sighs and his hands move through my hair again. "I don't like talking about my childhood, Annie. In fact, I've worked really hard to block it out."

"I get it. And if you really don't want to, I'll drop it. But if there is some part of you that wants to tell me, I promise to be a good listener and not bring it up ever again if you don't want me to."

A soft smile touches the corner of his mouth. "No one would ever accuse you of not being a good listener. In fact, I think you're made to listen too much."

I reach up and pinch the fabric of his soft T-shirt near his chest and tug lightly. "Tell me. Come on, I have a sick card. Let me use it."

Will opens his palm faceup. "Let me see it."

I sigh dramatically and pretend to pull it out of my pajama bottoms. I slap it against his palm. Will holds it up to the light for inspection and then takes an imaginary hole punch and makes a clamping sound with his mouth. He hands the card back. "Yours is only a day pass. Expires at midnight."

"Deal."

He casts his eyes to the ceiling like he's looking for inspiration on where to begin. "Uh—okay, well. In a nutshell, I grew up in a dysfunctional home. There was a lot of fighting and cheating happening between my parents. My dad slept on my floor a lot and openly spilled their baggage when he really should have shut the hell up about it." Will's tone is hard as granite on that last sentence, and before I realize what I'm doing, I roll over to face his abdomen. Maybe it's because he gave me permission, maybe it's because something about me feels free with Will—I don't know—but I don't hesitate before looping my arms around him.

He doesn't stop brushing his fingers through my hair and across my neck. Doesn't make me feel like this is anything out of the ordinary. My arms around him feel as natural as breathing.

"Go on," I urge.

"If you saw me back then—in high school and before—you wouldn't recognize me," he says with a sad sort of smile. "I wore polo shirts, Annie. And glasses. And I never socialized, ever."

"Wait . . ." I squint up at him. "Do you ever wear glasses now?"

"Only at night after I take my contacts out."

My ovaries quake at this news. It's too much to handle, so I swallow, make a noncommittal *hmm* sound, and then wait for him to continue.

"I busted my ass all through school because I thought"—he adds one short laugh—"I thought it would help. I hoped that if I could be the perfect son for them, if I could help take care of my brother and make sure that we never added additional stress, then . . ."

"Then they'd be happy."

"Exactly."

Our eyes connect and his words resonate somewhere deep inside me. "I relate. Although in a slightly different way. Because for me, it was that I was trying to keep life stress-free for my grieving siblings." My gaze moves to Will's shirt as I feel painful tugs of my past against my heart. I'm not sure I've ever said that out loud before—or even realized that it was true. But now I feel almost outside of myself, as I watch a younger Annie try to pick up the pieces for her siblings. Cutting her hands in the process and never telling anyone she's bleeding.

I don't realize I'm frowning until I feel Will's thumb brush against my brows, relaxing them.

"It sounds like we both put our needs in the back seat during critical times in our lives."

And yet we're both seeking different paths to soothe ourselves. He doesn't want anything to do with relationships, and I want the ultimate one.

I blink back up at him. "So did it work? Did your perfection pay off?"

His jaw flexes against memories. "No," he says quietly. "I graduated as valedictorian and got into MIT, but Dale and Nina were still toxic, surprise, surprise. They couldn't do anything right in each other's eyes, and as a result, Ethan and I couldn't do anything right either. I think they deeply resented their lives. So to answer your question, no, they were not affectionate."

"I'm sorry, Will. You didn't deserve that from them."

"Yeah . . . well, it all worked out, so it's fine. After my graduation ceremony, I came home, and my mom was crying because my dad found out she'd cheated again, and then"—he frowns at the wall—"she screamed at me for not taking out the damn trash that morning. So I snapped. I packed a bag and I left. I just couldn't do it anymore. Instead, I stayed in a hotel for a week and then joined the military. I felt awful for leaving my brother behind like that, but I needed to get out, and the Air Force was giving away free T-shirts outside the grocery store." He smiles self-deprecatingly.

"Wow." I try to process everything he just said, not fully being able to imagine that kind of life. And to be honest, if I were in Will's shoes, I can't say I would feel differently about relationships either. It would be difficult to jump into one when he's seen so much pain around the one relationship that was supposed to be stable for him.

"The really sad part is, my parents are doing better now, because after my brother and I were out of the house, they finally got a divorce. They said they had always stayed together for us—and we should be grateful they gave us that time as a complete family unit. How messed up is that?"

"That's rough. Do you ever see them now?"

"Occasionally, but not often. I don't have any desire to hang out with them for a full weekend and pretend that my childhood didn't nearly destroy me. And I'm not brave enough to actually fight with them over it either. So I just avoid them."

"I don't blame you, Will. I wouldn't want to either." My eyes trace the lines of his face, and I feel a protective anger rise up toward anyone who would ever dare treat him like he wasn't the most wonderful person in the world. Like he wasn't precious and valuable. "How long were you in the military?"

"Six years active duty, two in the reserves. I served as a Security Forces specialist."

"You didn't like it?"

He shrugs lightly. "Sort of. It was mentally and physically drain-ing, and it left very little room for living life outside of it. I was ready for something different by the end. I have a friend who intro-duced me to the agency I'm with now, and I started training with them while I was in the reserves. The rest is history. I already had plenty of hand-to-hand combat training from my military career, but with the agency I was also trained in evasive driving and other various weaponry courses."

"Does that mean you carry a gun?"

"Not to guard celebrities. Mainly when protecting politicians or people with a high-threat level. You have to have clearance for it."

Suddenly I think of Will in one of those high-threat-level jobs and having to use a weapon or be faced with someone else using one, and my arms instinctively tighten around him. "Have you ever regretted not going to MIT and choosing a different career path?"

There's a loaded pause that I don't miss. "I don't think I like the word *regret*. Every choice I've made has been valuable in some way or other. And the fact is, if I had gone to MIT back then, I proba-bly would have kept striving for academic perfection and returning home when I shouldn't. But the military forced me to get that space I needed—if that makes sense. It was somewhere my parents and their drama couldn't easily reach me."

My eyes drop to his arm. His flowers. I trace my finger over the petals. "So you were hiding in the tree from your parents."

"Yes," he says as his fingers trail down my neck and to the exposed skin where my pajama top has gaped open over my shoul-der. His touch grazes my book tattoo and I feel the smile in his fingertip. "So does that answer all your questions, Miss Inquisi-tive?"

"Not yet."

He groans.

"Tell me about your brother. What's he like? Is he antirelationship too?"

"My brother used to feel like I do. Against the entire idea of marriage and like we're better off without it . . . until recently."

"What happened recently?"

"He met someone and just got engaged." He pauses, and we only stare at each other for a minute—unspoken thoughts and feelings running like currents through the air. "I've been avoiding his calls because I can't bring myself to tell him I'm happy for him. Does that make me the shittiest brother in the world?"

"No. I think it means you have a lot of hurt still, and I'm willing to bet he probably understands."

Will grins and pushes a piece of my hair back from my face. "You see too much good in me, Annie. There's a very real possibility, you know, that I am just a very selfish asshole who uses women and lives according to my own whims just because I like life better that way."

I hum lightly and close my eyes, feeling exhaustion press over me again. "That's what you'd like me and everyone else to think."

Suddenly I feel Will's thumb trace my lower lip. "It's time to take off those rose-colored glasses, sunshine."

I tuck my chin and snuggle in closer to his stomach because he gave me permission and also because it feels so nice to do this. To just be close to someone and gain the affection I've been craving for so long without any pressure or fear of him not being the right one for me. "Not a chance. I love how pretty the world looks with them. You're a good guy, Will—I really hope you know that."

"Harriet would disagree. She thought I was making meth with your cold medicine."

I begin to doze in this lazy comfort. "It's the tattoos. She's always hated them. You should have seen how mad she got when she found out that Noah has a tattoo. Wouldn't let him buy anything besides vegetables from the market for a week."

"And what do you think about my tattoos now that you've really seen them?" he says, running the back of his knuckles against my jaw and hair. I've never been more comfortable with anyone in my entire life.

"I think they're not nearly as interesting as the man they're on. And that I've never felt safer with anyone than I do with you."

I feel his breath against my face as he lets out a deep sigh. "Annie. What are we doing?" he asks more to himself than me.

I don't answer. Instead, I slip into a deep sleep, and wake up hours later in the middle of the night, curled up next to Will's side in my bed. He didn't leave. And I'm terrified when I realize I hope he never does.

CHAPTER TWENTY-NINE

Will

"You're so freaked-out to wake up with me again," Annie says, eyeing me when I thought she was sleeping. I've been awake, staring at the ceiling for the last twenty minutes and reevaluating all of my life choices. And the text message I read when I first woke up.

"A little, yeah."

"You should be. I already called the pastor, and he's on his way to marry us immediately." Even though I know she's joking, my stomach dips and tightens. Unfortunately, not out of fear.

Annie sits up, hair cascading down over her shoulder, and props her chin on my chest. "Would it help if I tell you I'm not after you?" Her voice is still hoarse and her nose is stuffy, but she sounds much better than yesterday. I want to make her tea with honey.

I frown—and lie. "Yes. Is that true? Because last night felt . . . meaningful between us, and meaningful scares the shit out of me."

"I know."

"And then I slept over here again even though I have a very strict no-sleeping-over policy—and I'm spiraling out."

Her full pink lips curve into a delicate smile. Damn, she's gorgeous. Even puffy eyed and a little bloodshot. "I think what happened to us last night was friendship, which also might freak you out."

"It absolutely does."

"Why?"

I make a *tsk* sound. "Your card expired at midnight."

Annie is undeterred. "Do you really not have friends, Will?"

I sigh and turn my eyes back up to the ceiling. She's got me pinned here. I'm not getting away without telling her the whole truth about me. "My job keeps me busy. There's not a lot of time for friends."

"Which is intentional," she says putting a spotlight on my face. I knew I told this woman too much about me last night. Now she knows all of my weak points.

I cover her hand resting on my chest with my own. "Yeah. It is." I pause and she just waits. "After basically raising myself as well as my brother, when I left home and found some freedom, I decided I was done living for other people. I was going to be selfish for a while and enjoy the hell out of it. No relationships. No one to put huge expectations on me, and I can never be let down by someone if I never let them in in the first place. This job has given me the perfect excuse to stay busy and happy."

Annie scrunches her nose. "And now here you are. In my bed."

She adds that last sentence because she knows that this is a severe deviation from my plan. Intimacy of this kind is never something I've wanted . . . until now.

Annie rolls away from me back to her pillow, and we both stare at the ceiling. "Annie, the truth is, I really want to close myself off from you. But I also find myself wanting to tell you everything. What spell have you cast over me?"

She laughs and slides those beautiful blue eyes to me, peeking at me from the corners. "Do you have feelings for me, Will?"

I bark a laugh. "Annie. You can't just ask a person that. That's against the rules."

"Why?"

"Because . . . we're supposed to keep everything hidden and angsty. Keep each other guessing and miserable. That's just the way it works."

Her lips curve, and she slides her hand over the covers to gently link our fingers together. "Do you like me, Will?"

I hold her gaze and squeeze her fingers as her words tug the truth from me like they always do. "Yeah, I do, Annie. Do you like me?"

"Yeah. Against my better judgment."

I laugh fully at this and then scrape my free hand over my face. "It's why you need to run far away from me. Kick me out. Board up your windows. Lock your doors. I've got so much baggage, Annie . . . I'm not sure I'd be any good for you. Or that I'll ever be the marriage type."

She adjusts, rolling onto her side but not letting go of my hand. "I can handle myself, thank you." She grins slightly and my entire chest aches. "I'm not living in a fantasy world over here. You and I are two people who caught feelings but were never supposed to. Our lives are on different tracks that somehow managed to accidentally intersect along the way."

"So what do we do now?"

"We pine," she says dramatically but with a hint of amusement touching the corner of her mouth. "We stay friends."

"Friends."

"That's the only option for people who want different things, isn't it? So we'll be friends, and pine for a while, and then one day I'll be old and married with a slew of grandchildren here in Kentucky and you'll be a pirate on a ship somewhere in the Bahamas with a tiny man bun."

"Oh no," I say gravely. "You love pirates. Are you going to be longing for me while you're lying next to your very upstanding old husband?"

She nods. "Sadly, yes. But not as much as you'll be longing for the woman you left behind."

How is honesty so easy between us? Too easy.

"Either way," Annie says, sitting up and swinging her legs over the side of the bed, "you're off the matrimonial hook, Wolf Boy. And I have to go pee—don't listen," Annie says before disappearing into her bathroom and closing the door like we'd just discussed what's for dinner rather than admitted feelings.

So . . . good. Yeah. I'm off the hook. I should feel a great relief. Any second now the Great Relief will be kicking in. It's not. I don't feel relief, I feel frustrated.

I'm thinking with my emotions too much, that's the problem. I need to be logical. And logically, I have a career that will take me away from Rome no matter what. Logically, I've been happy living this way since I was eighteen. These feelings are just passing unexpected speed bumps on my open road of freedom. So what I need to do is ignore them and continue on with my plan. Have fun with Annie and then say goodbye with a clean break and no hard feelings when I leave. Even she thinks this is the best decision.

Yes. It's good. This is good.

A minute later, Annie surfaces from the bathroom and comes back to bed, not hesitating even a second before curling up next to me. "Do you want some coffee?"

I take in her long blonde hair, her soft blue eyes, and the curve of her mouth, and I throw all of my plans out the window and consider doing the one thing that scares the hell out of me: staying. Forget the open road of freedom. I think I have everything I could ever need in my arms.

But then Annie's phone vibrates on the bedside table. I grab it for her, but the screen lights up and I see the name: Brandon Larsdale (flower shop guy).

Wordlessly I hand it to Annie, and I don't even realize I'm hoping this guy is nothing but a flower supplier until she opens the text, not even trying to hide the screen from me at all, and I see the words: "Are we still on for our date this afternoon?"

So, not a flower supplier.

"You . . . have a date?" I ask her, frowning and hating how pathetic I sound asking it.

"Yeah. Kind of. I meant to tell you, but . . . I couldn't find the right time." She looks up at me. "I'm sorry. I should have told you sooner."

My stomach sinks. Annie has a date. "No, that's . . . totally fine . . . great even." I sit up and throw my legs over the edge of the bed.

"Will . . ." Annie says in a tender tone.

I give her a quick smile over my shoulder to try to keep her from feeling my weirdness. "It's all good, Annie. Really. This is the right thing. We just said that we're on different tracks and this is the exact course yours is supposed to take," I say, focusing extra hard on sounding normal and not like I'm filled with the jealousy of a thousand suns. Like I want to find this guy and shove him against the wall with my fist and warn him not to touch Annie or he'll die.

I go into the bathroom and splash water on my face and prepare to finger brush my teeth just so I can get a grip. She's got a date. Annie has a date this afternoon. With a guy. A guy named Brandon. A guy named Brandon is going to take Annie on a date.

Not sure why I'm listing all of these facts off like they belong on a wall with little red strings connecting all the clues. My behavior right now is ridiculous. Pathetic. It's not as if I didn't see this coming. It's literally what we've been working toward.

She told me up front her goal was to find her soulmate. Oh God, what if this Brandon guy is her soulmate? He gets to be her soulmate and I'm just her practice person.

I squeeze the toothpaste container too hard and the paste rockets across the bathroom onto the wall.

Annie enters the bathroom at that exact moment and wordlessly wets a washrag and wipes away the bright-colored toothpaste. I have to scrape my hands over my face because she looks so authentically beautiful and calm, and that only serves to make my nerves zing more frantically. Why am I acting like this? I'm never jealous. I never care if a woman I've been seeing goes out with another man.

I care if Annie does.

"Wilton," she says softly, taking my shoulders and angling me toward her. "Let's talk."

"We don't have to." I manage not to sound immature somehow. But I want her to know that she doesn't owe me any sort of explanation. She is her own woman and I am . . . just her friend.

"You came over and made me soup. And took care of me. And snuggled me. And told me you like me. And then saw a text that I'm going out with another guy. Of course I need to tell you what's going on."

"We're not together for real, so . . . it's all good. You don't owe me anything." See? This is why. This right here is one of the reasons I don't want marriage or a relationship. You can never predict what a woman's next move will be or when she'll do something that hurts like hell.

Annie seems determined to make me look at her. She takes my jaws in her hands. "But do you want to know who that was?"

"Is he your date for today?"

"Yes."

"Then I think I'm caught up."

She drops her hands away but continues to skewer me with her relentless gaze. "He's a guy who came into the flower shop last week while you were out of town. He's a vet and just moved into the town next to ours." She pauses. "We hit it off and he asked for my number. I told him up front that I wasn't looking for anything casual right now, and he said he feels the same, so I gave it to him because—wasn't that the goal the whole time? I want to get married. I want a family. I need to do this, Will. You don't understand, but I have to get married. I have this gaping hole in my heart, and I can't close it up. This is the only thing left to try to close it even though I'm pretty sure it's not going to work, and you're going to leave, and I'll get married, and it'll still be in there just empty and hurting." She's starting to cry.

I put my hands on the outsides of her arms tenderly. "It's really okay, Annie. You don't have to explain. I understand. You've got to do this for you."

She continues, though. "Brandon and I have been texting a little this week, and he asked me out for today. I didn't tell you even though I've wanted to because I was scared it would push you away, and, selfishly, I don't want you to go away yet."

I breathe out as I gently grip her biceps and tug her a little closer. "If there's anything I understand fully, Annie, it's acting out of selfish need."

She gives a sad smile. A brave smile. "He seems nice, though. We have the same goals. I had to say yes, Will. There was no reason for me not to."

I can't even get upset at that—because she's right. I'm not a reason. I told her up front I'd never be a reason. Whatever strange connection we have is a blip on the timeline of our lives. An interlude we'll look back on fondly. And soon, hopefully, I'll get back to real life, and Rome and Annie and everyone in this absurd town will only be memories.

I force a smile that I don't feel at all. "I'm happy for you, Annie. Really. And this is great timing, actually, because I've had something I've needed to tell you too." I pause. "I'm leaving soon."

She frowns lightly. "What?"

"After the wedding." I try to say this as casually and unattached as possible. "Don't worry—you're not pushing me away. And it's not because of your date with Brandon." The lie slips out easily. "My boss approved my reassignment to Washington, D.C., and I accepted."

I have to look everywhere but her face. If I look into her eyes, she'll see the truth. Amelia called my boss yesterday and said she was okay to be reassigned a new EPA (which feels like suspicious timing), and so the text I read this morning confirmed I've been cleared to move on to a new job after the wedding.

The thing is, I haven't actually said yes yet. I had planned to respond to Liv and ask if I could have a few days to think about it because I might want to stay in Rome after all. But this—Annie's impending date—is exactly the kick in the ass I needed to remember that whatever is going on between us is fleeting. I shouldn't change my entire life plans for a person I only met a few weeks ago. I'm following my own advice to Ethan and pumping the brakes. Or . . . I guess a more accurate metaphor would be flooring the gas and getting out of here.

"But . . . Amelia doesn't want a different bodyguard."

"Executive protection agent," I say weakly. "And she told my boss she was okay with it. It's going to be hard to move on from . . . her, but it's time. I need a faster-paced life. I can't stay here any longer or . . ." Or I'll start wanting things that scare me. Or I'll contemplate doing the things I've promised I never would. "I'll get bored."

In the movies, this is where Annie would feel hurt. It was meant to wound. To cut us both so I'll stop having these damn feelings and to show her that I'm not the good guy she wants. I've got a messed-up past and a messed-up heart that I keep clenched tightly in my fist along with a string of women throughout the country who will attest to the fact that I'll never release it to anyone else.

But this is Annie. And she does nothing as anticipated.

Her smile tilts into one that's so damn close to pity that my teeth clench. No one—and I mean no one—has ever been able to read me. But Annie does. It's like she has the subtitles turned on for my brain, and she doesn't feel hurt. She feels sad for me that I'm standing here and lying to her.

She looks down and clears her throat. "Okay, well good. I'm happy for you, Will."

"And I'm happy for you."

We're all happy, happy people!

After a painful silence, I finally ask, "So where are you going on your date?"

She narrows her eyes. "Why are you asking?"

I pull an offended look. "What do you mean, why? I'm your dating coach. It's my job to know everything about your dating life. This has nothing to do with the"—I lean in and lower my voice like I'm sharing a huge secret—"feelings we talked about earlier. Those are officially going back in the box where they belong from here on out."

She laughs quietly. "Well, if you must know, we're going to his nephew's Little League game."

My eyebrows fly up. "Little League? For a first date?"

She shrugs. "He's a family man, apparently."

When I laugh, I sound like a villain. "How perfect. I guess he's looking for a wife to make him pot roast on the weekends too?"

"I hope not. I don't know how to make pot roast."

I hate him. Whoever he is.

But you know what? Brandon isn't here with Annie now. I am.

"So . . . do you think he'll kiss you today?"

Her eyes fly wide open. "I don't know. Maybe? Oh gosh. Do you think he'll try?"

I cross my arms and shrug. "I would kiss you on a first date."

Her eyes hold mine—and they glint. She's reading my mind again. She knows exactly what I'm doing and approves. "Well . . . maybe we could practice a first date kiss? You know, just so I'm not caught off guard."

"Sure. Right." I nod thoughtfully. "As your dating coach, it's my responsibility to make sure you're prepared for that kind of thing."

"That's what I was thinking."

I edge closer. "So how do you want to do this? Like . . . role-play it?"

"Okay."

"Okay," I repeat while my heart pounds. "Time in," I say, already pressing toward her.

She takes her fingers and presses them quickly to my lips to halt me. "Wait. I have a cold. I had a fever yesterday. I don't want you to catch it."

"Do you feel bad right now?"

"No, I feel a lot better today, but—"

"Then give me the damn cold, Annie," I say quietly next to her ear. I feel her shiver lightly, but I know it's not from a fever.

I slide my hands around her lower back, inching along the terrain I'm beginning to find familiar. I have this small divot memorized. The one right above her perfect ass. I know that if I splay my hand against it and press her to me, she'll gasp lightly and then melt into my arms. I do it now, and after hearing the soft gasp that I'd like to capture in a jar and keep sealed away for eternity so no one else has the pleasure of hearing it, I begin. "Picture this: Your date is coming to an end. You're sunburned from sitting for hours on the bleachers, and while standing next to your truck, he hands you a Capri Sun he snagged from Pam's postgame snacks cooler . . ."

Annie laughs and shoves my chest playfully. "Stop it! That is not how it's going to go!"

"Fine. I'll be serious." I make my face somber. "Annie . . . I had a great time with you watching children never hit a baseball for five and a half hours—"

"Useless! You're useless!"

We're both laughing and Annie is trying to tickle me, but instead, I scoop her up and carry her into her room to throw her on the bed. "Do you think there will be a bed at the baseball game?"

"Absolutely."

"Thought so." I hover over Annie and dip my head into her neck, running my lips across her skin. "Annie, thank you for the best first date of my life. Can we go out again?"

She sighs as I lightly lick the tender skin behind her ear. "I think that might be acceptable—yes."

"Wonderful. How about next weekend? I know of a bouncy castle going up for an eight-year-old's birthday." I slant my mouth over hers before she has time to give me any sharp retorts, and she matches me kiss for kiss. Her tongue slides against mine, and her hands scale up my back. I'm shaking from how much I'm holding back. How much I want to peel her clothes from her body and consume her completely. It would be so good. We would be so good together.

But Annie's not mine.

So I ease up and somehow manage to pull away from her—

taking in her sad expression when I do. I kiss her cheek and her temple and her forehead. "I should go."

Annie nods and sits up with me, following me out of her room and standing in the open front door as I walk out. Before I go, I can't help but look back at her one more time. "Have fun on your date, Annie." I pause. "Maybe he can take you out for some chicken nuggets afterward."

She groans and rolls her eyes. "Shutting the door now!"

"Do you want to borrow a dollar for a soda in case he forgets his Velcro wallet?"

Bam!

CHAPTER THIRTY

Annie

"Thanks for agreeing to come with me to my nephew's game," says Brandon. He's sitting beside me on one of the metal bleachers that (as predicted by Will) is so hot it's burning through the denim of my overalls. "I know it's not normal, but . . ." He laughs and shrugs good-naturedly. "Well, honestly, this will be very normal for me now that I'm back. I plan on being more involved with my family than I have been in the past."

Ten points in the family-man box.

"I think it's great. Are any of your other family members coming?" I ask, thankful my cold medicine is working and my nose doesn't sound like Mr. Snuffleupagus from *Sesame Street* anymore.

"No one other than my brother, Rob," he says, pointing toward the middle-aged man standing on the field with his hands on his hips. "He coaches the team. And then my sister-in-law would normally be here, too, but she just had their baby two weeks ago, so she's staying home today."

Right. The one he bought flowers for. It seems like this guy is thoughtful in a big way. All the points for that.

"Do you have any other siblings in town?" I ask, while discreetly admiring his well-groomed beard and dark brown eyes. He's also wearing a team T-shirt, Little Grizzlies, and I find it incredibly endearing.

Brandon has comfy vibes written all over him. Potential dad vibes. Just like Emily and Madison told me I needed.

"Nah—it's just me and my brother. But our parents live in town too."

Wow. Another check mark. He has parents in his life. Which means I could have parents in my life, too, if we work out.

"I bet they are excited to have another grandchild," I say, feeling super proud of my small talk abilities today. This date is already proving completely different from my last one. I guess all the time I've been spending with Will has paid off. It's not even that we practiced specific things about dating all that much. It's more that I've learned over the last few weeks with him to trust myself and what I have to offer. He's been a safe place for me to . . .

Ugh! No, Annie, stop thinking about Will!

Brandon laughs a nice low laugh. "Oh, they are. And they're very eager for me to start adding some to the list as well. Which, I don't mind because I'm eager to start a family too," he says with an easy smile while looking out over the field. Not at all embarrassed that he just implied we'd get right to baby making if we work out. Funny how men can get away with saying things like that on a date and it's endearing, but when I did, I got left ten minutes into the date.

I suddenly jump when Brandon claps and yells, "Let's go, Hunter!"

He turns his face to me, and his smile only widens. It's such a nice smile I wait for my stomach to flip. *Go on, stomach, flip. Fine, a little roll then? Can I at least get a flutter? Listen . . . I'd settle for a twitch.*

Nothing. Dang it.

Oh, well. Not a problem. Long-term loving relationships are built on more than just flutters and stomach flips anyway, right? So even if I don't feel them now, it's totally fine. Tons of time for flipping later down the road. What I'm looking for is a partner. Not a roller coaster.

If only I hadn't just experienced a big stomach flip this morning, maybe this would be easier. Not only did Will make out with me until my bones felt like mush, but . . . he told me he has feelings for me. *Feelings*. And I told him that I have feelings for him. And now here I am on a date with someone else. It feels so wrong and backward and upside down. When two people declare their feelings, they get together, right?! That's how it happens. But of course I would fall for a man who doesn't believe in marriage. Who doesn't want a family. Who wants to remain as wild and free as a bird.

I knew I'd get feelings for him from the beginning, though, didn't I? I think something in me has known I was capable of loving him since the second I laid eyes on him.

But I would never in my wildest dreams want to try to change Will, and he doesn't want to try to change me. Neither one of us wants to ask the other to sacrifice anything. So our only options are to move on.

Digging into my mind for dating advice from He Who Shall Not Be Thought Of, I pull out a piece of memorized conversation. "So, Brandon . . . would you rather skydive or read a book?"

"Oh—good question." He makes a thinking noise and narrows one eye. "Read a book."

Ding, ding, ding. Right answer! *See stomach? This guy just keeps getting better and better.*

I angle excitedly toward him. "Me too! I love to read. What's your favorite genre?"

"Pretty much anything," he says, and then adds, "Well, not true. Anything besides romance."

Oh no.

I chuckle lightly to cover my despair. "Why not romance?"

He gives me a come-on look. "Because the whole genre just seems messed up. First, it sets unrealistic standards that no one can obtain, and, second, it's just . . . fluff. I'd rather read something that actually has substance, you know?"

Cue my internal crisis:

He hates romance.

But he loves his family!

But he just belittled an entire genre that I adore by calling it fluff.

But I've hidden my romance-loving ways for my entire adult life. What are a few more years?

Will's voice adds to the chaos in my head from when he read the romance book I gave him. *It was sexy as hell.* And there were a lot of profound moments too. Felt like free therapy. Ugh. That's not fair, though. I shouldn't compare Brandon and Will. They're two completely different men. As in . . . Brandon is turning out nothing like Will.

However, that thought is irrelevant because Will is leaving, and he doesn't plan to look back.

"What about you?" he asks. "What kind of books do you like to read?"

The sun seems to grow eight times hotter, if that's even possible. If you listen closely you can hear the sound of my sweat dripping down the back of my neck. "Oh, me? Well . . . I actually—"

Two figures suddenly catch the corner of my eye, trying to hop up onto the bleachers from the side, several rows behind us. Oh my gosh . . . this cannot be happening. What are they doing here?

"What's wrong?" Brandon asks, about to turn his head to look at the path of Will and Amelia, wearing baseball hats, sunglasses, and . . . is Amelia wearing a fake mustache?

I grab Brandon's jaw and tug it back in my direction. His eyes widen as I pretend to knock an imaginary bug from his jaw. "It was a bee. Didn't want you to get stung."

"A bee?" he asks, immediately standing. "I'm very allergic to bees." He's looking everywhere for the bee. Now I feel terrible.

"Oh—don't worry. It's gone! It flew under the bleachers."

"This one? Okay, we need to move, then, in case it has a nest. You okay if we scoot up a few rows?"

I cast a quick glance up and the only available seats are right next to Tweedle Nosy and Tweedle Mustache. Seriously, who does Amelia think she's fooling wearing a mustache? And it's not even stuck on that well. And Will . . . well, he's dressed normally and looks absolutely delicious in that hat, and that's why I can't sit by him.

"Oh, I don't think we need to. I'm sure the bee is—"

"I'm sorry, I know I seem overly paranoid here, but the thing is, I'd rather not have to use my Epi-Pen today if I don't have to."

And now I feel terrible that this man would ever think I was not worried about his safety. Or that having a deathly allergy is an inconvenience for me. "Oh my gosh, absolutely. Let's move."

"Great, thank you," he says, extending his hand for me to proceed him first.

When I turn and face Will, he immediately diverts his eyes and tries to hide himself behind the bill of his hat. He holds his hand up to tug the hat down farther over his eyes, and this makes me laugh. As if he didn't think he was distinct enough on his own, he's shielding himself with his tattooed arm. Nice.

I walk up the bleachers and stop just in front of Will. "Excuse me, sir, is this seat taken?"

Both guilty persons turn their eyes up to me and then to the man over my shoulder. "Of course! Have a seat there, young lady!" says

Amelia in the worst impression of a male country accent I've ever heard.

Will—the devil—bites his lips together to keep from laughing.

"Thank you," I say solemnly while taking the seat next to Will. Brandon takes the seat beside me and now we are one big awkward human sandwich. Should I just acknowledge that I know these two loons beside me and get it all out in the open? If I do, however, that might stir up a lot of questions. None of which I feel like answering.

Suddenly, Brandon's nephew steps up to bat, and Brandon shoots up from his seat clapping and shouting encouragements.

I take the opportunity to whip my head toward Will and Amelia. "What the helicopters are you two doing here?" I hiss.

"Just enjoying America's favorite pastime." If I could describe Will's expression in one word it would be *provoking*.

I shove my elbow into his ribs. "Don't you dare smile right now! You both need to go. Immediately. Amelia, you look ridiculous."

"Leave before I find out who wins the game? Never. We're not fair-weather fans," Will says way too over the top.

"Knock it off. And you," I say leaning toward Amelia. "Your mustache is falling off!"

She gasps and presses it back on with a grin. "It's pretty convincing, isn't it? It was a leftover from a Halloween party costume."

"No. You look suspicious and mildly alarming."

Will shrugs. "Told her not to wear it, but she insisted."

"You shouldn't have come at all! I don't need a bodyguard."

A smile touches his mouth. "Executive protection a—"

I hold up a menacing finger. "Don't you dare finish that sentence."

Brandon does the dad whistle through two fingers, and it's so loud I have to clutch my head. He finally sits back down when his nephew gets three strikes. He then leans around me to indulge in my worst nightmare: my date having a conversation with Will, the one man he'll never live up to. "Hi, I'm Brandon. And I guess you've already met Annie?"

I watch the moment Amelia slips back into character. It's painful.

She smiles so big her mustache unpeels in the right corner. "Hi there! M'name's Joe! And this here is my brother, Sam."

I watch in silent dismay as the two men's hands cross over me to join in a man shake. The sight of Will's butterfly hand clasping my date's very normal one makes me irrationally angry. I shouldn't be able to compare the two men so directly like this. It's not fair to Brandon. And when Will's eyes cut to me for the briefest of heated moments, I'm afraid that the thought *He licked my neck this morning* is projected onto my face. Will's invisible fingerprints all over my body are now glowing like a radioactive substance.

"Nice to meet you both," says Brandon.

"Likewise."

Brandon sits back and then leans into my side. "That's definitely a woman with a fake mustache, right?"

"It appears to be so, yes," I say, my gaze fixed forward, wishing I could drop the two people beside me into a black hole somewhere.

"I think moving to the country is going to take more getting used to than I expected."

"If it makes you feel better, I've lived here my whole life and I'm still not used to it."

He laughs. "Not sure it does."

Will crosses his arms, and his knuckles brush the back of my arm. My rude, *rude* stomach barrel-rolls. I want to glare at Will.

A conversation Amelia is having with the woman in front of her suddenly grabs my attention. "I've never seen you at these games before. Who did you say you were here to see play?" says the woman decked out in Little Grizzlies gear.

"Never seen us, huh? Strange. We're here every weekend to cheer on little Tommy."

"Timmy," Will corrects.

"Right. Little Timmy. Poor thing never was very good at baseball, but I tell him to keep on trying, just like his aunt!"

"Uncle," Will says.

"Uncle, right. Oh look, there he is getting up to bat!" Amelia stands up, her jeans (that is, Noah's jeans) swallowing her whole, and yells, "Go, Timmy!"

"That's my son . . . Matthew," says the woman.

Amelia pretends to squint heavily. "Well shit. That's what I get for leaving my glasses in the car. Brother, can you see Timmy?"

"No, brother, I cannot," Will says deadpan, and I want to push them both off the back of these stands.

Brandon, somehow oblivious to the Two Stooges scene happening beside me, asks, "How long have you owned your flower shop?"

Oh no, flower shop questions. This is what got me in trouble on my last date. However, I'm Annie 2.0, so I'm prepared for this. I crack my mental knuckles and prepare to wow him with a flourishing answer. "Four years."

Yep, wowed him.

Will bumps my arm intentionally. I toss a quick glare at him, and he widens his eyes with a keep-going look. Wait, so is he here to cheer me on or sabotage me? I feel like I'm on a spinning-teacup ride.

I sigh and turn back to Brandon. "What I mean is . . . four years in the brick-and-mortar shop. But before that I owned a flower truck and would sell out of farmers markets."

He looks genuinely impressed and interested. Another check mark. "That's really cool. Did you travel to other states or stay local to Kentucky?"

"I pretty much stayed within a fifty-mile radius," I say, and then realize this is the perfect conversational intro for a question that's become important to me as of late. "Um, which is actually why I think I'd like to travel more in the future."

"Go Timmy!" Amelia yells again.

Will shakes his head. "Still not Timmy."

"Rats." Amelia sits down.

"Do you like to travel, Brandon?" I ask while trying my hardest to block out the man beside me most definitely chewing wintergreen gum. His kiss would taste incredible right now.

Brandon grimaces. "I used to. But I traveled a ton in my twenties—I'm honestly pretty over it. I'm ready to finally settle in somewhere and just explore my own life around me."

One Month Ago Annie would be jumping for joy. Current Annie is deflating—especially as I realize I'm not sure what I really want anymore. Who I was and who I am becoming are meeting at an intersection and deciding who should proceed. All I know is, for Brandon getting so many check marks on my Perfect Soulmate List, I don't feel any physical reactions while sitting beside him.

It doesn't help that Will leans forward suddenly and addresses Brandon directly and with zero shame for eavesdropping. "But, uh, your girlfriend just said she wants to travel. Surely if she wants to, you'd go with her?"

Oh. My. Gosh!

Discreetly I reach behind me and pinch the back of Will's arm. His jaw jumps, but he doesn't retreat like I hoped.

Brandon looks just as startled as I do by this question. He laughs lightly to cover his unease. "Oh, well, she's not my girlfriend, actually. This is our first date. But, um, I guess if she really wanted to travel we could . . . figure it out." The way he says figure it out tells me he's just being polite. He has zero desire to travel. That's fine, though, right? I'm fine staying put.

"Great," Will says in a bland tone.

Amelia—or should I say Joe—sits forward. "You know? I've been known to do some traveling m'self. And to sing a few tunes as well. It's always been a big dream of mine to make it onto the big stage one of these days."

She's clearly having too much fun with this. I'm absolutely going to have to murder her later.

"That's . . . nice. Don't give up on your dreams," Brandon says, and he definitely gets extra points for not immediately shunning these two goons.

I stand up. "I'm so thirsty! Who needs a drink?"

Brandon stands too. "I can go get some bottled waters." Ugh, he's so nice.

"No! You sit down. Your nephew is about to bat, so you don't want to miss it." And then as I pass Will, I widen my eyes and flare my nostrils at him in a get-your-butt-up kind of way that he doesn't miss.

"Oh, uh, Joe, I'm going to get us something too. Keep your eyes peeled for Timmy."

"Well, hurry back now."

"This is not as charming as you think it is," I tell Amelia quietly as I pass. She pinches my butt cheek, and now I really hope Brandon isn't watching.

I storm toward the concession stand with Will following a few feet behind me. When we're finally out of eyeshot, I whirl around on him. "What in the Mary Poppins do you think you're doing?! Are you trying to sabotage me? Get in my head? Ruin my date?"

"No," he says firmly. "You were never even supposed to see us."

"Oh please," I say, rolling my eyes. "Joe back there could never go under the radar."

"I told her to leave the mustache in the truck."

"William."

"Annabell."

"You're ruining my date."

He scoffs. "That guy was doing it already."

"No! Don't do that." I wiggle my fingers in front of his face. "You don't get to say things like that and make me second-guess anything. Brandon is a perfectly nice guy. He's kind, he wants a family, he wants to put down roots. He wants everything I want. This date was going perfectly, and he's exactly what I've been looking for!"

Will's blue-gray eyes skewer me, and then he puts his thumb against my chin and tugs it back down. Neither of us say anything for a minute. No need to acknowledge that I didn't truly mean any of that—we both know it wasn't true.

Will inches closer so he can talk quietly. "If you want marriage and a family and all of that—fine, great. But don't try to delude yourself into thinking that you are still happy to settle for an un-adventurous vanilla relationship. You've been living in this town doing family events your whole life, Annie. You don't need a husband for that. What you haven't done yet is see the world. Experience new things. Live by your own desires. And if you settle for someone who's going to keep you from doing that, I'm going to be very upset."

He takes a step away like he's already angry at just the prospect of me marrying someone like Brandon. He picks up his baseball hat, rakes his hand through his hair, and then slaps it back on and paces back to me. "And you know what else?! You're one of the most passionate people I've ever met. What are you even doing here, Annie? You don't want to go to a Little League baseball game for your first date, where the only thing he's proving is he's going to put his family before you from the start."

I'm angry. He shouldn't be here. "If you know me so well, then where do I want to go for a first date, hmm?" I throw my arms out at my sides. "Where is this amazing place you think Brandon should have taken me?"

Will tilts his head. "Trick question. Because you want to be asked where you want to go for a first date." He steps even closer and brushes his fingers against mine. Like his body is pleading with mine for something. "And the problem with your failed date a few weeks ago wasn't because you were boring either. It's because you were bored, Annie. You want someone exciting and passionate and—"

"Someone like you?" I say in a sharp sarcastic tone. I threw that comment out on purpose and it hit a bull's-eye. Will's face falls and I give one short sad laugh. "What was the purpose of that speech, if not to get in my head? Which really isn't fair, Will, because last I checked, we were never an option. Did we not just lay everything out on the table this morning?"

He rubs the back of his neck and emotionally retreats. "You're right."

"And nothing has changed for you in the last four hours, has it? You're still leaving town after the wedding?"

He nods silently.

"Nothing has changed for me either. So please leave. Because although I know you mean well, this isn't helping at all. And frankly, it wasn't fair of you to show up here like this."

Will doesn't skulk off or pout like a man-child.

My breath catches when he steps forward, a blazing look in his eyes as he clasps my hands. "I'm sorry. You're totally right. I really didn't mean to mess this up for you today, I swear. I just wanted to . . . I don't know, make sure you were safe. Taken care of. And then I heard that guy already slicing away at the things you've been telling me you wanted to do—and when I thought of you having to sacrifice all of that . . . I couldn't handle it. I know your goal is to get married, but . . ." He lets go of my hands to cup my face. "Please just promise me you'll marry someone who sees you and loves you and who makes you excited and happy—not just someone who looks right on paper."

You. I want you, Will.

"I promise," I say softly, resisting tears with every fiber of my being. "You have to go now. And I'm going to give Brandon more than a ten-minute shot because maybe he has some adventure under all that beard hair."

Will winces like I punched him in the stomach. "You just had to mention the beard hair." His wince slowly unfolds into a smile that twists my heart into taffy. He then casts one tortured look at my mouth before stepping away. "I'll head out now."

"Thank you. And take Joe with you."

When I go back to the stands, Will and Amelia are gone. I hand Brandon one of the waters I purchased at the concession stand, but hold on to the small box of popcorn. He smiles kindly and thanks me. I can't help but notice that he doesn't have a dangerous black rim around his irises.

"So . . . did your friends finally leave?" he says as I sit down beside him.

I snap my eyes to him. "You knew the whole time?"

He laughs. "Absolutely. And that dude is in love with you, right?"

I breathe in and decide to stop playing games with myself and be nothing but honest. "Yeah, I think he might be."

"What's the deal there, then?"

I stare down into my popcorn. "We're both scared of different things."

"Been there," he says, in a thoughtful tone of voice that clearly has a story behind it. A story I'll never know because Brandon is not the man for me.

"Um, so Brandon, I don't think . . ." I pause to find the right words. Unfortunately, no inspiration hits.

He laughs and saves me. "It's okay, Annie. I'm not quite feeling a connection either if that's what you were going to say."

My shoulders slump with relief. "Oh good. I was worried I was going to hurt your feelings. Friends?"

"I think it's for the best. You want me to drive you home now?"

I look down at the water and popcorn and then at the baseball game. "Actually, if you're not eager to get rid of me, I think it would be fun to stay and hang out."

He smiles. "Absolutely."

And that—*John*—is how you tactfully end a bad date.

Later that night, I lie in bed restless and unable to sleep from unending questions somersaulting through my head. So I text the one person who has become my absolute safe place. "I can't sleep. Come over?"

Ten minutes later, even though it's against his rules, Will is slipping into my bed and wrapping his arms around me. He kisses my neck and my jaw and my temple and then with his arms around me, I fall asleep with my finger tracing the raised lines of his butterfly tattoo—scared of the day when I call and he's too far away.

CHAPTER THIRTY-ONE

Will

I rip a clump of weeds out of the front beds of Mabel's Inn. I don't fully know why I'm out here—at six A.M. no less. I just know that I woke up in Annie's bed at four thirty this morning after promising myself I wouldn't sleep over there again, and then immediately got up and went for a run to clear my head. I jogged through town to make sure everything looked safe (apparently, I've designated myself the town vigilante), and before going back up to my room, I noticed that Mabel's flower beds were overrun with weeds. So here I am. Hands and knees, ripping clumps from her garden like they cheated on me and I need vengeance.

But really, I am desperately trying to keep my mind from thinking about Annie. I can't figure out how to shut these feelings down. I've never had anyone stuck in my head like this before. When I close my eyes, I see her face. I hold her in my dreams, and I hear her voice in my ear when I'm waking up. I imagine leaving her after the wedding and my fists ball up.

I rub my chest.

It's time to talk to someone. Shifting from my knees, I sit in the grass and scrape my hands through my hair wishing I could scrape these thoughts out too.

Before I talk myself out of it, I pull out my cell phone. Miraculously, I have service right here in the dirt of Mabel's garden. I press the contact name open on my screen.

He answers on the second ring. "Will? What's wrong?"

"Why do you automatically think something is wrong? Can't I call my brother for no reason?"

"Not at six A.M. you can't. And not after ghosting me for several weeks." I hear the shuffling of covers and a female voice ask who's on the phone. Hannah. Of course she'd be in bed with him. They're a couple, and couples sleep together. All night. Side by side.

My mind flashes once again to Annie—the way she looked waking up on my chest yesterday morning. I think of her soft blue eyes flashing up at me under her thick dark lashes and the curve of her smile. And suddenly I think of seeing that every day for the rest of my life, and that painful tug in my chest happens again.

Ethan whispers to Hannah that he'll be right back, and then I hear a door shutting softly. "Okay, what's going on? You've been dodging all of my calls and texts for weeks, and now you're calling at the crack of dawn?"

"Hardly the crack of dawn. Some of us live a whole life before six A.M."

"I'm not one of them. I haven't had coffee yet, and I feel like shit before seven, so you better have an amazing reason for needing me this early."

"I'm sorry," I say, and my words are followed by a thick pause. "Not for calling early. I mean, I guess I'm sorry for that too. Or, no I'm not. You should wake up earlier. It's good for you." I clear my throat when I realize I'm nervously rambling. "I'm sorry for not supporting you, and for generally being an asshole about the engagement. I was never truly upset with you for proposing. I think I was just jealous and bitter that you were able to when I wasn't. And honestly, I didn't understand before . . . about you and Hannah."

"But you do now?"

"Support you guys? Yeah, I—"

"No," he says, quickly. "You said you didn't understand before. But you do now?"

Damn. I walked right into that one.

I drag in a deep breath. "I—uh—maybe." Shit, this is painful. I'm so used to being the one who has all the answers, who plows the way and teaches Ethan everything he knows. I've been protecting my brother from the world since we were kids. And now I feel lost and . . . terrified. "Ethan, how did you know that it was worth it to love Hannah?"

He laughs quietly on the other end as it sounds like he's opening a bag of coffee. "You make it seem like there was a choice in the matter. Believe me, if I could have chosen, I would still be living in my lonely one-bedroom apartment in SoHo. There was no choice in the matter, Will, and I'm thankful for it. I met Hannah and I fell in love completely against my better judgment."

Those words land with a dramatic superhero comic book *Thunk!* into my brain. I have no choice in the matter, my heart wants Annie.

"Okay then . . ." I say, thinking of how to rephrase my question. "How did you know your feelings were worth giving in to?"

"Hmm." He's quiet for a minute. "I guess when I realized it felt scarier to live life without her than with her."

Any other answer besides that one. Please. Any other answer and I would have been able to shove it under a rug. But that one . . . I can't dismiss it.

"Did you meet someone, Will?"

"Sort of."

"And you're scared?"

"A little. I've generally tried to not need anyone since I was a kid and realized that needing people usually ends in something painful."

There's a taut silence. "Hey, Will?"

"Hmm?"

"I don't think I've ever really said thank you before. For everything you were to me and did for me growing up." I sit silent, unable to form any words. Ethan continues, "I'm not sure I ever realized the differences in our childhood quite as much as just now when you said that. Because I don't have the same reaction toward needing people as you do—largely because when I needed you, you were always there for me."

"I wasn't there for you when I left after high school and joined the military."

"Are you kidding me? You sent money home to me every month. You even made it back to see me off to prom. You might not have been there day in and day out after you left home, but I never doubted that you were always one phone call away and you'd drop everything to be there for me. So . . . thank you."

I swallow and clench my jaws—only barely managing to get my words out without tears. "No problem."

Ethan chuckles lightly, understanding how deeply uncomfortable I am with, well, feeling my feelings. He has mercy on me. "All right. Now tell me about her," he says, and I hear the smile in his voice. I imagine it's smug and over-the-top. I wish I could withhold information about Annie just to piss him off, but unfortunately, I've been dying to talk to someone about her for weeks now.

"She's cute. Like in that wholesome, blindingly happy sort of way—but she has so much grit under the surface that it makes her almost dangerous. She's kind and empathetic, and so damn passionate and exciting in a way I've never really known before . . . and she's way too good for me."

He laughs. "So you love her?"

"That's why I called you, Mr. Hannah. I don't know. I don't know that I'm even capable of love. I mean . . . you were there, Ethan. You were right beside me when we had to close ourselves in my room and blare our radio just so we didn't hear the screaming matches between Mom and Dad. You heard the way he talked to her and how she would throw things at him. I'm so scared that'll end up being me one day, and I won't be able to leave. I'll be just like them—stuck in a loveless toxic relationship that doesn't seem to have an exit. How the hell did you get over that?"

"Quite frankly, therapy."

"Shit."

"Yeah. We had dysfunctional parents, Will. We spent our entire adolescence in an emotionally unstable environment and were made to feel like we were the problems most of the time. You more than me, obviously, because you shielded me from a lot. It's not something you just get over or choose to un-feel. And I think the day I came to terms with that was when I started truly healing. I'll never be able to shove it down with some elbow grease. It's going to take time, and work, and patience from my partner as I unpack it."

"I hear you, but I spent most of my life feeling absolutely miserable every day. I don't want to risk that ever happening again." Even though in my heart I know that Annie doesn't have the same hurtful traits my parents had.

"Will, we were children. We didn't have a choice. But you're an adult now—you always have the choice to leave a bad situation."

"What if I can't see that it's bad?"

"I'll tell you."

"What if I'll be the one that's bad for Annie? What if I'm like Mom and Dad and the only way to protect Annie is to not let myself have her?"

"Shit, Will. Have you been carrying that thought around this whole time? Is that why you've never settled down with anyone?"

My silence answers that question.

"That's a lie. You are a good person, with a damn good heart. You deserve love and to give love."

I have to clear my throat against the lump. And I wipe my face because apparently I'm sweating out of my eyes. "Thanks, man."

"Now, here's the flip side from a divorce lawyer: I'm still not convinced marriage is for everyone. So if you're one of those people it's not for, Will, that's okay. It doesn't make you a bad person or less worthy of happiness, or even love, than anyone else out there. It means you had a messier start in life than most people. However"—he says with emphasis—"if you are one of those people who always said he would hate it and then changed his mind—that's okay too. Just be honest with yourself about what you need, or else you're going to be miserable in or out of love."

I chuckle and shake my head. "And you said you're not good at six A.M."

"Yeah, well, don't make it a habit."

"Ethan?"

"Hmm?"

"I do love her. And I'm scared to death."

Ethan's sigh is dramatically long. "I'll give you the name of my therapist. She does virtual appointments too. Might want to consider twice a week for a while."

I laugh and wish I were near enough to give my brother a hug. I miss him and suddenly have the distinct feeling that I've kept myself too busy. That maybe the safety I thought my constant work was bringing me was actually hurting me.

Ethan and I hang up a minute later after I've told him to change the sheets on his guest bed because I'm coming for a visit soon. The second the call ends, I set my phone down and put my face in my hands. I'm not sure I feel much better, but I do feel closer to accepting my feelings.

I'm interrupted by a throat clearing to my left. I lift my head and find Mabel standing on her front porch in her light pink robe with a blue-and-white-checkered flannel gown peeking out the bottom.

"How long have you been standing there, nosy woman?" I ask her with a teasing smirk.

"Long enough to know that you love my Annie and you're scared and I would really like to pay your mama and daddy a visit," she says in her blunt fashion, and it makes me laugh. She smiles and doesn't say anything else, just opens her arms.

I stand and walk over to her before stepping right into her arms and letting her fold me in the most comforting hug of my life. Mabel doesn't say anything, she just squeezes me tight. I squeeze her back and bury my head in her neck, feeling a lot like the little boy who used to climb that magnolia tree just wishing for a hug like this.

Mabel doesn't release me, but she pats my back affectionately. "Now . . . should I be worried that you were lying in my flower bed at six A.M.? I swear the young people in this town are always doing something concerning."

CHAPTER THIRTY-TWO

Annie

It's not my day to visit my grandma, but I'm going anyway. Logically I know that she's not going to have any of the answers that I need—but I'm going anyway in some misplaced hope that she'll be having the most amazing day she's had in months, and she'll be my grandma again tonight, full of wisdom and grace and can tell me exactly what to do.

I haven't seen Will in a few days. Not since the night of my date with Brandon, to be exact. I think he might be hiding. That's okay, though. I've been hiding too. We're good at that.

He walked into the market yesterday, and I ducked behind a shelf and then abandoned my cart and crawled out. (Fine, I hunched over and tripped my way out.) The next day I saw him by The Pie Shop, and when we made eye contact, I blinked, and then he was gone. Ducked in an alley most likely. Just for good measure I texted him later that day.

ANNIE: You're avoiding me, right?
WILL: Yes. And you're avoiding me?

ANNIE: Yes. I'm confused and need some time.

WILL: Same. I miss you, though.

ANNIE: I miss you too.

So we got that cleared up, and now I'm just trying to figure out what in the world to do about him. Because I'm now able to fully admit to myself that I have feelings for him. Real ones. Ooey-gooey ones that could double as a butter cake. And that's very, very bad because Will Griffin wants to remain as single as a prewrapped slice of American cheese.

So what's one to do when she wants to be happily married more than anything just like her parents and her sibling, but has completely fallen for a man who will never be in a relationship? She moves on and gets over him. That's the only thing to do, right? She goes on more dates with other men. She reminds herself that Will Griffin was never Fred Astaire and she's not Audrey Hepburn, and when he gets on the airplane next week, he won't be coming back like Fred did.

Right? I don't know anymore. That's why I'm here.

But when I go into my grandma's room at her assisted-living facility, I find her sound asleep in her cushy recliner. She's in her powder-blue, long-sleeved, button-down silk PJ set because even with Alzheimer's, this woman remembers she will settle for nothing less than dressing to the nines at all times. She's always been that way. Pristine clothes. Freshly ironed each day. Don't leave the house without putting on your makeup and fixing your hair kind of southern woman.

I smile at the sight of her now, kicked back, sound asleep in her chair, *Wheel of Fortune* playing on the TV, casting her dim room in a subtle hue of blue. And for some reason, this sight makes me cry. I can't wake her up. It will only disorient her and make the night a mess for her and the staff. But I need her. I need someone to point the way for me.

I need my mom and dad.

How is it possible to miss people I barely knew so acutely that I have to hold my stomach and sit down on the couch, doubling over to silently weep? There are so many times in a day when I wish I could call my mom. I can't even fish into memories to find nuggets of her to hold on to. I don't remember her. And the woman who doubled as both a grandma and a mother to me has one foot on earth and one foot in heaven.

I'm scared.

But I can't tell my siblings any of this because, well, because that's just not what I do. I've never saddled them with my emotional burdens. They have enough as it is without piling mine on top. And Will is leaving, so it's useless to tell him.

So I cry silently in this blue room, soaking the tops of my jeans with tears until I feel a hand on my shoulder. I suck in a breath and look up into the eyes of Mabel. She frowns as she sees my face, and then uses the pad of her thumb to wipe tears off my cheeks. She silently urges me up from the couch and then whispers, "Come on, darlin', let's get out of here."

Mabel reaches across the table and holds my hand. "Tell me why you're crying, Annabell."

"I'm not sure there's only one reason."

"Give me your top five then."

We're sitting in the dim dining room of the assisted-living center. Dinner ended about two hours ago, so Mabel and I are the only ones in here. The room is decorated in deep burgundy and gold and navy, and every time I bring my grandma out here she remarks on how tacky the place is. I have to agree. It's a very nice facility, but something about it feels like a funeral home, which is unacceptable.

I make a mental note to bring in a fresh bright and colorful bouquet to put on each table tomorrow and talk to the facility manager about painting the room in a cheerier color.

"I'm not sure who I am anymore, Mabel—and I'd really like my mom to help me sort it out, but she can't because she's dead. And I never got to know her like my siblings did, and sometimes I resent them for that. And I don't know why I'm crying over my dead parents when I'm almost thirty years old, when I don't think I cried about them even in childhood." I suck in a breath. "Oh, and I've fallen in love with a bodyguard who doesn't believe in love and is leaving for good. Was that five? I don't know."

Mabel sighs. "Well shit, darlin'. You're running a whole race in that brain of yours." She squeezes my hand, urging me to look up into her kind eyes. "What do you need from me, sweetie? Advice? Or for me to listen?"

"Advice. I really need advice."

"Good, cause you were gonna get it either way." Her grin pulls one from me in return. "Truth be told, I've been waiting for this day. You've been overdue a good grieving for your parents."

I shake my head. "That's not what this is. I'm not grieving." I pause and Mabel just watches me. "I'm not. They died decades ago, Mabel. I've lived a whole life without them. I barely know anything about the people who gave me life aside from the crumbs that my siblings tell me. And the rest of their memories are bottled up in a woman who can't find them, and I'm this close to losing her for good," I say, holding up my thumb and forefinger to show the most depressingly small measurement.

I don't realize I'm crying during all of this until Mabel hands me a paper napkin across the table. I blot my eyes and thank my lucky stars that I didn't wear mascara today.

"That's grief, Annie. And it's okay. Grief—that mean son of a bitch—doesn't have a timeline or rules. It hits when it wants. Even with me—sometimes I feel all healed up, and then randomly I'll catch a scent that smells like my husband's cologne, and I'll lose it in an aisle at the market. It doesn't make sense, grief. And I've known you through it all, and I've never seen you grieve over your parents. Why?"

My lips quiver and I aim my gaze down at my lap. "I didn't think I was allowed to."

"But, honey, why would you think that?" Her tender voice rips my heart from my chest, and I feel like I'm bleeding out in the form of tears.

"Because I didn't know them enough to grieve them. But Noah and Emily and even Madison did. They have specific memories that I don't. I just have a hole in my heart that I can't seem to fully fill, and I'm not really sure why it's there."

Wait.

Suddenly, like a strike of lightning, I realize that I've been chasing the wrong things. I haven't needed a husband. Or even to find myself. I think this emptiness has been a result of constantly isolating myself from my feelings. I know who I am and what I want out of life—I've just been ignoring those needs.

"Don't your siblings talk about your parents much?"

Again, I shake my head. "No. And asking questions about Mom and Dad has always made everyone shut down. It seemed too painful for them to talk to me about their memories. So I quit trying— I didn't want to add more grief to their pain. I just stopped acknowledging my own sadness and focused on everyone else's instead. It's worked. It made them feel better and in return, it made me feel good."

"Until it didn't."

I sigh and nod. "Until it didn't. And now I've lived so much of my life without sharing who I am with them, that I don't know how to start. I don't know how to tell them that this version of me they've seen for so long is not necessarily true to me anymore."

"You say that. Exactly that."

"They'll be hurt, Mabel. My family loves me so much that to find out I've been lying to them all these years—"

"Exactly, honey. They love you so much. Honesty is a gift, Annie. And if you really love them, too, you'll be honest with them about who you are. And as for William . . ." Hearing his name mentioned suddenly in this conversation has me nearly jumping in my seat. "Don't give up on him."

"But Mabel . . ."

"Don't 'but Mabel' me . . . if you love that boy, don't give up on him, Annie. He needs someone to fight for him, like you've needed someone to fight for you. And I'm not saying it's going to look conventional, or anything like you've always pictured, or even anything like what your parents had . . ." She smiles and it's a smile full of memories. "But maybe it'll be something even better."

"Or maybe it'll crash and burn and hurt."

"Or maybe that."

I laugh until we both grow somber again. "What would my mom have said?"

"Hmm," Mabel says, pursing her lips and squinting her eyes. "Charlotte was all about living in the moment. I don't remember her ever thinking too far in the future about stuff—and sometimes that got her into a lot of trouble." Mabel smiles fondly, and I suddenly grieve that I haven't tried to talk to her about my parents sooner. "Your grandma used to come to me complaining about her wild girl all the time—but there was always a twinkle in your grandma's eyes like she couldn't help but be proud of her strong-willed daughter. So I don't know what she would've said exactly, but I have a feeling it would have been something along the lines of following your heart or your gut, whatever the hell you want to call it."

I doubt Mabel knows just how much I'm going to cling to those words.

"While I'm not your mama or your grandma, but someone who's lived a long time and loved deeper than I could ever describe to you, I'd say that I regret the things I never said way more than the things I have said. If you love him—be honest. With yourself and with him. And then take it from there. Don't deny yourself anymore, Annie."

I look at Mabel with a watery smile. "I love you, Mabel."

She waves me off like she doesn't need frilly words like that, but I see the way her eyes mist over as she looks away. "Love you, too, Annie-bananie."

CHAPTER THIRTY-THREE

Will

'm on surveillance duty today. I don't normally do this job because it's the bane of my existence, but the guy who usually sits in here during the day and watches the cameras around Amelia's property called me in between bouts of vomiting this morning and needed me to cover for him.

This is the only part of this job that I hate—sedentary, actionless watching. Not going to lie, it feels pointless. My time as Amelia's bodyguard here in Rome has been very uneventful. Which is amazing for her—boring for me. The threat to her out here has been pretty much nonexistent. Honestly, this town does such a great job keeping watch over her all on their own. I'm not even sure she needs a bodyguard here. If anyone catches wind of paparazzi or suspicious people resembling fans in the town, the phones start ringing. One by one residents trickle through the town square until everyone is alerted, and Amelia is safely taken out the back entrance to her truck and driven home.

Which is why I'm not needed. It would have been hard for me to leave knowing Amelia was in real danger, but the only danger to her right now is stubbing her toe on the front stoop of her house. Time to move on. It's going to be so great to keep busy and explore new places again. To not have to deal with Mabel's nightly chamomile tea checks. Or Phil's constant badgering about whatever sale he's running. Or this meddling town trying to petition Annie and me apart. Or the constant temptation to take Annie in my arms and make love to her with promises and plans. It's all too much. I've decided Ethan was right, and eventually I'd like roots and stability, but I'll catch it on the next round with someone I don't love as much as Annie. I'm not ready yet. I can't do it.

To kill the time, I do rotations of push-ups and sit-ups for a while. After that, and when my leg starts bouncing again, I set up my laptop in front of the security screens and open the web browser. I don't even know why, but before I realize it, I'm typing in the local community college. It's been buzzing around my head like an annoying fly ever since Annie asked me if I regret not going to school.

As I scroll through the website, I'm bombarded with pictures of happy students eating together at an outside table, studying together in a library, diligently taking notes in class wearing—you guessed it—big ole smiles. None of that looks appealing. But as I scroll down farther, I see a section listing their featured programs, and I can't help but wonder what I would do if I wasn't a bodyguard. In high school I had plans for becoming an engineer, but I don't think that was ever really my dream. It was just the most important-sounding career I could think of to impress my parents.

I did enjoy math, though. A lot. Still do.

My cursor hovers over Education in the list of programs, and I picture myself standing in front of a group of students, pointing to my name on the whiteboard. And then Annie steps through the classroom door with an apologetic smile and hands me the coffee thermos I left on the counter that morning.

I immediately slam the laptop shut.

"What the hell are you doing?" I mutter to myself as I run my hands through my hair.

Is this going to be how it is from now on? Am I going to constantly be thinking of Annie? What color overalls she's wearing that day? What she's been up to? Is she dating anyone? Is he going to be able to give her everything I can't? Will they have a family? Babies? Damn, he's going to sleep with Annie. He's going to hold her and touch her and . . . great, now I'm just pissed.

I'm irrationally angry toward a dude who doesn't even exist yet. I just need to text her. One text to see how she's doing, and then that will put my mind at ease.

But when I get out my phone, a perimeter breech notification pops up on one of my screens. Amelia is not expecting anyone because she decided to spend the day in the studio. My body immediately goes on alert as my eyes scan the monitor. Shit. Some dude wearing a T-shirt with Amelia's face blown up to maximum size has climbed the gate and is currently running up her driveway holding a box. So much for uneventful.

I jump from my chair and it topples over behind me. In two seconds flat, I'm out the door and running at full speed behind him. "Stop!" I yell, knowing he's not going to. Obsessive fans like this never do.

"I'm not going to hurt her," he yells over his shoulder, tucking the box under his arm like he's carrying a game-winning football to the end zone.

"Great, then stop where you are and we can talk!"

"Not until she sees what I have for her in this box."

Please don't be something nasty.

He doubles down on his sprint, but he's not fast enough. I catch up to him quicker than he was anticipating, and slam him to the ground.

CHAPTER THIRTY-FOUR

Annie

My sisters are finally home from their trip, and tonight is Amelia's bachelorette party at our house. She didn't want to go out and party—surprise, surprise—she wanted to stay in and watch an Audrey Hepburn movie. We still made her wear a sash and a veil, and we hung spicy lingerie all over the room. Oh, and we're all wearing penis necklaces. So that's fun.

The wedding is only two days away. All the details are finalized, and Amelia's dress came back from the seamstress today and it fits like a glove. Everyone seems to be remarkably calm about the impending nuptials. Not me. Because what it all means is that in three days, Will is going to be gone from my life for good.

I'm trying with all my might to pay attention to my sister's story about how in Mexico a male teacher got wildly drunk and went streaking down the beach and wasn't found until an hour before their flight the next day, butt naked on the beach, rear end pointed up to the sky, but my mind can't seem to stay put. Instead, it's willing my phone to light up with a text message from a bodyguard.

"And I didn't get to see it, but, apparently, his white ass was fried like a lobster!" Maddie winces and looks at me expectantly. When I smile, pretending I'm actually engaged in her story, she frowns. "You're not going to pull out the tally book?"

"Huh? For what?"

"For saying *ass,*" says Maddie with a duh expression.

"You get a freebie tonight."

All three women gasp.

"Something is wrong with you. You haven't recovered from your cold yet. Are you dying?" says Emily with a slight laugh, only 10 percent kidding but trying to convince us she's not 90 percent worried.

"I'm fine, Em. Just distracted." I unconsciously look down at my phone.

They all stare at me expectantly. "Distracted about . . ."

I look at them. "Stuff."

Maddie laughs. Emily groans.

"I swear you're harder to get information from than Noah," Amelia says with an affectionate smile.

I shrug, thinking there's only one person in this world that I've ever felt like telling everything to. Great, and now I'm sad. I'm never sad. I have this uncanny ability to see the positive in most situations, but I don't see it now. I have this sinking feeling that Will is gone from me forever—just as I knew from the beginning he would be. This whole situation has turned me into an angsty pessimist! How dare it!

"You've been over here huffing and puffing all night and scowling down at your phone like it pinched Grandma," she says, adjusting her body to face me on the couch.

"Speaking of Grandma, how was she when you guys went to visit her today?" I ask my sisters, knowing they went first thing when they got back in town this morning.

Madison throws a pillow at my face. "No freaking way are you distracting us that easily. Grandma was fine—now what's wrong with you, my angelic little buttercup? Your petals are drooping."

Knowing Maddie usually speaks in inappropriate innuendo, I look down at my chest.

"I'm not talking about your boobs, Annie. Did something happen with Will?" Madison jumps on the couch beside me so she can fix me with a closer-than-comfortable stare.

"Did he hurt you? That jerk, I'll wax him from head to toe!" says Emily, standing from her chair.

"Sit down, Emily. He didn't hurt me."

Emily folds her arms. "I'll only sit if you tell me exactly what he did to you and why it's making you wilt like a sunflower without water."

"So many flower analogies today."

Madison nudges me. "Is it that he wanted to take your lessons to the next level and have sex? Don't feel bad for waiting until marriage, though—everyone knows it comes with the territory of dating Angel Annie. Stick to your rules because you're going to have to put in a good word with the Almighty to get us into heaven with you! Heaven does accept plus-ones, right?"

I'm immediately angry. It's not a gentle movement on the meter from green to yellow to red. It's calm to livid in one second flat. At first, I try to swallow my feelings so I don't upset anyone, but then I hear Mabel's voice in my head: Tell your sisters the truth.

"Maddie, I need you to stop saying things like that. It's so frustrating to me."

Madison's head tips back a little, and her eyes widen. Everyone else seems too stunned to speak. That's fine because I have more than enough to say right now. "And please, I'm begging you to stop calling me Angel Annie. I hate it. I've hated it forever. I know you don't mean it as a bad thing—but it feels like one. It puts me in this suffocating little box that I can't climb out of."

"Annie . . . where is this coming from all of a sudden?" asks Emily, looking startled.

I sigh and then, yep, the tears finally catch up to my anger. "It's coming from years and years of swallowed feelings that I was too afraid to voice. And that's my fault. I haven't been truthful with you guys at all—and now I feel like you don't even know me."

"That can't be true," Maddie says, shaking her head and trying to catch up.

"It is—and I'll prove it. Will was actually acting as my dating coach because I did go out with Hot Bank Teller, and he bailed in the middle of the date because I was so boring."

Emily gets angry creases between her eyes. "That son of—"

I hold up a hand in her direction. "But it's not about him. What I realized is that I *have* been boring. I've been hiding so much of myself all this time to fit into the mold I accidentally made as a kid. I never really thought I was affected by the deaths of Mom and Dad like you guys were, but it turns out that my perfectionism has been one big coping mechanism. I never wanted to rock the boat or add more hurt or stress to anyone's lives, so I became this always-sunny version of myself, which . . . is killing me."

Tears start rolling down my cheeks now and instead of getting angry at me, Maddie tips forward and takes my hand. She doesn't say anything, just squeezes in a go-ahead sort of way.

"Y'all, I hate the No Swear Notebook. I loathe that thing. But I keep it up for you guys because it seemed important to you." I raise and lower my shoulders in an exaggerated shrug. "I don't even remember how it started! But truthfully, I could care less whether you guys curse or not. Oh! And yeah, it's true—I don't like casual sex. I'm an emotional person and I'll need an emotional connection before I sleep with someone. And I really need for you guys to stop turning that into a punch line."

"We didn't make it a punch line! Or . . . not intentionally," Emily says defensively.

"It always felt like one, though. Every time you guys call me sweet or refer to me as a cherub or someone who never makes mistakes—it feels like you're saying it in a belittling way."

"Okay—I do hear you, but roasting each other is what we do! It's how we show our love."

"And I understand that too. But you can't only refer to those aspects of me in a joke. You need to spread the teasing around. Make fun of my stinky feet, or that I snore at night, or some other random shit. Don't always go after my personality, because it starts to make it feel like a fault in me."

Maddie looks at Emily. "Did she just say shit?"

"I think she did."

I'm on a roll now, though. My adrenaline is pumping so hard I could walk outside and lift this house above my head. I could crack it down the middle with my bare hands. "And that's not all!" I say like an overexuberant infomercial host.

I dart from the room and return, pushing my box of romance novels. "I'm a romance reader," I say firmly, like this is the biggest reveal of all. "And sexy pirate romances are my favorite. I have fantasies of men in buckskin breeches wearing an earring and making love to me on the helm of a ship! But more important, I have fantasies of *Will Griffin* being the pirate to do it! And I've accidentally fallen in love with him and he's leaving in three days and he's never going to look back and now I've probably ruined my relationship with you guys too—and I'm so sorry."

I collapse into a heap on the floor now. Putting my hands over my face and crying into my hands. I've never been this dramatic in my entire life, and I'm sure that tomorrow I'll feel embarrassed about it. But for tonight, I just need to be authentically me. Messy embarrassing emotions and all. "I'm so sorry I haven't been honest with you guys. I just didn't know how. And now . . ."

Suddenly I feel bodies near me and arms wrapping around me.

"Shh, Annie! It's okay!" Maddie says with her face pressing into my neck so she can hug me tighter.

"We love you," Emily adds, brushing my hair back away from my face like the affectionate mother hen she is. "Everything about you. I'm so sorry you felt like you couldn't be honest with us or that we were making fun of how kind and sweet you are. I'm sorry we made you feel like that's the only version you could be of yourself around us."

Amelia is here too. "And I'm sorry that I've encouraged your constant sunniness. I—more than anyone—should have seen the signs that you were worn-out from always having to be perfect, but I didn't see it."

We are all four sobbing now. None of us really sound coherent, and yet we all understand one another perfectly.

"No, it's okay," I say to Amelia while reaching up and removing her penis necklace that's poking me in the eye. "It's no one's fault."

After a minute, Maddie stands up. "Because we're all being honest here, I have a few things to say too." She takes a breath. "I haven't been totally honest with you guys either. I applied to The Culinary Institute of America, and . . . I got in. I enrolled for this upcoming fall semester, and I'm going." She levels a firm look at Emily. "I'm going no matter what anyone has to say about it."

There's so much silence. I don't think anyone is even breathing. We're just absorbing.

And then . . .

"*Finally!*" we all say in unison before tackling Madison to the ground.

"Maddie! I'm so happy for you!" I say, kissing Maddie's cheek until it smooshes up.

"I hate you for leaving us," says Emily, "but I'm so happy that you are finally following your dreams."

"Does this mean you're not mad at me?" Maddie asks through her laughter.

I pull back and frown lightly. "Why would we be mad at you?"

She shrugs. "Why would I be mad at you for asking me not to call you Angel Annie anymore?"

"Touché."

"But actually—I have one more secret too. I think you're going to like this one, though." Maddie disappears into her room and comes back out holding . . . a box. She sets it next to mine and then tells me to look inside.

I open the flap and then laugh so loudly when I see a pile of bodice-ripping romances.

She grins. "I'm more into dukes and earls than pirates, though."

I press my hand to my heart. "You like men with *Big Duke Energy* too?"

"Oh yeah. I also have a Bookstagram account. It's how I actually learned about the term *stern brunch daddy*."

Emily then groans beside me and stands. "Fine. If we're all doing this, I don't want to be left out."

Want to take a guess what she goes and gets? Her own box. And as we all dissolve with laughter pulling her little mass-market paperbacks from their hiding place, we learn that Emily has a major thing for Scottish romances.

Amelia pouts because she doesn't live here and doesn't have a box of books. We tell her she can still be a part of our group, though, because we'll always have Audrey. She does, however, scoop up an armload of books from each of our boxes and sets them by the door to take home.

It's a good night and I feel a thousand times lighter. Mabel was right, honesty is a gift, and one I wish I had shared with my sisters

sooner. Then again, maybe everything is happening in its own perfectly messy timing.

After sitting together on the floor, penis necklaces around our
necks and unpacking a lot of the things I admitted to them—we
also talk about our parents and how I feel left out from their memories. Emily admitted that it's hard for her to talk about them, but
she would try to do better.

And then just when I thought I was going to get away from this
night without anyone being mad at me, Maddie pinches me under
the arm.

"Ow!" I say, ripping my arm away from her.

"That was for not telling us about John and all the shitty stuff he
said to you!"

"It was all too embarrassing," I say, shooting my gaze to the
ground. "Now more than ever because I'm head over heels for Will,
and he's already moved on before he's even left Rome. I haven't
heard from him in a few days."

That's when I notice all of the ladies sharing a look. A meaningful someone's-gotta-tell-her look.

"What? What is it?" I ask, feeling slightly frantic now.

My sisters look to Amelia to explain. "Let me start by saying,
he's okay—"

She no sooner gets the words out than I shoot to my feet.
"What happened to him?!"

"I didn't tell you sooner because he made me promise not to say
anything until most of the bruising has healed, so it wouldn't scare
you."

"Oh my God, bruising?!" I'm about to cry again. Is Will almost
dead? Images of him hooked up to a sad beeping machine in the
hospital plays in my mind.

"There was a superfan who made it onto the premises the other
day. He hopped the gate and then sprinted up toward the house

because he really wanted me to have a pair of his blue underwear to carry with me down the aisle as my something borrowed and something blue."

"Thoughtful of him," Maddie interjects.

"Will had to take him down, and the guy turned out to be really aggressive for someone wearing a T-shirt with my face all over it." I feel like I'm going to pass out. "Anyway, Will got hold of the situation pretty quickly, but the guy managed to get a few good hits in before that. But when Will tackled him onto the gravel driveway, his shoulder landed on a sharp rock and it made a big gash—" She cuts off as I whirl around and take off toward the door, grab my keys, and slam the door behind me on my way out.

CHAPTER THIRTY-FIVE

Will

I step out of the shower and look in the mirror. The swelling of my eye has gone way down, which is good, but my shoulder is still tender. I had to get five stitches—which in the grand scheme of things is nothing. The pain is manageable with Tylenol, and I'm just glad Amelia's safe.

The guy was arrested and taken into custody. Beyond that, it's out of my hands.

Suddenly I hear the sound of my door slamming, and I realize I forgot to lock it. Adrenaline kicks through my veins. I quickly throw a towel around my waist and fling open the bathroom door, ready to take an intruder by surprise rather than the opposite. And that's when I see her, standing in the middle of my room.

"Annie?" My shoulders relax for only a second before I take in how she looks. "What's wrong? Why the hell are you barefoot and wearing a penis necklace?"

She's breathing heavily as her eyes scan my body. "How dare you!"

"Me?" I ask, feeling drunk with how disoriented I am.

"Yes, you! I'm so angry with you I could tear you apart limb by limb."

She advances toward me and instinctively I take a step away. "What did I do?"

"Nothing, Will!" Annie's blue eyes are blazing. "And that's the problem. You were attacked and injured, and you didn't tell me. Look at you! You have a black eye and a big bandage on your shoulder, and you didn't immediately call me and let me come over and take care of you. You're not just avoiding me, Will, you're phasing me out."

She wags her finger at me. "Don't bother denying it because whether you like it or not, William Griffin, I know you." She doesn't even stop to breathe. The lung capacity on this woman is impressive. "But you can't phase me out. I won't let you! If you never want anything romantic, fine. But I can't go through life without knowing you, and talking to you, and holding your hand when I go on an adventure because you promised. Because I've never felt with anyone what I feel with you."

Her chest is heaving and her face is flushed and her eyes are teary.

"Say something . . ." she demands, some of her bluster failing now.

I laugh. "Oh, it's my turn now?"

"Yes, obviously that was your cue," she concedes, but then her eyes drop to my torso and the towel barely hanging on around my waist, and she frowns. "But you're naked. And I think I'm going to have a very hard time paying attention to anything you say while you're naked."

"I'm not naked, I'm wearing a towel—"

At that exact moment, said towel drops from my waist, and I am now, in fact, very naked. Naked and wet from my shower and standing fully frontal to Annie. I immediately cup my hands in front of me as Annie's jaw hits the floor. "*Oh my gosh,*" she says in a whisper that doesn't sound like she hates what she sees. Which is not helping the hiding of my groin issue.

"Shit—Annie . . . would you mind?"

She sucks in a sharp breath and covers her eyes. "Why do you look like that, Will?"

"Like what?" I grab the towel and fasten it back in place. Tightly this time.

"Like . . . so good!" she says, making me smile. "Will . . . you look like an underwear model. But without the underwear. Good gravy, I just saw your naked body."

"Could you maybe stop yelling that, though?"

"Sorry." Her hand is still firmly clasped to her eyes. "And you have a thigh tattoo!"

"I do."

"It's a wolf. You really are Wolf Boy."

"You had no idea how accurate you were all along. Okay, you can look again."

She doesn't move.

"Annie, you can uncover your eyes."

She breathes in and holds it. "I've never been in a room with a naked man before, Will," she says this quietly, like a confession.

I walk to Annie and slowly pull her hand down from her face. But her eyes are shut. I can't help but laugh. "Open your eyes. It's just me."

"Just me, he says. Like he's not the most gorgeous person my eyes have ever beheld." She raises her lashes tentatively—a squint at first—and then fully open.

"Thank you," I say softly. I'm not sure I've ever had anyone compliment me quite like that before. Or maybe it's that I've never had someone like Annie compliment me before. It shakes my already shaken self. "You're the most gorgeous person I've ever beheld too."

"Thank you." She smiles shyly.

"You were right, though."

"About looking like an underwear model? I know, you have the V that—"

I cover her lips with my fingers. "About me phasing you out."

"Oh," she said from the other side of my hand. I lower it. "Because you don't have feelings for me after all?"

I shake my head. "The complete opposite. My plan was to run as fast as I could away from you." I smile. "Thanks for chasing after me."

She blinks. "Always."

The tension between us grows—crackling and steaming to life. And more than anything right now, I want Annie. All of Annie. All of us.

"You should probably go," I tell her as my eyes drop to her mouth.

"Probably, yeah," she says stepping even closer and settling her fingers gently to my bare stomach. My muscles clench and I grit my teeth as her fingers trail lower to the top of my towel. "But I don't want to."

"Annie . . ." My plea is ragged from having to hold back from my own desire. I'm trying so hard to be upstanding here, but she's making it so damn difficult. "We haven't figured anything out yet between us, and if you stay . . ."

"I'm staying," she says firmly, leaving no room for argument. She knows who she is and what she wants and I sure as hell am not going to stand in the way of it.

I remove her fingers from the top of the towel, and a moment of hurt flashes through her eyes before I take those fingers and raise them to my lips to kiss each one instead.

CHAPTER THIRTY-SIX

Annie

I suck in a breath as Will's hands move to wrap around my hips—his face hovering torturously in the crook of my neck and the curve of my shoulder.

He kisses me once and pulls away to look into my eyes. That dangerous rim is overcome by the black center of his eyes—darkening and spreading. His jaws clench and he swallows, taking my hand and raising it between us. He slowly slides his fingers between mine and I don't think it's a good thing that I already want to moan from that small contact.

His smile slants. He knows.

"I want you to feel absolutely comfortable. We go only as far as you want—and at whatever pace you want. And if at any point you want to stop, just say it and we will." He says this while slowly unlatching one overall strap, and then the other. They fall to the floor with a satisfying *thunk*. The melting grin that takes over his mouth when he realizes I'm in a different pair of banana-print underwear (these bananas wear sunglasses) has my knees turning to jelly. Will holds me up—against him to be exact—and drops his mouth to my ear.

"Tell me what you like," he whispers, his words almost muffled from how they're pressing and nibbling against my skin.

His body is so hard and unyielding everywhere, making heat pool in all corners of my body.

"I don't . . . I don't know what I like," I say, the words barely coming out.

"Yes, you do." He runs his mouth against my jaw, sending shivers down my spine. He takes our interlaced hands and presses them above my head against the door. He's making a point: You know you like this. It's the same as the day we practiced, but different. So different because this time Will's mouth is kissing my neck. My collarbones. He's not holding back and I don't want him to. "You know. Trust yourself and then tell me, Annie. It's just me and you."

And he's right. I do know what I like and want, and somehow, having him trust and believe that about myself, sends a surge of confidence as well as a fresh wave of desire through me.

I decide to be brave.

I lower my hands to loop around Will's neck. He adjusts to look into my eyes—trying to read me as always. Trying to get one step ahead. Before he can, I rise up and firmly press my mouth to his. He sucks in a sharp breath and his hands grip me tighter.

I've been so measured and controlled and careful my whole life, and I can't bring myself to be that way tonight. I want to be lost for a while.

I hop up and Will catches me as I wrap my legs around his waist. His mouth explores mine in deep, hot caresses and before I know it, my back is landing gently on the mattress. I scoot up to the pillow, noticing that it smells like Will, a crisp, clean scent. He climbs over me and presses his mouth down onto mine, coaxing and so sensual I'm drunk and dazed.

"Beautiful," he says reverently after his hands slide up my hips and ribs and peel my shirt off. He kisses my stomach, and then runs his tongue around the rim of my belly button. "And you're so sweet." But this time, when he says sweet, I don't cringe. My stomach swoops because only Will can call me sweet in a way that does not feel sweet.

It doesn't take long for us to lose every stitch of clothing. And when we are skin to skin, I should feel scared. Terrified. Instead, the tops of Will's bare shoulders are backlit by the moon, and I study the shape of his muscles as they shift and flex. I'm relaxed and safe and joyful—and completely in awe of the way his body moves with confident ease. How his hands glide over me with tender care and expert precision. And for the rest of the night, we get lost in the sheets and Will teaches me things I never knew I needed to learn.

Time moves too quickly, and I know for the rest of my life I'll remember this night with Will in this room. I'll remember the flashes of his dark eyes, and his hands pressed into the mattress beside my face. His forearms flexing and our bodies together. I'll remember the taste of sweat and the smell of body wash and the warmth of our shower somewhere around two A.M.

And at some point, when the sun is starting to kiss the horizon just as tenderly as Will is kissing my shoulder, when we're both exhausted and in desperate need of sleep, Will pulls me back against his chest, wrapping his arm tightly around my body to just hold me, and I don't think anything could be more perfect.

CHAPTER THIRTY-SEVEN

Will

I hold Annie's hand as we walk through town toward the diner the next morning. It took a monumental effort for me to get out of bed and come with her to breakfast rather than asking her to take up residence with me in that room and never leave. She . . . Annie . . . Was . . . And I . . . We . . .

So good.

I've had sex before, and it's always been great, but never in my life have I made love to someone. And I can now say with absolute certainty—there's nothing like it. And now that I've had Annie in my arms, I can't imagine ever wanting anyone else.

We walk in companionable silence until something catches Annie's eye and she pulls me to a stop. "Hang on," she says, letting go to take a few steps backward and look over her shoulder. She gasps. "Oh my gosh, I knew it."

"What is it?" I ask, following her gaze to Comfort Quilts across the street. Through the glass I can see way too many people crammed into one place. "What the hell is happening in there?"

I can now feel the anger radiating from Annie as she pulls her hand from my grip and plants it sternly on her hip. God—her hips. No, not going there right now. "An impromptu town meeting, that's what." I watch Annie truck it across the street, ponytail swinging wildly behind her. I'm doing everything I can to keep up, but I've never seen this woman so determined. Except for maybe last night. (Again, not thinking about it.)

"I'm guessing you're not happy there's an impromptu town meeting?"

"Not when I wasn't invited to it. That can only mean one thing."

"What?"

She whips around just outside of the shop door. "They're talking about us."

"Oh. That's all? Come on, let's go get breakfast." I try to tug her hand to follow me, but she won't budge.

"Does it not bother you that they're all in there discussing our business without us?"

I laugh. "Not a bit. They're always discussing everyone's business without them."

She crosses her arms. "Well, I don't like it and it makes me mad."

Hearing this news, I know there's only one thing to do: step around Annie and open the door.

She nods once and precedes me inside. All of the local business owners are stuffed in here like prizes in a vending machine. The few shelves covered in bolts of fabric have been pushed to the back of the room to accommodate all the metal folding chairs. There's a small open area at the front, where Harriet is currently standing with a clipboard in her hand addressing the crowd. This really is a whole thing. How do these people have time for this? Someone had to bring all of these chairs and then set them up. Incredible.

When the bell above the door chimes, every head in the room

swivels to see who entered. You can tell they were already on edge with the prospect of Annie showing up, because when they realize it's her, there's a collective gasp and quiet murmurs begin.

"Uh—Annie . . . welcome . . . we were just . . ."

"Oh, save it!" she says, moving through all the chairs to get to the front. Metal folding chairs screech against the floor in an attempt to shuffle out of her way quickly. "I know what y'all are doing here, and you should be ashamed of yourselves."

And then Harriet steps in front of Annie to block her speech. The two begin to quietly bicker and I hang in the back, taking an empty seat next to Noah, who is by Amelia, who is by Emily, who is beside Madison. They each lean forward to wave and smile at me as I sit down. "Wondered if y'all would make it," says Maddie.

"Why are you guys even here?"

They each—including Noah—look at me like I'm out of my mind for even asking this. "Why wouldn't we be?"

"Because this is about your sister."

Amelia grunts a laugh. "And last month it was about Noah and how he refuses to give free pies for the local elementary school fundraiser—that didn't stop me from going. Popcorn?" She angles the bag my way.

"It's eight in the morning."

"So?"

"You popped a bag of popcorn at eight in the morning?" I ask, and she just shrugs. I look at Noah. "And why won't you provide pies for children?"

Noah glares at me. "I did provide pies. I provided twenty-five pies."

Amelia tsks. "Twenty-five rhubarb pies—and everyone knows that rhubarb pies are the worst pies, so it's like he didn't donate at all."

Noah folds his arms tighter across his chest—clearly triggered. "When did everyone get so damn picky about free stuff? I had a surplus of rhubarb that week. They should be grateful."

Someone in front of Noah turns around and glares at him. "No one likes the rhubarb pies, Noah. Just give us dirt in a cup next time."

"You know what, Jonathan, I'm going to take every single pie off the menu except for rhubarb pie until you all learn to be grateful."

Across the aisle, someone stands up and looks in our direction. "Before you do, can I get a fudge pie? I have family coming over tonight, and my mother-in-law swears I can't cook—I want to make her eat her words when I serve a homemade dessert."

Noah grumbles and then reaches into his back pocket and retrieves a notepad. "What time, Jane?"

"Can I pick it up around three?"

Annie and Harriet are still whisper-fighting in the front.

A man three rows up angles around toward us. "Noah! Can you put me down for a vanilla apple pie while you're at it?"

"I'm out of apples—take it up with James and his shitty farm."

James suddenly stands up from the front. "Damn you, there was a beetle infestation!"

"Hey!" Annie suddenly yells from the front of the room with one single reverberating clap. "Listen up! No more talking about pies. I have something to say. Harriet, sit down."

Amelia's bag of popcorn suddenly hovers in front of me. I push it away with a frown and focus on Annie.

She breathes in deep and then looks at me. I nod once, silently encouraging her to keep going.

Her shoulders square, and the woman looks fit for a court of law with how stern her expression is. Damn. It's sexy. "It's completely unacceptable for you all to gather together to discuss ways to break up me and Will."

Mabel tries to interject. "But honey—"

"No!" She holds up her hand. "Everyone needs to hear this. I am so tired of being treated like a child by this town. Just because half of you had a hand in raising me doesn't give you the right to make petitions and dictate who I can and cannot date. If I want to be in a relationship with Will Griffin—I will, end of story!" She snatches a brightly colored flyer from an audience member's hand. "And furthermore, just because you guys made a petition and everyone—" She cuts herself off as she frowns down at the paper in her hands.

I'm on the edge of my seat now. What is on that paper? And how is this suddenly the most entertaining thing I've witnessed in weeks?

She lowers the flyer and looks out at everyone. "Approves? You all approve?"

What?

I snatch a flyer from Phil, sitting in front of me.

"Next time, young man, just ask!" he says over his shoulder before Todd puts his hand on Phil's arm and pats it gently, earning a softening of Phil's shoulders before they eventually lock fingers.

"Wait," I say to Noah quietly. "Are they together?"

"Of course. What did you think?"

Well. The old married couple vibes make more sense now, that's for sure.

I turn my attention down to the flyer, and sure enough, it shows the final tally of town votes for our relationship: 250 votes in favor of me and Annie dating, 0 votes against. That can't be right.

This is me they're talking about dating Annie. I don't deserve her. This is bullshit. Every single person in this town should have voted against me. Do they not care about her at all?

Below the tally is an agenda for the meeting:

> Address Marvin using the mayor's parking spot
> Share official petition results for the Annie and Will
>   relationship: ruling in favor and support.

Harriet stands up again. "I'll admit that at first I was skeptical because of Will's media reputation. But the more we all watched you two together, the more we saw the realness in Will. He's a good man. And furthermore, we can see that you two are clearly in love and right for each other. We just want you to be happy, Annie. And we see how happy he makes you."

I'm still reeling from the word *love* used to describe me and Annie so casually. Mentally, I'm doubled over, hyperventilating, and trying to reach for something to hold on to.

Mabel suddenly shoots up from her seat. "But let the record show that I was always in favor of William from the start! Harriet only jumped on board recently."

"Oh, sit down. No one wants to hear you toot your own horn."

"I will not sit down," Mabel says indignantly. "Actually, I will, but only because my hip is acting up and I want to sit down. But not because you told me to."

Annie looks just as shaken by the L-word as I do. She blinks softly, hands the flyer to Harriet, and smiles. A montage of our night together runs through my head, and I assume it's doing the same for her. And then I see the moment she decides she's misled the whole town and needs to come clean.

Her brows pull together as she looks out over the crowd, and that's when I stand up. "Thanks for the votes, everyone. Jeanine, are you headed back to the diner soon?"

She blinks at me. "Uh—you can let yourself in, hun. Coffee's warm and Greg should be in the kitchen. Be there in ten."

"Sounds good." I go to the front, take a dazed-looking Annie's hand, and start pulling her with me. "And Marvin. You really gotta stop parking in the mayor's spot, man. Not cool," I say, shaking my head on my way out.

The second we are out the door, I stop and take Annie's face in my hands, pressing my mouth firmly to hers, stealing any words she was about to say right from her lips. Annie wraps her arms up around my neck and we both simultaneously deepen the kiss until we're full blown making out on the sidewalk. Weird town meeting forgotten.

A minute or two or five later, we pull away out of breath. Annie presses her fingers to her kiss-stolen lips and blinks at me. Neither of us knows what's happening anymore. And that's okay.

"Let's go get some breakfast, yeah?"

She swallows. "Okay."

I look over my shoulder as we cross the street and find no less than twenty faces peering out the window of Gemma's quilt shop.

CHAPTER THIRTY-EIGHT

Annie

After an abnormally quiet breakfast where Will and I didn't even come close to discussing what's going to happen to us after he leaves town in two short days, I went to the flower shop. It's closed today so that I could spend the whole afternoon putting finishing touches on the arrangements for the rehearsal dinner tonight.

Somehow I managed to block out all thoughts of Will and focus on my work. Just kidding! I literally zoned out no less than ten times when I realized I was replaying our night together. It turns out that even after reading all of those incredibly steamy scenes in my historical romance books, I was in no way prepared for how incredible the real deal is. What it would feel like to be fully known by another person. To love someone in a tangible, outward way.

And it was a lot of fun, so there's that too.

Anyway, I did manage to get the arrangements finished and loaded up in my truck and then unloaded again at James's farm in enough time to come back home and shower and get ready for the evening.

And now, as I stand here staring at the dress I bought for the wedding rehearsal hanging up in my closet, I consider not going.

"I can't wear this," I tell Madison, who's standing at my right.

"You absolutely have to wear this!" she says emphatically.

"It's the prettiest dress I've ever seen," Emily adds from my left.

The three of us continue to stare at the powder-pink, floor-length dress and marvel. I don't think I've ever worn anything so fancy. I bought it when I was in the throes of proving that I could be Audrey Hepburn in *Funny Face,* and I chose the dress because it was the same shade of pink as the overlay she wears during her big runway reveal. The reveal where she completely dazzles the crowd. But now I don't feel like I have anything to prove to myself, so I consider putting on my overalls instead.

"Oh no, you don't," says Madison, watching my gaze fall to my well-worn regular attire hanging behind the stunning dress. "You can love yourself and love dressing up in a fancy dress. The two can be synonymous."

Before I can protest, she's lifting my arms and taking off my shirt, and Emily is stripping my pants off my lower half. In a matter of seconds, I'm being zipped up in a dress that fits me like a glove. It's simple—a soft pink dress with a square neckline and thick sleeveless straps. Unlike the dress of Emily's I wore for my disaster date, this cuts off at the exact perfect spot for my curvy shape and short size—midway past my knees. But the wildest part is the sexy slit that extends up the side to my midthigh.

I feel beautiful and feminine, and can't help but smile when I look in the mirror.

And an hour later, as soon as I walk into the premises of the rehearsal dinner, of course John—the one man I'd like to never see again—corners me by the open bar. Noah and Amelia just had to go and invite most of the town. Of course John wasn't invited—but

Jeanine was—and I know from being warned by Amelia after the RSVP came in that Jeanine brought him as her plus-one.

"Wow, Annie . . . you look . . . incredible." He whistles as he eyes me head to toe in a way that I really don't think he should feel comfortable doing after he ditched me mid date, and is currently on a date with another woman.

Well, I feel incredible, but I didn't get this dress for him. Or for anyone really. I bought it and am wearing it because it makes me happy and confident. So much so that if someone were to call me Sweet Annie tonight, I wouldn't even be offended. Because it's only an insult if I accept it as one.

And thanks to Will, I will now forever and for always smile when I hear that particular adjective. Speaking of Will, I peek over my shoulder and look around the open-air tent to find him, but he's not here. There are beautiful warm string lights, big gorgeous bouquets (courtesy of me), tables with white linens, and people dressed to the nines everywhere I look—but no Will.

I turn back and almost forget I was midconversation with John. "Oh, thank you. You look nice too. Have a good night," I say, taking a glass of wine from the bar and preparing to turn.

"Wait, uh—Annie," he says in a sort of frantic rush. "I'm here with Jeanine tonight, but it's nothing serious. So I was actually wondering if you'd like to go out again sometime? Because the last time got cut short . . . by my emergency."

Ha! This man has some nerve still pretending it was an "emergency." And insulting Jeanine by asking out another woman while he's on a date with her.

Is this really happening? Am I getting my movie moment? The one where I've been completely transformed and am in my sexy dress, and I get to tell the loser guy who made me feel like cow poo to get lost in front of everyone? It would feel so good. I'll smile the entire time I deliver my monologue, *"I don't think so, on account of me being too boring for you."*

But then I realize that I don't need this win. I have nothing to prove to John, and I don't care to waste a single second on him.

"I don't think so. Have a good night, John." I walk off with my head held high and really hoping that Jeanine isn't actually interested in him.

I weave through a crowd of people I don't recognize who are flocked around Amelia and Noah. Music business friends, most likely. She hasn't invited many people from her Rae Rose life because she and Noah wanted to keep the wedding pretty intimate, but when I look closer, I do recognize Amelia's mom, Claire (her personal assistant), and Keysha (her manager).

But then I spot a little group of people I know gathered by the hors d'oeuvres table and am drawn to them like any true introvert would be at a large event.

"I'm telling you," Mabel says to Jeanine, Harriet, and James as I walk up to the huddled group. "I think there's a ghost living in the top floor of the inn." She says this so passionately that even I am lifting my brow and leaning in to hear the story.

"Mabel, there's no such thing as ghosts," James says with a good-natured smile before taking a drink of his beer.

Mabel gives him a duck lip expression and juts out her hip. "Then explain to me why I heard all those squeaks last night."

Of course I'm mid drink as she says this, which makes me spray it out of my mouth. I immediately cover my mouth, and Jeanine thrusts a cocktail napkin in my direction.

"Goodness, child," says Mabel with wide (far too innocent) eyes.

Harriet mutters something about mannerless heathen under her breath. Some things never change with her.

"I'm so sorry!" I pat my mouth a few more times and try to regain my wits. "There was a bug in my drink, and I didn't see it in time."

"Of course, hun. Well, anyway . . . like I was saying, there were all these squeaky sounds and then—even worse—moans." She shakes her head and then casts a sly look that only I would be able to see. And that's when I realize she knows all about what happened last night with Will and is teasing me in front of everyone. Traitor!

I clear my throat, willing my cheeks not to flame. "Yep! Sounds like a ghost to me. Better call someone about that. Well, excuse me, I need to go check on Amelia. See ya'll!"

I'm out of there so fast I nearly run straight into someone. Thankfully, a hand with a butterfly tattoo covers my wrist and stops me before my drink can end up all over either of us. I look up into the smiling eyes of Will, and my heart sighs with relief.

"You're here," I say, sounding far too dreamy even to my own ears. But you would sound like this, too, if you could see the man. He's in an indigo-blue suit that fits him to tailored perfection. Crisp white dress shirt underneath with the top button undone. The only tattoo showing is his butterfly, which for some reason, knowing what else is living under that suit, which no one else knows is there besides me, is driving me wild. I want to unbutton him one by one right here in the middle of the party. Strip him naked just like he should always be. His body is simply too good to keep covered.

He lowers his voice and steps closer and leans into me, his one rebellious lock of hair dashing almost provocatively over his eyebrow as he does. "You are the most stunning woman I've ever seen."

And just like that, my skin is tingling all over with remembered whispers of his body against mine.

"You look pretty stunning yourself." Too stunning. "Wait—am I distracting you from your work right now?"

He shakes his head and wraps his arm around my lower back to pull me in close to him. "I'm off the clock tonight. Well, off the clock for Amelia for good. My replacement from the agency showed up today. Danielle is over there in the black pantsuit. She's assigned to Amelia from now on."

I turn my gaze to the very stern-looking woman hovering on the outskirts of the event.

My smile falls along with all my hopes and dreams. "So that means . . . your job here is officially over?"

He glances away and then back to me. "It means I get to enjoy the night by your side."

"The night . . ." I repeat quietly, feeling just how final everything feels suddenly. How little time I have to say everything I feel.

"Will . . ." I wrap my arms around his waist. "I . . . want to say thank you."

His eyebrow goes up, and a cocky smile slants his mouth. "For last night?"

"For everything. For the tutoring and the friendship and—"

He cuts me off, playfulness dissipated. "Wait, wait, wait. Is this a goodbye speech?"

I shrug and then direct my gaze to the floor so I don't cry. "Well, tomorrow is the wedding. I'll be working all morning to set up and also after the wedding to clean up. And if your job here is done, then . . ."

Will hooks his finger under my chin and tilts it up. Before he says anything else, he bends down and kisses me. Long and slow. It's not an obscene kiss, but it's so tender my stomach quivers. My heart swoons.

He pulls away and then runs a finger softly across one of the barrel curls my sisters put in my hair earlier, his eyes tracing his own movements as he does. "No way in hell am I saying goodbye here in front of all these people, Annabell." He kisses me one more time. A quick peck just as a DJ begins to play soft background music while everyone mingles.

Will smiles. "Dance with me?"

I look around. "Uh, I don't think this is really a dancing sort of night. Everyone is just eating and talking."

"Come on, practice slow dancing with me," he says with a playful hitch of his chin. A who-cares-about-anyone-else look. It's what I love about him.

I nod and Will takes my palm in his and wraps his other around my waist as he pulls me in tight. Together, here in the middle of the tent, Will and I slow dance. His hand splays possessively across my back and then tucks our joined hands up between our chests. I close my eyes and memorize the way he smells and the feel of his suit jacket against my cheek. We sway in rhythm under the twinkling lights, and I can hear the sound of his breathing. His thumb glides delicately across the back of my hand in the most tender affection I've ever experienced. Suddenly, I want to beg him to stay. *Stay! Stay! Stay! Never leave. Forget D.C., we could be so good together. I love you.*

Off to the side, I see Amelia and Noah start to walk toward the clearing in the field where the ceremony is going to take place, and the wedding planner waves us all to follow. It's time to start the rehearsal.

Will bends down and kisses my cheek, and again I anticipate the saddest goodbye of my life. "Hey, do me a favor and wear those banana PJs tonight?"

"Why?" I ask.

He grins and looks every bit like the roguish fiend he is when he says, "Because I've dreamed of peeling them off you more times than you can imagine. I want to make it a reality tonight."

I laugh while simultaneously tingling with anticipation. "Peel them off. I see what you did there. Does this mean you're coming over later?"

"Leave your window open."

So this isn't goodbye yet? I get one more night with Will Griffin.

"You know you can use the front door now, right?"

"What fun would that be?" He lets go of me and gestures with his head for me to follow the rest of the wedding party to the field. "I'll see you tonight, Annabell."

"I guess you will, William."

I peek back over my shoulder while I walk away and find Will holding his phone in my direction. I think he just took my picture.

Will made good on his promise and climbed through my window an hour ago. Now, he holds me against him in my bed—my banana pajamas happily discarded to the floor. It's late, but my sisters still aren't home, and I assume they are staying at either Noah and Amelia's place or maybe even at James's house to give me and Will some privacy. I'm grateful. There's been so much change and so many revelations during the last few days that I feel like I've run a marathon. Or an iron man. Or run against Harriet for town councilwoman.

Tonight, Will and I never do get around to saying goodbye or what we'll do after he's gone or if there's even anything to be done, because every time I try to bring it up, he changes the subject. Instead, we make love and snuggle and Will kisses my forehead more times than I can count. And that's that. The next morning when I wake up and the sun is just peeking over the horizon, Will is already gone. And the latest pirate romance I was reading that was sitting on my bedside table is gone too.

Did he take it as a memento of me?

While making coffee, I tell myself not to worry. I'll see him at the wedding. There's no way he'd miss it. And there's no way he would actually leave without saying goodbye.

Right?

But then I think about last night and how he held me like he was afraid I was slipping away. How he kissed me, even after we'd made love, until my mouth was swollen. How in the light of his absence this morning, I realize that last night felt a lot like goodbye.

And that's when I realize that he's not going to be at the wedding. He's not even going to say goodbye—and he intended for it to be that way from the beginning.

How dare he.

CHAPTER THIRTY-NINE

Annie

The ceremony is set to start in about ten minutes. I've never loved a dress more than the ones Amelia provided for us bridesmaids. It's a mint-colored midi with a plunging V-shaped bodice and several layers of soft mesh overlay at the skirts, adding just a touch of princess whimsy. We've all been in James's house for the last two hours getting ready—Noah and his groomsmen on one side and Amelia and us bridesmaids on the other. But we've been kept separated so we don't accidentally get a peek at one another before the wedding.

I managed to slip out of the room we've been using as the bridal suite without Emily noticing, though, which feels like a real accomplishment. She's been barking orders and making sure everyone is toeing the line all morning. Oh, Amelia has a wedding planner, but even that woman seems to be a little afraid of Emily and has stepped back more than once to let Emily run the show. No one is fiercer than an elementary school teacher when it's time to get people in order and hold them to a schedule.

But I wanted a minute alone with Noah before the ceremony,

so after tiptoeing away from Amelia and my sisters, I knock on James's bedroom door, where I know Noah has been getting ready.

"Come in."

Inside, I find Noah standing by the window, dressed in his tux and gazing out over the farm that has been turned into a magical wedding venue. I was here all morning with a few hired hands setting up flower arrangements, so I don't need to look outside to know what Noah is seeing. Instead, I'm more interested in watching my big brother. I blink back tears, soaking in the sight of the man who's carried our family from far too young an age, about to marry the woman of his dreams. He gets to walk through life with her now—share his happiness and his hurts. And no one deserves a happily ever after more than him. I wish my parents and my grandma could see him now. They'd be so incredibly proud of the man he's become.

"Hi," I say, moving to stand beside him at the window.

"Hey, you," he says in a soft tone, reaching out to wrap his arm around my shoulder and pull me into a hug. Noah and I have always shared a special bond. Maybe it's because he's several years older than me so we never fought, or maybe it's because he and I are both quiet souls, but I always feel comfortable with him. And he's never called me Angel Annie, so that's a plus.

"How is it you're getting married today?" I ask him. "Just yesterday you were running through town in your Spider-Man underwear."

"How do you know about that? You weren't even alive yet when it happened. Dammit, is Mabel spreading that story out there today?"

"All morning," I say looking up at him with a bright smile.

He groans and stares up at the ceiling.

I pat his chest. "Are you nervous?"

He tilts his face back down and frowns. "Hell, no. I'm ready to get it done. Seal the deal and be married to that woman already."

"Good. No cold feet? Because I could pull the truck around if you need a quick escape."

"Only if Amelia is escaping with me."

I smile—so happy to see my brother like this. My heart tries to squeeze when I think about the man who's missing from this day, but I don't let it.

Just as expected, there've been no signs of Will today. Not even a text message or a letter or a sign in the sand. He just vanished, and a huge part of me is let down. I didn't expect him to stick around or anything—but I did anticipate him at least hugging me goodbye. Telling me that I mean something to him, even if it's just friendship. I went after him once when he pulled away—twice would just look desperate. If this is his choice, I have to let him go.

"I'm sorry he left," Noah says suddenly—apparently reading the expression that I wrongly thought I was keeping very neutral. "I heard he checked out of Mabel's this morning."

Oh.

I hadn't heard that. So I guess it is official. He really did leave.

I wave like, eh, no big deal! "He was always supposed to go." I give a big fake smile. "He's not built for settling down. But we had fun while he was here." Oof this hurts. Being fake happy. Being fake positive.

Noah chuckles. "Bullshit, Annie. Don't try to feed me any of that garbage. You miss him like hell, and you're mad he left."

"I don't have any right to be mad. He was up front about how he felt from the beginning." I can, however, be mad that he left without saying goodbye.

He gives me a sad sort of smile. "The problem is, you're trying to rationalize your feelings. I have bad news for you, the heart wants what it wants, and there's no talking it out of it."

"You sound like a fortune cookie."

Noah won't be quipped out of this conversation, though. "Did you ask him to stay?"

"Would you have asked Amelia to stay if she was determined to leave?"

He ticks his head to the side. "Good point."

"I just couldn't do it, Noah. I couldn't ask him to change his life for me. He would have ended up resenting me."

He turns to face me. "Believe me, I get where you're coming from. But hear me out. What if he was waiting for an invitation to stay?"

No . . . that's not . . . he wouldn't have . . . Surely, he knew . . . Oh no.

We're interrupted by a small knock on the door, followed by its opening creak. Amelia peeks her head inside. "Noah, can I come in—Oh, Annie! Sorry, I didn't know you were in here!"

I laugh and step back from Noah. "Are you kidding? It's your wedding day. You get to do what you want!"

She opens the door and slips through quickly, like there's a monster outside about to gobble her up. "If Emily sees me coming in here she's going to go berserk," she says, closing the door silently behind her. When she turns forward again, I watch my brother's face melt into something so tender I want to clutch my heart.

He breathes out in a rush as his eyes drop to take in her vintage-inspired wedding gown. It's made of delicate white lace and is fitted to her every curve. Loose cap sleeves of fine sheer lace cover her shoulders, and the neckline dips into a steep V. In the back, the dress flows out to the smallest suggestion of a train. It's a simple yet stunning gown that is the perfect contrast to Amelia's dark eyes and loosely waved hair, swept back on one side by a pearl-studded hair clip.

"Amelia," my brother whispers reverently as she crosses to him. "You're so, so beautiful."

She smiles. "Thank you. I know we're not supposed to see each other before the ceremony, but . . ." She breaks off as she approaches Noah and he takes her hand, lifting it above her head to spin her around and admire her from every angle. And then he pulls her into his chest and engulfs her in his arms. "I just needed to see you first. And my wedding planner keeps throwing tasks at me, and I love your sister, but I'm seconds from murdering Emily because she seems to be trying to one-up the wedding planner in her bossiness and—"

Noah captures Amelia's lips, showing no reverence at all for her makeup. And that's when I turn away and quietly leave the room—giving them the moment alone they need.

Unfortunately, seeing them like that does nothing to ease the pain in my heart. How am I going to move on from Will? How am I ever going to be held by another man and not wish the entire time that it was Will?

And the strange part is, I still think marriage is a wonderful idea and something I'd like to have one day—but I'm now seeing that it was the wrong thing to be placing on a pedestal of ultimate happiness. I was looking for the perfect person with the perfect traits and the perfect timing, when really, all my heart actually wants is to be fully known and loved. Someone to share the quiet moments with—someone to turn to when everything is good or everything is bad. Someone who wouldn't be mad if I snuck in to see him before the wedding and ruined traditions—but who'd be just as eager to be with me as I'd be with him. Someone like . . . Will.

The details were never as important as I thought they were.

In the hall, I'm not looking where I'm walking and run smack into a man. "Oof! Sorry."

"Oh, sorry Annie. Wow, you look so pretty," says James, admiring my light blue silk bridesmaid's dress.

"And you look very dapper." I return his compliment with ease even though I feel like shards of glass are pumping through my heart. I just want to get through this day and move on.

"Hey," he says suddenly, the look on his face changing. I'm afraid he's going to prod me with questions about Will just like everyone else, but he shocks me by going in a completely unexpected direction. "Is it true about Maddie? Is she moving to New York for culinary school?"

"Oh yeah, it's true. Can you believe it? We're going to have to be without her for two years." I laugh lightly. "Then again, that will probably feel like a break for you because you won't have to deal with her constant badgering anymore."

I expect him to laugh with me. He doesn't. He looks oddly troubled as he gazes blankly at the stairs that lead up to the bridal suite.

"Yeah. It'll be nice." He clears his throat. "Anyway. I'll see you out there." He winks and lightly squeezes my elbow as he passes. I watch him go, wondering if James has a secret too. Maybe I don't know him as well as I think I do.

We're all lined up in our places after having just walked down the aisle and are desperately trying to choke back tears as Noah escorts Mabel to her seat. The seat of honor where the groom's parents would usually be seated. Sniffles sound all around the audience as he kisses Mabel's cheek and whispers something in her ear before taking his place at the front of the aisle.

Noah casts one meaningful glance at each of us sisters, silently telling us how much he loves us. I'm a wreck. Holding in a sob has never been so painful. And then the music shifts, and the audience turns to look over their shoulders and Noah's expression guts me. His eyes lock on Amelia walking down the aisle, holding her bouquet of white, green, and pink flowers, her long veil trailing elegantly behind her. She sees him and smiles softly, her eyes misting over and her chest expanding with a deep breath. When she reaches Noah, he takes two steps forward to take her hand, like he couldn't even wait that long to touch her. It's only then that she releases the breath she took.

They stand together, gazing intently into each other's eyes as the officiant begins the ceremony and looking for all the world like they've found their paradise.

My eyes stray from my brother and Amelia to the sight beyond them. James is standing behind Noah, his pained gaze fixed heavily on a place just over my shoulder. Maddie. I steal one discreet look back, and find her smiling fondly at Noah and Amelia, none the wiser that a man is staring at her like every second she's not in his arms is torture.

I know that look.

And I can't help but mirror it as my eyes search the audience, acutely feeling the loss of the one person I love more than anything in this world.

The wedding was breathtaking. Romantic and tender; and even if I do say so myself, the flowers were stunning. Yeah, Amelia, you were a goddess, but let's face it—everyone is going to be talking about the flowers for years to come.

And now Noah and Amelia are slow dancing in the middle of the dance floor to "The Way You Look Tonight," the moon and twinkly string lights over their heads, swaying with their bodies so close it almost feels inappropriate to watch.

Also a little painful to watch, if I'm being honest, because it reminds me of dancing with . . . *ugh,* not thinking about him again.

I stand up from my seat at the reception table and grab my high heels from the ground, where I discarded them two hours ago when my sisters pulled me onto the dance floor with them. Every-thing is starting to wind down, and Amelia and Noah will leave for their honeymoon soon. The general atmosphere is relief. It's over.

The wedding is complete, Amelia and Noah are happily married, and everything can start slowing down and getting back to normal.

I tell Emily and Maddie that I'm going to get a drink refill, and I'll be right back, but as I approach the bar, I'm hit with a fresh wave of sadness when I spot Amelia's new bodyguard standing at attention off to the side of the reception. Suddenly I don't want to stick around any longer—and Amelia and Noah have been so wrapped up in each other the whole night they won't even notice whether I'm here for their send-off or not. So I set my glass down and then head for the parking lot, leaving the sound of Frank Sinatra and quiet murmurs behind me.

It almost feels wrong to get into my old truck dressed so elegantly. And yet somehow it's exactly right. There are a lot of things that I've realized have changed about me, but loving this town and this truck aren't among them.

But when I put my hand on the truck's door handle, a familiar playful and roguish voice sounds in my ear, and a hand with a butterfly tattoo reaches over my shoulder to push my door closed again. "It's me, and you're safe. I'm going to blindfold you now." A thin strip of black cloth blankets my eyes.

I gasp. "Will?! What are you doing?"

"Yes, it's me, Will," he says quietly and then clears his throat and speaks more firmly—theatrically—and definitely with more baritone. "But also—no, I'm not Will."

My heart is joyfully pounding. It's singing and running and skipping and I don't even know what's happening. I thought he was gone!

"My name is Captain Blackheart," he says before hoisting me up over his shoulder, making me squeal. "And you, my lady, are being kidnapped."

CHAPTER FORTY

Annie

I'm definitely sitting in a strange vehicle right now, next to Will—that much I know. And it's a truck, judging by the bench seat and the distinct smell of old gasoline, aka the scent of my life. But the question is, whose truck is this? Because Will drives his company's SUV usually.

Nothing makes sense.

And this blindfold is hot.

And I think I'm going to hyperventilate.

"Okay, wait. Can we just pause?" I ask, wanting so badly to go along with whatever this is, but because it's been a really long emotional week, I'm finding my natural tolerance for random fun set too low.

Will must hear the panic in my voice. "Of course."

"So I can take off my blindfold?"

"Yes, absolutely," he says gently, which feels like a balm to my nerves.

When I pull down the black fabric, my eyes blink against the fuzzy picture of Will in a black T-shirt and jeans, his hand casually thrown over the steering wheel of an old truck as we drive down a dark back road.

First things first. "Whose truck is this?"

"Mine."

"But you don't have a truck."

He clicks the side of his mouth and winks. "Ah, but I do. Well, this is actually an old Bronco. Got it for a steal, because I can't be in this town and not drive a truck. You should know this better than anyone."

I feel dizzy. I'm going to throw up. "What's going on, Will? I thought you were gone. I thought you'd left town this morning, never to be seen again—and now, here you are . . . driving a truck as if my world hasn't been crumbling this entire day." My voice is climbing the rungs of a ladder into a land of the hysterics.

He briefly looks at me and then back at the road. "Your world was crumbling?"

"Well . . ." I raise and lower my shoulders. "Sort of. Internally. Yeah."

Maybe I shouldn't have admitted that. Maybe I'm showing my cards too soon. But I don't even know what game we're playing because I thought he was *gone* about five minutes ago. And now he's mansplaining in his Bronco and having the audacity to look casual.

He shakes his head. "Why did you think I'd left town? Or that I'd ever leave without saying goodbye to you, for that matter?"

I laugh a stunted laugh. "Um, let's see. Maybe because you weren't there when I woke up this morning, and then you never texted or called or left a note, and then Mabel said you checked out of your room this morning too. What else am I supposed to think?"

Again he glances at me with furrowed brows. "But I did text you . . . this morning. I told you I wouldn't be able to make it to the wedding, but I'd see you tonight."

My mouth falls open. "No. You didn't."

"I did." He fishes his phone from his pocket and tosses it in my lap. "Look."

I tap the screen on his phone, pausing briefly to marvel at his new wallpaper photo: me standing in the flower shop the night we kissed for the first time. My heart shakes, and so do my hands as I slide open his phone and look at our text thread. Sure enough, there's a message he sent me saying those exact words. But above them is a little red exclamation mark.

"It never went through."

"What?" He cuts his eyes to his phone screen and back to the road, grimacing. "Damn service. I'm sorry, Annie." And then like I'm outside of myself, I watch his hand—my favorite hand in the world, reach over and lie across my thigh. "I would never ever leave without telling you. Never."

A heavy knot in my chest uncoils. I begin to breathe normally. "Good."

He smiles over at me. "Good. Now . . . can I finish my kidnapping, please?"

My dizziness spills into my stomach and turns into butterflies. Something is happening right now. My thoughts run to play catch-up now that all sense of dread is sliding away. Will kidnapped me for fun. He bought a truck. He hasn't left town. His hand is on my thigh.

I try but fail to smother a grin as I raise the blindfold back up over my eyes.

A few short minutes later, Will is putting the truck in park and cutting the engine. "I'll come around and get you," he says before getting out of the truck.

During his short walk around the cab, I try to imagine what in the world all of this could be about—but I can't come up with anything. Or maybe I'm just too scared to dare to. Either way, when

Will opens my truck door and slides my hips to the edge of the seat, my thoughts are lost as he leans in and lightly kisses my mouth. "Come with me?"

I nod. "Anywhere."

There's a heavy silence, and in it, I lift my hand to feel his smiling mouth against my fingertips. And then he hoists me over his shoulder, again quoting impossibly cheesy lines I recognize from a few of my favorite pirate romances. All ones in which a heroine gets kidnapped by a rogue pirate. I can't help but smile thinking of how much Brandon would scoff at this. How much my sisters would make fun of me. But Will doesn't just support my love of historical fiction—he reenacts them.

I hear his footsteps thud against wood and then a door opening and closing again. The faintest amount of warm light floods through the fabric of my blindfold. Will slides me off his shoulder to the ground and holds my waist when I sway slightly from all the blood rushing from my head. He turns me toward him and then I feel his fingers tenderly brush against my face as he lowers the blindfold.

Again, I blink the world into focus. My breath catches.

We're in a mostly empty house—except for all the things Will has clearly added. Warm twinkle lights all around the room. Candles lit inside the empty fireplace. And the most wonderful part— all different kinds of flowers strewn across the floor. A carpet of petals. A cloud of foliage. And surrounding it all, a cushy-looking pallet in the middle of the room.

Will takes my hand and when I look at him, wondering what this is all about, a piece of silver in his ear glints. I gasp. "You're wearing an earring!"

He chuckles. "Just for tonight. And just for you. I'll be your pirate, Annie." He smiles and it's so devious and sexy it makes my stomach swoop like a swinging ship. He takes my hands. "I couldn't make it to the wedding today because the trademark of every good romance novel is a grand gesture. And I wanted to give you one." He looks sort of shy and unsure as he gestures toward the room.

"Will . . ." I start, but he cuts me off, stepping closer and taking my face in his hands.

"Annabell, I need you to know, I've fallen madly in love with you."

I hold still. "But you don't believe in love."

He brushes the back of his fingers affectionately over my jaw and down my throat. "It was easier to say I don't believe in love, rather than admitting to myself that I was afraid I wouldn't be loved back."

I splay my hand over his chest. "Heartbreaking, Will. It's impossible not to love you."

He smiles and presses a finger to my lips, silencing me. "And then I called my brother, and as we talked, I realized that leaving this town without you was the scariest thought I've ever had. I need you in my life like I need air, Annie. You have wrecked me in the best way I could ever imagine, and I'll never be the same. Never want to be the same." He kisses my forehead. "I love you. And I know marriage is something that's deeply important to you—and what you want is deeply important to me, so . . . marry me, Annie. No one else."

I laugh as tears stream down my cheeks. Is this happening? It must be a dream.

"No," I say with a huge smile while shaking my head. "I won't marry you."

He stares at me for a second, wondering if he'd heard me wrong because my expression and my words are in conflict. "You . . . won't?"

Again, I can't keep from laughing as joy spills out of me. I step up to Will and link my arms around his middle, angling my face up. The dark rim around his irises has never looked more dangerous. More compelling. More lovely.

"I love you, too, Will. I love you more than I thought possible to love anyone. And that's why I won't marry you."

"Confusing."

"Isn't it?" I smile. "First, I want you to know that I heard you that night you explained why you're hesitant to get married—and knowing all that I do about you now, I would never ask you to jump into something headfirst and just trust me. I don't think that's true love. In fact, it would be crappy of me to ask you to put all those fears aside for my happiness. And second," I rise up to kiss him once softly on the mouth just because I need to. "I'm relearning who I am and why I love the things I do. So I'd like some time to do that before I decide to get married." I kiss him again. "But what I do want is to have a relationship with you—to go day by day and earn your trust while you earn mine, and we figure out who we are in this messy life together. If you're up for it?"

He grins. "I did already buy the truck."

"It's a great truck."

"Are you sure, though? Because, Annie, if marriage is really what you want deep down . . ."

"I've never been surer of anything. Besides, Will . . ." I laugh. "I only met you a month ago! Even if I wanted to get married, I wouldn't want a proposal this fast!"

He shrugs a shoulder. "Well, you are southern."

"Not *that* southern." And then I realize something as I gaze around the room he's so thoughtfully sprinkled with flowers and lights and cozy blankets. "Wait. Whose house are we in?"

"Mine."

"But you don't have a house."

"I do now," he says matter-of-factly.

And back on the spinning teacup I go.

"Oh my gosh. I'll pinch you, Wolf Boy!"

"Captain Blackheart."

I poke him in the chest. "Tell me what's going on! From beginning to end."

He relents with an easy smile. "Well, technically the house is mine in thirty days once I've officially closed, but it's pretty much mine already because Mary said it's fine if I go ahead and move in. It's been on the market for forever and needs a ton of work. Don't look too closely at anything."

"Willmont. You bought a house," I say, turning away from him to admire the place with new understanding.

He laughs. "Yes. I bought a house, and I quit my job, and I'm not going to D.C., because I couldn't. I didn't want to anymore. I found roots in this incredibly frustrating town, and I don't want to leave. I love it here. And I love you. And it sounds like a great new adventure to stay put somewhere—at least until we pick where to travel together first. Because I'm absolutely taking you all over the world."

"You're not a bodyguard anymore?"

"Executive protection agent."

"Will!"

He smiles one huge smile, with those perfect brackets around his mouth. "No, I'm not an EPA anymore. But I am officially registered for the fall semester at Rome's finest community college," he says like it's no big deal. Like this isn't life changing. "I haven't been able to get what you said out of my head that night when we talked on your couch. And I realized going back to school and earning my degree did sound pretty great—with the plans of . . . becoming a teacher when I graduate."

Okay, but it's adorable how embarrassed he looks all of a sudden. If there was a little rock in front of him, he'd kick it.

I touch my hand softly to his face with the wateriest smile I've ever had. "It makes sense. You're a good teacher."

He laughs. "But I think I'll stick to teaching math or science from now on."

"Probably smart."

"Annie?"

"Yes?"

"I love you."

I breathe in the smell of flowers and Will Griffin. My two favorite scents in the entire world. "I love you, too, Will."

"So if you won't marry me—will you be my girlfriend?" he says, dropping a kiss to the crook of my neck. "Before you answer, you should know that John is interested in you. At Hank's the night we kissed he asked if we were serious, and I told him no and I've regretted it every single day since."

Fireworks explode from my head. Hearts flood my eyes. My skin sparks from head to toe. "John who?"

"Good answer." Will swoops me up in his arms and carries me to the pallet, where he sets me down and lies beside me. He trails his finger languidly over my collarbones in no rush—because . . . we've got time. Forever.

"Did I ever tell you why I never talked to you before that day in the alley?"

"No," I say, feeling like I'm in a dream as I gaze up at Will bathed in the warm lights and smiling down at me like the secret to his happiness lives inside my bones.

"Because I knew once I did—it would be over for me. Some part of me has always known I would love you."

"Stop," I say, dragging out the word like I'm in pain and clutching my heart. "I can't handle any more emotional declarations, or I will die of bliss."

He smiles, dips his head to replace his finger with his lips, and murmurs against my skin. "There are worse ways to go. But I'd prefer you stick around. And I have several ideas of how we can fill our time."

Will's hand reaches under the pillow at my head and pulls something out. I laugh when I look down. He sets the book he stole from my room this morning onto my stomach and grins deviously at me. "I highlighted the portions you might be interested in re-enacting. They will, of course, require you taking off your pretty dress. Here, let me help."

I laugh until his mouth covers mine.

And no kiss has ever tasted this sweet.

The *Rome Gazette*

Last night, Rome citizens were treated to quite the adventure as Sheriff Tony was dispatched in the dead of night to investigate a break-in at Will Griffin and Annie Walker's residence. The two have reportedly been absent from Rome, Kentucky, for two weeks while in Paris on vacation, and were not expected home until the following day.

Around two A.M., Bud Appleton (neighbor) noticed two persons, one male and one female, attempting to break into the Griffin-Walker house through a side window. Sheriff Tony, upon arriving at the scene, charged the six-foot-one tattooed male and wrestled him to the ground. Having been alerted to the arrival of Sheriff Tony because of the obnoxiously loud sirens and bright lights from his police vehicle, onlookers flocked to the scene in order to get a better look.

Bud Appleton commented, "Was unlike anything I've ever seen before! Such commotion. Sheriff charged the man and took him down swift enough, but poor ole Tony was immediately flipped on his stomach and his hands were restrained behind his back."

Witnesses report the dangerous burglar then released Sheriff Tony in a remarkable display of compassion when Tony yelled, "Okay, okay, I give up! Let go."

When interviewed later, the male burglar commented, "It's my own damn house, Terry. Why do you keep referring to me as a burglar? You know me and Annie; and we've had a long day of travel, and we lost our house key and just want to go inside and go to bed. Please leave."

In an exciting turn of events, it seemed the late-night bandits were none other than the residents of the home: Will Griffin and Annie Walker, who have happily owned the home together for the past year.

Although Mr. Griffin was less obliged to talk, Ms. Walker, in her usual kind manner, remained outside to answer several of this reporter's questions. "Our trip to Paris? Oh, Terry, it was incredible! I brought you back a little Eiffel Tower like you requested. It was so romantic and everything I hoped it would be, but I'm eager to get back to the flower shop and finish our renovations on the house. We only have the porch left."

Unfortunately, our interview was abruptly cut short as Mr. Griffin stormed back outside, seized Ms. Walker, and carried her over his shoulder inside the home, shutting the door and all onlookers out, thus ending another eventful day in Rome, Kentucky.

ACKNOWLEDGMENTS

Well, friends, we did it. Another book of mine is out in the world (and currently in your hands), and I couldn't be more grateful. This never stops feeling like a miracle.

At the start of writing this book, I remember thinking this one was going to be so much easier to write than *When in Rome*! HA! Cue this being the most difficult book I've ever written. By the time I was finished, I had seven (yes, seven) nearly finished drafts of this story because Annie and Will kept demanding me to get their story right. The final draft, the one in your hands, is when it all came together, and I fell in love with the story and this couple.

So now, I will pledge my undying love to the people who helped me make it possible.

As always, first and foremost, I want to thank my very own safe person: Chris. My husband, my love, my absolute goofball, I love you. Thank you for encouraging me every day to take risks and to follow my heart. You are my heart, so catch me following you around for the rest of my life.

To my wonderful literary agent, Kim Lionetti, thank you so much for advocating for me and my books in so many ways. I also love that we can sit in a conference call together for fifteen minutes when no one else shows up and chat about *The Office* vs. *Friends*. Honestly, your friendship means the world to me, and your skills in this business are unmatched. Lucky to have you!

To my incredible editor, Shauna Summers, I am so proud and honored to work with you. Not only do you fall in love with my characters like I do, but you always encourage my voice and inspire me to have confidence in my writing, and I can't thank you enough for that. Having you as an editor (and friend) is such a joy and privilege!

To my brilliant, stunning, and creative gal pals at Dell: Taylor, Corina, Mae, and Jordan, thank you so much for your hard work and support and laughs! I want us to all live in the same city so we can be best friends.

To my family, thank you for listening to me drone on endlessly about my books and stress and joy and not putting me in the trunk of someone's car and telling them to drive away. I love you all!

And to my friends who I share stardust with, who send 400 reels back and forth with me, who I marco polo with after too much sparkling wine, who flew all the way to Nashville and taught me how to make a pizookie, who absolutely geek out over Taylor Swift with me, and who know all my secrets and also send me Nick Miller memes all day, thank you all for your love and support. Without you, this job and this life would be so boring.

And to my readers, I love you enormously. You have rallied with me when my indie books were in crisis, you have forced all your friends and family to buy my books even when they didn't want to, and you have sent me words of encouragement and even sweet little gifts when you knew I needed a pick-me-up like I was one of your dearest friends, and for that—I'll always be grateful!

Okay, I guess I should end this and go write the next book set in Rome, Kentucky! :)

Love, Love, Love,
Sarah

ABOUT THE AUTHOR

SARAH ADAMS is the author of *When in Rome* and *The Cheat Sheet*. Born and raised in Nashville, Tennessee, she loves her family and warm days. Sarah has dreamed of being a writer since she was a girl, but finally wrote her first novel when her daughters were napping and she no longer had any excuses to put it off. She is a coffee addict, a British history nerd, a mom of two daughters, is married to her best friend, and is an indecisive introvert. Her hope is to write stories that make readers laugh, maybe even cry—but always leave them happier than when they started reading.

www.authorsarahadams.com
Instagram: @authorsarahadams

ABOUT THE TYPE

This book was set in Hoefler Text, a typeface designed in 1991 by Jonathan Hoefler (b. 1970). One of the earlier typefaces created at the beginning of the digital age specifically for use on computers, it was among the first to offer features previously found only in the finest typography, such as dedicated old-style figures and small caps. Thus it offers modern style based on the classic tradition.